'A tense, unsettling and emotionally engaging whydunnit that grips from the first page'
Sophie Hannah, author of *Haven't They Grown*

'Gritty, tense, superbly plotted and the run-up to the end left me breathless and a bit of an emotional wreck'
Harriet Tyce, author of *Blood Orange*

'A complete triumph. An intelligent and deeply satisfying thriller with such vivid characters it's impossible to believe they aren't real'
Elizabeth Haynes, author of *Into the Darkest Corner*

'Superb. A rare combination of stunning twists and exceptional prose makes it the perfect read'
David Jackson, author of *The Resident*

'Layer upon layer of secrets, making for a perfectly paced page-turner. Past and present are woven together beautifully'
Robert Scragg, author of *What Falls Between the Cracks*

'Immersive and compelling, authentic and raw'
S.E. Lynes, author of *The Women*

'Everything you want from a novel – the grimy realism of the best crime, and the perfectly executed twists of the best psychological thrillers'
Dominic Nolan, author of *After Dark*

'Assured, gripping and with a twist I did not see coming. Fantastic'
James Delargy, author of *55*

'A mesmerising tale of justice and redemption, which will have you spellbound. One of the rising stars of crime fiction'
Trevor Wood, author of *The Man on the Street*

A RUINED GIRL

KATE SIMANTS

First published in Great Britain in 2020 by
VIPER
part of Serpent's Tail,
an imprint of Profile Books Ltd
29 Cloth Fair
London
EC1A 7JQ
www.serpentstail.com

1 3 5 7 9 10 8 6 4 2

Typeset in Garamond by MacGuru Ltd
Printed and bound in Great Britain by
Clays Ltd, Elcograf S.p.A.

A CIP catalogue record for this book is available from the British Library.

ISBN 978 1 78816 597 6
eISBN 978 1 78283 742 8

For my parents

Night. Real, dense, outdoors night. Nothing like the safe, half-lit gloom he's known from a life in the city. Here, the trees all around hold the darkness tight, pressing it in. Behind him, the distant thrum of the M32, but so low and constant that it's just a layer under the silence, like silt. Apart from that, nothing. Just the thud and scrape of his spade striking the earth, pulling loose, striking again.

There's a ghost of rain, cold and drifting so fine it might as well be dust, sticking to everything. But the boy isn't cold, because digging is hard, hard work. Has he ever even done it before? At his old house? He remembers the garden as he brings the spade down. The flowers. They spread and bloom in his mind, and he colours them in reds and purples and blues and the world is made vivid again. His mum grew them; he must have helped. He must have gardened.

But that wasn't the same as this. Gardening is for growing things.

This is something else.

The spade is starting to grind now that he's getting further down. The top layer was easy: twigs and leaves and mulch all softened from the winter above and the rot below. Now, waist-deep, it's getting stony. He stops, breathing hard. He lets the long handle fall against the side of the pit – he'll call it a pit, because that's as far as he can let this go, in his head. He pushes his fists into his spine, gets his breath back. Listening, watchful, although he's been here enough times to know how rare visitors are. Without passing by boat, on the water that's just a few feet away, it would be hard to know the clearing was here at all. He turns to watch the river, immense and silent, sliding blindly west towards Bristol, and then Avonmouth, and then the sea. He thinks of the thing they did at school about the water table. If he digs any deeper, any minute now he's going to hit it.

His pit isn't as deep as he wanted, but it'll have to do. He turns to tell the man, but he has to scan the blackness for a moment until he spots him, crouching, at the edge of the clearing. Head in his hands. Could be crying. The boy doesn't care.

He climbs out of the pit and switches on the torch, keeping the beam low to the ground. Right at the edge, there's the girl. Lying on her side exactly where he set her down. Facing him.

He wipes his forehead with the back of his sleeve. Considering the size of her, considering how he could practically circle her waist with his hands, getting her here from the car they had parked maybe half a mile away was like carrying a sack of rocks. Dead weight: that's what it's called. He had to keep shifting the load, her stomach folded across his shoulder. Closer to her than he'd ever dreamed, his hand splayed across the back of her thigh, holding her steady in the fireman's lift. The man could have done it but the boy wouldn't let him. That was the deal. He'd go along with whatever the man told him afterwards, but they would do this part his *way.*

He closes his eyes now and runs it back, cementing the feel of her in his memory. The swish of her hair, hanging down behind him, thick enough to feel it brush against his jeans. He replays the sensations of it, the bounce of her hands against the backs of his knees. Had he felt the contours of her chest, upside down, below his shoulder blades? Yes. He tells himself it's real, something recalled, not imagined. He had felt that. And the warmth of her skin, even through the clothes? Yes.

The beating of her heart?

He opens his eyes. Swallows hard.

Yes. He wants it badly enough, so he takes the blank and fills it with the detail and then it's there, in his version of it, for good. He remembers it all.

Half covered with the battered tarp, she is motionless. The tips of his fingers sing with the desire to reach out and touch her. They ache with it. The drizzle has sunk into her hair, binding the strands into damp cords; it's settled into a sheen on her face, catching scraps of light that skitter across the ground as the canopy of leaves shifts above them. Her eyes are closed. Her black-and-red checked shirt clings in sodden folds around her, and the tarp lifts and falls in the breeze, as if it is breathing. And she is beautiful.

She is beautiful.

He forces himself to look away, and pulls the sheet up over her head. Then he calls over to the man in a low voice.

'Ready.'

It's not a question. It's a command. He is in charge.

The man rises like he's a hundred years old, like it's the hardest thing he's ever had to do. Hands shoved deep in his pockets he comes over, close to where she's lying.

'Anyone finds it,' he says, jerking his chin towards her, 'it's on you.'

'I know,' the boy says.

'I still think we should burn it.'

The boy shakes his head, but the man is eyeing him. Wants convincing. So the boy says, 'The rain. Too damp. And even if we could, there'd be the smoke. The smell. Not worth the risk. This way is better.'

The man prods at the shape under the tarp with the toe of his shoe. 'Let's get it done then.'

'No!' The boy's shout is thin and high with panic, and the man snaps round and his eyes shine silver in the darkness. He puts his hands up, surrendering.

'Jesus. What?'

'Don't even fucking touch *her,' the boy says. Spits it. And it's all he can do not to drive him into the pit instead of her. Grab the spade and swing the edge against the side of his head. But he doesn't do it. He made a promise.*

Because she is his. Seven months he's loved her, and tonight he's done something for her that no one else could do, and no one else will ever know, and he will do every part of it himself, and that means she's his. It makes her his. *He breathes hard, staring at the man. Teeth tight. He could kill him. He could.*

The man steps back. 'Do it then,' he says. 'Go on.'

And the boy does. He sits at the edge of the pit like he's getting into a pool, and he lowers himself down. Gets his hands underneath her armpits, careful to keep as much of her covered with the tarp as he can. He starts to pull. At first she doesn't move, and then there's the sound of a tear, fabric, and oh god *he hopes he hasn't hurt her. He winces, but he keeps pulling, and all of a sudden the resistance is gone and she pitches in, shoulders hitting him awkwardly against the fronts of his thighs. He staggers back, recovers, and lowers her down. Softly. Soundless.*

He moves her so she's lying on her side, her back to the man, and lays the tarp out again, taking care to keep it a little way from her face.

'What are you doing?' the man says. 'It's not like she's going to suffocate.'

The boy takes a last look at her, at the smears of black under her eyes, the tiny silver gem-studded star at her neck on a chain so fine you almost don't see it. And then he starts to climb out.

Until the man says, 'Hold on.'

'What?'

From his pocket, the man brings out a flick-knife. He tosses it down, and the boy catches it.

The man half turns away, his lip curled like she is something disgusting. 'Clothes.'

The boy's heart stops still.

'Her clothes,' the man says again. 'They'll have fibres on them. From both of us – our hair. Particles. Say they find her. You want them finding those?'

The boy says nothing. The knife is impossibly heavy in his hand.

'Cut them off,' the man tells him. 'We're going to burn them. And ours, to make sure.'

The boy looks down at her. The rain is still falling, little puddles forming, black like oil.

He can't take her clothes. He can hardly bear to leave her in a pit, but naked? No.

'Now,' the man says. 'Or the deal's off.'

And so the boy doesn't have any choice. His heart convulsing in his throat, he kneels.

'Turn your back,' he tells the man.

'What?'

'I said turn your back. You don't get to look at her. Not… not like this.'

The man gives him a look of pure hatred. But he does what he's told and turns around.

The boy puts the knife in his back pocket, folds the tarp off, and rolls her onto her back. Her hair spreads like a wing over her face. He unbuttons her jeans, lifts her hips, and pulls, whispering, 'I'm sorry, I'm sorry,' so quietly he can hardly hear it over the tapping of the rain. He won't look at her.

A bird screams overhead.

'Get the fuck on with it,' the man says over his shoulder.

Through barely open eyes, the boy finishes the job, but he doesn't use the knife. He does it tenderly, without lingering. All of it: the shirt, jeans, socks. The rest. He piles the clothes beside him, covers her over again.

'Done.'

'Necklace,' the man says, peering down.

'I said *don't look—'*

'Necklace,' *the man says again, snarling now.*

The boy does as he's told. And when it's done, her hair catches around his fingers. As he unwinds it, careful not to uproot a single thread, he thinks of something else.

He looks up. 'What about her hair?'

'What about it?'

The boy blinks against the intensifying rain. 'Fibres. There'll be my hair in hers, probably.' He doesn't know if that's how it works, but the idea is taking hold now. He has to convince him. 'And yours. If they can find fibres on her clothes, I mean, why not in her hair? Not worth the risk.'

The man flinches, nods. 'Cut it then. Close as you can. Wrap it in the clothes, we'll burn it all later.'

The boy grunts, takes the knife back out, and flips it open. This time, he doesn't waste a moment.

'I have to,' he whispers to her. 'I'm sorry. I have to.'

He doesn't know it yet, but what he's doing now, it's going to be the cage around every dream he'll have for the rest of his life. And each one of those dreams, from which he'll wake choking for breath as if someone has forced an icy fist down through his mouth and taken hold of his heart, will end the same. An image of the girl he loved harder than anyone, the girl he would have given his life for, if she would have only let him do it, if it might have made her love him back:

Her skin, white as bone, streaked with earth and rain. The last filaments of her hair falling from her scalp as she stands, naked, her arms loose against the sides of her living, perfect body. Her smile as she comes closer and closer until her face is against his.

And her breath in his ear, and her voice, as soft as a blanket of snow.

'Thank you. Thank you.'

1

Now

Wren Reynolds pulls into the designated *Probation Service* bay, puts the Corsa out of its misery, and huffs at her hands. Almost March, but cold as midwinter. To her right, long wet stretches of overnight rain have darkened the concrete under the windows of B-Wing. Behind it lies a cloudless sky.

On the passenger seat, she finds the printout of the room booking. CB009, Community Building. The newest addition to the complex, tucked behind the original red-brick Victorian edifice and clad, inexplicably, in dusky pink weatherboard. Cold, clean air floods the car as she opens the door. The day is brisk and bright. The kind of morning a person would hope for, if they were planning a fresh start.

Her offender has six days left inside. Numerically speaking, at a few weeks off twenty-one years old, he's still a young man. But considering the average stay in Bristol is around seven months, with the best part of three years under his belt he'll be the grandfather of B-wing, part of the bolted-down furniture. One thing she knows: inmates do not come out the same as they go in, not if they serve as long as he has. Not even physically. He could be skinnier or fatter by now, or could have bulked himself up with weights and chin-ups the way they sometimes did. She recalls the photo in her file of the eighteen-year-old boy he'd been when he was sentenced:

heavy forehead and the dark, blank glare. Impenetrable, near-black eyes a person could trip into and never hit the bottom.

Wren takes a breath, then nods to herself. She's ready. She gathers her things: handbag, phone, files. Props, really; anonymous shields. It was the first thing she'd learned in training, day one, lesson one: don't give them anything of yourself. No pictures of your partner in your wallet, no mention of your kids, neighbourhood – nothing. Next to her, another student had asked a question. *Are you saying they're still criminals then, when they've finished their sentence?* The tutor, a PO himself, had laughed drily, and the students had joined in as if they understood. And for the sake of fitting in Wren had smiled, she remembers now, as she flips down the visor and smears on a layer of muted pink lipstick that she doesn't really like. But she hadn't laughed.

You had to try to believe in redemption. Forgiveness. You had to at least *pretend*.

She fishes under the passenger seat for the flask of coffee Suzy had left on the kitchen table for her, then gets out. Her shoes clack on the tarmac as she heads towards the entrance, sending a report across the still-empty car park. Beyond the buildings, an amplified voice orders prisoners around in the yard, the sound of it cutting through the drone of the traffic arteries to the east. The place is only just coming to life, and Wren is deliberately early. He is still theirs, but on the cusp of probation. This is the overlap of past and future, of incarceration and what comes next.

The reception doors slide open and she lifts the lanyard round her neck to show the ID card hanging from it. The woman behind the acrylic screen leans closer, pushes her glasses up her nose and peers at it.

'*Community Atonement Programme*,' she reads slowly, then turns her suspicious gaze up to Wren's face before softening in recognition. 'Oh right. It's you. What do you do now, then?'

'Same as ever,' Wren says, shrugging. 'Whisk them away for a new life free from crime.'

They deadpan that for a moment together before the woman breaks into a grin. 'Really, though?'

'It's still probation,' Wren says, looping the card off her neck and sliding it into the metal tray. 'It's the accelerated-release thing. CAP.'

The receptionist's face is pinched with the effort of dredging her memory.

'It's been on the news?' Wren offers.

'Don't watch the news.' Holding up an apologetic, *one-minute* finger, she disappears with the ID into a side room.

Wren leans against the counter and waits. It is the first day of her new job: probation and rehabilitation professional – not technically a probation officer, a distinction which has been made much of in the press. The project is a five-city programme, involving a total of 104 offenders being released between six and twenty-four months early. *Carefully screened offenders* – according to the CAP press release – *will make contact with those people most affected by his or her criminal actions, in order to understand and apologise for the repercussions of the crime.* Scrape away the jargon and the gilding and what's left is an emergency valve to release the pressure on the UK's critically overpopulated prisons. Let them out early, knock on some doors and make them say sorry nicely, hope for the best. Known briefly in the tabloid press as the 'Lout's Lottery'.

Known to people like Wren as 'The Knocks'.

As a bona-fide former PO, Wren is overqualified, and it has been a battle to get Suzy on side. There were other, better-paid jobs out there for Wren that would have appeased some of her partner's mostly valid concerns about belt tightening. And sure, the timing could be better, given that Suzy is about to start maternity leave. But they'll manage. She's pretty sure they'll manage.

Music from a poorly tuned radio billows from the back room as the woman returns.

'You're still National Probation Service?'

'Yep.'

'But just more optimistic.' The woman tents her fingers under her chin, pleased with her joke.

Wren points and winks, knowing better than to bother challenging the cynicism. 'You got it.'

'Proper job.' She slides the ID and a plastic key card through on the tray. 'All the way to the back, double doors, and follow it to the right.'

Wren thanks her and turns away, but after a few steps the woman shouts after her.

'Do you think it'll work? I mean, really?'

'Got to be worth a try,' Wren calls back over her shoulder. It's something she's found herself saying a lot lately.

Breakfast is only just over but the place is already dense with the high-volume catering smells of £1.27-or-less lunches: onions, meat, potato reconstituted from pellets. She mouth-breathes until she exits the wide central thoroughfare and emerges into the Community Building.

The mechanism on the door receives her card, then gives her a green light. She steps inside. The room is overheated and smells of new paint. There are two access doors – the one for visitors, and another on the opposite wall which, when unlocked, opens into B-Wing. Three of the walls are regulation grey, the fourth matches the questionable exterior.

Wren almost smiles. Carpet. Heating. She can practically feel the prison's Victorian founders turning in their graves. Sipping her coffee, she goes to the window that looks out onto the rec yard.

It is a grand view. The facility sits at the crest of Horfield looking north, away from the city, but the Community Building is afforded a broad, southerly sweep down to the best of Bristol, the postcard bits. Temple Meads; Suspension Bridge; St Mary Redcliffe; the blunt, unfinished-looking tower of the Wills Memorial. It strikes her that two hundred years ago when the first bricks of the prison were laid, most of that historic skyline hadn't even been built. All the same, someone along the line had made the decision to construct the place with its back to the city that had grown lawless enough to need it.

Or it could be that you're overthinking it, Wren tells herself. *Again*.

An office-supply clock on the wall informs her there are six minutes until the meeting. The prisoner will be on his way. She imagines him walking along the platform outside his cell, his shoes ringing out on the ironwork steps. Pausing every thirty feet for the warden to slide a new key in a new lock, and marvelling at his luck being chosen for the programme. Under the impression that release would be the end of all of it, of the shame and misery and boredom. The godawful food. Thinking that as long as he turns up to his appointments and keeps his curfews, everything he's done to get himself in there will be water under the bridge. And the people who have been felled and broken and twisted into tight, bloody shreds by the grief he's caused: all of those people might as well never have existed.

And maybe he'll be right about some of that. But not all of it.

Her phone buzzes as soon as she sets it on the table. Suzy. She lets her thumb hover over the green circle for just a moment before she makes the decision and cuts the call. Guilt needles her from a distance but evaporates a second later when she hears voices in the corridor. Something dark shifts in her chest and she clasps her hands together, turns them inside out and pushes until her lats creak, reminding herself that the nerves are just because the project is new. New protocols, interest from the press, brass with a point to prove, more at stake than just letting them out and keeping them out of trouble.

A beep from the lock on the other side of the room, the prisoner's door. She squares her shoulders, straightens.

The door swings open.

'Miss Reynolds.' The warden is not one she knows. Tall, thin, borderline friendly.

Wren hasn't been *Miss* anything for a very long time but she doesn't correct him. She nods, and he steps aside.

And there he is.

Robert Malachy Ashworth, formerly of Isambard Court, Southmead. White, six-two. His hair is unchanged, cropped tight against his angular skull, but his narrow shoulders are rounded now, like he's holding something in his belly. She wonders, briefly, if it's remorse. She doubts it.

Wren puts out a hand. He looks at it for a moment before turning his bottle-brown eyes to hers. The slightest frown gathers on his forehead but she doesn't look away. The seconds are marked off by the ticking of the plastic clock. She takes in the threads of crimson in the whites of his eyes.

In a soft baritone the warden says, 'This lady's your probation officer, Ashworth.'

'Right.'

Ashworth breaks eye contact, and Wren silently lets out the breath she hadn't meant to hold.

'Shake the lady's hand, bud.'

Ashworth does as he is told, with the air of a man who does as he is told.

The skin of his palm is soft and warm against hers. An unpunished hand. Letting go, he passes his gaze down towards her throat, then straight to his shoes.

Wren gives a nod to the pallid warden. 'I can take it from here, thanks.'

'Buzzer's on the wall,' he says before he leaves. 'Hit it when you're finished.'

The door closes, and they are left alone.

Somewhere in the building there is a short klaxon. Wren sits down, and invites Ashworth to do the same. The chair spreads slightly under her weight, and she crosses her legs to avoid the press of the armrests on the outside of her thighs. She smoothes her skirt across her lap, then unpacks: files, a single pen, notebook.

She takes her time drinking the remaining inch of coffee, then slides the cup aside.

'So,' she says. 'You're getting out. Congratulations.'

'Yeah.' His voice is dry with disuse, and his face is set as hard as concrete. 'They said I've got to do visits?'

'That's right. I'm going to take you round to see some people, and we're going to have some conversations. The idea is that you find out what your actions have done, long term. Understand the wider repercussions.'

'What people, though?' Not a blink. Maybe not concrete after all, Wren thinks; maybe something older. Volcanic rock, perhaps.

'There's a list. Victims of the crime. Obviously in your case there's going to be... more to it.' She lets that sit for a moment, daring him to ask her why. Eventually she says, 'For you, it's your victim, and people connected to your accomplice.'

'Accomp— you mean Paige?'

She nods.

'And by *victim*, you're saying I've got to talk to Yardley.'

'Being the man you burgled and assaulted, yes,' she says. Settling into it now, hitting her stride. 'That qualifies him as the victim.'

Yardley, a former counsellor at Paige's school who'd also acted as a consultant to the care company responsible for her, had been the first to reply to Wren's letters. She'd expected the victim to be the most reluctant, especially in the circumstances, but she'd been wrong. *People change,* he'd told her later on the phone. *If I didn't believe that, I'd be in the wrong job.*

Ashworth sinks lower in his seat. 'What am I supposed to say to him?'

'*Sorry* is usually a good place to start. *Sorry I cracked your head against that wall. Sorry I stole that big shiny twenty-grand bracelet that hasn't been seen since.* That sort of thing.'

He says nothing to that.

'And then there is the small matter of his wife.'

A flinch, just a flick of the eyes.

'Do you know she's on four kinds of medication related to the trauma, Robert?'

'It's Rob.' He rubs his fingertips slowly across his eyebrows. 'And no. I did not know that.'

'Well, *Rob*, she is.' Wren flips open the file, making a point of finding the right page. 'First year after you broke into her home and tied her up, she lost her hair. Alopecia. Know about that?'

A shrug.

'Pretty much a recluse now. Can't work. Scared of everyone.'

He grunts, mutters something she doesn't catch.

'What was that?'

'I said, *I* didn't tie her up. Wasn't me.'

'Right.' Technically, it's true. 'I'm not alone in doubting that Paige would have thought of that herself though.'

Paige Garrett had still been a child. Fifteen, with a record that was not so much clean as immaculate. Non-existent. Which wouldn't have been so notable, but coupled with the fact that she'd spent the preceding nine and a half years in state care, in some of the roughest boroughs in the West Country? It was more than a big deal. It was a miracle.

Wren pulls the sheet of standard conditions from its plastic wallet and reads them aloud: he will report to her on a twice-weekly basis; they will form a plan regarding his accommodation and return to work; the breaking of any licence condition could mean recall to prison. *You will, you will not. If you do x, then y.* The state's last attempt at drilling in the causal nature of crime and punishment. He nods at each clause, until she is done.

'And then there's the special conditions,' she says. 'For the programme.'

He looks up. Full attention.

She reads him the list of names, the people they will be meeting. The victims, obviously. Paige's friends. Teachers.

'*Paige's* teachers?'

'Yes.'

'Why?'

'Because in the absence of a family, we have to go a little further to find the people who loved her.'

'But I didn't do anything to her!'

'You did,' Wren says. Ashworth opens his mouth to complain but she holds up a finger. 'You *did.* And you don't get to control what we do here. Understood?'

He gives her a long, flat look. 'Fine.'

She continues the list of visits: Paige's friends, the children's home where she lived – which had also been the home of Ashworth's younger brother, Luke. With every name, his stare slides lower until he is directing the full beam of it into the table, as if he is trying to set the thing on fire.

'Did they find Paige?'

She looks up slowly from the sheet.

Ashworth was the last person to see her before she disappeared. The private CCTV from Yardley's house on the night of the burglary showed her leaving, with him: her long blonde hair flashing white in the night-vision settings, her bare ankles glowing green under her skinny jeans and checked shirt. They went their separate ways. Ashworth was found a few hours later, and the bracelet he and Paige had stolen – solid platinum, set with almost a hundred diamonds and a single huge Colombian emerald at its heart – was already gone. Questions had been asked about their specificity, their *restraint* almost, in taking just the bracelet. There had been countless other things they could have stolen – paintings, antiques, huge quantities of jewellery dangling from mirrors and nestling in drawers. But one hot item was easier to offload than an armful, as Ashworth had put it, and so they'd made their choice. Upon arrest, Ashworth had initially claimed no knowledge of the theft, but then changed his story, saying he'd sold it and used the money to pay off a debt. But the bracelet isn't what interests Wren.

What bothers her is that Paige hasn't been seen since.

She watches for a flinch, a flick of the eyes. A tell. But nothing comes. 'Do *you* know where she is?'

'No.'

'No?'

'No.'

But she sees it, a glint of it escaping before he manages to get it locked down.

Fear.

But of what?

There are forms that need signing. When they're finished with the paperwork she rings the buzzer, and almost immediately footsteps sound in the corridor again. The heavy door swings open.

'All done?' the warden asks.

'For now.' She gestures to Ashworth that he can stand, that they're finished, but he doesn't move.

He nods, infinitesimally, at her folder. 'What about Luke?'

'Your brother?'

Another nod. 'Haven't seen him since I got here.'

Luke was the link between his older brother and Paige. He was just fourteen at the time, making him seventeen now. He'd been Paige's friend. Questioned on three occasions by the police about her disappearance, but his alibi was tight. The transcripts read like a seance: lots of questions, very few answers.

'He's not on the list, no. But there's no restriction on you getting in touch with him,' she says, tidying her gear away. The warden ushers Ashworth towards the door.

'Or my mum?' Just for a few seconds, the muscled, crop-headed facade falls away and Robert Ashworth is a boy.

The file under her arm is slim, but it doesn't hold everything she knows. It doesn't say how it feels to have your mother institutionalised. It doesn't say what a child like the one he'd been must sacrifice to survive in a world without a parent. She'd need a wheelie-bin to cart around *that* file, the one with all the humanity in it.

But that part isn't her job. And even if it was, she's not sure she'd do it for him, under the circumstances.

He glances up at her, granite-eyed and angry, and the boy is gone. 'Did you track her down too?'

'Your mum didn't know Paige. So no, she's not on the list.' Wren doesn't say that she tried – that Carrie Ashworth's last known whereabouts, the studio flat a social worker had arranged for her when she was finally discharged to out-patient care, had apparently only been her home for a few weeks. After that, she'd packed up and left without leaving a forwarding address, and without, it seemed, dropping in on her first-born before she did so.

'Luke might know where she is.'

'Your mother?'

'Paige.' He keeps his eyes hard on Wren's. 'He might know where she went. But I sure as hell don't.'

'Ashworth,' warns the screw. 'Now.'

Ashworth waits, resisting the pull of the hand on his thick bicep.

'We'll see,' Wren tells him, like it's nothing much to her. 'Plenty of time.'

Something like life flickers for a moment around his eyes, before he remembers where he is and crushes it. The warden jerks suddenly sideways as Ashworth releases his counter-balance and moves as bidden into the corridor. He gives Wren one last look before the door swings closed.

2

Before

Luke Ashworth closes the door behind him and signs in. He puts the bag down with a soft bump. Half the point of buying something like that, spending all that money, is the bag. It's made of white card, with ribbon handles. It hardly weighs a thing but his shoulder aches from carrying it home, carefully holding it away from his body so it didn't get dented.

He takes his time untying his trainers. Behind him he can hear Fat Jake and Cameron playing PS3 and, further back into the knocked-through house, cooking sounds from the kitchen. Pans and plates and instructions. The whole place is dense with a sweet tomatoey smell: pasta sauce. Meaning Paige will kick off again probably. She won't eat pasta, says it makes her fat. She's not fat. She's perfect. She's got hair Luke wants to twist his hand into.

By the front door there's a shoe rack thing with ten spaces, one drawer for each kid, although there's eleven of them in the home right now because of the twins. Luke pulls out his, the one at the bottom. Geraint had given him that one when he first arrived, said it was because he's closest to the ground, which was supposed to be funny but wasn't, and anyway Luke's grown since then so he can go fuck himself. Taped onto the front is a bit of card saying *LUKE A* because when he got to Beech View last year there was Luke Forbes as well, but he's moved out now, thank fuck. He puts the trainers in, side by side, careful even though they were like £25 and proper embarrassing. But he bought them cheap because then he had some left from his mum's auntie's birthday money. Two hundred Canadian dollars she'd sent – she's lived out there since before he was born. The cash came with a card and a letter, a load of her curly writing going on about how she'd really love to help more, even though he can't remember her ever doing jack-shit for any of them. He jams the shoe box back in, hard. The money was to make herself feel better. Because that's what people do, just sit around and think about their fucking selves while he's stuck in here with staff who couldn't give a fuck about anything except getting paid.

Fuck her, he thinks. *And fuck the rest of them.* But then a stem of guilt pushes out: not Rob, not his big brother. Rob's always been there for him. He comes twice every week, and he's coming tomorrow, and he said he'll have got paid so he'll take them to Maccy D's. Just for a second, Luke smiles. It's only five weeks until Rob turns eighteen. After that, he's going to do the guardianship thing. He's going to get Luke out.

The smile drops when Luke's eyes settle on Paige's box, and he remembers the problem. That if he gets out, that'll be it. They're not even in the same year at school.

Luke checks over his shoulder, then he sneaks the quickest of quick looks into her drawer. The label just says *Paige*. There's only one of her.

Her shoes are in there. Red converse. A tiny *34* printed inside them – he looked it up and it meant she's a size two or something stupid. There's a massive dent in the wire mesh of her box where she always kicks it shut. Yesterday she got sanctioned for it: Mel had done the whole *let's remember to respect our home* thing and Paige had given her the finger, which got her extra washing-up duty. He touches one of the shoes and something pulls tight in his chest like a thread.

'Forget your phone today, Mr Ashworth?' says Geraint from the doorway, and Luke jumps out of his skin like a fucking bedwetter.

Geraint laughs, and refills his spoon with cereal from the bowl he's holding – the bowl he's basically holding every minute of every shift he works. Drops of milk cling to his hipster beard, and he wipes them off, glancing back into the TV room. From the sounds of it, Cameron's beating the shit out of Fat Jake. Even though Geraint is *right fucking there* watching.

'I'm only asking because you weren't in the book for anything after school, Lukey, so we were getting worried,' he says, but he's not even looking at him and he sure as fuck doesn't look worried. 'And you didn't call. So I was wondering whether you'd forgotten your phone, because that would be an excuse for not letting us know.'

He raises his eyebrows then, like he's doing Luke a massive favour.

And then he clocks the bag, mouths the name of the fancy shop that's printed on the side. And a smile spreads across his face and he goes, 'Ohhh.' Like it's funny. 'Little ladies' man. Anyone we know?'

He gives Luke this big wink, making out they're on the same side. They're not on the same fucking side, they're not even on the same planet, and Luke's jaw is suddenly locked and then the hot thing happens. Burning in his ears, spreading like actual fire all across his cheeks and the whole thing's fucked now if she comes out; she's going to take one look at his face and laugh herself stupid because he's a blushing little *twat*—

'Are you all right, Luke?'

Before he can stop himself he says, '*Fuck* off, bellend,' and it comes out proper loud, and pissed off. There's a scramble from the TV room and Cameron and Fat Jake appear like magic behind Geraint. And they see Luke's face and fall about because obviously he's the colour of a post-box and out of nowhere he thinks of a gun and *one day I'm going to shoot the fucking lot of you. I fucking swear.*

Geraint's *we're-just-mates-having-a-chat* face disappears and he tips his head. 'Luke, I'm just asking you to say where you've been. I need to log it.'

'I said fuck off.'

Fat Jake says, 'Uh-oh, Lukey, careful you don't go mental,' and Cameron takes the cue and says, 'Unless you want to share a room with Mummy in the nuthouse,' and turns to high-five Fat Jake. Geraint steps in front of them because Luke's squaring up now, rage and shame blistering across his face.

'Come on, then!' Luke shouts. 'If you want a beating, you fat *cunt*, come on!'

Geraint blows out his cheeks. 'OK. Formal warning. Come on, mate.'

'I'm not your fucking mate.' He knows exactly what's going to happen now and he Doesn't. Fucking. Care. He turns and runs.

'Looks like you're feeling pretty angry, Luke,' Geraint calls behind him. It's always *it looks like you're feeling* and *what I'm hearing is.* No one ever says what the fuck they mean; it's all in fake language that's meant to make you feel like they give a shit. Luke powers up the stairs. He might be skinny and short but he can outrun any of the staff, maybe get the drawers against his bedroom door before Geraint's even on the top landing. Anything to not have to say in front of all those pricks that he was late because he'd gone to that shop.

The shop – the *bag*. The bag's at the bottom of the stairs. If he stops running he's going to get sanctioned, but if he doesn't go back down, Geraint's going to open it. Or Cameron will, or Fat fucking Jake. And he can't let that happen. He can't.

Luke stops on the stairs and he's eye level with the bottom of Paige's door and there's a light on in there. Music. Judging by the clattering of plates in the dining room he's guessing he's got five, ten minutes until it all kicks off with Paige, the nightly battle about getting her to eat. He turns around and Geraint's standing on the bottom step. He's got the bag, but he's holding it in the hand the others can't see, pressed against his leg.

'Forgot something?' he asks, nodding towards it but not holding it out.

Luke goes down. Takes it. There's no resistance. He wants to say thanks, he should say thanks, but Cameron and Fat Jake are still there. Geraint points to the office, weary like he just can't be arsed with the sanction any more than Luke can. He's one of the only staff who bothers recording them, which makes him a dick, but he doesn't take your phone away and he never does restraints unless he's got to. Geraint clicks the light on and Luke follows him in. Doesn't even need to be told.

Once the door's shut behind them, Geraint says, 'Remember to breathe.'

Luke lets it out. He hadn't noticed. He hardly ever does until he gets the silver sparks flicking around in his vision, telling him he's about to pass out.

By the time Geraint's written the sanction up – Luke's got to pick up all the manky crab apples from the grass outside – the food's on the table. Luke runs upstairs to hide the bag and when he gets back to the dining room everyone else is eating. Everyone except Paige, who's in her room, and Mel, who's up on the landing, trying to coax her down. From what she's saying, the manager, Mr Polzeath – Ollie, he wants them to call him, so they don't – is coming that evening so everyone's got to be fed and ready for his usual bullshit *chat*.

Mel's all right by Luke. She's decent about the rules; as long as people play nice she'll let the small stuff go, and she doesn't shout. Or, she does sometimes, but not with Paige. Anyone shouts at Paige, she just shrinks, puts her arms round her head, and after that she's pretty much gone. *Withdrawing*, she calls it.

Sometimes with girls it's hard to know who's actually mental and who's just acting it.

Luke stabs at his pasta, thinking about chipping off little bits of the plate underneath, thinking of how sharp they'd be, and whether they'd cut your tongue up if you ate them, or if you'd be able to swallow them without chewing. And if you did that, whether they'd cut your stomach up, too. And if your stomach got cut up bad enough to go to hospital, whether they'd let your mum out to come and see you.

Fat Jake says, 'I swear to god, if you don't stop doing that with your fork you're getting shanked.'

Luke jabs a bit more and the fork screams on the china. Fat Jake smacks his hand down on the table and the plates all jump.

'Take it easy now, Jake,' Geraint says in a flat voice.

Paige stays in her room the whole time, and Mel comes down looking weary when everyone's nearly finished. She says something into Geraint's ear and he sighs, tells her to at least sit and eat hers then, while it's still hot. Luke eats slowly, dragging it out so he's last, so he can take the plates into the kitchen. When he looks up, Mel's leaning back and pushing her placemat away. He gets up to stack the plates.

Mel hands him hers and says, 'Anyone seen Luke? There's some lad here clearing up who looks just like him, but it can't be.' And she gives him a wink like he's six years old and Luke misses his mum so much he could punch someone.

Misses her like there's a vacuum where his lungs are supposed to be.

It's way too cold in the kitchen. The massive extractor fan's on, sucking out the sauce smell but taking the warmth with it. Paige hates that fan. She says the people that build these places, they don't think kids are going to notice stuff like that, but she does. And extractor fans like that do not exist in normal houses. You've got something like that on the wall: you're running an institution, not a home. He notices the fan every time now. Luke puts the plates on the side by the sink and out of habit more than anything he checks the knife drawer but it's locked.

Exactly like they do in normal homes. Cunts.

The music from Paige's room gets louder the second he opens the fridge and it makes him smile because it's like she's saying, *Yeah, thanks, Luke. You're lovely to me.* There's half a pack of celery left over from that manky stew the other day. Luke unzips his hoody and tucks the celery inside, then grabs one of the diet yogurts Fat Jake has to eat. Then he goes back through the dining room, fast, and up the stairs. He thinks of her chewing the celery he's brought her. Smiling. *Thanks, Luke.*

He goes to his room first to get the bag – he'd put it in his backpack under his bed. Pulling it out he notices one of the corners of white card has got crushed. He tries to pinch it to straighten it out but it just makes it worse, and then his finger goes through. Whole thing looks second-hand now. Fuck's sake.

He's swung it against the wall before he's even noticed he's got the ribbon handles in his hand.

Sparks in front of his eyes again. He's not breathing. *Breathe, you fucking freak. How hard can it be?*

In the boys' bathroom he puts cold water on his face and looks in the mirror. Rob says he blushed too when he was Luke's age but Luke doesn't remember it, reckons he's just saying it to make him feel better. Luke tries to see his brother's face in his own but it's not there. It's like they're opposites. Rob got their dad's dark eyes and clear skin and big square jaw. Luke got fuck-all.

He dries his face, goes to her room. Time to do it, stop dicking around. He breathes out slowly, nods once to himself, and knocks.

'It's me,' he says. 'Luke.'

She lets him in, closes the door behind him. She's brushing her hair, wearing full make-up and that blue dress with the bit missing so you can see a big teardrop shape of skin above her belly. Tight and smooth like stretched rubber. She's pulled the dress down a bit on the legs to cover the dressings on the cuts she did a few days ago. Three and a half weeks ago she was still fourteen. She looks about twenty-three.

'I'm just off out,' she tells him, but she doesn't move.

'All right.'

'I'm only going round Leah's.' She puts down the brush, folds her arms. Her phone with the unicorn sticker is in her left hand, where it always is. He does not look at her tits.

'All right,' he says again, and then he remembers the bag. He lifts it towards her. He hasn't even thought of what he's going to say.

'What's this?' When she meets his eye there's a smile on her face but it's the kind of smile you give a little kid who's done you a drawing and you can't tell what it's supposed to be.

'I bought it.'

'Yeah?' She laughs and it's actually like someone's turned the lights on. 'Yeah, I can see that. They don't give you bags usually when you rob stuff. What I mean is, why did you buy it?'

'It's six months,' he says, and then he wishes he hadn't

because the smile disappears. 'I mean, since you got here. But I mean it like a good thing, Paige, I meant…'

'Yeah. OK. I know.' The dancing thing in her voice has gone. But she takes it, thanks him. She slits a nail across the little sticker holding the top edges together. She lifts the tissue paper out, and then the dress. It's made of this thin, silvery-grey stuff and she holds it up high and waves it back and forward. Smiling at it, her head on the side.

'It's beautiful. Like a raincloud.' And she turns and wafts it down onto her bed and stands there watching it settle. She doesn't look at the label and she doesn't put it on. 'I love it, Lukey. But you really didn't need to.'

She takes his cheeks in her palms and squashes his face so his lips crumple in the middle and he jerks back, and the kiss she was going to put on his forehead stays on her beautiful lips. She makes a sad face for about half a second.

Then she says, 'Gotta go,' and picks up a handbag. She puts her phone in it and shoves something else inside too. Shiny packages, foil-wrapped squares joined together in a line.

'Paige,' he says, but the rest of it dies in his mouth. He knows what they are but what the fuck. He's *sure* she isn't seeing anyone.

A couple of weeks ago, at Leah's place, they all got caned and did truth-or-dare. And they made him admit he was a virgin. On the way home, she told him it was OK.

She said she was, as well. She promised it was true.

'It's nothing, forget it,' she says now, covering the johnnies in her bag with a pair of gloves. When she stands up, she looks different. She's wearing these earrings he hasn't seen before, gold and weirdly grown-up, somehow, the shape of them. She sees him looking, touches one, and winks. But it's not real. It's the face he's seen her putting on when she goes out, last month or two.

And then she nudges him out, follows him, locks the

bedroom door behind her. She goes down the stairs. While she's getting the Converse on Luke remembers the celery and the yogurt but it's too late now. Paige is out of the door and gone and she closes it so softly no one even notices except for him.

From his bedroom window Luke watches her. Even though she's too far away for him to see it, he thinks of the tiny wisps of hair that always get free at the edges of her neck, and the moles right in the middle of her back, on one of the bony bits of her spine. She's not wearing a coat, even though it's freezing out there. She's so white anyway, and that tiny dress makes her look blue.

Dead. His own voice says it in his head. *She'll look exactly like that when she's dead.*

She walks to the end of the road, stops for about fifteen seconds, and then a car drives up. Big shiny thing, but he can't tell the colour because of the streetlights. Dark, but it could be anything from red to black. She doesn't stick her arm out, and he realises it must have been waiting for her. Waiting, but out of sight. Luke wipes the wet glass, trying to get a better look. He thinks of the binoculars in his drawer, but there isn't time.

Paige gets in. The red brake lights go out the moment her door closes, and then it indicates left for a second. The indicator's cool, a moving line of LEDs like an arrow sweeping to the edge of the car.

It heads up towards Fishponds. Leah's is about three streets away in the other direction.

Later, in his dream, Paige kisses him once on the chest. Then she bursts, and she's just dust, and he wakes up with his heart shuddering like a pneumatic drill. Thick, crawling loneliness comes for him then, filling up his lungs, and even when he feels his way out into the corridor to crouch by Paige's door and listen for the damp sound of her sleeping, he can't breathe. He can't breathe at all.

3

Now

Ashworth's hands are in his lap, his seatbelt still on even though they've stopped. Wren gave him the morning to get settled in to the bedsit, and picked him up mid-afternoon. Now, he's staring out through the windscreen of the idling car, watching the rain. Or, more likely, watching the house, the one they've just arrived at after a stop-start hour on the road.

148 Shakespeare Terrace. Portbury, halfway between Bristol and the sea. Leah Amberley's house.

Knock number one.

There are roses outside the front room, but horticulture doesn't appear to be an enthusiasm shared by the wider community. Everywhere else: swollen IKEA chipboard leaning against pebbledash, faded plastic slides and ride-ons for long-gone toddlers. There are a couple of dozen roads just like it behind them, deep into the sprawl of suburbia.

Someone has wound fairy lights round the white poles that hold up the narrow porch over the front door. It isn't even dark yet, but those little bulbs are already going on-off, on-off, illuminating nothing much but the grey. And if that isn't a metaphor for a single girl squandering the best years of her life in a shithole, Wren doesn't know what is.

She clears her throat, and feels behind her seat for her

bag. Her phone tells her she has three missed calls, and she recognises the number before the voicemail even connects – it's the guy at HR who has been trying to get hold of her for the last week. She drops the volume so Ashworth can't hear, and listens.

Wren, hi. I'm not sure you're getting these messages. Can you call back? There's a few gaps in your file I need to chase. Just admin, nothing bad! It's Gary, he says, and he starts reeling off the number. She follows the instructions to send it the same way as the preceding three messages – *Press 2 to delete* – then drops the phone back into the bag.

'You ready?'

Ashworth frowns for a moment. 'Are there – has she got kids?'

The expression on his face, he might as well be asking if there are alligators.

'No.'

The rain is coming down so heavy by now that everything is slick and glossy. The daylight is sagging into evening. A van corners towards them, headlights on, and just for a second the glare projects a weak silhouette of the wet windscreen onto Ashworth's face. Like he's crying from the top of his grade-one head to his chin.

He looks out the window. 'I don't see why she's even on the list.'

'She was Paige's best friend.'

'Yeah but, so? I mean, Leah was my mate, too. It's not like I robbed *her*, is it?'

'Your mate? She come and visit you inside much, did she?' They both know the answer to that: Wren's seen the contact log. It wasn't just Leah who'd failed to visit. No one had come. Not his brother, not even his mum.

He sighs and she looks away because it is too intense, menacing, what he gives off. He's only been out a matter of days, so maybe it's just the HMP still lurching along in his veins. Sometimes it takes a while to clear.

'I just – I don't want to do this,' he says. 'With you there.'

Wren grabs her bomber jacket off the back seat. 'That's the thing about getting caught doing stuff you wanted to get away with, I suppose, Rob. You have to do stuff you don't want to do, to make up for it.' The wipers do another one-two before she kills the engine. 'You have to suffer,' she tells him brightly. 'You ready?'

He goes for the handle. 'All right. If I have to.'

There is no fence or gate. They go straight up the path. He has as much spring in his step as a man going to the gallows.

She gives him a nod. He knocks.

Movement inside, and then the door opens. Leah is preceded by the biting smell of bleach, and is wearing yellow rubber gloves. She is in her nursery uniform, a navy polo shirt with a logo of two teddies chucking a ball. She has straightened, highlighted hair. Make-up she must have spent a good chunk of her shit salary on.

She stares at Ashworth for a moment, and if Wren didn't already have her signature on the appointment document inside her file she'd have thought that somehow this visit had caught her by surprise.

'Fuck. *Rob.*'

She takes a step forward, lifts her arms. Wren moves in before she connects, getting between them like a barrier, before she realises she's got it wrong. Leah doesn't want to bash the shit out of him. She's trying to hug him.

The rain clatters down. There isn't room for both of them on the square of dry under the porch, not even if Wren was the same size as Leah, which she hasn't been since she was about eleven. But Leah is in no rush to invite them in. Her face tightens as she rocks back onto her doormat, looking Wren over like last night's condom.

Wren doesn't take it personally. The only thing she is interested in is what the hell is going on between these two people.

Leah was Paige's friend. She was her *best friend.*

Ten minutes later, the three of them are sitting facing each other across a flimsy kitchen table. Scraps of bhangra drift in through a broken window pane, the missing shards inexpertly replaced with duct tape. Leah took her time making tea, and now three mugs sit between them.

The protocol is that Ashworth reads his script first. With the acrid tang of Leah's interrupted cleaning still thick in the air, Wren passes him the three sheets of paper, his script that he will be reading at every visit they make. It is the culmination of weeks of work: taken from statements, redrafted by Wren, approved by her boss, ratified by SIO and the state-appointed solicitor seconded to the CAP, then finally agreed by Ashworth himself, by post a week before release. The full *mea culpa*, while his audience of one sits across from him, blank-faced.

Wren folds her arms and gives Ashworth a nod. 'When you're ready, then.'

He clears his throat, and begins.

'On the evening of the seventeenth of November 2012, after I finished work, I made a phone call to Paige Garrett, who lived at Beech View children's home in Kingswood, Bristol. I arranged for her to come and meet me. I was driving a car I had stolen from the garage in which I was a trainee.'

Wren fingers the handle of her mug, conjuring in her mind Paige's face, her footsteps. Imagines the hammering of her heart under the Superdry jacket she was wearing.

'I picked her up. We drove to the house of James Yardley, who had been Paige's counsellor at school. When we arrived at the house, I told her to wait until I found an open window.'

By the time police were made aware, the private firm providing the Yardleys' security had selected the relevant footage from the family's nineteen-camera array and sent it to their designated platform on the Avon and Somerset Police server. Faced with the overwhelming evidence, Ashworth had coughed for every charge without ado.

'She kept saying she didn't want to do it, but I needed her there. I went into every room in the house while Mr Yardley followed me. We could hear his wife, Lucilla, downstairs, crying and trying to get help. She was very upset and was threatening to call the police, so I instructed Paige to tie her to a chair in the kitchen.'

Minutes pass as he reads, summarising the hour of panicked action – the travel, the break-in, the confrontation, the search. As he reads it aloud in flat, faltering staccato, Wren searches every pause, every trip of his voice for clues to anything he's not saying, clues that could lead to what really happened to Paige. But there's nothing. He might as well be telling a story about total strangers.

Then, right at the end, something changes. His eyes move over the final line but his mouth closes, and he looks away. Apart from the suck and thump of the washing machine under the sink, there is silence. Leah, sensing the shift, starts inspecting her chewed fingernails.

'You need to finish it,' Wren tells him.

He takes a deep breath. 'I ran out of the house, we went different ways. I didn't see her again.' He lays the paper down on the table, almost reverently folding his hands across it. And looks up. 'I don't know where she is, Leah.'

No one could doubt the sincerity in his voice. But if nearly three years in prison was going to teach a man something, it was the ability to lie convincingly.

'Right. Well,' Leah says, scraping her chair back and standing. 'That's that then.'

Wren looks from Ashworth to Leah. 'Nothing you want to ask?'

'No. I've done what you said, I've heard his thing.' Leah takes Wren's half-full mug to the sink. 'What else do you want me to do?'

Give a shit, possibly? Wren wants to shout. But instead she tilts her head and says, 'You know the victim, is that right? James Yardley?'

'Sort of.' In the immediate aftermath of the crime Leah had been quoted in a couple of local news stories, appealing for information about her friend. Both times, she'd mentioned Yardley: once she was featured in an accompanying photo sitting with him, holding a framed headshot of herself with Paige. The angle of the piece was more a response to Yardley's instant forgiveness of Paige – *she's just a vulnerable child who made a very bad choice*, was the phrase he used – but it was clear from the coverage that Leah and Yardley had been brought together by their lobbying efforts. 'He's all right. Didn't deserve it. End of.'

Wren tries again. 'This is your chance, Leah. Don't you want to know anything else about what happened? Why Rob did what he did?'

Leah eyeballs her. 'Firstly, he'll tell me if he wants to, otherwise it's none of my business. And secondly, are you really expecting us to have some kind of heart-to-heart in front of you? I don't even fucking know you.'

'Sure, fine,' Wren says, trying not to think of all those empty check-boxes in the debrief paperwork. 'How about telling us what it felt like when Paige disappeared?'

'He's not here about Paige going missing.'

'Not exactly, but—'

'I was cleared of that,' Rob says, and takes an angry last mouthful of his tea before handing the empty mug to Leah. 'All I did the time for was the burglary.'

'Aggravated,' Wren adds.

'I don't even know why you're here, if I'm honest,' Leah says, turning to fill the washing-up bowl.

Wren has to raise her voice over the sound of the boiler heating the water. 'The programme is for people affected by the crime to have the chance to understand it.'

Leah twists the taps off but keeps her back to the room and starts dunking the mugs. 'I understand it.'

Wren wants to shake her. *You can't understand it. No one understands it.* Any of it: why Paige chose that moment to throw her entire future away, in such a spectacular fashion; where she went. What secrets Ashworth is keeping.

The answers, Wren is certain, are right here in this room. So why doesn't Leah want to know?

'We're done here then, right?' Leah says, drying her hands and gesturing back through towards the front door. 'You can go now.'

Without any good reason to delay her, Wren has no choice but to do as she is invited. 'Come on then, Robert,' she calls to him as she heads into the hall. *One down,* she thinks.

As Wren pauses to put her shoes back on, she catches a murmur from the kitchen, and glances back at them. Leah is close to Ashworth, her lips moving.

'...at my grandad's,' she's saying.

Ashworth lifts a quieting finger almost imperceptibly. Indicating Wren with an imploring flick of his eyes.

4

Before

Everyone else is in bed. Luke crouches with his ear against the office door. Mel's voice is low and muffled, and Paige has so far said pretty much nothing. If he hadn't been at his window to see her come along the road ten minutes earlier, he'd hardly have known she was in there.

'It's not just because it's my job,' Mel says.

'Yeah, right.'

'Paige, there are a lot of people out there who care about you—'

'Only cos they want the money—'

She laughs but not like it's funny. 'Well, OK, if you say so. But the rules say if you're gone that long we need to have it agreed.'

'It's in the book.' Paige is chewing her thumb, he knows from her voice.

'But you weren't where you said you'd be, were you? Mr Polzeath went out looking for you after the house meeting. He was – very disappointed.'

Silence from Paige.

It's just after half-two in the morning, and Paige is on a half-ten curfew. Luke would know if it had changed. But the police haven't been called, so surely Mel *must* have known where she was. No one else gets to go missing for four hours without the police coming. It just doesn't happen.

Except it does. For Paige it does. He thinks back, works it out. Third time in twelve days.

There's the scrape of a chair, someone getting up. Luke freezes. *Shit.* He scans his mental map of the safest place to go. Dining room. He slips noiselessly behind the door and presses his ear against the wall. It's thin, and he can hear them better.

Mel's saying in a hushed voice, 'Well I'm going to have to put something down.'

'It's already in the fucking book!'

'Not just about you being out late, Paige, even though we both know you're not being truthful there. I mean about *that*.'

Luke would do anything to know what she's talking about.

Paige says nothing. Luke imagines Mel watching her, head on the side, waiting. No one says anything for a really long time.

Eventually Mel sighs loudly, frustrated.

'I need a coffee.'

There's a pause, and then footsteps, and the office door opens. Luke drops to the floor and crawls, fast, under the dining-room table. She'll have to walk right past him to get to the kitchen but it's a big table, it should be enough to hide him.

'Stay here. I mean it,' Mel says to Paige. Even though she's whispering now she sounds worried, not angry.

Her feet appear, close enough to touch. Luke holds his breath, pulling his knees in tight. As she passes into the kitchen he realises that, once she's out there, the angles mean she might just be able to see him. Especially if she switches on the dining-room light on her way through. She's going to find him, and then Paige will know. Can he just get up and pretend he's sleepwalking? Or that he came down for a drink and fell asleep? No. Fucking *idiot*, of course not.

But she goes straight to the kitchen and flicks on the light. He hears Mel fill the kettle and flick it on. Paige opens the office door just long enough to call out, without bothering to keep her voice down. 'Black with sweetener, thanks for offering.'

Luke grins. She's a cheeky cow sometimes.

The kettle starts to rumble, and Mel gets her cigarettes out, puts one in her mouth while she rummages for her lighter. Making sure he doesn't touch any of the chair legs surrounding him, he shifts a few inches to the side so he can peer through. Mel's reaching up to unbolt the garden door. There's the scrape of the key in the lock: it's almost rusted shut. There's fuck-all to do in the garden, just a couple of sagging footballs and knee-high grass, so no one goes out there except to smoke. Mel gives the door a few hard yanks to get it open, then squeezes herself through the narrow opening, phone in hand. A flick of flame and her face glows bright for a moment as she lights her cigarette. She doesn't fully close the door behind her, so he can hear the sounds of the night outside.

The security light out there hasn't ever worked as far as he knows, but he can see her face clearly because she's got her phone out now. She's rubbing hard at her forehead with the wrist of the hand holding the cigarette, like it's the toughest night of her life. Luke edges a bit closer. If Paige comes out he's screwed but he's got to know who Mel's phoning, what she's saying.

The harsh, tarmacky smell of her cigarette finds him and there's a flash across his mind of his front room at home; him coming back from school, and his mum there, jumping up and grabbing the ashtray and squealing with laughter, trying to run round him to hide it outside and him laughing too. Laughing even though he hated her smoking, used to shit himself about her getting cancer, because back then cancer was still the worst thing he could think of.

He tries to block the thought that always comes after he remembers being at home, but it happens anyway. His front room that's not his any more. The height chart they had, marking off how tall they were whenever it was Christmas or back-to-school or birthdays, gouged into the doorframe of the sitting room so they couldn't even take it with them when they had to leave. His stuff gone, and Rob's and his mum's stuff gone, all their photos and everything, and a new family there instead. All the curtains changed, and everything painted white. And in his room, where he grew up, there's a baby. He blinks hard to get rid of it, and concentrates on Mel.

She's got the phone against her ear now, smoking as she speaks. He can't hear all of it but whatever she says, it's quick. *I knows* and *yeah buts* and it doesn't take a genius to see she's not being listened to.

'I'm just saying – no, she's not *bleeding*, but there's a mark – nothing, I'm not implying – I *know* what I said, I'm just saying if someone else sees – *OK!* All right. Fine.' Then, after a deep breath, 'I'm not comfortable about this, I want you to know that. She's – this could go very wrong. For us, as well. Fine. Yes. *Yes*, I understand.'

The blueish light goes out, and Mel shoves the phone into her back pocket, fury on her face. Luke shuffles back to the most hidden place, makes himself as small as he can. There's the sound of her coming back in, locking the door, then the fridge opening and shutting and the ring of a teaspoon against a mug. The light flicks off, and Luke wills himself invisible, as Mel's slippers pad on the carpet towards him. The stink of the smoke follows her like a cloud. She goes inside. Luke sags with relief, waits for the door to close, then moves back over to listen against the wall.

Mel's voice first. 'OK. Look—'

'No. You look,' Paige says, and it's obvious she's been in

there getting angrier and angrier. 'It's my fucking body. I get to do whatever I want with it.'

Softly, 'You're a *child*.'

'Fuck's sake! It's one little mark!'

'It's not about how big it is. It's where it is. It's what it looks like.'

'Yeah, well. Like I said, we were mucking around.'

'So you really are sticking with your story. That it was Leah who did… *that*.'

'Yes.'

'Even though you know that if someone at your school sees it – your swimming teacher, for example – they're going to have your social worker right up in your face about it.'

A pause. 'Whatever.'

'I know there are things you don't want going in the book, sweetheart—'

'I said, *whatever*.'

'I really don't want to make it difficult for you, but if someone else sees what I've seen—'

'Yeah, well, maybe you shouldn't have fucking seen it at all! Maybe you shouldn't have been eyeing me up in the first place!'

'Oh, Paige, come on! I've had swimming cossies longer than that dress! How could I *not* see it?'

'By not staring at my arse? How about putting down that you're a fucking pervert in the book? I mean, I know you look like a fucking dyke but I didn't think you'd go for *little girls*!'

Luke's eyes go wide. There's nothing from Mel, and there's nothing from Paige, not for ages.

He has to screw his eyes up tight to hear what Paige says next.

'I'm sorry. That was—'

But Mel cuts her off. 'OK. All right. Know what, I think that's enough.'

And she means it, she's not even going to do a sanction, it's like they're past all of that. She sounds completely beaten. Luke can feel the regret coming off Paige through the wall. Mel cares about her. She can be spiky sometimes but he trusts her; she cares about the kids, she's the only one who does.

Paige says, 'No, look, I'm sorry, I really am.'

'Yep.'

He hears the creak of a chair: they're coming out. He creeps quickly back under the table. The door opens.

Whispering now, Paige says, 'I'm sorry you had to wait up for me.'

Mel sort of laughs again. 'Well, that bit *is* my job. The curfew isn't really the problem here, Paige.'

They say goodnight and Mel takes the mugs back into the kitchen without bothering with the lights, then goes back to the hall. From where he's crouching Luke sees her dig in her jeans and pull out a phone again but this time it's her personal one with the diamond bits that have mostly come off. Not the shift phone. She pauses, like she's deciding whether to do something, but then she tips her head straight up at the ceiling with her eyes shut, and sighs, and sticks it back in her pocket. And then she's gone. He listens to her climbing the stairs, following Paige.

There's movement up there for a bit, toilets flushing and tiptoe-footsteps along the landings. Then the staff bedroom door closes and so does Paige's. It's not until Luke gets up that he realises how fucking freezing he is. He's only got shorts and a T-shirt on and his feet are numb and his arms are prickled with goosebumps.

He's about to go up but he stops. *Office door*. He remembers the sound of it closing, but not the crank of the lock.

He pushes the door, and it opens. He steps inside, quietly pulls it to. His eyes are already used to the dark so he leaves the light off. Without making a single sound he goes to the desk. He sits on the swivel chair, puts his hands on the keyboard. When he moves the mouse the screen comes to life and he's straight in, no password, nothing. He thinks, *fucking hell*, and he's grinning as he opens the file on the desktop marked *Current Residents*. He starts looking inside for anything on Fat Jake.

But he changes his mind when he sees the folder marked *Garrett, Paige*.

He lets the little arrow hover for all of about ten seconds. If he knows about her, he can be a better friend. He clicks twice. He starts to scroll down the documents. There are dozens of subfolders, called things like *Medical* and *Education* and *Previous Placements*, and he can't decide where to start. He highlights all of them and does the thing to send them to his email, but the thrill of it is buzzing through him and he's not thinking and before he realises he's clicked the wrong icon, the printer on the shelf behind him whirrs into life and the noise of it is like a fucking train through the silent house.

A sound upstairs. A door opening.

Shit.

Shit shit shit.

He opens the print queue but he doesn't know how it works, because who prints stuff? And the thing's spitting out paper and whatever he clicks – *delete*, *pause print job* – doesn't do anything. He's on his feet now, reaching up to the stupid machine that's sucking and clattering like it's laying a road. He tries to pull the thing out and get to the power button wherever the fuck it is and make it just *stop*.

All of a sudden there's silence again, the red light blinking. It's out of paper. He slumps back into the chair almost laughing. Relief swarms over him, and the blood thudding in his ears slows.

And then there's a buzz, and the striplight above his head goes on.

He screws his eyes shut against the sudden glare and when he opens them again she's there. Paige. Standing in the doorway, wearing a T-shirt that only just covers her knickers.

'Luke.'

He doesn't move.

She rubs a fist into her eye and blinks at him. 'What are you doing up?'

From the corner of his vision he sees that red light going on and off on the printer that's still making a wheezing cool-down noise. In his head he tells her *don't look*. Says it silently again and again like he can programme her. *Don't look. Just don't look.*

She yawns. He's never seen her with no make-up before, and it's like seeing her underwater, or asleep, like something he's not supposed to see. He opens his mouth but he hasn't got an answer.

She shrugs, already bored. 'Go to sleep, Lukey. You've got school.'

Paige turns away, switches off the light, and Luke's breath solidifies in his throat.

It's where it is, Mel had said. *It's what it looks like.*

In that second, when Paige turned away and her T-shirt lifted with her arm, what it looked like was a pinched circle, blotchy and red, like a string of beads had pressed into her flesh, hard enough to leave deep pits. Back of her leg, right at the top, just underneath the lace edge of her little shorts.

What it looked like was teeth marks.

5

Now

It is a café chosen by a perfect storm of necessity and conveniently steamed-up glazing, and in any other circumstance Wren would have walked right by. But she's starving, Ashworth is sullen, it's shitting it down, and so it'll have to do.

Inside, the atmosphere is heavy with atomised grease. Wren goes to the counter and orders a tea and a ham sandwich. She calls over to Ashworth for his order but he just shrugs and says he'll have the same. He gets up and goes off to the gents without another word.

Wren chooses a table, and starts an internet search on her phone for Leah's grandad. But even if she does track the old guy down, what possible justification could she invent for visiting him? *Your granddaughter mentioned you vaguely to my offender, I want to know why*? No. She pockets her phone when the order arrives, and taps the backs of her nails on the thick mug, watching the rings rise and spread in the surface of her tea.

Thinking. Trying to ignore the inane pop music from a tinny speaker in the kitchen out the back. And thinking.

Wren has never claimed to be any genius of psychology. She understands that it takes a while to get a decent understanding of someone, or a situation, a relationship. To date, she's spent maybe eight hours with Ashworth, not including the time spent on his files. No one would expect her to have a measure of a person in that time. But what just happened in there with Leah Amberley: that didn't make any kind of sense.

Ashworth returns from the gents drying his hands on his trousers, and Wren waits until he's folded himself into the booth opposite her.

Elbows on the table, she appraises him.

'Do you know how long it took to get the CAP from an idea to a thing we're actually trying out, Rob?'

He bites into his sandwich, chews, and gives a slow shrug. 'No.'

'I'll tell you.' She takes a sip from her mug, eyeing him over the rim. The tea is disgusting, as if the teabag had just come to the end of a long and arduous career. 'Twenty-two months, start to finish.'

'Right.'

'Best part of two years. A development panel of four core members of staff, maybe three dozen expert consultants. Thirty-odd drafts for the Department of Justice guidance, nine for the briefing to the minister. Fourteen versions of the handbook. Thousands and thousands of pages of research, evidence, projections. That kind of thing.'

'OK.'

She leans over the table. 'We got all the details down. How far we follow the sphere of the crime's influence. The way we approach the victims. Reporting, safeguarding, analysis, briefing, debriefing. Per diems. Do you want to know the one thing we couldn't decide on?'

'Nope.' He sends a cascade of sugar into his tea from a glass container.

'Outcomes. How we measure forgiveness, and remorse. At what point we can say, yep, this man has understood the gravity of his crime, and sincerely tried to apologise.'

He draws his finger and thumb down the corners of his mouth. 'I did apologise. I tried *sincerely* to apologise.'

'You didn't have to try very hard though, did you?'

'Are you saying I did it wrong, in there with Leah?' Black nothingness in his eyes where anyone else might have a smirk, or a wavering arrogance, or worry. Anything at all.

'I'm asking you,' she says, resting her chin on her fist, 'how come Leah isn't angry?'

Ashworth sighs and lets his eyeline drift high. He has a way of doing silences that make you feel he's already said all the things that matter to him, and that no one has been listening, and now he's given up.

'She was Paige's *best friend*, Rob. You got any idea what that means when you're fifteen?'

'Yeah.'

'Do you, really?'

Little buttons of muscle pop in and out at his jaw. 'No,' he says eventually. 'Is that better?'

They sit in silence for a while. The plates are collected and Wren looks through the file. The next visit is the children's home where Paige had lived. Beech View. She can feel his eyes burning into the sheets on the table.

And the thought strikes her all at once, like a kick to the back of the knees: maybe she is out of her depth.

If this was a normal probation case, there would be none of this cat-and-mouse. There would be meetings and agreements and no grey areas. Doing this job, Wren doesn't take other people's shit to heart: she wants them to go straight, because fewer knackers on the streets is fewer knackers on the streets. And until now, her job hasn't been to treat their personality or make them care. They can be who they want to be, and they very rarely surprise her. Big hard bastards and cocky little twats and everything in between. Some of them were for real and others were fronting, desperate to hide how shit-scared they were of the real world outside. Some of them wanted everything she could offer; some of them couldn't wait to get her off their backs and get up to their old tricks.

But none of them had got to her like Robert Ashworth.

Wren straightens up, remembering the other thing. 'So, what was that about Leah's grandad?'

He shakes his head like he doesn't know what she means.

'Because you know that's not something I'm going to be able to just forget about, right?'

'Why?'

She frowns. 'What do you mean, *why*? Because it's my job, Rob.'

He cocks his head, looks at her too closely. 'But it's not, though. Your job is to do what we just did. Tell everyone what an arsehole I am, so they've got someone to blame.'

'That's not exactly—'

'But if they want to forgive me, surely that's OK too, right?'

It's true. It's also true that there is something distinctly *off* here.

As they'd left Leah's house, she'd hugged him. Hugged *him*. The man who'd roped her best mate into an aggravated burglary. The missing persons file is still open, but it's been dropped to a rolling six-month 'weed-date', when some lowly DC will make a handful of maintenance calls to check for news. Without fresh evidence, that isn't going to change.

Wren looks down at her hands. She lets go of the folder, and the blood slowly returns to her knuckles.

When girls like Paige ran away, they took their phones and their money and one of a handful of things happened. They were found and returned. They stayed on the streets and reappeared on the system some other way: drugs, crime, sex work. If they disappeared permanently, it was never good. It almost always meant other people were involved, and those people rarely had that girl's interests at heart. At best, it meant serious exploitation. At best.

And Paige's closest friend – her lieutenant, her confidante, the girl who should have done her hair before their prom, and been maid of honour at her wedding and godmother to her kids – had welcomed Robert Ashworth into her home. She had buried her face in his shoulder like she'd been chalking off the days until she could hold him again.

They drive back to his place in silence, more or less.

Nearing his flat, he turns to her. 'When can we start looking for Luke? And my mum?'

'What do you mean, *we*?'

'You're going to help me. I need to find him.'

She shrugs, feigning disinterest, but she's interested. Him needing something from her can only be a good thing.

He lowers his voice. 'Please, Miss Reynolds.'

Wren sighs. 'If I'm going to help you do that, Rob – and I'm not saying I will – there's going to have to be a bit of give and take.'

'Like what? How much are we talking?'

She glances over, and the face on him; she actually laughs aloud. 'You can't bribe me, Rob.'

They arrive outside his block, and Wren pulls over and cuts the engine. 'I'm talking about the truth. About Paige. I want to know what happened.'

He gives her a long, slow nod. 'The truth.'

'If it's not too much to ask.' Just for a moment she lets herself believe that this is it. The moment where he cracks under the weight of the guilt. *I can't carry it around with me any more.* That kind of thing.

Her hope is short-lived. He gets out, closes the door behind him, and walks away.

She winds down the window. 'Bright and early tomorrow then, Rob,' she calls after him. He lifts the back of his hand in return, and then he's gone.

After he disappears into the stairwell, she waits a few minutes until he reappears on the second-floor walkway, his hands in his pockets. A woman is trying to navigate the narrow path with a buggy, and he pauses to let her pass. Without him seeing, the mother turns back to get another look at him. Probably caught off-guard by his chivalry; the strong, brooding atmosphere of his face. He is the kind of bloke women like the look of. Kind of bloke girls trust.

Number 28, his flat, is halfway along. He doesn't look down until he has his key in the door. When he turns, he gives Wren a nod. *I know you're watching me*, the look says.

I know you're watching me and I'm not going to give you a thing.

6

Now

Wren can hardly open the front door when she gets home. The barricade is an increasingly alarming collection of boxes, stacked along the narrow hallway in what Suzy probably imagines is an orderly fashion. Stamped along the edge of the largest container are the words *CuddleClose Co-Sleep Unit*.

Before she knew Suzy, she'd assumed that police officers were as neat and ordered off-duty as the job required them to be when on shift, but she had been very wrong. Even after ten years on the force, Suzy is as sloppy a homemaker as it is possible to be. Radclyffe, their curly-coated retriever, bounds down the stairs at her. He leaps up, knocking a smaller package to the floor with his tail and getting his claws caught in her buttonhole.

She scratches under his collar and unhooks him. 'I'm home,' she calls out, replacing the fallen parcel on top of the pile. She pictures their joint account, supine and emaciated, begging for intervention.

'Kitchen,' comes the reply.

Suzy is standing at the stove, stirring an impossibly huge silver pan that Wren has never seen before, an apron tied around her spherical stomach. Her cousin Marty, from an echelon of her vast and spreading family in which both the men and the women are built like Vikings, is sitting at the kitchen table surrounded by paperwork. Wren nods to Marty and pecks Suzy on the cheek.

'Who is this woman, Marty?' Suzy says archly, laying the spoon on the worktop and turning around. 'I'm not sure we've met.'

'That's not fair,' Wren protests. It is true that she's been working later than usual, but they've been over it already. She gets a couple of beers from the fridge, uncaps them and puts one in front of Marty.

He looks at the bottle longingly, but pushes it away. 'Sorry, can't,' he says, gesturing at the variously sized sheets of paper spread out in front of him.

'Oh, the new job?' Wren asks him. 'How's it going?'

'They've put him straight on the news desk,' Suzy says without turning.

He rolls his eyes. 'You know how you said they'd be bastards?'

Tipping the bottle into her mouth, Wren nods.

'Well, they're bastards.'

She swallows and laughs. He's recently changed careers, surprising everyone who knows him by eschewing the gardening he's always loved in favour of journalism. He is a huge man, but was always happier when his work involved planting saplings than sledgehammering patios. Whether or not he'll have the nose or the hide he needs to make it as a hack is yet to be seen.

He glances at the clock, swears softly, and starts hastily shoving his research into his shoulder bag. 'Evening shift. Should have been at my desk half an hour ago,' he says, getting to his feet. Then, to Wren: 'Can I have a word?'

'What is it?'

He looks to Suzy, who shrugs and goes back to her pot.

'Younnis Ibrahim,' he says to the table.

Wren stares at him. 'My Younnis Ibrahim?'

Ibrahim was a rapist who'd been controversially freed ahead of schedule. He also happened to be the last offender on Wren's caseload before she'd started on the CAP. It hadn't ended well: he'd been recalled to prison two weeks after release, and was awaiting trial for assault. Wren glances at the papers Marty is collecting up, and realises what he's saying.

'Tell me you're not writing about it.'

'Just a little thing, pre-trial kind of…' he says, trailing off.

'Bit of a coincidence they gave you that as your first story, isn't it?'

'No arguing in my kitchen,' Suzy says sharply.

Wren raises her eyebrows and asks him, with exaggerated generosity, 'What did you want to know?'

'They wanted a kind of profile, human angle.' The discomfort is so tight across his face, Wren almost feels sorry for him.

'I can't give you anything that's not already in the public domain, Marty, you know that. The court will have all the—'

'Not on him,' he says, looking up. 'On you.'

Her stomach wouldn't have lurched harder if she'd been dropped out of a plane. But she keeps her face pleasant and her voice level. 'Things must be pretty lean at the *Southwest Observer* if they're doing a profile on a probation officer.'

'It's because of the CAP. A lot of interest in it.'

'Interest? It's not interest, Marty, it's an agenda. They were fanning the flames before we even got started.' He opens his mouth to protest but Wren shakes her head. 'The answer's no. I don't want to see my name in it.'

He sighs, shoulders his bag, kisses Suzy on the cheek and leaves the room. Wren follows him. She gets between him and the front door before he has a chance to open it.

'I want you to promise,' she says, covering the latch with her hand, 'that you won't make this about me.'

'OK,' he says petulantly. 'Fine.'

Wren forces a friendly, 'Bye, Marty,' and opens the door, standing aside as he murmurs a farewell and leaves. The moment she closes it behind him, the smile hits the floor. She stands for a moment with her forehead resting on the wood.

She hadn't expected this. It's no surprise that the paper's editor, ex-tabloid and as right-wing as they come, would be against anything remotely progressive in the judicial system. But that isn't the issue. If Marty had seriously been sent over to dig the shit on Wren, that makes it something else.

But then, it was only ever going to be a matter of time. She shakes herself and goes back into the kitchen.

'It wouldn't hurt, you know.' Suzy is still busy with her pan. 'It's his first gig, after that massive slog at uni.'

'You're not serious,' Wren says. 'Do you not remember them baying for blood after Ibrahim went back inside? They'll be all over the front garden.'

Suzy gives her a look. 'Let's not be dramatic, chicken. It's not exactly O.J., is it?'

Wren, wanting the subject changed, takes a deep swig from her bottle and goes to join her at the hob. She slips her hands around Suzy's waist and rests her chin on her shoulder.

'What *is* that you're making?' Wren asks, kissing her ear. 'And will I be expected to eat it?'

'Chutney, and fuck off,' Suzy says, shrugging her away. Pregnancy makes the skin more sensitive, she'd told Wren that before. It wasn't to be taken personally.

Radclyffe's claws clack on the floor tiles as he comes in, his lead dangling from his mouth.

'Take him out, will you?' Suzy asks. 'And careful of the boxes. Most of it's going back.'

'Again?'

The last few months, the house has become a thoroughfare for short-stay items of nursery furniture and baby equipment. Each item painstakingly chosen, eagerly awaited, then falling short of Suzy's expectations in some way upon receipt. Too mumsy, too pretentious, too cute, too boring. Cheap and nasty, or suddenly *beyond our budget*. But it isn't the continual shopping itself that bothers Wren. It's what it says about Suzy's decisiveness, her ballsiness. The things she seems to be losing.

Wren walks with Radclyffe for nearly an hour in the early-evening drizzle. When he pulls back to inspect a piss stain outside the florist's, she takes his hint and goes in, emerging minutes later with a flamboyant armful of dahlias. Not even Suzy can stay grumpy in the face of dahlias.

Then, on a roll, she buys the least repellent-looking alcohol-free wine she can find at the offy, and catches Suzy's favourite deli minutes before it closes. She picks out olives, cheese, pastrami, some fancy little crackers. Sex food. Food for feeding a little of to your lover in bed, just enough to build the reserves back up before...

Well.

Before hauling one's arse out from under the covers to put the next disc of the boxset in the player, if she is entirely honest.

Radclyffe's tail slaps damply against her thigh as they head home, and at the second pass, things are better. Suzy has finished making the chutney and is reading, lying on her side on the living-room sofa, her belly buttressed by a V-shaped cushion that appeared a few weeks previously. Wren produces the dahlias with a flourish, and Suzy laughs.

'I don't deserve five seconds of you, you know,' she says, inelegantly hauling herself upright. In the time it takes Wren to lay the flowers on the low wooden table, Radclyffe has beaten her to the warm spot beside her.

'Yes, I love you, I do I do I do,' Suzy tells him in her pouty dog-voice, accepting a lick on the cheek before shoving him gently to the floor. She wipes her face with the heel of her hand and smiles up at Wren. 'But I love your mamma even more.'

Wren sits, and Suzy puts her head on her shoulder. She even smells different these days: there's an earthiness, something animal. Her body has become a foreign environment, glinting with magic or hostility with a change of the light. It is somewhere Wren has no access to. But it is temporary, of course. That's what everyone says.

'They're taking me to the pub tomorrow after the day tour,' Suzy says glumly.

Wren had forgotten it's her last shift before she goes on maternity leave. 'But that'll be fun, won't it?'

'No.' She groans and glowers at her belly. 'I can't even get pissed, thanks to *you*,' she says with mock accusation at the baby, who responds with a kick that Wren can see through the stretch of Suzy's sweatshirt.

They both laugh. Shifting closer, Suzy says, 'Really though, I'm sorry I've been grumpy.'

'It's OK.' Wren pats her leg, then gets up and goes out for the plates. The TV is on by the time she gets back. She sets the food out and puts a bit of everything on each plate. Radclyffe's tail thumps on the rug, but he's a good boy and he stays where he is, eyebrows seesawing with the effort of not eating.

Suzy says, 'It's not OK, though, is it? Doesn't even count as mood swings if you're mardy *all* the time. I had a new PC in tears yesterday. Know what I said to her?'

'Nope.' Wren takes an olive.

'I said, if she wanted a job cuddling bunnies, she should have got a job at the cuddly bunny farm. In front of the whole team. Poor bitch.'

Wren snorts, spits the stone into her hand. 'She going tomorrow?'

'I fucking doubt it. Probably spending the evening sticking pins in a little fat doll with shitty hair and chevrons on the shoulders.'

'Your hair's not shitty.'

'Oh, but I am fat?'

'You're just… beautifully…'

'If you say *blooming* I swear to God I'll flay you bloody.'

Wren smiles. 'I'm sure she'll forgive you,' she tries, but Suzy just makes a *pff* sound and snaps a cracker. Wren can't help thinking: *six months ago, you wouldn't have given two shits what a baby constable thought.*

There is a pause. 'Come,' Suzy says, a little whine curling at the edge of her voice. 'To the thing, the… *send-off.* Will you?'

'Can't. Work.'

'Shit.' Suzy reaches for the remote, switches off the TV and faces her. 'Shittety shit. God, I'm so selfish, I forgot. The new offender. How did it go?'

Wren makes a vague grimace. 'Fine,' she says. It would have sufficed for anyone else. Not Suzy.

'Fine.' A pause. 'Huh.'

'Yeah. Nothing out of the ordinary.'

Suzy's eyes narrow further and Wren laughs, aiming for breezy. She peels off a slice of charcuterie, folds it and pops it in her mouth. But Suzy isn't distracted.

'You know, just starting the visits. Doing the school where the victim worked tomorrow.'

'Are we talking about the same case?' Suzy asks. 'Young guy, aggravated burglary?'

'That's it, yeah,' Wren says. Another sheet of pastrami, because Suzy's not going to be eating it.

'With the teacher.'

'Guidance counsellor.'

'Right.' Suzy puts her plate down. 'So, this offender. Do I know him? He got a name?'

'Ashworth. But you know how it goes. I'm not really supposed to talk about it.' Technically, the confidentiality clause goes for both of them, but it's an edict that has never stopped them gossiping about their cases before. Wren can practically hear the thin ice cracking.

'Right. Loose lips sink ships.' Suzy initiates a game of eye-contact chicken that Wren knows she is going to lose.

The simple thing, of course, would be to just tell her. That the case involves the girl who went missing, three years ago, the one Wren had got so upset about. But she knows exactly where that conversation would lead and she just does not want to go there. Because the fact is, even as their rock-solid unit of two is swelling inextricably to accommodate three, she's finding more and more space between them. And it's not Suzy's fault. It's just that since their focus has shifted onto becoming a family, all Wren can see are their differences. Suzy is someone whose family adores her, someone for whom even the word *family* has an entirely different meaning.

And alongside that, she knows that Suzy is never going understand how, with a past like her own, Wren couldn't just let Paige's disappearance be forgotten.

To Wren, that's not just a difference between them, it's more like a gulf, a widening chasm. And it's just not an option to start talking about it now, when they're so close to becoming parents together. So she doesn't mention Paige's name. Instead, she clears up the plates, and tries not to notice Suzy's worried gaze following her from the room. Because although Wren's whip-smart girl has become temporarily forgetful, and tearful, and *moody as hell*, the one part of her that the tornado of hormones has left one hundred per cent intact is her perceptiveness. It is what makes her a brilliant cop. She can smell avoidance at a range of miles.

Long term, the black shadow that trails behind Wren is going to have to be thrown into the light. She's always known it. But that's OK. Right now, she's got a job to do – for Paige, and for herself.

She doesn't need long term.

7

Before

Luke crumples up the brown paper bag with the rest of the cold chips in it and pushes it away. Across the restaurant there's a dad staring at his phone, ignoring the two little lads with him. They're dicking about, sticking chips in straws and blowing them at each other and falling about laughing. Then the dad – hard bastard – looks up, straight at Luke, who drops the grin that had crept up on him. Luke looks away but he can feel the eyes still on him, driving into him like he's a fucking paedo or something. Twat – he didn't mean anything by it, was only because of the kids. Reminded him of him and Rob, how they must've been little boys once.

Rob comes back from the gents. He's drying his hands on his trousers – he's always done it, says it's because Luke was scared of driers when he was a kid. Sitting down, Rob turns round to see what Luke's trying to avoid looking at and clocks the dad, who's started hissing at the youngest one. The boy's saying he's sorry and has started to cry, leaning his head on the washed-out reverse of a life-size Ronald McDonald sticker on the window. The older one's staring at his feet. They want to go home, anyone can see it. Home to their mum.

Rob turns back. 'It's like they have dad exams.'

'What?'

'Like you have to prove you can be as big a wanker as possible before you're allowed kids.'

Luke snorts, but it's not funny is it? The kid's bawling now, and the dad's pointing his fat finger in the poor little fucker's face. Rob leans over and gets in Luke's eyeline.

'Take it easy, mate,' he tells him, and Luke realises that his hands are in fists. He shrugs.

As they get up and walk to the door Luke can hear the dad saying, '—them to think you're a little fucking poof? Do you? Stop fucking crying.' Then, rounding on Luke, 'Fuck you looking at?'

Luke's heart is a tight balloon in his chest taking up all the breathing space and the twat's standing up now and he's massive.

The older kid's going, 'Dad, don't, Dad, please.'

And Rob's coming back, pulling at Luke's jacket, going, 'Luke? *Luke. Lukey*. Come on,' and to the other guy he says, 'Sorry, take no notice. Sorry.'

And they're on the pavement then, running, and Rob's pulling him along – 'Let's get the fuck out of here, seriously' – and Luke looks back and the kids are staring at him. The little one's red eyes are wide. Scared shitless of his own dad and he'll have to get in the car with him in a minute and then what.

Luke has made it worse. *Fuck*.

There's a gap in the hedge round by the drive-through bit. Rob ducks in first, holding some of the brambles up out of the way for Luke but bungling it so they both get scratched to fuck anyway.

The overgrown sprawl of hedge thins out and they're on gravel, then a cracked-up path, edged with concrete posts at intervals, the wire fence long gone.

Rob's laughing, saying, 'What were you going to say to him?'

Luke ignores him. They're in the trading estate bit now, heading for the park. Breathing hard, Luke slows down.

Rob zips up his jacket. 'Do yours. It's cold.'

'I'm not a fucking baby.'

'All right, *Jesus*. I'm only saying.'

They walk in silence until they're nearly at the field.

'What was that about, then? Back there?'

Luke shrugs.

'Mate, you've got to let stuff go, you know?'

'No. I don't.'

'You don't have to take on everyone else's shit.'

'Whatever.'

'It's not like you haven't got enough—'

'I said *whatever*.'

'—shit of your own, I was going to say.'

Rob sighs, reaches inside his jacket and pulls out a pack of Lamberts and lights one. Luke gives him a sideways look, and Rob rolls his eyes.

'What? Don't you fucking start. Had enough earache from…'

But he doesn't finish it. Doesn't need to.

It's like a spell, talking about their mum. You say her name accidentally and everything changes. He tries not to think about her. Concentrates on the sounds – their feet crunching stones against fractured concrete as they walk. The smell of Rob's fag. All he wants to do is shake the picture of his mum from his mind, but the effort of not-thinking makes it gain traction. Her alone in that room with the window looking onto the corridor and the nurses' station, the blind on the outside so she can't close it, so she doesn't

so she doesn't

so they can watch her.

Luke pulls out the button that he keeps in his pocket. She wanted to sew it back on for him last time he saw her. They wouldn't let her have a needle so she went off and came back with glue, and it was funny, at the time, because it was so stupid. What damage could she possibly do with a *needle*, she'd asked him, rolling her sunken eyes. He'd made himself smile back, even though he could think of plenty of things. But he didn't tell her any of them.

He picks the very last ridge of glue off with his thumbnail. He turns the button over in his hand. Then he lobs it as far as it'll go.

Rob says, 'Want to talk about her?'

'No.'

Rob pulls on the cigarette a few times, eyeing him as they walk. 'And are you talking to—'

'No,' Luke says, cutting him off because if there's one thing he wants to do less than talk about his mum, it's talk about Mr Yardley, the counsellor who comes to school on a Tuesday lunchtime to try to make him talk about his mum. And Luke's fine with talking to him in general, but he's not saying a fucking word about *that*. Yardley's all right, he doesn't push it, and he doesn't give him any bullshit cliché stuff about how it'll all be all right in the end. But the fact of it is, Luke's already said both the things he's going to say.

She got sectioned.

My life went to shit.

That's all there is.

Rob flicks the fag away, tucks his hands in his armpits, and leaves it.

They reach the field, and Rob finds a football in the hedge. He's dribbling it back, shouting, happy. Luke runs at his brother and makes a play for the ball but Rob turns and boots it off towards the goal frame. He chases after it and he's so fast; Luke's forgotten how fast his brother is, he's like a racehorse. Rob pulls his jacket off after a bit and he's been working out because his shoulders have rounded out like watermelons where they used to be just bony corners like Luke's. Luke has to try to catch him, but he hasn't played in months and they've only kicked it around the goal for a bit before he's had enough.

He stands there bent over for a while, his hands on his knees, getting his breath back. When Luke looks up, Rob's leaning against the goalpost, his head tilted. Watching him.

'So are you not going to ask?' Rob says.

'Ask what?'

Rob folds his arms. 'I said, on the phone. Had some news for you?'

'Right.' Luke squints up at him. 'Go on, then.'

'About the guardianship. About you coming to live with me.'

'What about it?' Luke flexes his hands in his pockets. It's going to be bad news. The next thing out of Luke's mouth is going to have to be *thanks for trying*.

'I talked to your social worker. We went through all the forms and everything. She's doing the assessment and she reckons it'll be all right.'

Luke presses his eyes shut until they feel all right again, dry, and when he opens them Rob's swinging his bag off his back and unzipping it.

'You've got to fill these in,' he says, taking out some sheets of paper. They're crumpled at the bottom and Rob tries to smooth them out before he hands them over to Luke. 'We've both got to go to this family court thing and then I get to be your guardian. Until Mum gets better. And we'll get our own money for your food and clothes and all that, direct payments.'

Luke's bouncing on his heels. He can't help it. Rob's birthday, just over a month away. Thirty-four days. He thinks of his room at the home, what it looked like when he arrived and how fucking amazing it'll be to pack everything up into his bags again and get the fuck out of there. Rob's place is proper tiny, he'll be kipping on the floor probably, but Luke doesn't care. There'll be no more sanctions and no more waiting all morning for Fat Jake to finish his wank before he can use the shower and no more *those are angry feelings you've got, Luke* and *looks like you're getting pretty frustrated there, Luke*, and no more—

Paige.

No more Paige.

He stops bouncing.

'I can't.'

The smile slides off Rob's face like it had been stuck on with Vaseline. 'The fuck you talking about, *you can't*? You telling me you want to stay in Beech fucking View?'

Luke doesn't answer. Rob stares at him a bit, and then he starts nodding.

'That girl. Whatshername.'

Luke keeps his mouth shut. He *knows* Rob knows her name. He's seen him looking at her when he visits. There's a reason they're out here, and not in there, and that look Rob's got, that's the reason.

'Seriously, *that* girl?' Rob says, and a cloud goes across his face that makes Luke look away. 'Is that what we're talking about here? You can't leave cos you've got a hard-on?'

'It's not like that, all right?'

'No? Tell me what it is like then. Tell me why I wasted all that fucking time trying to help you.'

'I can't—' Luke starts, and then he takes a deep breath. 'I can't leave her behind. Something bad's happening with her.'

'Bad like what?'

Luke shrugs. He can't say about the car she got into without admitting he was spying on her, and he definitely can't say about the bite mark or the johnnies. Even the jewellery she was wearing a few days ago – if he told Rob about that, what would he say? *Presents don't mean she's being pimped out. Johnnies just mean she's a slut.* He knows something is wrong, but Rob's not going to see it.

'Bad like *what*, for fuck's sake? What do you mean?'

Luke doesn't let his gaze drop but he can't make himself explain.

'Nah, mate,' Rob says, shaking his head. He makes it so he's looking down at Luke, chin out, and Luke sees the thing about his brother that he doesn't like to see. 'Nah. You've got to be fucking careful what you're saying here, little man. You need to keep your head down and your nose out, right?'

'Just forget it,' Luke says. His face is burning, and there's tears coming out of him now because he doesn't want Rob being pissed off at him but he can't make him understand. He wants to go and live with him, he really fucking does, but Paige has got no one else.

Rob's face changes and their dad disappears and he says, 'All right, Luke, mate, come on. I'm just saying.'

'Yeah, well, fuck you.' Luke's shoulders are right up and he wipes the back of his hand angrily against his nose. 'You've got no fucking idea.'

Because someone's got to help her and no one's doing it. Even Mel's acting like nothing's going on when it clearly is. Paige is out more nights than she's in. And she needs to live somewhere safe, where people give a toss about her.

Rob's holding his shoulders. 'Come on, mate. Calm down. You've got to breathe, Luke.'

It comes to Luke so quickly then that he can't believe he hasn't thought of it before. Can *he* get her out of there?

He does as his brother says and breathes, then ducks Rob's grip and takes a step back and his vision settles. It's like he's taller, growing with the idea itself, filling out, because maybe—

Maybe he *can* get her out. Maybe *he's* her chance. All he needs is evidence.

He takes a deep sniff and wipes his eyes on the back of his sleeve. And he smiles.

8

Now

Ashworth, who has stared wordlessly ahead the whole way here, becomes suddenly animated as Wren turns across the threshold of the school grounds and enters the car park.

'Used to pick Luke up from here,' he says, craning his neck to see the buildings. 'Every Thursday.'

'Yeah? Why?' Wren has been there herself at kicking-out time and it's the same as any other state comp. The kids walk themselves home.

'Keep an eye on him,' he says, defensive. 'Let people know he weren't an easy target. Why else?'

A clutch of girls swings past the front of the car, sharing a secret. Mid-teen, every aspect of their uniforms hitched up or nipped in for maximum impact. Ashworth watches them, then clocks Wren's raised eyebrow, and looks pointedly away.

She checks her phone. Since the previous day, she's left two messages for Leah Amberley, on the pretence that there's an additional form she needs her to sign. So far there has been no reply, which if deliberate is a mistake on Leah's part. All it tells Wren is that she has something to hide.

Putting her phone away and getting out of the car, she spots the head teacher striding across the car park to meet them. Ahmed Bashir is as straight-backed as he is broad-shouldered. Late thirties, with one of those double-grasp handshakes Wren knows for a stone-cold fact he's learned from management training. She doubts he's done a day's teaching in his life, especially in a school like Westmead.

Wren gets the shake first, then Ashworth.

'Ms Reynolds, so good to meet you in person,' he says. 'And, uh, Mr Ashworth. Welcome.' They follow him into the building to sign in.

'There are a handful of students in our sixth form who were contemporaries of Paige's who've agreed to come and meet you, and some teachers,' he says. Wren knows from their exchange of emails that he'd never met Paige personally, hadn't started at the school until after she'd gone missing. To Wren he says, 'I'm afraid I haven't been able to find any forwarding address for Luke.'

Wren nods, thanks him for trying.

'Not at all. I did try to get someone who had been involved in the Care Ambassador project – Oliver something? – but hit a brick wall there I'm afraid.'

'Oliver Polzeath.' Polzeath and his wife Alice owned the chain in charge of the unit that had been home to both Paige and Luke. Paige had been a Care Ambassador, part of an initiative set up by the council.

'No matter,' Wren says. 'He's on our list for a visit anyway.'

They follow Bashir along a corridor and through another set of doors into a bright atrium. 'This is the new IT department. You'll be in what we call the Outside-the-Box room.'

She forces a smile, thinking instantly of Suzy, making a mental note to tell her later. It's the kind of mindless management crap she just loves to hate.

'Are we likely to get this finished before the students break for lunch?' Bashir asks, with an apologetic wring of his hands. 'Just to minimise disruption.'

'Of course,' Wren says, knowing that it's got nothing to do with disruption and everything to do with exposure. If one un-briefed student recognised Ashworth, the place would be swarming with local news decrying the presence of a convicted criminal on school property. 'We'll do what we can.'

'Bring you some coffee maybe, help you get started?'

'Yeah,' Ashworth says.

'No, thank you. We'll be fine,' Wren says, then, turning to Ashworth, 'Ready?'

'Not really,' he says emptily.

Wren pushes open the doors.

The room has been laid out like an interview, but one where the panel consists of half a dozen teachers and the same number of teenage girls. Straight lines of desks facing two chairs. The entire place falls silent as they go inside.

Less like an interview, actually, and more like a courtroom.

Wren thanks everyone for coming, and then makes them all stand up. Once the tables have been pushed against the walls, she rearranges the chairs into a ring, and sits down.

'That's better.' She gestures Ashworth to take the chair beside hers.

He scans the room. 'Where is he?'

'Who?'

'Yardley,' he whispers, eyes darting.

'Not today, Rob.'

His shoulders drop with relief, but it's soon replaced by confusion. 'Then why are we *here*?'

The chairs fill, with a scramble from the girls to ensure they sit together. All but one of the girls is white, each indistinguishable from the next with their long, straightened hair and skinny jeans. The one black girl is dressed the same and has an armful of highlighted braids twisted into a fat knot behind her head.

Every pair of eyes in the room is staring right at Ashworth. Unease, edging into panic, twitches on his face.

She can't force him to talk. But that look on his face, the

shame, the desperation: *that* she can use. *That*, in answer to his question, is why they are here.

Wren starts her spiel.

'Everyone in this room has been affected in some way by what Robert Ashworth and Paige Garrett did to a member of staff at this school. As you all know from the letters I sent, what we're here to do today is talk about that crime, and the ways in which your lives have been altered by it.'

She turns to Ashworth, who is busy trying to drill an exit into the middle of the carpet by staring at it. 'We're going to start by introducing ourselves, Rob.'

He looks up. Clears his throat. 'I'm Rob. Robert Ashworth. I'm twenty-one.'

'Go on.'

'I'm unemployed, but I've done some training in—'

'Why don't you tell us what you did?' the black girl says suddenly. Her chin is up, defiant, and she's staring Ashworth hard in the face. 'Cos this is kind of bullshit otherwise, isn't it?' She transfers her glare to Wren. 'I didn't come here to hear about his career plans.'

Wren feels Rob looking at her for guidance.

'Where did Paige go?' the girl goes on. 'After you knocked off Mr Yardley's place? Did you kill her?'

'*Lily*,' commands one of the teachers, a woman with strings of magenta and purple beads round her neck and pink streaks in her curly brown bob. A plastic A2-size portfolio leans against her chair. Art teacher, Wren guesses. 'That's not what we're here to do.'

'No? Then what *are* we here to do? Tell him we forgive him?' She scowls. 'Well, I don't. I don't forgive him. Paige was doing *fine*. And then this piece of shit got her into stuff she would never have done.'

The art teacher stands up. 'OK, come on. Outside. We need to talk.'

'Come on, Miss, I'm just saying—'

'Outside, *now*.'

The girl gets up, delivers a death glare first to Ashworth and then to Wren, and does as she's directed. The art teacher closes the door behind them, re-entering half a minute later alone.

'We've decided that it's maybe best that Lily doesn't participate after all,' she says. 'There's quite a lot of anger there still. It's not appropriate for… this.'

'But that's exactly what we're here for,' Wren says, doing her best to hide her frustration. Ashworth needs to see it. *She* needs to see it.

But the woman is back in her seat. She shakes her head tightly. 'No, not today. I'm sorry. My duty of care is to the students.'

'Paige was one of your students,' Wren says.

'Indeed she was,' the woman says, missing the implication. She reaches down for the folder and lifts it onto her lap. Laying her hands in it she says, 'I brought along some of Paige's artwork. Would you like to see it?'

Ashworth closes his eyes.

'Yes,' Wren says.

The teacher goes to the whiteboard and uses circular magnets to attach a large rectangle of paper to it, maybe a couple of feet in width. 'This was for a year ten project. The last term before she disappeared.'

It's a painting, black into greys into browns in the background, reds and purples and blues in the foreground. The whole thing like a bruise.

'We were doing a project about emotion, and how artists have expressed their feelings through their art,' the teacher says.

Chairs scrape as the participants turn to peer at it. An amorphous border of shadow made from layer upon layer of handprints, the fingers pointing towards the centre. Wren can picture Paige painting it: coating her hands in a hundred different shades of dark and placing them on the sheet, repainting, turning the sheet, printing again. Soft hands. Not even fully grown.

'Paige spent hours on this. She came back in during the lunch break and asked if she could finish it. We don't get that very often.'

In the centre of the sheet there is a figure. The proportions are all wrong – legs too short, fingers lumpy and overlong – but it is recognisably female. Arms wrapped around her naked body. Protective, futile. Next to Wren, Ashworth is staring ahead. Through the wall, actively avoiding the whiteboard.

'The prompt Paige was given to work from was "anticipation". For reference, these,' she says, drawing out another few sheets and positioning them alongside Paige's picture, 'are what some of the others produced.'

Other students had painted abstracts of bright colours, sparks, smiling faces with eyes gripped shut. A line of fireworks with their fuses just lit.

'I thought she had misunderstood. Her classmates had taken the word to mean excitement about the future, that kind of thing. But to Paige, anticipation was about what she expected to happen.'

One of the girls sniffs, and another covers her face.

Wren turns to Ashworth. 'You want to respond to this at all?'

He rubs his hand over his mouth and shifts his gaze briefly from his feet to the teacher. Wren wants to shake him. She wants to kick the chair from under him, make him look. But it is as if the picture is invisible. It is nothing to him.

She had been nothing to him.

And all he says is, 'I didn't hurt her.'

*

After Ashworth has read his script, the remaining time in the classroom is spent listening to the stories of the people who'd known Paige. They damn her unintentionally with faint praise. She wasn't stupid, but not a genius; cheerful, sometimes, but also moody. A teenager, essentially. Wren is left with the impression that none of them had known her, not truly.

There is a conversation about a fight that broke out once, a few months before Paige disappeared, in which a boy Paige's age had started a rumour about Robert and Luke's mother. One girl recounts how Paige had been present when both brothers had ambushed the boy outside the school in retaliation, and how she'd stuck up for Luke when he was disciplined later.

'She was pretty tight with Luke,' one of the girls says, 'even if she didn't exactly hang around with him here. She kind of *got* him, you know? All the stuff about his mum. Because of what happened with her family, I suppose.' She addresses this to the floor, then glances up to see Ashworth's response, but he is unreadable.

The art teacher leans forward and says, gently, 'It must have been very hard for Luke.' Glancing at Ashworth, she adds, 'And for you, I should think.'

Everyone looks at Ashworth, who shifts in his seat and glares hard out of the window.

Bashir calls the meeting to a close ten clear minutes before the lunch bell, and Wren deposits Ashworth back in the car for safekeeping before heading back in to find Lily. On the way, she tries Leah again but it goes to voicemail.

Wren finds Lily in the library. She's wearing glasses, a textbook open in front of her. Even from the other side of the room it's clear she isn't reading it. Wren is right next to her by the time she looks up.

'What do you want?' she says, in a whisper.

'Can we talk?'

She sighs, annoyed, but relents, and Wren follows her out to a heavy door that leads to stairs at the back of the building. The fire door thumps shut, and Lily folds her arms, glaring.

'You get what you came for?' she asks, her voice echoing in the hollow stairwell.

Wren gives a loose nod, non-committal. 'Would have liked your input.'

'Yeah, well. They just wanted to have it over and done with. Like everyone else. Forget it ever happened.'

'What makes you say that?'

'People thought she was OK before but— I don't know. Say what you like about Mr Yardley, no one could believe she'd done what she did to him. I mean, seriously – tying the wife to a chair? What the fuck?' She shakes her head, incredulous.

'What *do* people say about Mr Yardley?'

She rolls her eyes like it's a stupid question. 'I don't mean like that. Just – fucking do-gooder. All caring and bullshit.'

'Paige was your friend?' Wren says, trying a different way in.

'Why else would I have been in that room?' There is a practised disdain on her face but she is young and it is only thin. Transparent to the forgiving eye.

'Had you known her long?'

Her gaze drifts, defocusing. 'She got moved around a bit but we went to primary school together for a while, year four and a bit of year five. Then she got a new placement or something and I didn't see her until she started here in year eight.'

Wren smiles. It isn't hard to imagine them together as little girls – Paige's hair still white-blonde, Lily maybe in braids and bobbles. 'How did she get on here, really?'

Lily starts to pick at a loose thread on the cuff of her

sweatshirt. 'She was… things were tough for her. I mean, obviously they were tough, or she wouldn't have been in care. Her mum was a smackhead or something, hadn't even tried to contact her in years and years. I mean, can you imagine doing that to a kid?'

She didn't want an answer, and Wren couldn't even begin to formulate one.

Lily sighed. 'But I mean, even before that. She was one of them people who've got like a shit-magnet, you know what I mean?'

Wren tells her she does.

'Even when we were little, crap just used to happen to her. And then as soon as she was old enough to bother about boys she had this way of picking out the bastards.'

'Bastards? In what way? Who are we talking about?' Wren has read Leah Amberley's statement to the police maybe a dozen times. She was asked explicitly whether there was anyone Paige seemed afraid of, or whether she'd ever talked about anyone being abusive to her. The answer had been no. No and no.

But Lily is looking at Wren like she's defective. 'Robert Ashworth not strike you as a bastard? She hung out with *him* a lot.'

'They were a couple?'

'I don't know. They hung out. I didn't say she was *with* him.'

Something about the way she says it makes all the circuits flash in Wren's head. 'But there was someone else?'

'Maybe. I thought so but…' she trails off, shrugs. 'She kept it way secret. It was kind of the reason I didn't see much of her in the last few months before she… before it happened. We'd been friends all that time and then she started being, I don't know. Secretive. Closed-off.'

'Did the police ever ask you about Paige?'

'For like five minutes. I told them what I'm telling you.'
'It wasn't followed up?'
'Why would it be? There wasn't anyone else there that night. Just Paige and *your guy*.' She looks away, wraps her thin arms around her ribs.
Wren waits for a moment before saying, gently, 'It hit you hard.'
The girl's expression goes through defiance and derision before settling into what looks like its natural state: a sadness so profound Wren can almost feel its weight in the gravity around her.
'I just laid low for a while, after she disappeared. I mean, I say that, but actually I couldn't get out of bed, once the search was called off.' Her eyes go misty, and then wet. 'Not for weeks. I was off school for like three months. Couldn't eat, couldn't sleep. By the time I got back it was all over, they'd forgotten her and that – that *wanker* you brought here was in prison. And we all just had to get on with it.'
'Paige never contacted you?'
Lily snorts. 'Give me a fucking break.'
'Why do you say that?'
She drops her head backwards and closes her eyes. 'Because she's very fucking obviously dead, that's why.'
'We don't know that.' Wren forces herself to maintain eye contact.
Lily's mouth hardens, defiance sparking. 'Yeah we do. They said she didn't use her phone from the day before she disappeared. She was *glued* to that phone. And anyway, she didn't have any relatives or she wouldn't have been in Beech View. So even if she was alive, where would she have gone?' Lily leans against the wall, looking away. 'I never really felt like a kid again, after what happened. Everything changed.'
'Is there anything I can do to convince you to come and tell this to him?'

'No.'

'You're—'

'Yes, I'm sure,' Lily says, and she looks it. 'I thought I could do it but I can't. I'm too fucking angry, do you know what I mean?'

'That he got her to do the burglary?'

She gives Wren a look between pity and disgust. 'No. That he killed her afterwards. They had him on video, for fuck's sake, leaving with her. What other explanation is there?'

Wren knows every frame of the tape by heart. Paige and Ashworth leaving the building, her fleeing as if running for her life. Exiting the frame stage left, and disappearing into thin air.

Lily bounces herself off the wall and crosses to the door that leads back into the library. Before she goes, Wren thinks of something else.

'Listen, one last thing. You said you think there was another guy?'

'I've told you I don't know—'

'Who he was, I know. But what made you think there *was* someone?'

'She had money. Nice things, shoes, bits of jewellery. Had this kind of, I don't know, swagger, I guess?' She puts her hand on the doorframe and sighs. 'Last conversation I ever had with her was me basically asking if she was on the game. She went *ballistic*. Said just because she had a few nice things, didn't mean she was a whore. I hadn't called her a whore but, you know. I didn't even think it might have been Luke's brother at the time, or I would've told someone. Because that's not right, is it – he only got to her because his brother was in the same house. It's fucking sick. We were *kids*. Anyway,' she says, shaking her head, annoyed she's got sidetracked, 'she wouldn't talk to me after that. Not even to say hi. Last I saw of her, she was getting into a taxi outside school, like a really nice-looking one, you know? She saw me looking, and she gave me the finger.'

She lets out a long, sad breath. 'Two weeks later she was gone.'

9

Before

He's spent such a long time choosing the card that the woman behind the desk is starting to give him evils. It's for his mum, her birthday. Thirty-seven tomorrow, and he's left it too late to post now. He's choosing between one with these peas with googly eyes saying *Hap-pea Birthday!* or the one with the *18 Today!* badge on because she's always saying she wishes she was. But he turns the badge over and sees the safety pin and that's the decision made.

He pays and then he gets going. Out the shop, right to the back of the mall, to the toilets. The real reason he came. Because there's fuck-all privacy at Beech View, and the boys' shitter at school might as well have no doors at all, the number of times he's seen them scaled or kicked in. With what he's got in his bag, he's not taking any risks.

He goes straight to the cubicle at the end, folding the front of his jacket across his face because the whole place stinks. There are globs of paper on the floor and the striplights are flickering, but none of that matters. In here, the walls are solid and go up to the ceiling, and there's two kinds of lock on the doors.

The cubicle door swings shut behind him, and he does the locks: the normal one and the fuck-off slide bolt at the top. He flips the seat down, sits. Opens his bag.

After Paige had gone back to bed, he'd found a way to delete the print job, but it had already got through twenty-six pages. And he's going to read it. It's her private stuff, he knows that, but when it all pays off, she'll understand. And she'll thank him.

He pulls the wedge of paper out of his bag, and smooths it out across his lap. He starts to read.

10

Now

They get to Beech View for 9.10 a.m., as requested. The Polzeaths didn't want Ashworth there when the children were on site.

Alice Polzeath answers the door so abruptly that Wren suspects she'd been standing behind it, waiting. She is blonde, late forties. Neat as a pin in shirt, pristine jeans and pink suede ballet pumps. A cross hangs delicately from a fine gold chain that rises and pools on the bones and recesses of her clavicle. Nervousness jumps in her every movement.

'You'll have to sign in,' she tells them after a cursory handshake each. She gives Wren a tablet with a form on the screen.

Wren uses her finger to scribble something that looks roughly like a signature, then holds it out for Ashworth to do the same. She glances over at the driveway, spotting the immaculate white Land Rover Discovery tucked up the side of the building.

'That one yours?' Wren asks benignly, for the sake of something small to say. 'Nice ride.'

A glint of pride thaws the deliberate severity on her face. 'I've had a new one of those every year for a decade. Lovely cars.' She puts her hand out for the tablet.

'Pretty high tech,' Wren says, handing it back. The security is a totally different story than it had been when Paige and Luke were residents. Different *genre*.

'We had to make a lot of changes, after what happened. Ensuring the children's safety was obviously the first thing we had to deal with,' she says. It's clear she's doing her best to be friendly, but it's hard to picture her getting her hands dirty working with actual children. Probably she doesn't. Her company, Acumen Social Care, is responsible for over fifty children across seven sites. James Yardley had consulted for the company, being something of an expert in children's mental health, but as far as Wren has been able to make out, Alice's own responsibilities rarely involve direct contact with the children.

She locks the screen away in a cabinet beside the door, and leads them into a large, newly painted sitting room. Perching awkwardly on the arm of a sofa, she says, 'Security was something we could solve quickly just by paying to solve it. Other things took more of a long view.'

'Like what?' Wren asks.

'Like their expectations. Of themselves I mean. Most of the children we get only really know adults who've, for whatever reason, not made the best of their lives. We try to drum into them that just because everyone around them was drinking or on drugs or in prison, that doesn't have to be *their* future too. A lot of the kids looked up to Paige.' A hand comes up to flutter around her throat. 'Saw her as an example of how someone can do well, despite it all. And then *that* happened and,' she shrugs, 'they sort of lost faith, I think.'

She leaves it hanging in the air for a moment, then gets to her feet again. 'I'll get us some drinks.'

Wren leaves Ashworth where he is, following her into the stainless-steel kitchen.

'Are we expecting anyone else, Mrs Polzeath?' she asks her. 'Your husband?'

'He's out there,' she says, indicating the kitchen window. 'But it's ex-husband, actually.'

'Oh,' says Wren, unsure of the etiquette. 'I'm sorry. I assumed that—'

'You assumed wrong, I'm afraid,' she says, accompanying it with a tight smile that does little to disguise the sadness. 'This is the first time I've seen him in months, if you don't count handovers for his weekends with my son.'

Wren takes a step back to look out of the window in the kitchen door. Oliver Polzeath, balding and slightly plump, is sitting on a once-white plastic chair, palms up in his lap, perfectly still with his eyes closed. He wears suit trousers and a smart shirt but neither look right, like he is unused to wearing them. His shoes, she notices, sit paired neatly next to him, his bare feet flat on the scrubby lawn.

'What's he doing?' Wren asks.

'Meditating, I should imagine. *Men*,' she says conspiratorially, with a sardonic eyeroll that could curdle an entire dairy. 'He used to drink – now it's *Buddhism*.'

As if he can hear them, her ex-husband opens his eyes and looks straight at Wren. He gives her the slightest of nods, then stands and stretches. Wren turns her attention back to her host, who is filling the kettle.

'So, is anyone else coming?'

'No. I wasn't able to locate any of the staff members from that time either.'

Wren frowns. 'None of them?' She'd seen the copies of Beech View's staffing records from Paige's case file: she'd had half a dozen key carers, let alone the casual and agency workers.

'I'm afraid not. We had a very high turnover of staff, after the crime.' She closes one stainless steel door and opens another.

Wren glances about and locates a two-kilo barrel of instant

coffee next to a catering-sized cutlery tray on the worktop. She slides it over. 'No forwarding addresses?'

The kettle reaches its crescendo and clicks off. 'No.' Alice Polzeath spoons brown granules into cups with the uncertain dosage of a committed cafetiere user. The back door opens, and in walks Oliver.

Without looking up, his ex-wife says, 'Oliver, this is Wren Reynolds from the Probation Service. And,' she adds acidly, 'Robert Ashworth is in the sitting room.' She takes the mugs and the tray and busies past them.

Wren holds out her hand to him. He tenses his jaw a few times before he confers a cursory shake. 'I'm not entirely sure what you need me here for,' he says. It comes with a hint of either annoyance or apology, Wren can't tell which, and then he bends to tie the laces on the shoes he's put back on.

'What's that, like a grounding thing?' she asks him, trying to break the ice. 'The bare feet.'

'Something like that.' He straightens, moves his hands into his pockets as if he can't quite work out what to do with them. There is none of the beatific calm about him that she had expected from someone who'd just finished meditating. He brushes at an invisible mark on his shirt. 'I don't have any involvement in the children's homes these days. Strictly Alice's domain now.'

'I see. What did you move on to, then?'

'Other projects.'

Friendly, she thinks. 'Social care?'

'No.'

Wren nods. 'I see. I don't mean to pry, Mr Polzeath, but was your move away from social care a result of what happened with Paige, would you say? We're here to talk about the lasting effects of what—'

'I hardly even remember her, if I'm honest,' he says, cutting her off. 'Let's go through.'

Wren follows him, frowning. From his background, she'd guessed he'd be business-like, but this is… different. Hostile. It comes off him like a broadcast.

Back in the living room, Ashworth is sitting exactly as she'd left him, unmoving, eyes on the carpet. Alice is standing as far away from him as it is possible to get while remaining within the same four walls, grasping her mug and staring intently out of the window.

Wren sits, and invites the others to do the same. 'We're ready then, Rob,' she tells him, and hands him his script.

Ashworth straightens and begins to read. He speaks mechanically, while the Polzeaths listen. Blowing steam from the surface of her drink, Wren looks around the room. There are the pencilled beginnings of an unfinished mural, a torn and taped poster of a tattooed footballer. The built-in bookshelves either side of the chimney breast are devoid of books, instead housing jumbles of DVD and game cases, a couple of dusty board games and margarine tubs of lidless pens.

Three grand a week per child, these places cost. More than three times what it would cost to send them to Eton.

But it isn't even about the money. Fact is, it isn't a *home*. But that's what it had been to Paige.

They are coming to the end of the script. Throughout, Oliver Polzeath stands in a motionless at-ease, hands clasped behind him, eyes front. Once, Wren sees him stealing a glance at his former wife, followed by an infinitesimal shake of his head, as if dismissing something that is hard to dismiss.

'We went different ways,' Ashworth says finally. 'I didn't see her again.'

The room exhales. 'Is that it, then?' Oliver says to no one in particular.

Wren stays where she is. 'You don't have any questions?'

He shakes his head. 'It was years ago. My memory of it all is rather sketchy, like I said. This man's served his time, right?' He shoots a questioning look at Wren. 'I do have places I need to be, I'm afraid.'

'We can't force you to stay,' Wren tells him. A shell as hard as that, she knows, forms for a reason. Either there is something painful underneath it, and he can't bear anything getting in, or there is something dangerous that he can't risk letting out.

'Alice, Robert,' he says, nodding. Then to Wren, 'I presume that's my role finished, then? I won't need to hear from you again?'

'Not if you don't want to.'

'I don't.' Then, with the smallest of smiles as if to ameliorate the offence, 'Goodbye then. Good luck.'

Only after he leaves does Wren realise that he hadn't looked at Ashworth once.

The front door closes, and Mrs Polzeath sets her still-full mug down on the coffee table.

She takes a deep breath. 'Can I be honest?'

Wren leans forward. 'Absolutely. Anything you like.'

'Well. I wanted to say how it affected me. Personally, I mean. Paige meant a lot to us here at Beech View. She was our Care Ambassador, you know; we chose her because she was a good girl. Studied hard, stuck to the rules, wanted to make something of herself. And then these boys,' she says, gesturing helplessly at Ashworth, 'they mucked all of that up for her.'

'*These* boys?'

'Him. His brother. It was such a waste, you know? Her getting involved with *them*.'

'You can leave Luke out of it,' Ashworth says, stiffening.

'I'm sorry?' Mrs Polzeath says with a syllable of confused laughter.

'Luke's done nothing wrong,' he says, fixing her with a glare.

She folds her arms, and that's the end of her patience. To Wren she says, 'He was infatuated with her. Did you know that? Followed her around.'

'Rob did?' Wren asks.

'*Luke*. The whole time she was here.'

'This isn't about him,' Ashworth practically snarls.

Alice casts him a long look, then sighs, defeated. 'You wanted to see Paige's things?'

They follow her up the staircase onto a strip-lit corridor. All the doors leading off are closed except for one. She pushes it wide open and stands aside.

'This was hers. She was happy here. As it happens, it's vacant right now, though we're getting a new boy in a few days.'

Stepping inside, Wren catches her reflection in a full-length mirror that's been screwed to the wall. Her face is blank, professional. The room is small, hardly bigger than the single bed and the desk it contains. Through the window is a view of the recently trimmed back yard. On the desk is a cardboard box, the flaps open.

'They left everything for us to deal with, the police,' Alice says. 'As if we didn't have enough to sort out. I'd rather hoped someone would come and take it away, but there you have it.'

Ashworth stands just behind the threshold. 'In you come, Rob,' Wren says, waving him over. He moves like a condemned man.

'Fuck's sake. Why are we doing this?' he whispers.

Wren doesn't answer, just unpacks the box, laying the things out for him with Alice Polzeath standing by the window, watching. There are girls-range scents, a hairbrush, a metallic handbag, a few exercise books. Wren flicks through one marked *Drama – Y10*.

'She played Juliet,' Alice tells her, nodding at the book.

'My husband pulled a few strings to get her cast – he knew the head rather well. Always went the extra mile for her.'

'For Paige?' Wren asks, wondering how this thoughtfulness could possibly make sense from a man who claimed not to remember her. 'Any particular reason?'

'Not just her,' she says, bristling slightly. 'We did whatever we could for all of them. Prided ourselves on it.'

Wren closes the book and hands it to Ashworth. The handwriting on the front is bubble-shaped, with a little heart above the *i* in Paige's name.

'I was told she had been given quite a few gifts, before she went missing,' Wren says.

Alice frowns. 'Not that I know of.'

'Really? Is there nowhere else she might have kept her things?'

'This is all we have.'

Tucked into the bottom of the box is a silver-grey dress made of chiffon or silk, delicate and graceful. Way too sophisticated. Wren gets it out and shakes it, dislodging something solid wrapped inside.

'Ah yes,' Alice says quietly. 'She left those hidden like that at the bottom of the wardrobe, apparently. They're from her mother.'

It is as if something has taken hold of Wren's heart and squeezed. It's a bundle of letters, the addresses on them handwritten in a long, looping hand. *Paige Garrett, c/o Children's Social Services*, followed by the address of the social services office that had been responsible for her. Before she can wrap them back up, Alice takes them from her.

'Some of the parents do actually visit, but as far as I know, Paige never had any communication from her mum apart from these. And they were already very old by the time she came to us,' she says, flipping through them and pointing out the postmarks. They're all dated from the same six-month period, more than a decade previously. On the back is the name Leanne Garrett, and an address in a sink estate in north Bristol.

Rob puts out his hand and, after glancing at Wren, Alice gingerly hands them to him. But he doesn't want to read them. He straightens them into a neat stack and wraps them back up in the dress.

'She said she was going to find her one day,' he says. 'I was going to help.'

It is the most intimate thing he's said about her, and he seems to immediately regret it, glancing up as he goes to return them to the box. The fabric slips against itself and the letters fall to the floor. Wren gathers them up.

'And did you have any real intention of doing that?' Alice asks, with a high note of accusation. 'Or was it just part of the grooming?'

A hard knot of muscle bulges at Ashworth's temple.

Article 6. The offender must actively engage in the programme, and be willing to discuss the crime to the full satisfaction of the affected party.

'Rob,' Wren starts, the letters still in her hand.

'I didn't *groom* her.'

Alice gives an incredulous scoff. 'Really? It seemed to me that you saw a good, wholesome child who was doing well with us, and you used her.'

Fortified by his silence, she squares her shoulders. 'Paige trusted us to care for her and you lured her away. You used your brother to get close to her and then you decided that close wasn't enough. You had to ruin her too. Isn't that right?'

Too late, Wren sees the change in his face and knows what is coming. Ashworth launches at the other woman, so quickly that in the time it takes for Wren to get her arms locked around his elbows, holding his back tight against her chest, Alice only just manages to shrink back against the wardrobe.

'Not him,' he growls. '*Not him*, you *bitch*, all right? He loved her. He did his fucking best for her. You leave my fucking brother *alone*.'

'Robert,' Wren hisses into his ear. 'Cool it. Don't mess this up.'

Alice, coughing and eyes wide, darts out of the room and down the stairs.

As Wren holds him, waiting for the fury to subside before she releases her grip, a wave of clarity nearly knocks the wind out of her.

She's been looking at it all wrong. It wasn't ever about wearing him down.

The key is Luke.

Alice Polzeath watches from the bay window, as Ashworth, wordless and compliant, straps himself into the passenger seat. Wren stands on the pavement, the adrenaline still crackling in her blood.

'You are one lucky little shit,' she spits at him. 'Stay here, don't fucking move, or you're going back to Horfield faster than you can say *immediate recall*.'

She locks the door, points a finger at him through the window, and goes back inside. Alice stays hovering in the hall by the door. She's already said she isn't going to make a formal complaint, but that hasn't put a dent in the righteous indignation.

'I'm going to need a signature on here,' Wren says, handing her the forms, 'and here.'

The woman scribbles angrily. 'I don't want to see him, or hear from him, or even hear from *you*, ever again.' She hands the clipboard back. 'He's an animal, just like his brother. I should never have agreed.'

'You feel very strongly about Luke,' Wren observes softly.

The cup of coffee she's holding becomes suddenly

interesting to her. Wren waits as she takes a long, slow drink from it.

'Mrs Polzeath.'

She wipes her mouth of nothing at all. 'The police questioned Luke after she disappeared, several times. We already knew he was... overly keen on her, let's say, but it turned out he'd broken into her records here. Read everything we had about her.'

Wren keeps her face impassive, but it rings like a bell in her head. *Is that true?*

'Why would he have done that?' she says, then, 'Do you think Robert and Luke were, I don't know, working together, somehow?'

Alice rubs her face with her hand. 'I don't know. But Luke was *obsessed.* Oliver found him more than once *asleep* outside her room. I mean, does that strike you as normal?'

'That's not what I'm asking,' Wren says levelly. 'Do you have any reason to believe that Luke was involved in the burglary?'

'I gave my evidence, Miss Reynolds. This whole thing,' she says, gesturing expansively to include Ashworth, Wren, the bedroom, possibly the years in between as well, 'is not about me. But no one ever sees that, do they? People like me put their whole lives into caring for the young, and something like this happens and we still get blamed.'

'We came here so Robert could apologise. No one's blaming you.'

'Really? And did he apologise?'

'Yes.' Albeit minimally.

She rolls her eyes and moves past Wren, heading back into the kitchen.

'Mrs Polzeath,' Wren says, following her, 'all I want to do is ensure that Robert is held properly accountable. We're on the same side.'

She turns back, drying her hands delicately on a stained tea towel. 'Are we now.'

'Yeah. Tell me what I'm missing.'

She sighs heavily. 'Do you know what we do here?'

'Tell me.'

'We look after damaged, unhappy children. We care for them. We feed them when no one else wants to.' There's a break in her voice, and she looks away, clearing her throat.

Wren realises that maybe she's made a mistake here. From what was in the files, she'd taken the Polzeaths for a power-couple with a string of businesses whose security had been shamed. In all the police interviews and social services reports she'd read, she'd just assumed that their concern was merely corporate; that they'd simply appropriated the anxiety about Paige's welfare expressed by her friends and reconstituted it as their own, to deflect attention from their failure to care for her properly.

Every one of those judgements had been made by her own prejudice, and she hadn't even seen it happening.

'Look, I didn't know Robert Ashworth any more than anyone did here,' Alice says finally. 'He was a family member of one of our children. End of story.' She looks Wren in the eye. 'Is that all right? Are we finished?'

Wren can't push it any further. She puts out her hand, thanks the other woman.

And as she walks down the path back to the car, where Ashworth waits sullenly like a caged beast, she feels the rectangular block of Paige's letters beneath her shirt, their secrets rigid against her skin.

11

Before

Sun's going down, and he's getting cold. He's been waiting for her round the edge of the music block because Tuesdays she's got counselling in there half-three to half-four, but he must have missed her coming out. It's ten to now, and the caretaker's locking up.

Luke sticks his shitty phone back in his pocket and cuts through to the main building. School seems all right when it's just him there. Without the people, it's not that bad. Same for Beech View.

Same for anywhere.

He goes out the front, ten-foot shadow in front of him, a muddy sunset mirrored in the glass of the art block. Through the gates, and he's out. He starts the walk back to Beech View.

Heading through the park and out onto the road, he's thinking about the thing he's supposed to be handing in on *Jane Eyre* in the morning.

He steps off the kerb. There's a massive blare of a car horn, way too close.

'Bloody moron!' the driver screams at him. 'Watch where you're fucking going!'

And he's still standing there on the pavement, every muscle jittering and his breath coming in quick snips like a rabbit's, when he hears his name. A hand on his back.

'Shit, Luke, what the fuck?'

It's Paige, and he opens his mouth to say something – what a dick that driver was, or whatever – when there's someone else there too, running up behind her. It's Mr Yardley, the school counsellor.

'Narrow escape there, Luke,' he says, looking him over. 'You all right, mate?'

'Yeah. What are you doing here?' Luke asks, before realising how it sounds and adding, 'Sir.'

'Just walking over to yours, as it happens.' Yardley takes a last drag of his cigarette – roll-up, liquorice paper. 'Doing a bit of training with the staff.' He blows the smoke out in a thin stream, squinting at Luke through the flop of wavy brown hair in front of his eyes.

Paige says, 'That'll be good then, Lukey. You're always saying how you wish you could have more counselling, and now you can!'

'Fuck off,' he says, trying and failing to keep half a smile off his face. She's a sarcastic bitch sometimes.

They start walking, awkwardly. Luke wants Yardley to fuck off for at least ten different reasons, the main one being who the fuck walks home from school with a teacher without getting the royal piss taken out of them the next day?

'We had that panel thing,' Paige tells Luke, like she's not even bothered there's a middle-aged man walking next to her. 'I tried to find you but you'd already gone.'

The panel – fuck. Mel had reminded him about it this morning. Free pass for the afternoon – social workers and the council and Mr and Mrs Polzeath. They're trying to get some contract with the council to open another load of kids' homes.

'Go all right?' Luke asks Paige, but it's Yardley who answers. 'Pretty dull,' he says.

Luke hadn't known Yardley would be there. Yardley says,

'They wanted me there for the *liaison*.' He puts little speech marks round the word with his fingers, and Luke sniffs a laugh.

'So stupid,' Paige says. 'One of them wanted to know if I'd *recommend* Beech View to other *young people*. I mean, what the fuck is that supposed to even mean?'

'Like you'd be in that dump if you had the choice,' Yardley says.

Luke and Paige look at him. 'What?' he says. 'You've both told me that.'

He's right, it's a dump, but it's *their* dump, and he should know that. It's like how you can slag off your brother but if anyone else does it they get a smack.

Yardley changes the subject, saying how Paige did such a good job with the panel. She's got this Care Ambassador thing where she gets asked about stuff to do with how the home gets run, and even though there's nothing in it for her, she goes along, does what they ask her. It's because she actually cares about it. He's seen her talking some of the younger ones down when things have kicked off. She does all that, but there's no one looking out for her, not properly.

But then he remembers what he read in her file, and the dark thing takes shape in his throat again and he tucks his chin in and keeps walking.

'You don't fancy it yourself, Luke? Being an ambassador?' Yardley says.

'No.'

Yardley laughs. 'Man who knows his own mind, aren't you?' But he takes the hint, and hangs back to do something on his phone.

Luke waits until they're out of earshot. 'Twat,' he says.

Paige wrinkles her nose. 'I don't know. He's only trying to help. I think he does actually get it, a bit.'

Luke rolls his eyes.

'He was in care for a while, you know. He told me.'

'Bullshit. *Yardley?* He pulls a face to say he doesn't buy it.

'You don't trust people much, do you?' she says, laughing.

He doesn't have to answer it. *She's right though,* he thinks. *I do not trust people one little bit.*

Not even you.

Then they've arrived at Beech View and Luke swings the gate open and heads up the path. And when they get to the front door, without having any reason to do it, she puts an arm around him and gives him a squeeze. His skin lights up like she's plugged him in to the mains. He'd wanted to talk to her but he can't now. He goes solid, and she immediately pulls back.

'What's up, Lukey?' she says, hurt all over her face.

He shrugs, and the opportunity's gone. She goes inside and up to her room.

Luke takes his shoes off. He's got to put it away somewhere, whatever that feeling is when he's close to her now, since he read what he read in her file. He knows what a massive arsehole he is for reading it in the first place. She'd never talk to him again if she knew. He wishes he'd never seen it.

But it's too late for that now.

MTP, it said, which he had to look up. *Medical termination of pregnancy*.

She'd had an abortion. When she had just turned thirteen.

And it's nothing to do with the baby, he's not that much of a dick; it's her business and he didn't even know her then.

It's that she looked him in the eye and told him she was a virgin, and it was a lie. And he wants to forgive her for that.

But he can't.

12

Now

Forcing herself to keep her eyes shut despite having been wide awake for hours, Wren shifts onto her side, tucks herself around Suzy's sleeping form and tries again. If she gets up now, that'll be it, all hope of another few hours' rest gone. So she does the breathing exercises that never work, and the mindless alphabetical lists that are supposed to beat insomnia. But nothing helps: she can't even bore herself to sleep. Not with her mind being drawn, as if magnetised, towards what's in her glovebox.

Eventually, she admits defeat. Careful not to disturb Suzy, she slips out of bed. She blindly, noiselessly selects underwear from the drawer and a shirt, skirt and jacket from the wardrobe, then goes out, taking her time to close the door without a click.

Ten minutes later, she's showered, dressed, and writing Suzy a quick note to leave on the kitchen table. *Couldn't sleep,* it says, *thought I'd go out for breakfast and make an early start.* She pauses, considers redacting the lie. But it's half true: it *is* work. It's just not the kind of work she's going to do in a café, any more than she'd risk doing it at the kitchen table. Because how would she explain it if Suzy came in? *They're personal letters that I don't have any permission to read, but I just couldn't stop myself*?

No.

So Wren clicks the pen a couple of times, adds a few kisses at the bottom, and leaves.

She drives vaguely north without a destination in mind, then turns after a while into a side road up near the UWE campus. She quiets the engine.

And before she can change her mind, she unclips the latch of the glovebox. She takes the bundle of letters out, slips the first one from its envelope, smooths it against the steering wheel, and starts to read.

It takes her a whole hour. The story the letters tell is piercingly familiar to her, so much so that several times, as she finishes one and opens up the next, she finds that her hands are shaking.

There is a hope in the first few messages, a mother's promises that Paige must have believed, early on. *I'll come back for you.*

I'm trying really hard.

I love you very much.

As time passes, though, the promises sound emptier and emptier, the positivity dwindles into nothing, and the letters get shorter. Strained questions about how Paige is doing, about her friends and activities, until, without anything new to say, they tail off altogether, and stop.

Wren finds nothing at all that could shine a light on what might have happened to Paige in the end. What had she been hoping for exactly, to make this risk worthwhile – a threatening note from Ashworth tucked in there? An incriminating photograph? A conveniently damning diary entry, like in one of Suzy's beloved psychological thrillers?

All they are is a record of someone else's pain. Each letter is leathery with age and handling, as if they have been taken out over and over again, read and re-read. At first, maybe Paige would have cherished them. But if Wren's own childhood taught her anything, it's that no fifteen-year-old who'd been left in the system as long as Paige was going to read these letters about love and reunification and happy-ever-after and truly believe that the mother who wrote them meant a single goddamned word of it. Not when all the other evidence pointed, as it did, in entirely the opposite direction.

By the time the sun's rising, Wren is squaring the corners of the bundle ready to stow it away again, and her face is a ruin of tears. Most of it is for Paige, for this dereliction of a blameless girl who just wanted a proper home and someone to care about her. But some of it, Wren has to concede, is for herself.

A cholesterol-bomb of a drive-through breakfast inside her, Wren stands on the walkway outside Ashworth's flat, knocking. She's redone her makeup and is ready with an easy lie about a head cold to explain the redness in her eyes. Not that Ashworth is the type to ask after her health.

There's a finger-thick view between the rollerblind and the window frame into the kitchenette. Clean crockery stands in the drainer, and a pile of folded clothes sits on the arm of the sofa. But there are no lights on.

'Rob,' she calls again. No answer. She bends down to shout through the letterbox, making a note to talk to the landlord about the draught from the flap-less catflap. He's taped some cardboard on the inside but it's hanging down from one corner now. She does have a spare key to his flat, but it's only to be used in emergencies.

'Robert. Come on, seriously.'

It's day three. And day three is James Yardley, the victim.

Straightening up, Wren checks her watch. Thinking of Code 17.

In the event that an offender absconds, the Probation Officer must inform their immediate supervisor or equivalent at the earliest opportunity.

It's been ten minutes. She thinks of the office, and of her boss, his desk heaving with unfinished paperwork.

Hi, Callum, she'd have to say. *Afraid my offender's done one. Yeah, I know we're only three days in. Yeah, I know you're going to have to call the Home Office. No, I don't think the press are going to be all that kind about it either.*

Wren leans her forehead against the door and bangs, hard, until her fist hurts, and then she pulls out her phone and punches in his number. She listens at the letterbox for the sound of his phone ringing. Nothing.

The touch on her shoulder makes her actually squeak. She spins around.

'Sorry,' he says, hands up.

'Where the hell have you been?'

'The river.'

'What?'

'Walking. I go every morning.' He takes a step back and unhooks the plastic bag dangling from his wrist. 'Needed supplies, too.' Inside there are two cans of a vicious-looking energy drink, ibuprofen, and a Twix. 'Knackered,' he says. 'Couldn't sleep last night.'

The proof is all over his face. Not so much bags as bin liners under eyes that are redder than they are white. He's dressed, at least, and he smells showered. More importantly, he hasn't absconded.

'Let's go,' she says, heading towards the stairwell.

In the car, after he's sunk both cans and the chocolate, he leans his head back against the headrest and closes his eyes. 'How long have we got?'

'Not long enough for a nap, if that's what you mean.'

With some effort, he opens his eyes again.

'I'm going to the office later,' she tells him. 'See if I can dig anything out on Luke.'

That wakes him up. 'Yeah? Like what?'

Wren shrugs. 'Try to track down his last social worker, take it from there.'

'Can you find my mum, too? Like tax records or whatever? Find them both?'

'I'll do what I can, Rob, like I said.' They hit the A4 and join the stop-start stream out east towards Bath. 'But you need to co-operate with this. All right?'

He nods. 'You're the boss.'

They crest Brislington Hill and start the descent down towards the Keynsham bypass, fields on either side now.

Wren looks away from the road for a moment to glance at him, desperate to know what he's thinking about. He stares straight ahead, an old, old look in his eyes. Like a general at the end of a battle where everyone died.

'She'll be eighteen in a week,' he says.

'Maybe she will be, Rob,' Wren agrees, keeping her eyes hard ahead. 'If she's alive.'

They find James Yardley in his back garden, kneeling on a green gardener's pad with several trays of brightly coloured bedding plants beside him. A drift of something sweet, maybe jasmine, is carried past them. It is a warm morning, and Wren envies his freedom to potter. His housekeeper, who buzzed them through the huge electronic security gates, excuses herself once her employer has seen them, leaving Wren and Ashworth to cross the lawn unaccompanied.

Wren calls a hello and Yardley gets to his feet, visoring the sun from his eyes with one hand and lifting the other in greeting.

'Wren,' he says. He is an unremarkable-looking man, late forties, average height, with the light hair and darker skin that comes from plenty of leisure time in the sun. He turns to Ashworth.

'And Robert.' He pauses before carrying on, handling the

tension and letting it slip like a fishing line. 'I was going to say it's a pleasure, but I don't really know what it is,' he says, unguardedly.

A breeze blows a thick flop of hair across his face. As he pushes it back, Wren sees the first shade of dread in his eyes as Ashworth returns his gaze.

'Let's go over to the deck, shall we? Have some coffee.'

Of all the people on Wren's list, it was Yardley who had signed up first to the programme, who had been most keen to get involved. She hadn't even needed to call him. He was a very well-connected man, having been involved in remodelling children's residential care and insisting on psychological support for any child finding themselves a ward of the state. The moment the plans of the CAP were announced, he'd lobbied everyone from the Justice Secretary to the governor of HMP Bristol to Wren's own boss at the Probation Service. He'd made the case that the project should include Ashworth, and his request had, unsurprisingly, been granted. He wanted reconciliation, forward momentum, proof that prison was not the only option, he said.

'Nice place you've got,' she says, following him. Lush climbers grow up well-maintained trellises, and somewhere nearby there is the sound of water.

'I guess so.' He twists to regard his home as if he hasn't given it much thought. There is an easy poise to him, a humility, and she finds herself understanding Lily's remark about everyone's shock that he'd been targeted.

Ashworth lagging behind, they come to a wrought-iron table, and the young woman who let them in reappears with a tray. It's shady here, and Wren wishes she'd brought her jacket. She'd assumed they'd be invited inside.

Yardley waits until the coffee is unloaded and the woman is out of earshot. 'She's a lifesaver, that girl,' he says, picking up the coffee pot and pouring. 'Helps Lucilla, my wife. Comes every day.'

'What does your wife do now?' Back then, she'd been a journalist. The bulk of the Yardley money, Wren knows, is his family gold, though. You didn't get a house like that from a career in counselling.

Yardley finishes pouring and squints at her. 'Do? She doesn't do anything, not any more.' He pushes a little jug of cream and the sugar bowl pleasantly over to Ashworth, then notices a beetle making its way slowly across the table. Gently, Yardley blocks the insect's path with his hand, encourages it to crawl onto his skin, then reaches over to release it onto a glossy fig leaf. 'PTSD,' he says by way of explanation. 'She gets flashbacks. Common thing with trauma. Wakes up screaming, and cries half the afternoon.' He offers this information pleasantly, as if they are discussing the best way to prune a wisteria.

Wren glances back at the house. At a downstairs window – the kitchen – she catches half a second of a face, before it disappears.

'Did Lucilla change her mind about taking part?'

'She's rather unwell, I'm afraid. Something of a relapse.' He flicks a look at Ashworth.

'I understand, but wouldn't it be worth my asking if I could—'

'*No*,' he insists, raising a hand. 'No. I'm absolutely serious. She is not strong enough.'

The face reappears, and stays long enough for Wren to take in the details of it, and the headscarf. If she hadn't already known that Lucilla Yardley is in her early forties, Wren would have put her at least ten years older. More.

Yardley passes Wren a cup and she thanks him, takes a sip. It is excellent, of course – no catering tub of Nescafé here. 'And you? How have you been, would you say?'

'Since the—' He breaks off, suddenly unsure of himself.

'The *attack*,' Wren says, remembering the training. *The victim may appear to need the vocabulary approved.* She gives Ashworth a look, wanting his engagement. But he doesn't move, just sits with his arms folded.

'At first I did exactly what I tell everyone not to do. Bottled it up, you know?' Yardley replies pleasantly, lifting his cup to his lips. 'But after that, I spent a lot of time working through it. I'm getting there. Couldn't carry on at the school, though.'

Wren senses the admission is hard to make. 'Why not?'

He shrugs. 'It was all anyone saw. Kids and teachers, everyone. I was the victim – they'd either walk the other way when they saw me coming, or they'd want me to talk about how terrifying it was.' He pauses, examining his hands. 'I kind of – and honestly, despite what I do for a living, it's taken two years of therapy to be able to say stuff like this out loud and not feel like a proper tit but – I lost my sense of self.'

Ashworth raises his eyes to Yardley's. 'Your… what?'

Wren glances down to his hands, which are now curled into fists in his lap.

'We're here to listen, Rob.'

The older man says, 'But what's done is done.'

'So what are you doing now?' Wren asks.

'A lot of this,' Yardley says, gesturing apologetically to the garden. 'Spoils of privilege, being idle. I did try retraining, actually. Physiotherapist. I have this need to get involved in people's problems, help people be their *best selves*.' He rolls his eyes slightly at himself. 'Narcissism, I suppose, if I'm honest.'

From anyone else it would be woolly, irritating, but somehow the self-deprecation balances any of that out.

Ashworth gives an almost imperceptible shake of his head, and looks away.

'And what happened?'

Yardley brightens into a sheepish smile. 'Silly of me really. It turns out I'd rather underestimated my squeamishness – all those broken bones and injuries were just a bit much for me. So I just do one-to-one now, psychotherapy, a few bits and pieces for groups. Emotions can get pretty icky but at least it's not as bad as bodies.'

She laughs, ignoring Ashworth's scowl. She hands him his script.

'We want to hear every word of this, Rob. OK?'

He sighs heavily and takes it. In his defence, he reads dutifully, workmanlike and clear, no skipping parts or mumbling. Yardley listens with his elbows on the table and his head in his hands, a frown of concentration sitting heavy on his brow.

Ashworth finishes, and for a moment, nobody speaks. And when Yardley looks up, a vertical wet streak shines on each cheek for a second, before he briskly wipes them away with the heel of his hand.

He straightens up, and does an admirable job of summoning a smile. 'I forgive you.' He states it, enunciating every word slowly, like he's practised it in a mirror. There is a moment of silence. Then, the smile falls and is replaced by a look of bewilderment.

'No,' he says. 'Actually, I don't think I do.' He looks at Wren, almost apologetic. 'I thought I had, but now we're here…'

Wren glances at Ashworth, who's staring hard at Yardley.

'There's no expectation that you have to forgive him, James,' she says. 'That's not why we came.'

'No. No, I know that. I just rather wanted to put a line under it, you know?' He turns to Ashworth, seemingly unperturbed by his glare. 'What I can promise you, though, is that I am trying. To forgive. I'm working on it.'

He doesn't get an answer.

'Rob,' Wren prompts.

'*What?*' Fury in his eyes.

Yardley clears his throat. Then he stands, sudden enough to knock the table. 'OK,' he says, almost to himself. 'Maybe I was wrong.'

He's leaving. She can't let him leave.

'Let's talk about it a different way,' Wren says quickly, aiming to sound coaxing but overshooting, ending up closer to desperate. 'Let's talk about the material side of it. About the stolen bracelet. What did it mean to you?'

But Yardley is gathering the coffee things back onto the tray.

'Mr Yardley. Please.'

He stops. When he speaks again, his eyes flash with fear, or bitterness.

'I think I have maybe made a mistake. I thought I'd never fully recover from it unless I embraced this.' The cups clatter on the tray as he lifts it too abruptly, as if he expected it to be heavier. 'I'm sorry. I'm sorry to have wasted your time.'

'Five more minutes,' Wren calls after him, standing.

He doesn't stop. 'I think you better leave,' he says over his shoulder. 'As quickly as possible, please.'

'Do you know what?' Wren says to Ashworth as they get in the car. 'I've had enough.' She slams his door, rounds the bonnet, gets in and slams hers too for good measure. 'You don't get to do this.'

'Do what?'

'Fuck it up.' She can't even look at him. 'You couldn't just say thank you for forgiving me?'

'No.'

'Why? Tell me *why*, Rob!'

But he doesn't tell her a thing. He closes his eyes and leans back into the headrest.

She forces herself to take a breath. She's livid, her stomach rigid with it. She hadn't even *started* with Yardley. He'd known Paige, she'd liked him. His name was on half the Care Ambassador documents Wren had dug out from the Children's Services archives. If she had a proper chance to question him, she was sure he'd have some theory about what had happened to her.

'You wanted him to kick us out,' she says.

'Why would I want that?'

'Because you're avoiding any kind of conversation about where Paige is!'

Ashworth laughs. 'That again.'

Wren lets out a wordless shout of frustration.

Ashworth flinches, shock splitting the indifference on his face wide open. 'You're fucking mental, you know that?'

'Where did she go, Rob?'

'I've already told you, I don't—'

She leans in, right into his face. It's against all the best practice guidance and she doesn't give one particle of a shit. 'Where. Is. She?'

Ashworth blinks. 'You really want to know.'

The rage drops out of her all at once. 'Yes,' she says. 'I do.'

He turns away from her. 'Then help me find my family.'

She wants to floor the car out of anger. But she reins it in and forces herself to go smoothly, respectfully, to the end of the drive. There is no case for misinterpreting Yardley's instruction: he wants them gone. The automatic gates are already open when she reaches them, and she drives slowly through. In the rear-view mirror she watches the gates judder as their motor completes their opening arc and reverses, beginning the return, shutting them out.

Her one chance to talk to the victim, to properly mine what he knows, what he saw, is closing. The space between the gates narrows.

Wren pulls up on the kerb, yanks the keys from the ignition, barrels out of the car and runs full tilt. Because she can't leave. Not yet.

The gates graze her hips but she slips through, seconds before they lock behind her. Yardley, who must have been watching on the monitor, comes jogging down the drive, his face a confusion of anxiety and fear, with an undertone of rage that he is clearly trying to hold back. And all things considered, he has good reason to feel every one of those things, especially the last. Hasn't he gone out of his way for Ashworth, when most people would want him locked up for good? And how did Ashworth thank him?

'Look, I said go,' he calls. 'This is not what I thought it would be. I don't—'

She puts her hands up. 'Please. It's just me.'

'What do you want?'

Letting her hands drop, she opens her mouth to try to convince him to let them stay, to try again. Then she remembers something about that face in the window. That fear – and Yardley's fury, right before he kicked them out. He hates Ashworth. He doesn't want to hate him, he believed that he could cure himself of it, but he failed. The hurt has gone too deep. Putting the two of them together, getting them to understand each other – it had been like trying to talk oil into making peace with water.

Wren looks at the house behind him. She knows its angles and divides from the countless viewings of the tapes. The way the apex of the long, slated roof has bowed slightly with age in the middle, the way the ancient oaks frame it at both ends.

Right there, she is within a few feet of where Paige disappeared from view.

Wren makes her decision.

If it goes wrong, and he reports her, the whole thing is

screwed. But his *anger* – that is something she hadn't banked on. She only has this chance to use it.

'Do you want to know what happened to Paige?'

'Wh— what?' he says, sagging as if someone has put a pin in him. 'What do you mean?'

'Ashworth knows.'

He stops dead. 'Why do you think that?'

There is no way she's telling him what Ashworth has just said. Anyone can claim they've got information to trade – she knows that, and so will Yardley.

'He's the only one who was with her that night. He said nothing about where she might have gone, the whole way through the investigation and the trial. Nothing. I don't believe him. He knew a side of her that no one else had seen.'

Yardley watches her. 'You haven't got any evidence.'

'Not yet. But he knows something he's not telling. And I think you can help me find out what it is.'

13

Before

Luke piles out of school the moment the bell rings. Doesn't need to bother with the usual tactic of taking ten minutes over a piss or suddenly remembering that *really important* thing he has to do before he goes, so he can leave after everyone else. Because today's a Thursday, and if anyone even thinks about giving him any gyp on his way out on a Thursday, they'll change their mind pretty bloody quick when they see his brother at the gate, waiting for him.

Rob's in his usual spot, leaning against the sign. He's never been a student at Westmead but the kids dodge him when they pass like they know who he is. People don't look Rob in the eyes for long, because it doesn't take long to see he's *hard as*. Even from the other side of the playground.

Luke strides out across the tarmac, waiting until Rob looks up and catches his eye. And when he does, Rob grins and raises his hand. Luke's shoulders relax.

They high-five and start walking back to Rob's place. Rob's still got his work stuff on: blue rolled-down overalls and a T-shirt with the name of the garage where he's apprenticing on City and Guilds. There's a black streak of grease on the side of his face. Luke points it out and Rob starts rubbing.

"They wanted me to stay and finish putting in a gearbox. I

had to say you were ill so they'd let me out,' he says, smearing the dirt. 'Gaffer was proper miffed.'

'Sorry. You didn't have to.'

Rob rolls his eyes and smacks Luke on the back. 'I know I didn't *have* to. Don't be soft, mate. Want to show you the new place.'

He's moved flats because the social worker told him he'd need to show he had room for Luke, so the guardianship application had a chance. His last place, you couldn't even open the door properly because the bed was half blocking it.

'It's bigger. You're going to like it,' Rob tells him. 'Even got a bedroom separate from the main bit. It's yours, once you're in. Soon as it gets approved they'll send over the first lot of cash and we'll get a bed and that. Four to six weeks, social worker reckons.'

Luke balls his hands in his pockets a few times and then he just comes out with it. 'Is it just me you can have?' He looks at his shoes. Rob's frowning at him, he can see him out of the corner of his eye, but Luke keeps his eyes down.

'Not planning to open a children's home, if that's what you mean.'

'No,' he says, and he's not going to lose his nerve. 'But what about if there was someone who needed somewhere, just for a while?'

Rob stops. Luke tries to style it out, carrying on walking, but eventually he has to stop too. He turns and Rob's got his arms folded. An artic goes past and blows Rob's bomber jacket against him, and he must have been lifting a lot more lately because the chest on him, it's huge now. Luke goes back.

'What are we talking about here?' Rob says. 'Are you talking about that girl?'

'No.'

'Are you though?'

'I just thought if we could change it just a bit so that she—'

'*No.*' Rob dips his head, forcing Luke to meet his eyes. 'Because let's get one thing fucking clear here, Luke. The guardianship is for you, OK? No one else.'

'But I thought, later on, you know, once the dust settles—'

Rob jabs a finger in his face. 'Do you want to live with me?'

'Yeah,' he mumbles to his chest.

'Right. So let's do that then, Lukey. The application's in. Play the fucking game.'

Luke says nothing for a minute and then, quietly, 'Can we just look at it, though? As a possibility. Just, maybe?'

Rob growls in frustration. 'I don't know! I don't even know if that's a thing. Maybe, all right? But just – leave it. And stop thinking with your dick.'

Luke smiles. It's not a no.

They need milk and some food, Rob says, and Luke sinks a bit because he knows what that means.

'Do we have to?' he mumbles, but Rob pretends he doesn't hear.

They make a detour to the place they haven't been to for a while, just behind the City Road. Luke sighs and goes to step off the kerb but Rob holds him back.

'Just a sec,' he says, and he gets everything out of one pocket ready. A few notes and a handful of change. He tucks the notes carefully away and gives Luke the change. There's maybe a couple of quid, mostly fives and coppers. Last time they did this, he was sure the woman at the counter knew what was going on.

He doesn't say anything but Rob gives him this look and says, 'It's not much, mate. Just a few bits and pieces.'

'I can just wait and eat at the home,' Luke says.

But Rob shakes his head. 'Wouldn't be much of a big

brother if I couldn't even get you fed, would I?' He folds Luke's hand over the coins. 'Take your time counting it out,' Rob tells him. 'And wait—'

'—until you're clear. I know.'

Luke goes in first, gets a pint of milk then has a careful look at stuff right at the front of the shop. Will he buy the plain beans, or the ones with little sausages? He picks both of them up, makes a big thing of taking out the glasses he hardly ever uses and reading what they say on the back. The shop woman is watching the little telly next to the register.

She doesn't even look up when the bell at the door rings and Rob comes in.

Forcing himself not to look at his brother, Luke changes his mind about the beans, picks up some noodles instead, then goes to the desk. He pushes the stuff across the counter and she gives him a big smile that takes over her whole face, and rings it up.

She says, 'And how was school today?'

'Fine,' he says.

'One nineteen,' she says, and then she looks up and frowns at the door and the bell rings again and he thinks it's Rob leaving, already finished. But it's not, it's an old guy coming in, and she calls out hello, starts having a chat with him. Luke gets out the change and he hates this bit but she's looking at the door now and he has to get her distracted or she's going to clock it. He drops the coins, pretty much throws them at the floor, and they roll everywhere.

'I'm sorry,' he says, careful not to swear because you never know. 'I'm really sorry, hold on,' and he starts scrabbling round.

And she does what they never do. She stops talking to the old guy and comes to help him pick them up. Blocking the door as she crouches down.

Grabbing on the floor for the money, Luke glances back

and he's right, Rob's still inside, but now there are three people blocking the exit. The woman finds the last coin and hands it to Luke, and as he takes it, Rob passes her, slipping out of the shop with his coat so obviously concealing something that Luke can't believe she doesn't run down the street after him. But she doesn't. She lets Luke count the coins out, gives him his milk and noodles in a used placcy bag, and says goodbye.

When he catches up with Rob he gets a grin and a slap on the back. 'Close one,' Rob says.

Luke doesn't think it's funny. His heart's still going like anything because what just happened was too fucking close. Rob nearly got caught. And if he got caught, what then?

They go under the tunnel to the back of the block and up the concrete steps. His flat's on the third floor but he stops on the first. Luke follows him along the walkway, waits while he knocks on a door with a flowery net curtain hanging behind it.

It takes ages but eventually a woman opens the door. She's about a hundred and ten, and she squints at Rob for a bit before her leathery face cracks into a big smile.

'What you got for me today then, my lover?' she says.

Rob opens his coat and inside there are two bottles of wine. 'You're a red girl, aren't you, Marge?'

'Ooh, lovely,' she says, peering at the bottles.

He quickly thumbs the bright yellow *£3.99!* labels off and he tells her twenty for both of them.

'That dear, are they?' she says, peering at them.

Rob shrugs. 'It's really good stuff. Not that I know about wine, but my auntie, you remember? Lives in France?' She nods back at him, without certainty. 'Says it's really great stuff. But no probs, Margey. Derek's been on my back for a sample for weeks.'

He shrugs, turns as if he's leaving.

'No, love, I'll have them,' she says. 'Treat myself.' She balances the bottles on the radiator and shuffles inside, returning with two crumpled notes.

Rob takes it with a wink and says goodbye. As they walk away, he hands both of the tenners to Luke.

14

Now

The main CAP area is a jumble of mismatched office desks and conference chairs. When the programme was launched, Wren's team had been shipped off to new offices near Temple Meads, all glass and greenery. Not for long. Once the minister had done her bit with the cameras, they'd lasted all of about three days before they were moved back to where they'd started.

Her end-of-week supervision should have been half an hour, but they've already been in the overheated windowless room at the back of the Probation Service offices for forty minutes. The building backs onto the motorway, and everyone inside it speaks at an embarrassed shout.

Callum Roche, a senior probation officer seconded to the project to oversee Wren and the two dozen other CAP officers, folds his arms on the table and rubs his temples with nicotine-stained fingers. 'Run this past me again then. Your offender *is* attending the meetings.'

'Yes.' Wren glances at the clock.

'You're on schedule. He reads the script.'

'Yes.'

'And he's behaving. You haven't got any broken conditions.'

Wren had known where this would go before she even sat down. 'That's right.'

'So?' He spreads his hands. 'What's the problem?'

'What I'm saying is, his motivation for staying straight is going to be stronger if we find the brother.'

Roche gives the cynicism a good long soak before he speaks again. 'Let me explain something to you, Wren. No one wants this to work. I mean, sure, maybe the yogurt-knitters at the *Guardian*, but everyone else, they're praying for this to fail. I'm having to call the *Southwest Observer* every fucking day to stop them following our offenders, trying to catch them out.' Wren flinches at the mention of Marty's new employer, but Roche is on his feet now and doesn't notice.

'And don't even ask me about the national press,' he says, going over to a filing cabinet and yanking the long drawer open. 'I got called an "anarchist" by *The Sun*. An anarchist!' He selects a file, slams the drawer shut, and slaps it on the desk. 'We go one day over budget, they're going to know about it.'

'If I can put him back in touch with Luke, the brother, he'll have that connection with the straight and narrow, back in the family bosom,' she tries. 'By the time they get to publishing the stats, he might even be in established employment, if we can give him a reason to stay there.'

The key with Roche, Wren has learned in the few months she's worked with him, is to frame everything in terms of outcomes. He's a National Probation Service veteran, his career stretching back over half a dozen home secretaries and twice as many massive budget cuts. She's been told he'd once been a genuine activist. But the Callum Roche she knows, the SPO in charge of daily business on the Community Atonement Programme, got this job by being a reliable box-ticker, plain and simple.

He narrows his eyes at the file and lays his hands on it. 'We have eight days intensive contact per offender. You're telling me you need, what?'

'A week.'

'An extra *week*?'

'Four days, then,' she says, holding up fingers. 'The brother dropped off the social services radar two years ago. I've had a sift though his old caseworkers already but no one's got a current address.'

He makes a *pff* sound. 'Nope. No way I can justify that.'

'Two?'

He takes a deep breath, pulls a face as if he's giving it some thought, but then shakes his head. Little flakes of dandruff drift onto his shoulders. 'Look. I'm glad you care, it's lovely, it's really…' he says, wafting a hand in the air, 'inspiring. Whatever. I can see you want the best for him. But neither the budget nor the timeframe give a shit about that stuff. Just sign him off and move on.'

Fingers poised to open the file in front of him, he pauses, remembers something. 'I know we went over this in the pre-release but tell me again: the girl's mother, what was her name?'

'Leanne.'

'You didn't get anywhere finding her, right?'

'Complete dead end. Why?'

'Having lunch with an old colleague from care placements, thought I'd double check.'

'Yeah, I already covered that. She went out of borough, no forwarding address.'

He nods. 'Drugs, was it?'

'Yep. Could be anywhere by now. Or, you know…' Wren says, making a face and not needing to finish the sentence.

'Poor kid,' Roche says. Then, looking up, 'You done that bloke yet? The school shrink? Been on my back from day one.'

He means Yardley. 'The victim, yeah. Saw him this morning.'

'Satisfied customer?'

'It went fine.'

Before she'd left Yardley's driveway, she'd pressed her business card into his hand, telling him she could meet him anywhere, any time. He said he'd think about it, but she's not holding out much hope. Something about him had descended like a portcullis during that meeting with Ashworth.

'Well, thank fuck for that,' Roche is saying. 'Seen it all, after that. Victim of a violent crime practically begging to have a chinwag with the offender. And the effort he went to for the kid. Paige.' He shakes his head, baffled. 'At least someone gave a shit about her. Makes up for the absent mother, I suppose.'

He slides a folder across the desk. Wren's next offender: Liam O'Shea, late thirties, domestic assault. 'He gets out ten a.m. Monday week; all the prelims have been done.'

He runs her through it, but Wren isn't listening. She's still thinking about Roche's take on Yardley: how much he'd clearly cared for Paige, how even after the crime, he'd taken on the things a parent should have been doing for her. How would that have made Paige feel, if she'd been around to see it?

Wren blinks, shakes the thought away. It is important not to go down those kinds of routes, she knows. They are too dark. A person can get lost.

Roche, who has stopped talking, gives her a wry look. 'Am I boring you?'

She makes herself laugh. 'Just thinking about the next steps.'

Placated, he flaps the cover onto the folder, the meeting over. 'I used to be like you, you know.'

'Like what?'

'You know. Obsessed with it. Wanting to get it all right,

wanting to *understand* the crime,' he says, putting quote marks round it with his fingers like it's some out-there concept.

'Sure I'll get it out of my system eventually,' she says.

'Here's hoping.'

She gets a coffee from the machine by the lifts and heads to her desk, checking her phone as she goes. If Roche isn't going to give her the time she needs, she'll just have to prioritise. She's already fairly sure she's exhausted the leads she has on Carrie, Rob and Luke's mother: the wall of confidentiality from the professionals who'd known her had proven too high and thick to breach, and as far as friends and family went, she seemed to be little more than a ghost. So what matters now is finding Luke. Even in the absence of a parent, or a relative, there must be somebody out there with a clue. Someone who cared about him.

She stops walking. The only route is to find the staff he'd known. Someone at Beech View must know something. And if the Polzeaths and James Yardley aren't going to help her find him, she'll have to do it herself. With renewed resolve, she tucks her folder under her arm and takes the stairs two at a time.

But as she comes onto the office floor and rounds the corner, she slows. Perched on her desk, casually flipping through a notepad, is a blond man in his twenties.

'Oh, Wren!' he says as she gets close. He lets the notepad slap shut, hops off the desk and puts out his hand. 'Gary, HR,' he explains. 'We met before your interview? I've left you some messages?'

'Messages?' She shrugs. 'Sorry. Must have missed them.' She puts her bag on the desk. 'What are you doing here?' Her monitor, which she definitely shut down before the meeting, is turned on and displaying a webpage. A government crest in the top corner: Department for Work and Pensions.

'Oh, just, you know,' he says, following her eyeline to the screen. 'Thought I might as well log in while I waited.'

'But this is *my* desk!'

'No harm in a bit of hotdesking, is there? But listen, there's a couple of background bits I need to fill in. Have you got a minute?'

'Background on what, the offender?'

'No. You.'

Shit.

'What kind of background?' she asks brightly. 'I've worked for the NPS for years. I'm not new.' Have they run new checks, something they hadn't needed when she first started? Because before, she'd made sure everything was airtight, rock solid. She'd made absolutely sure.

His smile is beginning to snag. 'Just dotting a few *is*, nothing to worry about. School history needs validating.'

'Why on earth do you need that?' She smiles, trying to buy herself a few seconds. 'I mean, they really go that far back, do they?' She scans her options. Does she even have options?

'Yeah, kinda,' he says, conspiratorially now. 'Not unheard of for people to totally falsify degrees, even.'

'Excuse me? I haven't falsified *anything*.'

'OK.' His hands go up. 'Look it's just my line manager trying to get promoted. She wants everything perfect, especially on your thing because it's so high profile. I should have had your certificates before you even started. Have you got them?'

'Professional ones? I'm sure I can—'

'No. GCSEs.' He picks up his A4 pad from her desk, draws a finger down a handwritten list. 'Just – English and Maths. You said you got Bs?'

She nods, smiling. Mute.

'And the school was – which one?'

Keeping her voice level, she says, 'I think it's changed names since I was there.' If she doesn't respond to the confused frown on his face, maybe it will just go away. 'How about I just get you the certificates?'

He clicks his pen a few times, eyes on hers. Then the door to Roche's office bangs open. They both look round at the sound and Roche spots them, glares, and cups his hands around his mouth.

'Fuck you doing?' he calls. 'I thought there weren't enough hours in the day to get the job done.' He strides over.

Double shit.

Gary tucks the pen into his jacket and nods to Roche. 'HR,' he says, holding out a hand. 'Need some background on Miss Reynolds. Secondary school.'

Roche ignores the hand. 'Firstly, it's *Ms* Reynolds, and secondly, I've seen all the records we need. All right?'

Gary fish-mouths for a second and then, to Wren, says, 'Scans'll be fine. Soon as, right?'

Roche watches contemptuously as Gary slinks away. 'Fucking bean counters,' he says. 'Never trust a man in shoes that shiny.' The two of them instantly look down at Roche's own footwear. Which gleams.

'Ah,' he says, rubbing the sole of one over the toe of the other. 'Wife must've done that.'

After he's gone, Wren sinks into her chair, not knowing whether to laugh or cry. She wakes her mouse and drags the cursor to the top right to close the window, then stops. Across the top, *G. S. Kitchener – Staff ID 337LN2.*

She checks behind her. Gary S. Kitchener is gone. Gingerly, she looks back at the screen, holding her breath as she minimises the window. Behind it, there's a screensaver of a shirtless, tanned man and a slim young woman in a bikini, astride an elephant. That shirtless man is Gary, which mean the icons dotted all over this picture of his idyllic trip to the Far East contain his access to all the local government staff records. Dates of employment, payroll information, addresses – including clearances for staff employed by private contractors.

Private contractors like Acumen Social Care.

Wren doesn't waste a second. She scans the icons, finds the database and gets in. The system is divided up into departments, so she makes a path straight through. Social care > Children's > Auxiliary Providers. Checking over her shoulder every half a minute, she changes the date parameters, sets the location, and after a bit of scrolling, she hits Beech View.

She swaps the mouse to the left, leans into her screen, scribbling fast with her right hand without even looking at what she is writing.

'Excuse me!' A shout from the stairwell; no need to look round to identify who it is. 'Excuse me, Wren! Don't use that computer for a minute!'

She flips the notebook over, closes the browser window, and in three clicks, she's logged out.

By the time Gary Kitchener is close enough to see what she's doing, she isn't doing anything at all.

15

Before

She's in the Occupational Therapy room, painting a tiny chest of drawers. The nurse tells them to wait at the door, and goes over to talk to her. On the far wall, there are faded posters of sunsets and mountains with little messages on them like *Mistakes Are Proof That You're Trying* and *A Smooth Sea Never Made a Skilful Sailor.*

'You've got your boys here to visit you, Carrie,' the nurse calls over. Their mum, still holding the paintbrush, turns her head slowly to where the nurse is pointing, and blinks a few times. Just from that first second, Luke knows what this visit's going to be like.

He lifts his hand in a slow wave. Rob just shoves his hands in his pockets and waits.

They take her to the day room and sit at a tea-stained laminate table, the kind with the chairs attached. It's the only room with a view, but there's always a slight trace of stale piss in the air, with pine over the top like someone's tried to cover it up. Rob goes to the visitors' kitchen and makes tea.

Their mum rubs her temples. 'I'm sorry, Lukey, I'm a bit bleary this evening.'

She says it every time. It's the medication she's on. He's asked the nurses whether she'll come off it, and they've just nodded and shrugged and said, 'All in good time,' or, 'We'll see.' The kind of stuff people say when they don't want to say *no.*

One of the other patients is sobbing in the corner with a man – her husband? – patting her on the hand and looking around the room like he's just realised there aren't any doors. Heart FM drifts in from the nurses' station where it plays all day long.

His mum stops rubbing her head and looks at him suddenly as if she hadn't known he was there.

'Look at you.' She takes hold of both of his hands and draws them towards her mouth to kiss them. 'My baby,' she says.

Turning into a man, he thinks.

'Turning into a man!'

While I'm just rotting in here.

'While your daft old mum's rotting in here.'

He looks away. 'You're not rotting.' She rubs his hands too hard, squashing the bones together. He knows not to take them away. 'Or old. They're just making you better.'

'Except they're not,' she says darkly.

It's been fourteen months and a week since she got sectioned. The night it happened, he was upstairs in his room, had his headphones on so he didn't hear the door go when she left. The police asked him about it later while they were still out looking for her. He remembers the too-hot room and the too-sweet tea the woman cop brought him while they waited for the social worker. *Can you try to remember what time she might have left? Did she seem happy to you today?*

Did she say anything that made you feel worried about her, Luke?

Fact was, he worried about her all the time, but that night hadn't seemed any different than usual. She went out late a lot. Not drinking or anything, not with anyone. Just – he didn't know. Walking, she said. Sometimes for hours and hours. And yeah, it used to scare him, when she'd come back and her voice would be weird and croaky like she'd been shouting, her eyes and her face all puffy and red. She'd stand there at the door to his room watching him while he pretended to be asleep. A few times, he'd woken up with her next to him under the covers, still wearing her coat and shoes, curled up in a little ball. When that happened, he'd get out and tuck her back in. He kept a sleeping bag jammed down the back of the sofa for nights like that.

But whenever she went out, she'd always come back.

Until the time she didn't.

They'd found her down near the river, right out near Hanham, sheer bloody luck that someone had seen her. Lying on the ground, in a clearing. Just so happened that some guy on a narrowboat had got a log stuck in his propeller and had to moor up. Apparently, he'd scrambled through the bushes and there she was. Naked, although Luke only found that out later, from a kid at school who'd put it together because his dad was a copper who couldn't keep his fucking mouth shut. She'd been gone more than twenty-four hours by then, and she was in the cells for another three before the mental health people came and sorted it out. Psychotic incident, they said. Hypothermia on top.

He goes down there sometimes, that spot in the woods where they found her. Just to sit, or lie down like she did, staring up at the trees. He doesn't know why he does it. The first few times he thought maybe it meant he was going mental, just like her. But then he'd told Rob about it, and Rob had just nodded and said, 'Yeah. I go there sometimes, too.'

The first place they'd taken her was OK, and they'd reckoned she'd be out within a month. She had her own room, and there was a woman with blue hair whose job it was to talk to Luke about what was happening. But then something happened – money, one of the nurses had said – and the woman with the hair went. They'd moved his mum twice since. This place seemed more like a big waiting room with beds. He could feel the sadness, feel it hardening against his skin.

She sniffs and pulls her hands away. There's a smile on her face. You could never tell when that was going to happen, that change.

'Do you know what I miss, Lukey?'

'No. What?'

Rob comes into the room then with the teas. 'Milk was running out,' he says, putting them down. One of them's normal, one of them's way too dark and the other one's got no milk at all. Luke pushes the good one towards his mum, and Rob takes the in-between one.

Ignoring the tea, their mum says, 'Our garden.'

'What?' Rob says, blowing steam.

'I miss our garden. I bloody loved that garden.' There's a weak smile that could go either way. 'We had a little, what was it called? The thing that the bees liked. In a stone pot.'

Luke dredges his memory of the little patch of green behind the house. How they'd take the sofa cushions outside and put them on the patio slabs, drinking lemonade in the sun. They had their dinner out there sometimes, trailing the extension cord through the kitchen window so they could have the radio too. Fish-finger sandwiches wrapped up in kitchen roll like a picnic.

'You must remember the plant,' she says, squeezing up her face. 'How can I not remember its name?'

Luke meets Rob's eye for a second, both of them thinking the same thing: how every time there's something she can't remember, if they don't change the subject soon she'll get on to how the electric therapy thing has scrambled her head.

'We had that sprinkler,' he says.

'Oh!' she says, and it's like a light's gone on. 'Yeah! And you two running about in it – you'd scream and scream! Remember?'

Rob gives a short laugh. 'What I remember is Luke hiding and connecting the tap up and turning it on when we weren't expecting it so we'd get soaked.'

His mum slaps the table. 'He did! The little shit! And we lost him that time, didn't we, and he'd put a pallet against the wall and made a den.'

'I called the police,' Rob adds, grinning.

But Luke's not grinning. Because Luke knows what comes next when she's like this, what always comes next.

And Rob knows, too.

'And they came!' she shouts, her eyes bright, unnaturally bright. 'The police! Oh, it was so *funny*! We looked everywhere and I was screaming up and down the street and it was just the funniest thing,' which it wasn't; it was a lot of things but funny was definitely not one of them, 'and everyone else came out to see and stare at us!'

Luke tightens his hands around his mug while she pulls everything out of the memory, producing the details like endless handkerchiefs from a magician's sleeve.

'And that mean old cow over the road came over shouting about us bringing the neighbourhood down! God, we had a laugh about that, didn't we?'

Around them, other patients are stirring, moving away or getting anxious at the switch she's making. She has two settings these days: she'll either shrink herself down into a tiny little corner of her head and turn her back on you completely, or else she's like a TV version of herself with the volume and the brightness stuck right up, with no off button.

Luke exchanges a glance with Rob, both of them recognising the peak. A nurse comes in, drawn by the volume. She pauses at the door for half a second like she's assessing what she sees, and Luke's mum clocks her. Something passes between them, and the nurse gives a little nod, then leaves the room.

And practice has made perfect, because Luke's called it, almost to the second. The joy slips back out of his mum's eyes.

'We had a laugh,' she says again, but flat this time. And just like that, she's a million miles away, somewhere he can't reach her.

She leans slowly back in her chair. And then she slides down onto her knees. On the floor.

'I don't want to live like this.'

Rob gets up and goes over, kneels down. He takes her hand. 'You're all right, Mum,' he says. 'We're all going to be all right.'

'No, we're not,' she says. 'Nothing's going to change. I'm not any better. And what if I was? What then? Who's going to give me a job when I tell them I've spent the last year and a half in the nuthouse?'

The work she'd got had always been a bit sketchy, bits and pieces of cleaning and nannying, nothing that ever seemed to stick or go anywhere. Not that she hadn't tried. The attic room she'd made into a kind of studio had been rammed with drawings she'd spent half the night working on: tiny ones on the backs of envelopes, massive huge things on broken pieces of plasterboard she'd pulled from skips when she was out walking.

If I can't make something beautiful I might as well die, she'd said.

It's the sort of thing Paige would say, Luke realises. The thought bites into him, lurches instantly down into his stomach. What does that mean, then, if Paige is like his mum? What does that make *him*? He gives an involuntary shake of his head to dislodge it.

'You'll find work, Mum,' Luke tells her, vaguely, but he still has Paige's hair, her impossibly smooth skin, slinking around in his mind. He checks the time. He wants to get out of here.

But Rob's not moving. 'We are going to be OK. I'm going to sort things out.' He drops his voice, like it's a secret, but he won't look at Luke. 'We're not going to have to worry.'

'Why?' She drags her hands down her face and sighs, crouching still like she's making herself smaller. Small enough that the world won't notice her.

Rob ducks his head to get hold of her eyeline again. 'We're going to get someone really good, Mum, and they're going to make you better.'

Luke coughs hard, staring fiercely at the side of his brother's face, but Rob won't look up.

The idea of a smile twitches at the corners of her mouth then drops, forgotten. She looks away and then she mouths something.

'What's that, Mum?' Rob says, going closer.

'Peony. The shrub. The bees liked it. It was called a peony.'

Just for a second, Rob's nostrils flare. Then he pulls her hands closer, harder.

'I mean it. *Everything's* going to change.'

Luke storms ahead and doesn't speak again until they're on the bus. He sits at the back, Rob in front of him, knees wide apart. Beads of rain track and merge sideways across the black windows. Luke texts Mel because he'd told her he'd be back by seven.

Thnx Luke but I'm not on shift tonite, she replies. *I'll pass it on. C U Thurs.*

Rob is frowning at his own phone, messaging someone, but he's angled it so Luke can't see who. Luke kicks the back of his seat until he looks round.

'What?'

'What was that about?'

Rob shrugs like he's got no idea what Luke's referring to.

'With Mum. You said, *everything's going to change*. What did you mean?'

'Nothing. It's not a big deal.'

'You can't just say stuff like that to her!'

'She needs hope, Lukey.' He rings the bell and gets up.

'Not if it's bullshit she doesn't!' Luke says, following him down the aisle.

'What if it's not bullshit?'

The bus lurches to a stop and then they're on the pavement, facing each other. Rob's putting his phone away. Luke's fists are balls of iron in his pockets.

'She's going to expect you to make it happen,' Luke says. He thinks of her there now, sitting on her bed like she does for hours and hours. She'll be thinking about what Rob meant, how he's going to make everything all right. And what happens when she realises he was just talking out of his arse?

'Maybe I've got a plan, though. You think of that?' Rob's mouth tightens and Luke takes a step back. 'What about trusting me, huh?'

'I do trust you,' Luke says mechanically, because he does. Doesn't he? It's what they've always done. When you can't rely on jack shit except one person, you hold on to that person and you don't let go.

Except now it's changing. Rob's changing.

Rob rolls his eyes and lets out a long sigh like he's had enough of him. He says he'll ring in the morning. And then he walks away. No hug. No slap on the back. Nothing.

Luke opens his mouth to say something, to pull them back together somehow, but then the worst thing comes into his head and his throat just goes hard and there's nothing but that thought. Right in this second, standing on the street with the turbulence from the bus lane rushing past him, lifting the back of his coat and making him totter like he's made of nothing at all, it's all Luke can think, over and over.

I hate you.

16

Now

Pulling out from the car park under the offices, Wren edges into the traffic and flicks on the radio. It's almost five, and the office car park is disgorging itself like clockwork.

The lights change, and as she puts her foot down her phone rings.

It's Yardley.

She snatches it up and answers it without even checking her mirrors.

'Just a second, one moment,' she says, cradling it between ear and shoulder. She pulls over into the first side street she comes to, across someone's driveway, then thanks him for calling her back.

'It's – it's not a problem,' he says. From his voice she infers he doesn't want to be overheard. Because of the wife? 'Look, I'm just returning your call to be decent to you, but I really don't think I can help you.'

'OK, look, that's fine. Mr Yardley—'

'James.'

'James. Could we meet? Just us, I mean. And off the record, if you're worried about that.'

There is a blast of a horn behind her, and she turns to see a Volvo, its driver gesturing angrily for her to move. She makes an apologetic face and holds up a finger, turning her attention back to the call. 'I just need half an hour. Less, even, if it's difficult.'

'No,' he says, 'it's not that. I just don't have anything to add. There was an investigation. The police tried. I did everything I could.'

'I know you did.' Another honk from the Volvo. 'But no one found her.'

A long pause. 'They didn't, no.'

'Look,' she says softly. 'I'm sorry. I know you've been seriously affected by what happened. And I'm doing this job because I want to put it to rest, make sure Robert really pays for what he did. And I'm sorry to have to remind you of all of this again—'

'I can assure you I never forgot it. But I have to ask,' he says, and Wren winces, knowing what's coming. 'This is beyond the remit of your job. Why is it that you're so interested in Paige?'

'She was a very vulnerable girl, and she's gone. Just disappeared.'

Yardley doesn't respond.

Reluctant to let the silence gain traction, Wren says, 'I read her case file. People gave up on her. I just think she deserved better.'

'No,' he says. 'No, I don't think that's it.'

Wren sighs heavily. In for a penny. 'OK. Look. We all have our… histories.'

'Ah. You were in care.'

But he's already had all he's going to get. 'It's not about me. It's about Paige.'

'I understand.'

'So, will you help? I think that if I can find Luke, he'll be able to help.' It's as close as she can get to the truth without telling him what Ashworth had really said, his offer of an exchange. 'I need to find anyone who might know where he is. Not just the people who came forward in the investigation. You knew her – you knew *him*. So help me. Please.'

She waits, screwing her face up in anticipation. The woman in the Volvo brings herself alongside, rolls the window down and gestures in no uncertain terms for Wren to do the same.

Down the line comes a long sigh. 'All right,' he says at last. He names a café on the Christmas Steps, in the middle of town. 'Has to be early though. Seven o'clock tomorrow. If I'm not there, I'm not there – don't call, all right? I can't afford to let Lucilla find out. She's not strong enough.'

They say goodbye and Wren, shaking with excitement, puts the Corsa back into gear and moves off, the Volvo woman giving her a final character reference via her open window.

She's only just shifted up to third when her phone buzzes again. It's just a number this time, not a contact saved into the phone's memory. She answers the call and taps the hands-free icon.

'It's Gary Kitchener,' the voice says. 'HR.'

Wren tightens her grip on the wheel. 'Gary, hi. How's things with—'

'You used my login to access confidential information,' he says. His voice is low, and she knows why. File security has got ludicrously tight in the last few years. Even as a vetted employee, if you want information beyond your clearance, it has been a long time since you could just go and ask someone on the next pay grade up to get it for you.

'Oh, did I?' Wren says, as casually as she can.

'You know you did.'

'I guess you should have logged out, then. Before you left.'

'It leaves a digital signature, you know. So I can find out exactly what you did.'

'What *you* did, you mean. I hadn't been logged on to that machine since lunchtime, and the only one using it was you.'

'I'm going to have to report it,' he hisses.

'Of course. Let me know who and when, and I'll pop over too. I should let them know, really, how you left yourself logged in to a random computer so that the payroll data of everyone on the entire intranet was wide open.'

There is a pause.

'Just delete whatever you accessed, all right? Everything you got on,' another pause, the sound of a mouse clicking, 'Oliver Polzeath and… Melanie Pickford-Hayes. What did you want with this stuff, anyway?'

'Take it easy, Gary. It's nothing I couldn't have got myself,' she lies. There are forms, e-signatures, triple bastard air-locks. They both know that, but they also both know that he is weeks into a new position himself, still firmly in the three-month trial phase. Admitting what's happened would likely cost him his job. 'Anyway,' she says, 'better go, driving. Health and safety. Toodlepip.'

Fixing the phone into the holder so she can see the map, Wren hits the new link road to the airport. Melanie Pickford-Hayes hasn't been employed by the social care division for years, but once Wren had her name as Luke Ashworth's key worker at Beech View, creeping around on Google for ten minutes had given her a fairly confident hit for her current whereabouts. A livery yard just outside Chew Magna.

Another beep from the phone.

I'm going to need those records, Gary's message reads. *I'm beginning to think you're hiding something.*

17

Now

There had been kids at school who had been into horses, Wren remembers. She follows the satnav out of the village, then pulls off the narrow lane, the stables on her left silhouetted against a savage pink sky. Always girls, and usually the quieter ones. She's never given it much thought, but as she slows into the entrance of Melanie Pickford-Hayes's livery yard, she guesses the common denominator is the feeling of responsibility. You had a horse in a shed, you had to look after it, or it would die. Wasn't a million miles from keeping a house full of motherless children, when you looked at it that way. Or a million miles from power.

There is a sign on the gate prohibiting entry but it is unlocked, and Wren pushes it open. Two blocks of wooden stables face each other, the muddy space between them leading to a series of fields. Horses scrape and sniff behind their doors as Wren passes, scanning the place for any sign of human life, but the place appears deserted. The smell of fresh manure hits her in a warm drift at the same moment that her heel sticks. She totters, struggling to dislodge it, then loses her balance and goes down, hitting the wet muck with both knees.

'Help you?'

A woman materialises, striding towards her, a faint curling

smile on her face at the sight of this inept stranger. She is dressed primarily in well-worn jodhpurs and mud. Wren, prevented from getting up unaided by a combination of her weight and the consistency of the ground beneath her, forces herself to smile through the humiliation and lifts a hand in greeting.

'Are you Melanie?'

'Who's asking?'

'I'm a— I'm just—' Wren starts, struggling to right herself. 'Bit of help?'

The woman gives a brief laugh, leaving Wren with the sense she is someone who does so rarely, and heaves her up.

Discounting the ruined tights, it turns out Wren has got lucky. She takes up the woman's offer of some blue roll to clean off the worst in the tack room. Wren follows her into what is little more than a corrugated iron shed, riding paraphernalia hanging along three of the walls and a little makeshift countertop running along the back.

Wren accepts the wad of tissue paper and starts rubbing at the muck on her skirt. 'I'm trying to find out where Luke Ashworth might have got to. You were his key worker, right? Knew Paige Garrett?'

'Luke,' the woman echoes. She folds her arms across her stomach, instantly suspicious. 'Who are you, exactly?'

'Wren Reynolds. Probation Service. I'm working with Robert Ashworth?'

Melanie darkens. 'So they let him out.' She turns her back, angrily flicking the switch on an electric kettle.

'On licence. He's part of the Community Atonement Programme, you might have heard about it?'

She snorts. 'Oh, right. That. Where they make them tell everyone how sorry they are. That working, is it?'

It isn't a question that requires an answer, but Wren shrugs mildly and says, 'It's in its early stages at the moment.'

'And how come he gets chosen? Because you lot think he's safe, yeah?'

'Not safe, exactly—' Wren starts, but Melanie turns to her then, face like a gathering storm.

'No, he's not. You're damned right.' She flings open the fridge door for the milk, slams it shut, then turns back to Wren. 'What do you want from me?'

'I'm trying to piece together what happened,' Wren tells her. She glances around and finds a bin for the blue paper, now sodden brown mulch in her hand. 'There seem to be some… inconsistencies, in what happened to Paige.'

'But that's not what he went away for.'

'No.'

'So why are you here asking questions about her then? It's done and dusted. He went to prison, now he's out. She disappeared. Whole thing's over.'

Wren regards Melanie. Her face is ruddy, the hair pulled back severely from her forehead, each one of her forty-something summers etched deep on her face. She can only be a few years older than Wren but she wears those years like a heavy coat she can't shake off. No ring, and – if she's the owner of the camp-bed in the corner, replete with a duvet and pyjamas folded on top – likely no family waiting for her at home either. Around her eyes, the start of that crimson wateriness reserved for lifelong drinkers. Wren glances up at the shelves and yes – there's the bottle of no-brand vodka, tucked behind a tub of equine supplements.

There but for the grace of God.

Wren nods slowly. 'You cared about those kids.'

Melanie drops a single teabag into a single mug. 'I don't want to talk to you.'

'OK. I'll pass that on to Robert Ashworth. He'll be so pleased – hates it when people hold him to account. Anyway…' Wren lets it trail away, and makes as if to go.

The kettle clicks off, and Melanie sighs heavily. 'All *right*,' she says, before unhooking a second mug. 'Five minutes.'

They take the tea outside. There is a bench that looks out across the Mendips, behind which sinks a bloody sun.

Melanie lights a cigarette and blows a thin spear of smoke towards the hills. Talking as if to the horizon, she says, 'What do you know about social care then, Wren Reynolds?'

'How do you mean?'

'I mean, I'm looking at you,' she says, looking anywhere but, 'and I'm seeing a professional, well-turned-out adult woman who I'm guessing was previously a well-turned-out little girl. Brought up in a nice clean home, with a mum or dad who got you to school on time, did your homework with you.'

An image streaks across Wren's mind. Herself aged nine or ten, lifting a corner of the towel that hung across her bedroom window, watching the cats in the lamplit street. The flat freezing, the power off. No one home. Darkness.

But she looks the other woman in the eye. 'You got me.' She doesn't even have to worry about the memory showing on her face. Years of practice she's invested in that veneer.

Melanie nods. 'And that's great for you, it's what every child should have.' She fills her lungs with smoke again, exhales. 'It's what Paige should have had. She was a sweet, sweet girl. I told the papers that – I called them, tried to get their help. They just weren't interested.'

The papers hardly covered Paige's disappearance at all, and the story had been quickly trumped by other tragedies. A twelve-year-old suffering concussion when falling out of a canoe at a theme park, as Wren remembers it.

'Because she was just a kid in care,' Melanie says. 'Normal kid goes missing, you've got desperate parents ringing the police every day, ringing the media, quitting their jobs to find them.'

'Couldn't someone at the home have done that? You?' It slips out before Wren can stop it.

Melanie rounds on her, instantly defensive. 'I had ten other kids. *Ten!* And that's not just normal happy children who you can play Scrabble with on a Sunday evening—'

'I *know*, Melanie—'

'—these are damaged, frightened, angry young people. Half of them abused by the people they thought they could trust. All of them shunted around their whole lives. And when I wasn't at Beech View I was stacking shelves half the night. But what, you think I didn't care?'

'I didn't mean—'

'You reckon I just thought, *oh, whatever, she's probably fine, move on*? I *loved* those kids. Luke and Paige and all the others. I was the *only* one who gave a shit. You want to point a finger, try starting with the families. Try Paige's fucking mum, who decided drugs were more important than taking care of a defenceless three-year-old.'

Wren opens her mouth, then closes it again, and looks away.

There is a moment of quiet. Melanie sighs, stoops to pick a dandelion by the leg of the bench, then goes over to the fence ahead where a horse has wandered over. And Wren does what Suzy always tells her to do at times like this. *Breathe in, root yourself. The present moment is all there is.*

Except that's the problem with mindfulness, isn't it? All you really are is an amalgamation of the choices you've made or that have been made for you. That's all anyone really is, even the life in Suzy's belly, hurtling towards existence.

There is only the past. It can't be changed. And the injustice of that grips her hard, every moment of every day, like a curse.

'I miss them,' Melanie says simply. And when she turns around, the sky ablaze behind her, tears twinkle in her eyes.

'Those poor kids. Horrible bastards, half the time. But I'd do anything to have them back in my life.'

Wren says, 'Was Paige that unhappy?'

Melanie lets the horse lift the flower from her palm with its great lips, and strokes its nose with her free hand. 'I thought you wanted to talk about Luke.'

'I do, but—'

'No difference to me. Paige was up and down. Issues around food. There was some…' she pauses, choosing her words, 'health stuff.'

'Like what?' Wren asks, frowning. She hadn't read anything pointing to that.

Melanie clears her throat. 'I don't know. Confidential, I should think. You've got a file on her, haven't you?'

Wren changes the subject. 'But apart from that she was OK?'

Shrugging, Melanie says, 'Ran away a couple of times. Which didn't help matters when she disappeared. Police less likely to take it seriously.'

'When did she run away?' This is news to Wren, too. Is she missing a file somewhere? Because she's sure she would have noticed that.

'You'd have to ask Oliver Polzeath. He found her, talked her round.'

'Did he? They get on then?' From her hurried trawl of restricted data courtesy of Gary Kitchener, Wren has a number for Oliver that she hasn't yet tried. She's read everything he said about Paige during the investigation but does she need to try him again?

Melanie spreads her hands, non-committal, but there is bitterness on her face. 'She was very pretty, Paige. Charming.'

'What does that mean?'

'Men liked her.'

'Are you saying she and Oliver—'

'I'm saying men liked her. All of them, pretty much, same as boys. Who fucking knows? I thought I knew her but I didn't. The girl I knew wouldn't have done what she did.'

Wren remembers what Lily had said. 'Do you know about any boys she might have been seeing? Any men?'

'Robert bloody Ashworth you mean?' The horse swings its head and Melanie whispers to it, laying her hand against its neck. 'He definitely liked her but I don't think it was mutual. Maybe that's why he killed her. Got sick of the rejection. And before you ask,' she says, holding up a hand, 'no, I don't know any more than you do about what he did with her. Though God knows I wish I did.'

'There wasn't anyone else? Someone who bought her presents?'

There is a pause. 'No.'

Wren narrows her eyes. 'You're sure about that? Just that someone from her school thought—'

'I said no.' She leaves the horse abruptly, starts digging in her pocket for her cigarettes. After pulling one out and lighting it, she adds, 'We would have known.'

But they hadn't known she was involved with Ashworth, had they? Involved enough to go and burgle her school counsellor's house?

Wren waits, but nothing else comes.

'What do you think happened to her, Melanie?'

'I don't know.'

The pain of that not-knowing shines out of her like a beacon. Softly, Wren says, 'You took it very badly. When she disappeared.'

After a few moments, Melanie returns to the bench. She studies the glowing end of the cigarette. 'I was there eleven years. Few stints at their other places, but Beech View mostly. Do you know how many kids came through when I was there?'

It's a ten-bed unit, and much of the time kids are fostered first, with group homes being the last resort. So they are likely to stay a while once admitted. Wren does a rough sum in her head. 'Eighty?' she guesses.

Melanie shakes her head. 'By the time I left, we had files on a hundred and seventy-six. Some of them born and bred Bristolian, some of them from two hundred miles away.'

'It's a lot of kids.' Where is she going with this?

'Know how many of them had police records?' Melanie taps the ash.

'Most of them?'

'All of them – all but two. Paige Garrett, and Luke Ashworth. They were like this,' Melanie says, crossing her index and middle fingers together. 'Paige had a bright future. She could have been anything. Not many of them you could say that about. So when she disappeared, it felt…' she pauses, as if groping for something big enough to convey what it meant to her. 'It took a piece out of me. I'd believed we could help.'

'Is that why you left?'

'Nope.' She closes one eye and aims the cigarette like a dart at the fencepost. It misses by an inch and glances instead against a spike of barbed wire. Tiny sparks scatter into the grass. 'I left because Oliver Polzeath fired me, two days after Paige disappeared.'

Wren looks at her. 'On what grounds?'

That laugh again, acidic and angry. 'There weren't any grounds. I'd been a loyal member of staff for years, even though I was only on zero hours like everyone else. He'd always been oblivious of what that was like, as if we could just take or leave the work. Not like it's any surprise – have you seen their house? The flats they rent out in Clifton? The cars?' Her face clenches as if something has tightened inside her. 'Whole thing was just a business. Simple as. Every chance they got, they'd claw more money out of the council for it. Even if it meant using the kids. Some people, they'll manipulate literally anyone. Everyone, even the best-hearted children you'll ever meet.'

'How do you mean?'

A bank of cloud, black and close, is crowding out the sunset now. 'The Care Ambassador thing came with extra money to cover expenses. Pennies really, to them, but it went straight into their pockets. Constant corner-cutting, cheap staff not doing things properly because they weren't properly trained. All that fuss they made a few years back about redressing the balance between looked-after and normal kids, to get them funding for music lessons and dance and outward-bound stuff.' She scoffs, kicks at a stone. 'Think the kids saw any of that?'

'Did you tell all of this to the police, at the time?'

'I was never interviewed.'

'Why not?'

'I wasn't around. Ireland. Family reasons.'

'I thought you said you were busy working. Stacking shelves.'

'I said I wasn't around,' Melanie repeats, getting to her feet. 'Look, she's gone, all right? She's not coming back. The police couldn't find her, the Polzeaths couldn't find her, she's gone. So what's the point?'

'No one does that out of choice though, do they. Disappear. I just want to make sure she's safe.'

Melanie cocks her head, scrutinising Wren. 'But *why*?'

Wren maintains the eye contact. 'Because she could have been anything,' she says eventually. 'Like you said.' Then she lifts her bag to her knees and rummages inside. 'Also, I do need to find Luke,' she adds matter-of-factly. 'Any ideas?'

'No. Lost touch.' Melanie picks up the mugs and starts back off to the tack room. This is the thing about straight answers. You don't give them, you don't get them.

Following her, Wren brings out a pen and a scrap of paper. She leans on the plywood door and writes her name and number, and a short note. *Please do call if you remember something else.* She hands it to Melanie. 'If you think of anything, any places he had connections, could you ring me?'

Melanie goes to put it in her back pocket, and then stops. She studies what Wren has written, then casts her a narrow-eyed glance before folding the paper with utmost care, and slipping it into her jodhpurs. They say goodbye, the shadow of suspicion staying put on the older woman's face. Wren can still see it there as she drives away, half an eye on Melanie as she recedes, hands on hips, in her rear-view mirror.

The office is silent and still by the time Wren gets there. She makes herself a coffee, knowing it's a bad idea considering the awful night's sleep she had the night before and the early start she's got tomorrow. She fires off a vague, apologetic text to Suzy and turns her phone off before she gets a reply.

There's a cupboard at the back of the CAP office where they've got all the files of all the current caseload. So Wren clears everything from her desk, and she gets started. One by one she brings everything out. The entire archive on Robert Ashworth, which includes all the secondary stuff about Paige.

And she reads the lot. Every sheet and transcript, every note, because she has to make sure. It takes hours, but by the time the moon has nearly finished its slow ascent into the night sky, she knows that she'd been right.

There is nothing in Paige's records about having run away. There is nothing about ill health. Beech View had received a good inspection judgment, with almost no advisory improvements. It was James Yardley himself who'd signed off on the pastoral care elements – his report had been glowing, start to finish. There is a mention in there of the work that had been done with improving outcomes, the Care Ambassador programme. But, even though it happened in every children's home in every town in the country, absconding was serious. If Paige had run away, as Melanie had insisted, it *must* have been recorded, however badly trained the staff were. It would have ascended the chain of command – right to the top.

She doesn't get home until almost one. A note, written on the back of the one she'd left for Suzy that morning, sits waiting for her at the kitchen table: *Where are you? Keep your bloody phone on. Tired, gone to bed.* Beside it sits a gluey plate of beef stroganoff growing a skin.

Wren microwaves the meal and forks it mechanically into her mouth without sitting. Then, after washing her plate and checking Suzy is indeed asleep, she runs herself a bath and tries to piece it together.

There can be only one reason that there's no mention of absconding in Paige's file. Someone, at some point, must have removed it.

Why?

And if they removed that, what else is missing?

18

Before

Until he walks past it, he doesn't even notice that they've cut down the tree. He was just thinking how nothing had changed on Dulverton Road since he was last here, and then he sees the stump, fenced in by four of those plastic orange barrier things the council use, so he knows they're going to be coming back to dig out what's left, too.

And he doesn't know why but it really gets him. Right in the heart. Not that he climbed it or paid it any attention, back when they lived here. It was just always *there*. The roots are breaking through the pavement in about ten places. Luke touches the ragged surface of it, then straightens and walks on. His curfew is 9 p.m. – he's got to get on with it.

Their old house is number 72, up where the road levels out. The red Polo that belongs to the woman who lives there now isn't parked outside, but sometimes she parks around the corner. Once, there was no sign of it anywhere and then she just turned up out of the blue on a bike, so he doesn't even bother looking for it now.

He stays on the opposite side, getting closer – number 65 where those two old ladies still live, 67 with that kid in a wheelchair. He doesn't slow down as he passes 72, just glances over, long enough to do the check. Front room: dark. His mum's bedroom: dark. From the window above the door he knows there's a light on in the hall. He keeps the same pace right to the top, then goes left, and left again, down the alley.

The back gardens.

The gate for 72 is the sixth one from the top. He checks ahead and behind him before he stops, but there's no one around.

The fences are too high to see over, but there's the hole in that one panel where he once worked the loose knot of wood out, and he looks through it. The grass has been trimmed. There's a new picnic table with a plastic highchair, and there's a sandpit. But the plants are the same.

The peony, his mum's favourite, should have big pink flowers. He scans the garden as best he can through the hole, but he can't see anything the right colour. Maybe the flowers are small, or tucked behind something. He's already got a vase waiting for them, found it right at the back of one of the kitchen cupboards at Beech View. He'll only need a few of the flowers to make it look nice. The people in the house won't even notice they're gone.

He swings his bag off his back. Zipped up in the side pocket there is a pocket knife. It's blunt as anything, can't even do paper without leaving it all torn. But it'll be OK for the stems. He flips out the blade and slides it under the latch. The gate opens without a sound.

He goes in, closes the gate behind him, then squints through the gloom at the flower beds until he sees what he thinks could be the right thing. But when he gets closer, the flowers aren't right, they're going brown. No – mostly they've *gone* brown. Only a couple of them have any colour at all, just a few petals. A gust of wind gets under his jacket and it's freezing, and then he stops, realises what the problem is. It's fucking November. Nothing flowers in November. *Idiot.*

It'll have to do. Maybe he can pull off the brown bits; maybe once they're in water they'll be all right.

He gets to work. The stems are tough and he has to crack them against the blade to break them. He takes the two best ones that aren't totally dead, and then he finds three more that are still tight buds. Brown on the outside too but maybe they'll open up, who knows.

Stems in his hand, he looks around. There's no light at the kitchen window, but it looks different somehow. They've changed the curtain. And the back door's been replaced with a wooden one, no glass.

He gets to his feet.

When he thinks about it later, he can't explain why he didn't just leave. But he doesn't just leave.

He pauses in the shadowy garden, with the very last daylight thinning into night around him, and he takes a look at the house. He's so close, metres away.

None of their stuff is in that house. Rob's said it loads of times – *you can't miss it, it's just bricks; it's not even our home if we're not there.*

But Rob's forgotten something. There is something that's theirs: the height chart. It'll be painted over by now, he knows it will. But it was loose at the bottom, the wood. Maybe he could get it, maybe not. And what if this is his only chance?

He goes to the back door. Obviously it's going to be locked. He pushes down on the handle and there's a clunk.

It's not locked.

The kitchen smells of something he doesn't recognise, something it never smelled of when he lived there. Breathing silently through his mouth, he runs his fingers over the worktop – they've changed that too. Theirs was that plastic fake-wood stuff; this is the real thing, smooth and solid. The cupboard doors are cream now. His mum would shit: she hates cream, beige, anything boring like that. Calls them *non-colours*. On the wall there's a thing hanging, blocks of pink-painted wood cut out to spell the word HOME over the top of a heart.

He puts the stems down on the worktop and goes into the hall. There's no sound other than a clock somewhere and his footsteps on the carpet. The door to the living room is wide open, with the streetlamp outside making a big triangle of light on the wall. He touches the new paint on the inside of the doorframe, bends a little bit, getting up close, and he can just about make out some of the writing next to the lines that were drawn across it, marking his height. *Luke 20 months. Robert – 8 years old today!*

And it's while he's standing there with his fingers tracing the words in the wood that he hears the baby.

It scares the shit out of him to start with, that sudden gasp it makes like it's just been underwater. But then he realises what it is. He goes over to the sofa, where it's lying on the floor in a basket. Its eyes are open, one chubby fist waving above a stripy knitted blanket. He crouches down to touch it, and it opens its hand, grabs hold of his finger, so stupidly tight it makes him grin.

And then he freezes. It's taken that long for what it means to hit him.

If there's a baby in the house, there's an adult as well.

Then everything happens very fast.

The light goes on, and he jumps to his feet, jerking his hand away too hard. The baby screams, and there's a woman in the doorway, and she pauses like she can't believe that there's actually someone here, and then she starts shouting and she runs over and snatches the kid up out of the basket.

'Get out! Get out of my house! Get out!' she's yelling.

Luke steps backwards, puts his hands high in the air. And the woman's eyes snap up to above his head, and her eyes go wide, and she shields the baby and turns away and screams louder than he's ever heard a person scream before in his life.

And that's when he realises he's still holding the knife.

*

He cries all the way back to Beech View.

Mel's driving, Luke's in the back. She won't even look at him.

At first he tried to stop, just bite it back, but after a couple of minutes he can't do it any more and it just keeps coming out of him, massive juddering sobs like they've been growing inside him for weeks.

She says, 'For fuck's sake,' under her breath for the hundredth time. 'What the hell were you thinking, Luke?' There's another furious pause, and then she says, 'You are one unfucking-believably lucky kid.'

He knows it's true. He dropped the knife the second he realised what was happening, and he told the woman, shouted it, that he was Luke Ashworth, he used to live here, that Mrs Dias next door knew him. That he just wanted to get these flowers for his mum because she was in hospital. Bursting into tears probably helped, he thinks now, and the thought brings with it another wave of shame.

She made him wait outside the front door, did all the bolts, and talked to him through the letterbox.

'Don't even think about running away,' she'd said, crying too, 'or I'll just call the police, all right? You understand me?'

She asked for the name of the home he was in, already knew he was in care somehow, probably from the neighbour. And twenty minutes later, Mel had arrived. She put him in the car, didn't even talk to him, and went inside the house. She was gone half an hour, and the bloke came home too, the woman's husband, and they were all in there talking about whether or not Luke was going to spend the next five years or whatever in Young Offenders. And Luke just sat in the back of Mel's Clio, shaking, thinking about what was his mum going to say.

Or what she was going to do.

'If you pull anything like that again, Luke, I swear to God I'm going to call the police my fucking self,' Mel says now, eyeing him in the mirror, shaking her head. He's never seen her so angry. 'You were *this* close to a criminal record, do you know that?'

When they get back, he goes straight to his room and locks the door. He pulls the chest of drawers across it, and gets into bed without even taking his clothes off and pulls the duvet right over his head.

They come to the door about twenty times. First Mel, bringing food and drinks and saying things to him, saying he's got to let her in. And then one of the bank staff after Mel's gone home.

But he doesn't come out, not that night, not all day the next day. Mr Polzeath turns up at one point saying he'll have to break the door down but of course he fucking doesn't because it'll cost him to fix it. Luke won't even go out to piss, just uses a Coke bottle. Doesn't even answer when Paige tries to talk to him through the door. She comes back three times. But he stays curled up, facing the wall.

He doesn't want her to know, but Mel must have told her. Because when he creeps out in the early hours of Sunday morning when he really, really needs a glass of water and some food, there's a bunch of peonies lying on the carpet outside his door. *Grown in South Africa*, the label says.

19

Now

Something wakes her early, just gone four, and sleep is gone in an instant. She's not meeting Yardley for hours yet but Wren gets up, showers and leaves quietly, knowing from years of experience the futility of trying to return to sleep.

There is a coffee bar in Cotham, up past the hospitals, that never closes. The warm scent of new croissants blooms out at her as she opens the door, but she sticks with her usual espresso.

The guy behind the counter is new. 'Night shift? You a doctor?' he says, handing it to her and laughing mildly at her lengthy yawn.

She sips at the scalding paper cup as he gets her change. 'I work in probation.'

He makes a face like he doesn't believe her. 'At five in the morning?'

'What can you do? Crime never sleeps,' she tells him, and he laughs.

Back in the car, the radio mumbles benignly as she makes the familiar loop. Top of Blackboy Hill and out onto the Downs. She pulls over in the spot she always favours when she's up and out early, near the Observatory.

Killing the engine, she sits back. But as she scans the view, something Melanie said comes back to her and makes her get out her phone: the Polzeaths, and the property they had in Clifton.

The search is swift and productive. The first hit on Oliver Polzeath is a profile article she's already seen, published in *Community Care.* He'd originally trained in social work, and bought a near-derelict ex-hotel in Burnham-on-Sea to convert into a children's home back in the late eighties, and the business grew from there. In terms of a current property portfolio, though, there's nothing obvious. His ex, however, is a different story. She's a director of Positano Residences, listed out of an address in Bristol's most prestigious BS8 postcode. Wren digs a notebook out of the glovebox and scribbles down the addresses she finds associated with them on a property rental site. Then she buckles up, doubles back onto the Ladies Mile towards the zoo and enters the residential part of Clifton from the north.

Wren doesn't come up here often. Her work rarely involves these kinds of neighbourhoods, and if she and Suzy have a night out, they're more suited to what Stokes Croft or the Gloucester Road has to offer. When she does visit the opulent suburb, she's always accompanied by a faint sense of resentment. It's hard to stomach the comfort and wealth of the top of the pyramid when you've seen what it is to live at the bottom.

She finds the first, second and third addresses on her list within a few streets of each other. Each one is a penthouse in a different detached Georgian block, not dissimilar from the Lord Mayor's pile. She looks up through open curtains at a gorgeous ceiling with a modernist chandelier the size of her bathroom.

Wren presses away the frown that has formed involuntarily. How had Melanie put it, about the stipend for Paige's involvement in the Care Ambassador project? *Pennies really, to them, but it went straight into their pockets.* But it didn't add up. Aggregate resale value aside, the rents from the three flats she's just seen – enormous, luxury homes – must be netting the best part of five figures a month. So why would they bother pushing Paige into a scheme for the sake of a few quid of petrol money?

Wren finishes the coffee, remembering how unkindly she'd judged the Polzeaths before she'd met them. Can't care be a business, like any other? Just because it makes a ton of cash, it doesn't make it immoral.

Except her gut says it's more than that. It's not just about the money. Something is off.

It's getting on for seven – time to go and meet James. She heads towards the centre, the roads getting busier by the minute now, and finds a space opposite the court. Christmas Steps is a five-minute walk.

Wren orders a decaf tea and spots him at the rear of the café, rigid concentration sectioning his forehead. He sees her and gets to his feet.

'Look, maybe this isn't a good idea,' he says. He looks as if he's had less sleep than she has.

'It's just a chat,' she tells him, pulling out a chair.

He nods, sighs heavily and sits back down. 'I just – I don't know. I spent so long thinking how it would go, you know? Meeting him, talking it all through.'

'And it wasn't how you expected.'

He glances up, as if testing the waters, unsure of what he can trust her with. What he is safe to admit. He goes on stirring his flat white, four empty sachets of sugar at his elbow.

'How about you tell me what you've been looking into, OK? If I can help, I will.'

'I can't share details of the schedule with you,' she says. 'I'm sorry. It's confidential.'

'You've seen the Polzeaths?'

Wren shakes her head with an apologetic laugh. 'Honestly, I really can't talk about it I'm afraid.'

James nods. 'I can't help you then.'

'I'm sorry?'

'I've done my bit. I co-operated with the police, I went to court, I went out of my way to find you, to help with your programme. I wanted to forgive him.' He folds his arms. 'If you want me to do something off the record to help you—'

'This isn't for me. It's my job, it's about justice for Paige.'

He tilts his head. 'But is *she* part of your job?'

'What?'

'The answer is no. She's not, not really. And look, I already know it's personal. It's personal for me. I want to know what happened to her. But what you're requesting, what you're about to ask me about Luke, and Paige – yes, I do know what's coming, Wren, I'm not stupid – it's privileged information.'

'OK,' she says, deflated. 'Then I'm sorry you've had a wasted trip.'

'No,' he says, putting his hand out to stop her from getting up. Wren stays put. 'I *will* share,' he goes on. 'But it's quid pro quo. All right? I want to know what *you* know.'

He waits.

'All right?' he says again.

It's either accept it as it is offered, or walk away. She looks at the door. It's right there.

'All right,' she says to her tea. And she takes a deep breath, and tells him. Starting with Leah Amberley, the teachers, the girl at school. James listens intently.

'OK. Who else?'

'I spoke to a woman who worked at Beech View at the time. She had some things to say about the Polzeaths, who own the chain.'

There's a pause. 'Not Melanie Pickford-Hayes,' he says archly.

'You know her?'

'To a degree.'

'Meaning what?' Wren presses. It hadn't even crossed her mind that Melanie was anything other than honest.

'Meaning,' he says, unselfconsciously wiping milk foam from the corners of his mouth, 'you might want to have a look at her credentials before you get too cosy with her.'

'I wouldn't call it cosy – we've spoken *once*. All she said was that Rob was untrustworthy, which I already know—'

'You and the rest of the human race.'

'—and that the Polzeaths fired her.'

He raises an eyebrow. 'And she still has an axe to grind about that.'

'I don't know, we didn't—'

'It wasn't a question. She does. She never worked in care again.'

Wren frowns. 'How do you know that?'

He lets his eyes drift. 'You'd be surprised where a lot of sleepless nights and a decent Wi-Fi connection will get you. Strike you as odd that she left her… vocation? Or do you think professional misconduct might follow a person like her around a bit, stop her from getting other work?'

'Misconduct? How?'

'I remember Paige talking about her; she was a mother figure. She trusted her – she was supposed to look after her, wasn't she?'

'But surely if she had been a suspect the police would have insisted on interviewing her. She wasn't even in the country when the investigation took place.'

'Funny that.' James leans forward, his voice just above a whisper. 'Look. Beech View was a good home. The people there did their best. But there's no legislating for bad eggs. And that woman may not have been the guardian angel that she'd have us take her for.'

'What do you mean?'

'There were promotions in the offing – it was part of my

job as the liaison between the school and the social care places that I would sit on panels, did you know that? So I knew the staffing systems pretty well. There had been an incident with drinking on the job, as I remember it. She was… unreliable. But in retrospect it was generally agreed she must have known Paige and Rob were involved with each other.'

'So they were, you think?'

'To some extent. We know they spent time together, don't we?'

'But romantically?'

He shrugs. 'I don't know. But you know what teenagers are like: it's very likely. And I'd say it would have been nigh-on impossible for *her* not to know.'

'So why wouldn't she have done anything? Given how young Paige was.'

'Maybe she tried and failed? Easier to turn a blind eye? Or perhaps she let Paige get away with a bit of naughtiness. Melanie wanted to be the cool adult, the confidante.' He hesitates for a moment, then says, 'Without beating about the bush, she was an odd one. Got overly attached. No children of her own, got a little bit too maternal with them. And that combined with the drinking, I mean…' He shrugged.

'Are you saying that makes her a suspect?'

'I'm not saying anything. I've just – let's say I've seen first-hand how quickly the demon drink can propel a person from love to rage.'

Wren puffs out her cheeks. 'What about another man in Paige's life, was there any concern about that?'

'Man? As in, adult?'

'You tell me.'

He considers it. 'Not that I know of.'

'You're sure? Her school friend was fairly confident—'

He gives a slow shake of the head, eyes narrowed. Then he says, 'I'd say not. We talked about a lot, Paige and I. Took some time to get her to open up to start with but then – she trusted me,' he says simply. 'I can't be sure about Robert, but if something like *that* was happening, I'd like to think I would have picked up on it.'

Wren doesn't doubt Paige had liked James – he must have had an exceptional talent with teenagers to have that rapport with them. When she'd been at school herself, the counsellor was someone creepy in too-tight joggers, a person with whom you'd avoid discussing even the weather if you could. James's relationship with Paige though, the depth of it, it's something she hadn't expected.

'What changed between you and Paige? It sounds as if you were… I don't know.'

'Were what?' he says, looking up.

'I was going to say friends.'

'Ah. No. We weren't. I was a counsellor, she was a student. Strict code of ethics, just like I'm sure you have. We met every week. It was in a timetable. I was paid.'

'And what about Luke? You counselled him too, right?'

'I did.'

'After the burglary?'

James smiles, shakes his head.

'I just can't get hold of him,' Wren says. 'No NI number, no online presence, he just dropped off the social services radar. All I want to know is whether you think he might have known more than he let on.'

After a deep sigh, James says, 'Luke Ashworth was not the subject of any suspicion.'

'He *was* interviewed. Twice.' Luke had maintained he knew nothing of the burglary until everyone else did.

'Because he knew her. They were friends.'

'I heard they were more than that. Mrs Polzeath said he was obsessed with her.

James shakes his head. And it's frustrating: if he had been

that close to Paige – whether he would admit it or not – how could he be so clueless about Luke?

'With respect, I'm not sure you're being totally straight with me. You're probably the one person who knew them best. Someone they relied on,' she says, changing tack. He doesn't strike her as someone susceptible to flattery, but it's worth a shot.

'Even if I *could* find him for you. You think he'll tell you anything he didn't tell the police?'

She shrugs. 'Maybe.'

James checks his watch. 'I'll dig out my notes. I didn't write everything down,' he warns. 'I'm thorough, but I've never overdone the paperwork. But you never know, maybe Luke mentioned something that might help. I'm not promising anything,' he adds. He asks for Wren's email, writes it down.

'Does Robert have email? A phone number?'

'Phone, yes, but I can't just—'

'Not for me,' James says, laughing, holding up his hands. 'Christ, it's not like I'm going to take him out for a pint. I was thinking Luke might want it, if I was to get in touch with him.'

'No,' Wren says firmly. 'Robert desperately wants to get hold of Luke. If we find Luke – if you find him – I don't want to put them in touch just like that.'

'Ah. You want to keep your leverage.' He regards her with amused suspicion, and she realises how manipulative it sounded.

But she doesn't correct him. Because leverage is right. A bit of power is exactly what she needs.

20

Before

The photo guy has been there for an hour with Mr and Mrs Polzeath and Paige and some woman from social services. They've got some big-deal bid coming up, trying to get a contract from the council for more homes, and they're doing a brochure. So the whole kitchen's gleaming. Even the flickery striplight that's been blinking on-off since Luke moved in has been fixed.

They've got Paige in there obviously because it's her they really want the pictures of, but also Fat Jake. Even though Luke said he'd do it, and he knows he's not exactly Ronaldo but seriously, Fat Jake? It's bullshit. They're going to be in the kitchen pretending to cook something, and no one's allowed in while they're setting it up.

Luke goes into the dining room, and Mr P is in there, watching TV in a suit and tie. Some news show. Luke's got homework under his arm, he's got this bit of *Hamlet* to learn. He flops and gets sheets out but he can't keep his mind on it.

'Didn't have you down as a thespian,' Mr Polzeath says, straightening up and reaching out to turn the TV down.

Luke has got no clue what he's talking about, so he says nothing.

The sound goes off and Mr P's looking at him. 'I've been

hoping to have a chat with you. I know you've been having a bit of trouble lately.'

Luke gets up. 'I'm fine.' He is not in the fucking mood.

'Actually, Luke, this is important. Could you sit down, please?'

This is what they do. Start off pretending that they're on a level with you, and then switch to telling you what to do and expect you not to notice.

'Right,' he says, and he sits down, his face going instantly molten because he knows what's coming. It was three days ago he got caught in Paige's room, and he'd started to think maybe they'd stop bringing it up. He's already had to have two separate 'chats' with Geraint and Mrs P.

'Geraint told me about what happened the other night. In Paige's room.'

'I was literally just sitting there!'

He gets the eyebrows for that. 'That's what you told Geraint, yes.'

'You calling me a liar?'

Mr P doesn't answer. Just looks at him until Luke looks away.

Quietly, Luke asks, 'Have you told her? Paige?'

'I don't want to do that, Luke.' He takes a big breath, pushes his shoulders back and Luke knows he's building up to some bullshit speech the way he likes to. 'But look. Here at Beech View we take respect very seriously. We respect you, and we expect to receive respect back, the social teams respect us because of it – it carries on like that.'

Luke can feel the stems of his eyes trying to roll. 'Yeah.'

'The point I'm making is that it starts with you. Everything we do starts with the clients.' The word he's looking for is 'kids', but Luke leaves it. 'Part of our job is to teach you respect.'

'Right.' There's nothing about respect that Luke can learn from this prick who rocks up once a month in his forty-grand car when someone important wants a look round.

Polzeath gets up, walks over to the window and stands with his hands on his hips, legs apart like he's delivering a speech. 'I can see that you're very fond of her. She's a very – magnetic person. And beautiful too, right?' he says with a smile.

Luke glances at the door. If she comes in, he'll literally die.

'But being in someone else's room without permission, Luke. It goes against the values of our—'

'Right. Yeah. Can I go?'

He's annoyed. Big man doesn't like being interrupted. 'Luke, what were you doing in her room when she wasn't there?'

There's no way he's answering that. Not honestly, anyway. *I like being surrounded by her stuff*? *I want to find out what she's not telling me*? *I love her*? No.

'I told Geraint. I needed her copy of this book. For school.'

Mr P raises his eyebrows. 'Sorry, Luke. I know that's not true. And it's not respectful to lie, either.'

No point replying to that. So he doesn't – but when Mr Polzeath realises Luke's saying nothing, he comes right over, crossing the whole fucking room in two steps like he's had enough pissing about. He gets right up in Luke's face. Luke can smell the sweat on his skin, the toothpaste on his breath.

'You need to tell me, Luke.' He speaks low now. 'What were you looking for?'

Luke ducks to the side, gets up, and sprints to his room. He shuts the door and sits leaning against it, getting his breath back.

It's then that he realises that this isn't about something he's done wrong. Mr P wants to know what he knows. Which means one of two things. Either he thinks she's hiding something, and he wants in on what it is. Or he already knows what she's hiding, and he doesn't want Luke to find it.

And either way, Luke's going to have to find out.

*

When Mr P leaves, Luke takes his homework to the dining room. He's given up on the Shakespeare and got his maths spread out on the big table. Mel comes out of the kitchen where they're taking the photos. She stops when she sees him, raises one eyebrow.

'What?' Luke goes back to the book, pulls his finger down the page. *Simplify* $4^3 \times 4^2$. 'Got homework.'

'Yeah?' He looks up and she's smiling at him. 'Didn't fancy the desk in your room? Why's that then?'

And he knows she's only kidding, teasing him about listening in on what's going on in the kitchen, but now he feels like a dick and he closes his book with a smack and says, 'Whatever. Fuck's sake.'

Mel doesn't care. She gives a soft laugh and comes round the table, pulls out the chair next to him.

'I'm glad you're not hiding in your room any more,' she says.

Through the kitchen door they can hear Mrs Polzeath directing the photo shoot, the excitement rising in her voice. *Jake, just take a step back – and perfect. Beautiful, Paige!*

Mel leans in, whispers, 'You'd think she was modelling bikinis in the Caribbean, wouldn't you?' and rolls her eyes.

A laugh escapes from his nose, and he grins back. They haven't spoken much since what happened at Dulverton Road. She pulls his textbook over and puffs her cheeks out, flipping through *Laws of Indices*.

'This stuff make any sense to you?'

'Kinda,' he says, shrugging. Thing is, it does. He *gets* maths, way more than English, where everything's about convincing people that your version of it is the best. Maths, you either get it right or you don't. There's no grey area.

'Mrs Shah says I've got a talent for it.'

'Yeah?' Mel nods, grinning. She holds his eye until he looks away.

This is where she's going to bring it up, tell him how disappointed she is in him about breaking into the house. That, or give him one of those horrible gentle bollockings about Paige's privacy. She liked him, but now he's just a massive fuck-up to her like everyone else.

Except, that's not what happens. She puts a hand on his shoulder. 'You're doing great, Lukey,' she says.

That's all. *You're doing great.* She's letting him get away with it, and he doesn't know if it's the gratitude or what but suddenly he's got both his arms around her.

There's a click and the sound of the kitchen spills out, but somehow Luke doesn't react, not straight away. It's because of Mel, hugging him back. It's the first time he's had someone that close to him in weeks and weeks. Months.

By the time Luke sees him, Jake is there filling the whole fucking doorframe, a face on him like he's won the lottery. He's got a phone in his fat fist, way up above his head. His eyes lock with Luke and then quick as spitting he's taking a photo, Luke with Mel.

Behind him, Paige's voice, savage with fury. 'Give it back!'

Jake jolts forward as she crashes into him, shoving past to get to the phone that Luke can see now is hers – of course it is, it's got the sparkly unicorn sticker on it. But he's massive and she's like a little fairy so he just sort of clamps her behind him with his other arm. While that's happening, Luke springs away from Mel, standing up so fast he knocks his chair back and it cracks against the wall.

Fat Jake's piggy face splits into a grin as he raises the phone even higher, further out of Paige's reach. Luke realises he's never seen anyone else hold it. Not even touch it. Her whole life is on that phone, it's like a part of her body.

'Well, fuck me,' Jake says, looking from Luke to Mel and back again. 'You sure you're her type, Luke?'

'Piss off,' Luke spits, his fists shaking by his sides and his face white hot.

'Give me my *fucking* phone back,' Paige screams. She's kicking him as well now, but she's just in her socks and he doesn't even seem to notice.

Jake looks up at the phone still held high, scrolling with his thumb. 'Such a *cute* photo of you guys!' He'll be texting it to himself. Then he'll be texting it to Cameron. Or those dicks he hangs around at school with, Luke thinks, with a feeling like paper crumpling in his chest.

Jake taps the screen and turns his attention back to Luke. 'I mean, I know our Melanie likes pussy and everything—'

'That'll do,' Mel says, sighing like he's boring her. She's not angry, not even with him saying *that* to her.

Mrs Polzeath's half in and half out of the kitchen, whisper-shouting at Jake to *stop it, now*, clearly more concerned with what the woman from the social is going to think.

Mel says, 'Give the phone back right now please, Jake. I'm only telling you once or it's straight to sanction.'

Luke's staring at Jake, frozen with rage. He says one more fucking word—

Then Paige wrestles herself free. She disappears into the kitchen and when she reappears, seconds later, she's got a saucepan, one of the heavy silver ones with a long handle. And it's like everyone sees what she's about to do, but no one does anything because they can't believe that she's actually going to swing it, maximum force, into the side of Jake's head.

There's a horrible dull thud as it makes contact. The phone spins across the floor, and Paige scrabbles for it.

Jake goes down like a sack of rocks, hits the floor on his knees and then keels sideways. Conscious but not moving, this creaking sort of moan coming out of him.

Mel's the first one to snap into action. 'Shit,' she says, and in an instant she's crouching next to him. 'Oh, Jake. Come on, buddy, let me see.'

Just for a moment, the whole room freezes. Blood, loads of it. Oozing out between his fingers where he's clutching at his temple.

Paige covers her mouth, backs away. She shoots a panicked glance over to Luke. She wants help, and his heart skips. He opens his eyes wide, jerks his head to the door.

Go.

Everyone's watching Jake. Mrs Polzeath's got her hands over her mouth, doing jack shit to help, just trying to get the woman from the social back into the kitchen. Mel's shouting instructions at people who are just standing there looking horrified like they've never seen someone smacked before. No one notices when Paige backs out of the room.

Fat Jake is sobbing, his voice high and shaky. 'I'll fucking kill you,' he's saying, his eyes tight shut and blood spreading across his mouth, bubbling wetly when he speaks. 'You fucking bitch, I'll kill you.'

Luke expected her to run out of the house, but he finds her in the store cupboard on the first floor, under the stairs to the boys' rooms. It's musty in there, airless.

When he's settled next to her, she says, 'I can't believe I just did that.'

They sit in pitch-black silence, the rise-and-fall sound of the drama downstairs reaching them in muffled bursts.

'I'm not normal,' she whispers. He feels her move, bringing her knees up, hugging them to herself. 'I just – I just *lost* it.' Then, almost like she's fine with it, she says, 'He's going to kill me.'

Luke turns, tries to make out her face, but it's totally black. 'He deserved it, Paige.'

'No, he *didn't*!' she says sharply, and he wishes he could take it back. 'No one deserves that. What kind of a headcase *does* that?'

Luke doesn't know how to answer.

There's an ambulance, the sirens getting louder and louder until it stops, right outside. Commotion in the hall.

'I'm always going to be a fuck-up,' she whispers eventually.

'That's not true,' Luke whispers back. He wishes he could make it real and not something coaxing and empty like the staff say, like his mum's nurses say.

'It is true,' she says. 'You can't go through all of this and be normal. You can't do well.'

'How do you mean?'

She shrugs. 'None of us are exactly geniuses, are we?' She must feel him flinch because she says quickly, 'I mean, I'm not saying you, Lukey, I'm not saying you're thick. But people like us, we don't end up doing well in school, or going to uni, or getting really good jobs or anything. It's like it's all mapped out, you know? And everyone tells us we've got the same chances as anyone else. But it's bullshit. We're all broken up. You can't start off with what we've got here and make a go of your life. Sorry, but you just can't.'

Luke wants to say that it's not true – that Leah's doing OK, that Rob's all right, too. But it goes hard in his throat, because Leah's wiping arses for minimum wage, and what is Rob, really? A thief. A scammer.

There's a vibration on the floor and her message tone, the sound of a duck quacking, and whatever was pulled tight in there is cut loose, and they giggle.

Paige gets hold of the phone, and when she finds it she's suddenly lit by the glow of the screen. She inputs the unlock code quickly, but he sees it anyway. 7031. She hasn't been looking too perky for a week or so, but in that light she looks like death. Her eyes are ghostly, and he wants to look away, but they pull him in.

'What?' she says, sensing his eyes on her. She angles the screen away.

'Nothing, I'm not— I wasn't looking,' he says, hurt.

But she doesn't notice. She chews her lip, frowning as she texts.

Then something comes to him. 'What about Yardley?'

There's a slight pause. 'What about him?'

'You said he was in care.'

'Oh, right,' she says. 'Yeah.'

'And he turned out OK.'

She leaves that hanging. 'But look at everyone else. All our parents. Your mum. Both Jake's parents were addicts; Cameron's never met his dad and his mum's a pisshead *and* on the game. My mum was a junkie.' Paige shifts her weight on the hard floor, and rests the side of her face on her knees. 'She sent me all these letters when I first went into care, saying how she didn't want to do it but how she was a terrible parent,' she says bitterly. 'But all that soon dried up. She's probably dead in a ditch somewhere by now.'

Being really, really careful not to touch anything he shouldn't, Luke lifts his hand, feels for hers. 'I know.'

'Do you?'

His eyes flutter shut and his face bursts into blistering heat and he thanks God for the dark. 'No,' he tells her. 'I'm sorry. I don't know anything about what you've been through.'

She squeezes his hand back and if it wasn't for the shame of the lie, of only really knowing anything about her because he's read her file, that pressure on the back of his hand would have been the high point of his whole fourteen months in Beech View. But it's over as quickly as it happened, and she moves her hand, and the moment's gone.

'Sometimes I think I see her, you know? Like outside

school, or on the bus. I see people look at me for a minute and I always think, *is that her*?'

Luke's eyes are adjusted now and he can just make her out, the shape of her face, frowning hard.

'It just makes me so fucking angry. I'm angry all the time. And I lie, I let people down, I do such stupid things, and I'm always trying to tell myself it's not my fault. But it is. It's *me* making these shitty choices, not anyone else. I just need to forgive her, and everyone else who should have helped. And then I could be a better person, Lukey.' A tear slips down her nose, and she sniffs, then rubs it angrily away.

'But I can't,' she says simply. 'I can't forgive them. I never will.'

21

Now

Wren puts down the parenting magazine she's been reading as soon as Ashworth steps out of the interview room. Not a moment too soon, either: the guilt has been ratcheting up with every page as she realises how many things she hasn't prepared for, hasn't even discussed with Suzy. Sleep arrangements, buggies, breast vs bottle, the whole nine yards. But even as she flipped the pages, she hadn't really been concentrating. Too many things cycling in her head: Paige and Luke, Paige and Rob. James, Melanie, Gary. All of them. And, because of what she's got planned for her extra-curricular work that evening: Leah Amberley, first and foremost.

But that is for later.

'How did it go?' Wren asks him. The interview was for shift work in a hospital laundry, a shade over minimum wage to reflect the unsociable evening and weekend hours. He hadn't wanted to go. She didn't blame him. 'Think you got it?'

Ashworth shrugs. 'Maybe. Think you could probably have found me something shitter though, if you'd tried.'

'You think you can find something better without my help, Rob, you go right ahead. But if they offer you that and you turn it down, you don't get a safety net. Benefits have got a whole lot tougher.'

He stares at her. 'I'm not going on benefits.'

'No?' She holds the double door out of the waiting room open for him and they head along the corridor. 'You'll be needing to take whatever you get offered then, unless there's some grand plan you've not told me about.'

'What's that supposed to mean?' he snaps, but before she can answer he downgrades it. 'I haven't got any fucking plan. Obviously.'

They retrace their steps through the labyrinthine hospital and outside. She sees him to the bus stop, says goodbye, then gets in her car. For about ten seconds she tries to talk herself out of making the trip she's got planned, but her dogged curiosity wins in the end. She just can't let go of what she overheard between him and Leah.

The drive out to the smart suburb of Westbury is smooth and uncomplicated, and she arrives outside the nursery she's tracked Leah down to with twenty minutes to go. She tucks herself in a space facing the road, with a full view of the bunting-strung entrance in her wing mirror. By ten to six there is a steady flow of parents pulling up. Wren watches them hurry out of their cars, emerging minutes later clutching sleepy toddlers with tiny backpacks. The stream thins to nothing by ten past.

The lights inside flick off and one by one the staff make their way to their cars. Wren scrutinises each face, but Leah is the last to leave, zipping a padded coat up to the neck and striding out towards the street with the obvious resolve of someone catching a bus. Good: it would be much harder to wring a conversation out of her if she had a car.

Leah doesn't miss a beat when Wren falls into step next to her. 'You again. Got bored of hassling me on voicemail?'

'Slightly. I just want ten minutes of your time.'

'Yeah? Well, I just want a villa in Ibiza.'

'I'm not here to cause any trouble.'

Leah sighs heavily and stops dead. 'What do you want,

then? Because you sure as hell don't seem like any probation officer I've ever heard of.'

Wren has given this a lot of thought. It's clear that Ashworth has some kind of sway over Leah, and trying to get information out of her about him isn't going to be easy. So she goes at it sideways.

'It's not about Rob,' she says. 'It's about Paige, and about Beech View.'

Leah raises her eyebrows, suspicious. 'Right.'

'Look, I want him to keep out of trouble, for everything to go smoothly for him. That's my job. But I want to talk to you because between me and you, I've got concerns about the home Paige lived in.' The slightest softening of Leah's face, making Wren's pulse skip with anticipation. 'I think, of everyone, you're going to know what I mean.'

'Concerns like what?' Leah says, not giving anything away.

'The kind of concerns that make news.'

Leah uncrosses her arms and starts walking again. Wren follows.

'She's not coming back. I don't see what difference anything I say is going to make.'

Matching her pace, Wren digs in her bag for the pack of cigarettes she's bought for the occasion, and offers one to Leah. 'You know they own seven homes across Bristol and South Glos now?'

'No.' Leah glances at the cigarettes, refuses with a shake of her head, then mutters, 'All right then,' and takes one.

'They do.' Wren lights the cigarette, considers taking one for herself but remembers Suzy, and puts them back in her bag. 'Sixty, sixty-five kids at a time.'

Leah shrugs, but even in the gathering gloom Wren can see her flinch.

'Look, if there's something going on that means those kids aren't safe—'

'Like what?'

'Any of the adults there who weren't… wholly appropriate.'

'We need to talk in fucking riddles for a reason?'

'Let's start with the care workers. Did you hear anything suspicious about a Melanie? Mel?'

'I know the name. Wanted to be Paige's mum, by the sounds of her. And Luke's. Why do you ask?'

'Just some things I've heard,' Wren parries.

'From who?'

There's the sense of a thaw so Wren tells her. 'James Yardley. You know him, right?'

Leah's face instantly brightens in recognition of the name. 'I do, yeah. He's a good guy.'

'How so?'

'Paige liked him. I don't know why she and Rob ended up doing what they did to him, and it's none of my business. But Yardley, he was OK. Carried on going door to door trying to find clues when the police got bored with looking for her. He was different. Didn't want anything in return.'

'You're sure about that?' Wren asks, because not for the first time she knows how it would look to an outsider.

'Meaning?'

'Meaning it's not exactly a traditional friendship. Wealthy, powerful, decent-looking older man with unsupervised access to a vulnerable, beautiful girl?'

But Leah shoots her a warning look. 'Don't even go there. That man did everything he could've done for Paige. I'm not kidding. Anyone tells you otherwise they're talking out their arse. You think I wouldn't have noticed, if he was a nonce?'

'OK, I didn't mean—'

'Well, then, don't say it. There's enough arseholes in the world without decent people getting accused as well.'

Wren raises her palms, surrendering. Then Leah says, 'Those two posh wankers still running it?'

'The Polzeaths?'

A nod.

'Alice is still in charge. But she's separated from Oliver now.'

'*He* got pretty cosy with her.'

'With Paige?'

The younger woman inhales deeply. Wren hasn't smoked in years but her blood sparkles with the memory of the nicotine. 'Made a thing of trying to take her under his wing a bit. The way they do when you look like her.'

'What are you saying, Leah?'

'Nothing.'

They take a left, heading towards the main road into the centre. The traffic crawls along beside them, and Leah increases her speed. 'Look,' she says. 'I don't trust you. I've got no reason to trust any of you, for the same reasons that Paige didn't trust any of you.'

'Any of who? I'm not—'

'You're no different. Saying one thing and doing another. All of them, social workers, teachers, the fucking Polzeaths. They do just enough to tick the boxes. They took what they wanted from us, they decided who we got to be, and they let us get on with it. People like us don't stand a fucking chance. So don't come round here telling me how you care what happened to her. She got fucked over and spat out, just like Rob and Luke and everyone. Even worse for their favourites. I did fucking warn her.'

'Warn her about what?'

'That she couldn't trust them!'

'But why?' Wren persists.

'Just leave it!' Leah shouts. 'Leave me alone!'

The hand holding the cigarette is shaking now. Wren's chance is getting away from her.

'What do you mean by favourites, Leah?' Wren asks softly.

Leah stops dead and faces her.

'Enough. Stop calling me,' she says. 'I've done my grieving for what happened. I don't want to talk about it any more.'

Wren goes for her trump card. 'OK. But I need to speak to your grandad. Could you give me his details?'

'Why?' Her contempt seems to evaporate in an instant, and she looks as if she might cry. 'What's he got to do with anything?'

'Just need to discuss with him what he's got that Rob's interested in.'

'It's none of your fucking business!'

Wren tilts her head. 'I'm afraid it is.'

'Please,' Leah says, her voice cracking. Her bravado shimmers and is gone, as if she's suddenly shed a decade. 'Please. I've caused them so much hassle, they're only just trusting me again. Please don't involve him.'

'I don't have to, if you'll give me a straight answer.'

'It's just a couple of boxes,' Leah whines, her eyes on the pavement. 'Some stuff I was holding for Rob while he was in prison. And I can't get them for another week and a half, like I told Rob. It's at my grandad's. He's on holiday in Spain and I don't have a key.'

Wren digs in her bag for her card and hands it over.

'What's this?'

'My number. Just get the boxes, and call me. And I promise I won't phone again.'

22

Before

'You need to take a break,' Mel says, putting the mug down on his desk. 'It's gone eleven.'

Luke picks it up without looking at it, takes a sip, but it's not coffee, it's hot milk. He pushes it away.

'Help you sleep,' she says.

'I don't want to sleep.' He's got tests all the next week, and yeah, they're not GCSEs, but if he can't prove to himself he can pass them, he's not going to believe he can do it for real next year. He's got to prove Paige wrong.

'Half an hour then,' she says, and she turns to leave.

'Where's Paige?'

Mel sighs.

'I just want to know.'

'She's at a swimming gala.' She goes to the door.

'At eleven o'clock?'

Mel shrugs slowly like she's had this conversation before and she can't be arsed to have it again. 'She helps clear up, doesn't she?'

'Not until eleven o'clock she doesn't. Where is it, Easton?' If it's the pool in Easton he could go down there, walk her back; it's only twenty minutes.

But Mel doesn't answer his question. She just eyes him.

'Where, then?' There's the big new place, Paige calls it

the competition pool, down in Hengrove; if Cameron's out maybe Luke can nick his bike, probably do that in half an hour.

'She's getting a lift back,' Mel says as he brings maps up on his screen.

He looks up. 'Who off?'

Mel sighs. 'Lukey—' she starts, and she takes a deep breath like there's something big to say.

'All right, whatever, fine,' he says quickly and his face instantly catches fire. He turns his back to her again, flips a page, pretending to make a note. He hears the door click and he thinks for a second she's left.

'Luke,' she says. He turns round, finds she's still inside. The door's closed behind her.

'What,' he says, his voice flat.

'You need to give her a bit of space, love.'

He turns, scowling. Shame or rage or something else tears at him right in the gut, but she's smiling at him, and it just makes it worse and before he can stop himself he says, 'Yeah? Fuck off. Mind your own fucking business.'

But Mel acts like she hasn't heard him. 'I'm only saying it because I can see how much she means to you.'

'You don't know anything about anything,' he says. 'Just leave me alone.'

'All right, Luke.' She opens the door. 'Half an hour,' she says. And then she's gone.

He closes his eyes then and just sits there. She doesn't know. There's no way she could know, because what happens to him with Paige, it's like it's more than a human being can manage. When he's with Paige it's like he's going to physically split open. Like his skin is just too tight, how he feels is all just too big. And he knows he doesn't hide it properly, and he doesn't make her laugh and he's never got anything good to say, anything that'll make her think he's got something to offer her.

And that's the fucking bottom line, isn't it?

He *doesn't* have anything to offer her. And he's going to be the strung-along and spat-out friend, the loser, every time. And it's just fucking bollocks because he *could* make her happy. He would hold her together and forget everything that's happened before and he wouldn't ever judge her, and they could start again and make things OK. But she won't let him. And Mel knows it, and everyone knows it, and he wants to die.

She's never going to love him back.

And if he can't have her—

There's a swing of headlights across his bedroom wall. In two seconds flat he's beside the window, careful not to stand in front of the glass. He leans over to the desk, snaps the light off. Watches.

In the street, the car is still but idling. It's big, maybe the car from the other day but he can't really tell. It's dark and polished.

The headlights go off. But nothing happens.

He reaches towards the drawers, but he doesn't take his eyes off the car. Second drawer down, right at the front so he always knows where they are: the binoculars he got from his grandad when he died.

Slowly, in case his movement draws attention, he loops the strap round his neck and lifts them to his eyes.

The angle down onto the street is awkward, and the base of the streetlight is in the way so he can't see the driver. Paige is in the front passenger seat. She's got her feet on the dashboard. Trainers, bare legs. She's leaning forward like she's folded in half, and he can see her hair is wet, knotted up in a tangled bun.

She's nodding. Saying something, bringing the heels of both hands to wipe under her eyes. Then she's leaning towards the driver, whose arm is around her, their hand on her neck.

Luke squints, moves to the other side of the window, keeping low. He still can't identify the other person.

Whoever it is, he doesn't want them there, next to her. Fingers on her bare skin, touching her perfect body that is not theirs to touch.

He waits five, ten, fifteen minutes. And eventually, the headlights go back on. Paige turns, reaches behind her for her bag. She gets out, closes the door without slamming it. The passenger window goes down, she leans in, and out of nowhere he thinks—

Slag.

Luke lowers the binoculars and wipes his eyes.

And when he looks back, Paige is on the pavement and the car is moving, making a slow three-pointer in the street. And then, now the angle's changed, he can see who the driver is. He knows from the shirt, and fleshy neck, and the close-cropped hair that's thinner now than it was when Luke first met him last year. He doesn't even need the binoculars.

It's Oliver Polzeath.

23

Now

Apart from the contractor trying to resuscitate the venerable photocopier that they'd only been given the week before, Wren is the only one in the office. She slings her bag over the back of the chair and shakes the mouse to revive her screen.

There are two emails from Gary Kitchener, the first short – *I'm going to need those certificates sooner rather than later. When can I expect them?* – the second even shorter: *Please confirm you're getting my emails.* She bashes out a reply – *Are photocopies OK?* – then gets down to what she's gone there to do.

Twenty minutes later, she's sending four articles and a couple of paid-content Companies House documents to the printer. And while she's waiting, she sends a two-word text to James Yardley.

Call me.

Wren emerges from the building into a sideways flurry of rain. Keys ready, she bolts from the door to the car, but she isn't fast enough. She shuts the weather out as soon as she is inside, and as her breath returns she inspects the damage. Her white shirt is almost translucent with water, the thick straps of her bra clearly visible beneath it.

James had returned her message immediately, saying he could meet her in an hour. But now she only has ten minutes, and she is soaked through. Maybe if she turns the heaters on full blast? She makes a brief effort to tidy her hair, then turns the key.

Nothing happens. She tries it again – not a peep. Had she left the radio on? The headlights? She checks everything, knowing as she does so that even with the whole array draining the battery, the hour or so she's spent in the office couldn't have flattened it completely. She brings up a map on her phone to the place she'd agreed with James. It's a half-hour walk.

Isn't going to happen. She feels in her bag for her phone and calls him.

'No problem,' James says after she explains. 'I'll come and get you.'

'No,' Wren says, 'I'm going to have to deal with the car—'

'Rubbish, not in this rain. We'll wait for it to stop, then I'll bring you back to have a look. Call me old-fashioned but I'm not going to leave a woman stranded.'

Wren relents, thanks him, and hangs up, then repositions the mirror and tries again with her hair.

Just before he arrives, it occurs to her that the car might need taking to a garage. Which would mean the places in the car that are usually safe for storing confidential things might be breached. Holding an A4 document wallet over her head, she gets out and opens the boot. She shoves the detritus to the back and lifts the rigid felt cover, then the spare wheel, and retrieves the plastic bag in which the letters from Paige's room are wrapped. Back in the dry, she empties her handbag and places the bundle right at the base, then repacks everything on top of it.

James appears in a matter of minutes, in a car worth about thirty of hers. He looks thoroughly amused about her predicament.

'Yes, hilarious,' she says drily as she climbs in, conscious of the combination of damp skirt and pristine leather upholstery. 'Hope you're not precious about your seats.'

'Couldn't give a monkey's,' he tells her. With a swift glance around the spotless interior of the car Wren decides this is not true, but she can live with that.

'I passed that café you mentioned,' he says as he releases the handbrake and rolls the steering wheel with a casual palm. 'Totally rammed.'

So, with the rain clattering all around, they go somewhere else. A café bar he knows. Newly opened, with a covered patio garden that means he can smoke, he tells her. Wren makes a beeline for the ladies as they go in, and when she comes back, James is sitting just outside the French windows beneath a gas heater. In front of him is a silver wine cooler and two glasses.

'What happened to the coffee?' Wren says, making a display of checking her watch.

James laughs. 'After-work drinks.'

'Isn't that usually an evening thing?'

'It's nearly half-five,' he offers.

'Just a small one then,' Wren relents. The wrought-iron chair screeches unhappily on the flagstones as she pulls it out.

He cracks the seal on the screwtop. 'Sauvignon OK?' he asks, already pouring. He starts to chat about his day, makes her laugh with a story about a disastrous batch of jam he'd tried to make. Wren warms up, to the conversation, to him. The wine is good.

After a while she shrugs off her jacket, feeling it buzz as she hangs it on the back of the chair. A text from Suzy.

Can't remember a thing you said when you left. You working late tonight?

Wren glances at the half-empty bottle.

Afraid so. Sorry love. She hovers over the X button, adds two kisses and then two more, and hits send.

James fingers the stem of his glass. 'Problems at work?'

Wren frowns. 'What?'

He nods towards the pocket.

'Oh,' Wren says, making a vague gesture, dismissing it. 'No, nothing.'

James indicates her glass for a top-up. 'Well, I'm starving,' he says, finishing the pour with a professional twist, and waving an apron-clad waiter over.

While he orders a couple of things from the list of tapas on a chalkboard by the window, she roots in her bag for the printouts.

The waiter leaves. 'Right then,' James says, pulling the sheets towards him, 'business.'

'It's about the Polzeaths,' she tells him. 'Shortly before Paige's time.'

He pauses to retrieve a pair of reading glasses from his top pocket. 'Don't laugh,' he warns her as he puts them on, glancing over the rims.

'We all get old,' she says.

It is from a North Somerset local newspaper. The story, which appeared first in April 2011 and was followed up just once three weeks later, details the death of a fourteen-year-old girl.

'Makayla Slater,' James reads. 'Am I supposed to recognise the name?'

'No. But she was in care too. Burnham-on-Sea.'

He takes a mouthful of wine and regards her over the half-moons. 'I only ever worked in Bristol. I don't—'

'I'm not saying you knew her. Read to the end.'

She sits back, folding her arms. According to the story, Makayla Slater had been found dead in her bedroom at an address in Burnham. Reading between the lines, Makayla had enjoyed a close relationship with the police in the months before her death, but previous to that, there had been high hopes for her. After unearthing the initial article, Wren dug around for anything else the internet could yield on Makayla's history. There was enough there to piece together a picture of an athletic girl, active in her school drama club, with a fondness for Justin Bieber. There was a brother, Jake – and he'd gone right to the top of Wren's list of people to find. But what is missing in the piece is the obligatory soundbite from the heartbroken parents.

James removes his glasses. 'You're going to have to help me out. I mean, now I see it, I do vaguely remember this being mentioned. It's a very sad story, but what's the connection?'

'I only came across it because of a comment someone had left right at the bottom,' Wren says. 'She was in care.'

James drinks. 'OK.'

'The home is run by the Polzeaths.'

'OK.'

'*OK?* A girl dies in their care, and a year or so later another girl disappears without trace? How is that OK?'

James looks mortified. 'No, look, that's not what I meant,' he says, lifting his hands in defence. 'I just – right. Look.' He pushes the papers away. 'I don't know how much you know about looked-after children, but it's not actually that unusual, suicide.'

'We don't know it's a suicide.'

He turns the article to face her. 'Narrative verdict. Doesn't look like foul play was suspected, if that's what you mean.'

Wren takes the printouts. 'But what about this, here.' The Companies House documents she'd paid for showed how, not long after Makayla Slater died, Oliver Polzeath's business was wound up. Fast forward another two days, and a new company was founded by Alice Polzeath, without Oliver's name on the documents. Acumen Social Care. That company took over control of the Burnham home and, a few months later, bought Beech View. Some other documents in the stack list James as a consultant, and she knows he'd been heavily involved in creating a framework for improving outcomes for looked-after children. Local government even used Acumen at one point as a very favourable case study. So they must have been doing some things right but not everything, not by a long shot. She turns the Acumen sheets back to him, tapping the relevant section. 'They're hiding something. Making it look like he's not involved when everything else says he was. It's suspicious as hell.'

James refills Wren's glass with the last of the wine. 'So what, you think they *killed* Makayla Slater?'

'I'm not saying—'

'Because I thought it was Robert Ashworth you're after? Or are we saying it's a conspiracy?' He's being kind but the implication – that she's not quite making sense – is unmissable.

'That is absolutely not what I—'

'But actually,' he says, interrupting her again but with such gentleness that she's blindsided by what comes next, 'that's not the question here, is it?'

She carefully sets the glass down. 'What is that supposed to mean?' she says steadily.

'*Why* do you care, Wren? I mean, I know you say it's about *justice*,' he says, waving away the protest that she was about to make, 'but, without meaning to blow my own horn, I'm a psychotherapist. I can see there's more to it than that.'

She finds something resembling an exasperated laugh. 'There *isn't*. I told you before. I'm just doing what I'm paid to do.'

He raises his eyebrows. 'You made it your job,' he says, nodding slowly. 'You wanted this case.'

'I didn't.'

'I think you did.'

Maybe it's the wine, and maybe it's the gas burner overhead, but suddenly the heat is too much. She excuses herself, gets up unsteadily, and goes to the ladies. She splashes water on her face, then eyes her reflection in the mirror, pink and a little wild.

Don't fuck it up, she tells herself.

When she gets back, James has tidied up the papers. He lays his hands on the table and says, 'What else have you got? Other leads?'

'Nothing.'

'Really? What's next then?'

Wren shrugs. 'There's a box of Ashworth's stuff he's keen to get his hands on but the likelihood that there's anything—'

'What kind of box?'

'Belongings he wanted stored while he was inside. He had Leah look after it.'

'Hmm. Interesting.'

'Why? What do you think's in there?'

James taps his lips. 'Who knows. But if it's important to him, that'll mean it's got something in it from his life before prison, no? Which might give you some pointers.'

It is a vindication: maybe she isn't on a wild goose chase. 'She promised she'd ring once she'd picked it up from her grandad's house but I can't exactly rummage through his stuff…'

'No. Certainly not.'

They exchange a look. It doesn't need any more than that.

And then the food arrives, and with it, a second bottle. Noticing Wren's glance at the clock, James gives an apologetic shrug. 'Have to make the most of going out when I can manage it,' he says. 'It's a rare event these days.'

He lifts the wine from the cooler and sloshes out two generous glassfuls.

'So, Wren Reynolds. Tell me about yourself.'

She sips her wine. 'What do you want to know?'

'I don't know – who are you? What do you do for fun? Who's the husband,' he adds, nodding at the ring Suzy gave her for their two-year anniversary.

'More like wife,' she says, though in truth they've never formalised it. 'We're having a baby,' she says flatly, and out of nowhere.

He swallows a mouthful of wine urgently and coughs, puts his hand up to suppress a laugh. 'Once more with feeling?'

'*We're having a baby!*'

He smiles, but it isn't funny. 'I'm sensing some ambivalence.'

'I can't wait,' she says. Why is she talking about this?

'Well, then.' He raises his glass to hers. 'Congratulations!'

The baby is due in two weeks. And all she feels is a crouching, muffled terror.

He leans back. 'I've got a daughter,' he tells her. 'Twenty-two, now. And when she was born, I was just devastated. Couldn't see how my life was going to be any good, ever again.' He is looking at her as he speaks, enquiring, offering her a way in, a way of talking about it. But he'd have to try harder than that. And she'd have to be drunker.

'Honestly,' she says. 'I can't wait.'

And just like that, the evening has peaked. They talk for a little longer, James orders shots, but the sense of it plateauing and falling off is undeniable. Then somehow they are in a taxi, and James is laughing because she can't spell the name of her road for the driver.

'What's Robert Ashworth's place like?' James asks as they pull away. He moves his seatbelt aside so he can turn to face her. 'I mean, is it a shithole?'

'Do you want it to be?' she asks, reaching up to grip the handle above the door. The movement of the car coupled with the wine is making her feel downright nauseous.

James gives that some thought. 'I want to say no. Otherwise

all that expensive therapy hasn't worked, has it?' That self-deprecating smile.

She is drunk, drunker than she's been in months, and even as it comes out of her mouth she knows it isn't a good idea.

'You want to see?'

Fifteen minutes later they are outside Ashworth's building. They get out, tell the driver to wait.

Wren gazes up to the balcony, struggling through the bleariness to locate Ashworth's flat. 'It's up there, third floor. The one with the catflap,' she adds, pointing it out.

James stands so close she can smell him.

'I wonder what he's doing. What does he do all day when he's not with you?'

She shrugs. She suddenly feels very tired. She wants to go home, to have a shower and get into bed next to Suzy.

'Not found work yet?'

She hasn't heard back about the hospital laundry job yet and she knows that's likely to mean it's bad news. She shakes her head which only increases the dizziness. 'Man of leisure,' she says, then without thinking she adds, 'Doesn't seem right, does it? The whole thing is just—'

'Unfair. Un*just*,' he says, then darkens. 'When Paige is just forgotten somewhere—'

'*Dead* somewhere,' she says suddenly. The vitriol that comes with it startles even her. 'I think she's dead, actually.'

He narrows his eyes. 'You think he did it.'

Wren sags. A huge emptiness is opening up inside her and she just wants to get out of there. 'I'm sorry, I'm just…' She turns back to the cab. 'Need to sleep. Let's go.'

'Wren.'

'Come on.'

'*Wren*,' he says again. This time, he puts his hand on her arm, and when she meets his eye there is a concern there that almost floors her.

And then there it is. No warning, no trigger. It is as if the fury and heartbreak she's compressed inside of her this whole time suddenly reaches breaking point. The tears don't start as a soft welling-up but as a rush, and the whole thing disrobes itself to her at once: the injustice of it. The permanence of her own past, and Paige's past. The details of them colliding, merging into one, or facing off like mirror images of the same damned thing.

She turns back to the cab, takes a step but misjudges the kerb and ends up on her knees. Her handbag slips from her shoulder and lands, upended, over the pavement.

'Shit,' she says, half choked.

James lifts her under her shoulders so she is upright again, and gets down to collect the things she's dropped. 'Here,' he says, handing her the tissues.

She unfolds one, hides her face in it, forces herself to breathe slowly.

Then she remembers the letters.

She looks around her, wildly trying to locate them. He's holding her bag, and she lurches out at him to get to it.

'Woah,' he says, handing it to her. Everything is already packed back in. 'You all right?' He opens the cab door and helps her inside.

'I'm sorry. Fuck. What a m-m-mess.'

James gets in next to her and puts a hand on her arm. 'Don't. It's OK.' He instructs the driver to take her home first, and they pull away.

She forces a few deep breaths and gets herself under some kind of control. 'This is basically the most unprofessional night of my entire career. It's the wine, I'm so sorry.'

'Is it?' He laughs softly. 'That looked like more than just the wine.'

She doesn't know this man. But it is delicious, the

proximity of that release. What would it be like, to just be honest with someone?

'Is it about the baby, Wren? Or Paige?'

Like breathing air after a lifetime underwater.

Shut up, Wren, she tells herself. She tightens her jaw. *Just shut up.*

24

Before

Leah's got her own place. Got it pretty much the day she turned sixteen, said she got lucky having a social worker who reckoned she was OK to leave care, get direct payments, the lot. And fair play because she's doing all right, and she's doing this part-time thing at college learning how to look after little kids. Her flat's not far from Beech View but Luke came on Cameron's bike. He didn't ask to borrow it, so Cameron's going to go mental. Luke thinks about that for a second, and finds that he doesn't give a fuck.

Luke and Leah, they're standing in the kitchen end of her bedsit, waiting for the water to boil in the saucepan on the cooker. She hasn't got a kettle.

'I've got some of those little packets of hot chocolate, want one?' she asks. He nods, and she opens a cupboard and digs around for them. Calls out to Paige on the sofa, 'Hot chocolate?'

'Low fat?' Paige wants to know.

Leah finds a packet, reads both sides. It's just the normal kind, but she pulls a *whatever* face at Luke.

'Yeah!' she calls back, grinning at him.

'Go on, then.'

Luke loves being at Leah's. It's easy.

'They had them in the waiting room when I went for the

interview,' she says, tearing it open. She tells him about her new job; it's kind of waitressing but in an old people's home so sometimes she has to feed them as well. 'Which is bollocks really,' she says, pouring on the water. 'It's not what they said I'd be doing. But no one else wants to do it and I'm not going to let the old fuckers starve, am I?'

'Thanks,' he says, taking the mug and blowing.

She leans back against the worktop, staring out the window. 'One girl there, she says she's not spooning anything into anyone's mouth for the money we get. And it's not even like she needs the money. Lives with her parents, spends the whole lot in bloody Topshop. But,' she says, heading over to the sofa, 'they'll have to pay me more when I'm seventeen. I'll probably be able to live off it then.'

She puts a mug in front of Paige, who's been brushing her hair for the last ten minutes, looking like she's a million miles away. Luke had messaged Leah and she'd said he could come over after school because she was on earlies. He thought he'd have her to himself because Paige would be swimming, but she was already there when he turned up. He hadn't seen her at school.

Paige lays the hairbrush down and picks up her mug. As she brings it to her lips, her cuff slips and there on her wrist is this delicate little silver watch. Luke frowns at it, and Paige, realising what he's looking at, glances at Leah, who's trying to dig something out of the back of the sofa. Not meeting his eye, Paige unclips the strap and stuffs it in her pocket.

'Got it,' Leah says, yanking out the *Grand Theft Auto IV* disc. She loads it up, sinks back into the sofa, and gives him that look, warm but waiting. 'What's up then, Lukey? You just come down to scrounge my hot chocolate, or what?'

He looks into his mug. He'd wanted to talk to her, but he can't now Paige is here. He starts talking about getting sent out of maths earlier but it trails off.

There's a silence, until Leah says, gentle as mist, 'Paige said you got in some trouble with the home staff.' He flinches and reddens, says nothing. 'All right,' Leah says. She passes him a controller for the knackered old PS3. 'Maybe you just came over for some company, then.'

'I don't like being on my own, either,' Paige says vaguely, brushing again.

'Yeah, well. Good job you're so friendly, isn't it?' he says, and if she doesn't spot the anger in his voice she's as stupid as she is fucking beautiful. 'You're getting *plenty* of company.'

Paige puts the mug down. Leah eyes both of them. She loves a barney, Leah, loves winding people up, but she's not smiling.

'What's that supposed to mean?' Paige says, looking at the floor.

And it gives Luke courage. He knows he's right about Polzeath. Something is going on.

'You're not exactly discreet.'

Leah gives Paige this look like *what the fuck?* Luke watches whatever it is passing between them.

'You going to tell us what's going on, Paige?' he says. What he means is, *please, please tell me you're not fucking him. Please*.

Leah places her mug very carefully on the table that she's covered in photos of random stuff she's cut out of a magazine. Then she slaps her legs and gets up. 'I'm going for a fag,' she says.

Frowning, Luke points at the ashtray literally right there in the middle of the table, noticing the empty pack of Lambert & Butler, folded up into a cube like how Rob does it.

Leah says, 'Yeah, but—' and she glances at Paige, who flashes her a warning.

'What's going on?' Luke asks.

Leah, suddenly cheerful, says, 'Passive smoking – don't want you getting cancer as well,' even though she's never cared before.

'I've given up,' Paige says to the table.

Leah looks from Paige to Luke and back again, and then she leaves the room. They hear her footsteps on the metal stairs down to the ground floor.

Paige and Luke talk at the same time.

'Look I wasn't spying on you but—'

'It's not what you think, Luke—'

Paige laughs nervously, and he doesn't get why she's not angry with him. He's basically just admitted to stalking her.

Paige clears her throat. 'What did you see, Lukey?'

He shrugs. He can't look at her. 'Enough,' he says.

'Whatever you think you saw, just forget it.' She says it like she's trying to be tough. It doesn't work.

'No,' he says flatly.

She sighs. 'Please. Just… just leave it.'

'Leave what, though?' He picks up the fag-packet cube and turns it over in his hand. 'You're going to have to tell me.'

She sighs. 'It's none of your business.'

No. He's not having it. He reruns what he saw the night before, Polzeath's paws on her. What is he, forty-five? Fifty? Older?

She brings her knees up, holds on to them. Her bare arms, still tanned from the summer, but still skinny despite the swimming. And out of nowhere, a picture in his head: holding one of those arms in both hands and snapping it like a twig.

He grits his teeth and it goes away. He says, 'Why are you doing it?'

'I don't want to talk about it.' There's a sadness on her face that he's never seen before. The answer swirls out at him, wraps itself around him.

She cares what he thinks of her.

'I can save you,' he says. He didn't mean it to come out.

Her forehead knots and then she smiles. 'Save me from what?'

'*Him.*'

She shakes her head. 'It's not like that, Luke. It's—'

'Please don't fucking say it's complicated.'

'Well, it is.'

Luke can't believe what he's hearing. It's like they're not even having the same conversation, or like she's been brainwashed. 'But he's forcing you into—'

'He's not! We— I know what I'm doing, all right? Just leave it.'

'I'll tell someone. Mel. You don't have to do this, Paige.'

'Luke, don't. Just forget it.'

The sound of the door opening behind them, but he doesn't turn. Panic in Paige's eyes. She's said something she shouldn't have said.

'Paige,' says a voice from the doorway. Luke turns.

It's Rob. *Rob*, here. Luke opens his hand: it was Rob who made the fag-packet cube. And Leah, standing just behind him. Paige takes her chance and darts out of the door, followed by Rob, who just gives Luke this little raised-eyebrow look that says, *yeah, what you going to do about it?*

And all Leah does is stand aside to let them go.

Leah's going to the warehouse, and she talks Luke into going. She can see how fucked off he is about Rob showing up.

'Come on,' she says, pulling on her coat. 'We'll have a spliff, clear your head.'

He's so churned up he thinks *what the hell, why not*. He gives her a backy on the bike all the way, and she clings on round his waist. He tries to pretend it's Paige, but then he gets hard so he stops, willing it to go away.

They found the warehouse months ago, and it's basically theirs, no one else goes there. He can't quite remember the way but Leah shouts directions until he recognises where he is – the Feeder Road out to the Avon, the bridge, then the secret route in. There's an alley between two metal fences and it stinks of piss but the weeds are knee-high and blooming with bright blue flowers. He thinks of his mum, and he wishes he could show her.

He rolls to a stop by the chained-up gate and looks up. It's one of those big brick places – they call it the warehouse but it could have been a factory or anything, they don't know. Beyond the fence there's a massive open entrance, a load of twisted rusty junk outside, like it vomited all its rubbish and no one got round to clearing it up.

They find the loose bit and climb through, darting across the scrub before anyone sees them. Loads of signs tell them how dangerous it is.

'Fuck *me* it's dark in here,' Leah says as soon as they're inside. They stand there blinking for a minute, getting used to it, then they make their way up. It's got these creaky as fuck steps that you have to be really careful on.

'Remember last time?' she says, laughing, heading over to the steps. Her voice echoes in the emptiness.

'Still get the nightmares,' he says, adding, 'you bitch.'

Last time, Paige had been there too, and the two girls had scared the shit out of him pretending to fall. Quite high up there's a whole step missing and the board underneath it is smashed too so it's basically an open hole. Bolted into the wall under the broken section of stairs is this big iron grid thing. It turned out Paige and Leah had spent an afternoon seeing if they could drop down to make it look to anyone above them like they'd fallen, when actually they were just hanging on, ready to climb or drop down the last bit.

At the broken step, Leah pauses and looks down.

Luke's right behind her. 'You could seriously die falling down there,' he says as he comes to the gap.

'*You* could, maybe. Me and Paige are little mountain goats though, aren't we?' She laughs, and he holds her arms and pretends to give her a shove, making her scream. 'Stop it!'

He lets her go first, then clings to the scaffolding pole bolted to the wall and steps carefully around it. He has to almost stretch into the splits to do it.

They go up, and the door to the roof is stiff with rust but Leah shoulder-barges it and then they're out. The sun is going down, a messy riot of orange that turns everything in front of it to silhouettes.

Leah goes right over to the edge and stretches out her arms. She turns, her back to the drop, and grins at him. 'Let's sit on the edge.'

'No chance,' Luke says. Even standing several metres back like he is now is making his knees forget how to lock. He goes over to the raised bit he prefers, where some kind of vent that's a good height for sitting on sticks up against the flat roof. You get all of the view but you don't feel like you're going to die any second.

She follows him, sits, and gets her tin out of the little fabric bag she takes everywhere with her.

'What you need is a bit of a calm down,' she says, opening the tin.

Luke watches her unpack the little box: baccy, Rizla, resin.

He chooses his words carefully. 'Is she seeing him, then?'

She keeps her eyes on the papers, sticking two together with a lick. 'I think that's her business, isn't it?'

'Just asking. Wondering if, you know. Paige likes him.'

She sighs. 'Luke. Rob's a mate. There's nothing to get paranoid about.'

'Would you tell me?'

'*Course* I would,' she says, winking. But it's got to be a lie because Paige and Leah are close like *that*. Even though

Leah's older. They knew each other from before, Paige told him ages ago. Back when Leah was still in care.

In Luke's head, the veins of it connect. Leah had been in a home in Burnham-on-Sea. The one the Polzeaths ran.

Keeping it casual he says, 'What was it like when you were in care, Leah?'

She laughs. 'What do you think? It was shit.'

'Like what, the staff?'

She rolls a tube of card for a roach, shrugging like he's stating the obvious. 'Everything. The house was a dump, the staff mainly couldn't give a fuck, the other kids were mental – usual shit. Same as what you've got, probably.'

'And the owners?'

'Didn't see them much, but yeah,' she says, dismissing it. 'They were pretty bad. I stayed out of their way. Same owners as you've got. That arsehole Polzeath. All about the money.'

'Oliver?' He frowns like the judgement is a surprise to him, like he thought he was an OK guy.

'That's him. There was this one girl, it's a really sad story actually. She was his little favourite. Probably shouldn't say this but she came off like she thought she was better than the rest of us. Used to see her and Polzeath having these private chats all the time; he'd ferry her about. Fucking creepy,' she says, arranging the tobacco in the V of the paper.

'Do you think he was – you know?'

'Screwing her?' She holds the little block of resin, puts the lighter to it. 'Hell of a risk if he was.' The brown block crumbles between her fingers onto the waiting tobacco. She runs the tip of her tongue along the glue line and rolls the whole thing shut. 'Honestly though, I don't know. We weren't close.'

'So why was it sad?'

'She topped herself,' she says simply.

'Seriously?'

'Yep. Shit, innit?' She inspects the joint and puts it between her lips, lights up, takes a drag and says, 'Makayla, her name was. Slater.'

Luke stares at her. 'She have a brother?' he asks. Because Fat Jake's surname is Slater.

She frowns. 'Yeah. I think she did. He was in a different kids' home.'

Shit, Luke thinks. *Poor Jake.* The kid's a total twat, but still. *Shit.*

'Did she kill herself because of him? Polzeath?'

Leah shrugs. 'Don't know. Maybe.' She takes another pull, holds it in, hands the spliff to Luke. 'Why are you so interested?'

Luke says he's not, just asking. He takes a deep pull of smoke, holds it in his lungs as he passes it back to her. It's strong, but he doesn't cough. He lets it snake out into his blood, feels it sparking up the cells of his skin and it's like he's coming alive. When he opens his eyes, Leah's grinning at him. But he's not ready to let go, not just yet.

'I'm going to kill him.'

'Who, Polzeath?' Leah gapes at him, then she cracks up. 'For what?'

'I mean it.'

'Fuck's sake, Lukey. You don't half take stuff seriously.' She leans over and puts the joint back in his mouth. 'Forget I said anything. He's a bit of a creep, he's got a big ego and a fat wallet and he can seem like a dick. He's not Adolf fucking Hitler.'

He makes himself laugh then and says, 'All right, fine.' But it's not fine. It's like the world's just tipped up and no one else has noticed. What's he actually supposed to do, just sit there?

They all think that's what's going to happen. That he'll shut up and stay out of it, because he's just a kid and if she wants to whore herself out for pocket money, she can.

They're wrong.

25

Now

'He's going to kill me for giving this to you,' Leah Amberley mumbles as Wren lifts the second cardboard box out of the boot of a borrowed car and into the back of Suzy's battered Kangoo. Her own car is in the garage, being looked at by another of Suzy's legion of cousins.

'You're not giving it to me. I'm delivering it straight to him.'

'Without dicking around with it?'

Wren lifts a corner of a cardboard flap. 'Leah. I've got better things to do with my time than go through his old pants and,' she pulls out an electrical cord, 'clippers, or whatever.'

'Yeah, well. He's still going to bollock me.'

Wren's head is pounding from the wine the night before, and the fumes from the dual carriageway next to them aren't helping her nausea one bit. It's barely past dawn, so she hasn't even been able to properly sleep it off, but this is more important than nursing a hangover. She hadn't expected the call that quickly – Leah had already said she wouldn't be able to get hold of Rob's stuff for another week or so. But the grandad had been unwell and cut his holiday short, and she'd gone round to see him as soon as he'd got back last night.

'Yeah, well,' Leah says, watching but not helping as Wren

shoves the boxes side by side. 'Good job I had you on my back about them,' she says, nodding at the boxes as Wren shuts the boot.

'Yeah? Why's that?'

Leah opens her driver's door. 'Just got a text from my grandad. He's got the police there – just got burgled.'

'What? When?'

'Early hours this morning. Amazing he didn't wake up. Whole place turned upside down, even the garage where Rob's stuff had been. I only missed it by a couple of hours.' Leah sits behind the wheel and goes to pull the door shut.

But Wren gets in the way. 'What was taken?'

Leah frowns at her. 'Just some tools, I think.'

'Just that? No electrical stuff, jewellery, anything valuable?'

'I don't… I mean, he didn't say so—'

'But was there anything valuable in the house?'

'Well, yeah, of course there was a few things, but it was just the tools—'

'What kind of tools? Were they expensive?'

Leah sighs petulantly. 'Normal DIY stuff. Look, can I go?'

Wren stands back, leaving Leah to pull the door closed and starting the engine.

As the little car pulls away, Wren bangs on the window. 'Wait.'

For a moment it looks as if Leah is going to just drive off anyway. But she stops, winds the window down. 'Jesus, what?'

'Does Rob know where your grandad lives?'

'What? Yeah, I think so.'

'Did he know he was coming back early?'

'No, of course not. Why would he?' Her face drops as the implication dawns on her. 'No, come *on*. Why would he do that?'

Because he guessed Wren was going to beat him to it? As

far as she knows, he thinks the old man is still on holiday, that he might not get hold of his gear for another week – but communication between these two has hardly been transparent. Wren stands back to let Leah go, her mind already fast-forwarding to getting the crime number. DIY tools taken, nothing else? She dismisses the chances of a coincidence on that basis: the tools could be a smokescreen. Before she's even back in the car she has Suzy's number up on her phone.

But then she pauses.

If she really and truly thinks Rob was involved, it isn't Suzy she should be calling, however neat the shortcut to the information would be. This is a potential recall to prison. Protocol is, in the first instance, to pass the concern to her immediate superior. But what would Callum Roche do? If *anything* is found linking Ashworth to the scene, the very first thing that will happen will be the police applying for recall, and immediately after that, Wren will be requested to turn over her notes. She'll be interviewed. She remembers with horror what she shared with James last night. If it gets out that she went on the piss with a *victim* – well, she'll lose her job faster than blinking.

Decision made, she puts her phone away, and reopens the boot. Maybe Ashworth is involved, maybe he isn't. But she's not going to dig her own grave.

She stops on the way, methodically unpacking and repacking both boxes to examine the contents, replaces everything exactly as it was. She half expects to find the missing bracelet, but the possessions that are apparently closest to Robert Ashworth's heart are disappointingly mundane. A games console, a couple of old photos. She cracks open the three games cases, hoping for secret notes, cash, drugs, anything, but all they contain are the games. There are clothes, an early-generation tablet computer, a phone, and some bike gear.

At Ashworth's block, she slides the boxes into the lift, one on top of the other. They're not too heavy but they're bulky, so she's going to have to take them one by one to his door. On the first trip between the stairwell and his front door she notices, with a slump of the heart, that the kitchen blind across his window is rolled all the way down. It isn't ideal, but by the time she returns to the stairwell for box two, she has a plan. All she needs now is luck.

Three knocks, and the door opens, almost as if he had been waiting for her.

'Delivery,' she says, indicating the two boxes beside her. 'Your stuff.'

His face lights up – the closest to real emotion she's seen from him since he went for Alice Polzeath's neck – and he makes a grab for them. As he bends for the first one and takes it inside, she executes the manoeuvre exactly as she planned it. The beaded cable that operates the rollerblind is inches from the door. She reaches in and gives it a yank in the time it takes him to get the box over the threshold.

The blind lifts. She has an inch, maybe two, of unrestricted view into the flat. It will have to do.

Once he's got the second box into the kitchen, he goes to shut the front door.

'You're very welcome,' Wren tells him.

'Thanks,' he says. And the door closes.

She moves away from the door, passing the window. Checks the walkway is clear, and then stops, bending to fiddle with a shoelace. And through the window, she watches for as long as she safely can, taking it all in.

Ashworth tears open the flaps of the first, then the second box, dumping the clothes, the games, even the photos on the floor. He drops into a crouch when he finds – what is it, the tablet?

He turns and she ducks, then slowly rises, careful to keep out of sight.

The phone. He is clutching the phone with his eyes clamped shut, a look of beatific relief on his face.

26

Now

They're driving to the hospital for a scan, in the Kangoo. Suzy is still in her yoga gear from her morning session. Paul, the cousin with the garage, left a message to say he had news about Wren's car, but between meeting Leah, dropping in on Rob and getting back in time for the antenatal appointment, she hasn't had the time to go over yet. Just thinking about her abandoned car, and the way she'd ended up tits-deep in wine, causes a shudder of guilt.

Yardley had texted first thing that morning – *Still working on Luke, you getting anywhere?* But she hasn't replied. Although she does have something. She has a lead on Makayla Slater's brother, Jake.

She shakes herself and lets her hand drop from the gear-stick and onto Suzy's leg.

'Oh, cool,' Suzy says, glancing at the hand but not responding to it. 'You are a solid human being still, then.'

Wren sighs. 'What does that mean?' She leaves the hand where it is but it feels like an intrusion now.

Suzy looks out of the passenger window. 'I've hardly seen you. At all. Did you even come home last night?'

As she turns, Wren sees with equal quantities of shame and sadness that her eyes are red and swollen. She's been crying.

'I'm sorry—' Wren starts, but Suzy sighs and moves her leg away.

'I don't want you to be sorry,' she says. 'I want you to *want* to do this with me.'

'Do what, the scan?'

'Everything! The baby, the family thing, being a couple. That sort of shit, you know?'

'Sweetheart, I *do.* Of course I want it. Wasn't it me who talked you round when you were lukewarm for all that time?' Although the memory of that now feels as if it must have been tampered with somewhere along the way. Who had they even been, a year ago?

Who are they now?

Suzy rubs her eyes angrily, fixes her glare on the windscreen. 'There's this PCSO. Gemma something. Up the duff, thirty-two weeks. Showed me this series of photos her husband's been taking.' There is an unnatural brightness in her voice. 'Standing sideways in a doorframe, you know? To show how she's getting bigger every week.'

'Ugh, how *cute*,' Wren groans, glad of the reminder of their common ground.

'Really? Because I thought it was quite nice,' Suzy says.

Wren adjusts her grip on the wheel and says nothing.

'Are you going to tell me what it is?' Suzy says blankly to the dashboard.

'There's nothing wrong.' Wren feels for her hand but it isn't there.

The Kangoo struggles up St Michael's Hill to the hospital, the engine sighing in relief as the road levels out before the turning to the car park. She finds a bay and pulls in.

They sit in silence for a few moments before Suzy turns to face her. 'Wren. Please. You're not… It's like you're not even here.'

'It's just work,' she says. 'Just a lot on.'

'But why? The whole point of the job change was that it would be less stress. *Your* words.'

'I'm *fine*.'

Suzy, the woman she's chosen to split her life with, studies her face. Concentration in her irresistible eyes, and then a look of horrified realisation.

'Oh my God,' she says. 'There's someone else.'

'There is *not*!'

Suzy waits, then eventually she shrugs, defeated. 'Do you know what? It doesn't matter. It doesn't matter what it is. What matters is that you aren't ready for what's about to happen to us. You either don't want the baby, or you don't want me, or you don't want either of us. Whichever it is...' She shakes her head. 'I'm not doing this.'

'Love, come on.' Wren puts out a hand.

'Don't.' Suzy shifts her bulk left to undo her seatbelt. *Our child,* Wren thinks as the seatbelt slides back across the tight, low swell of Suzy's bump.

Except – except it isn't *theirs*, not really. It isn't Wren's child. Not because of the genetics, or the conception. None of that really makes a difference. In the early days of it, the days of studying the plastic sticks for the two blue lines, she'd found with relief that Suzy's pregnancy had indeed felt like it belonged to them both, truly and fully. Because they were genuinely close, and tight, and solid.

No, the problem is something else. She hasn't acknowledged it because how does a person do that, two weeks before the due date? But it is there, as sure as an ulcer in the gut.

Suzy can't get the seatbelt catch to release, but bats Wren's hand away when she tries to help.

'Just – just leave it.'

Wren sighs. 'Do you want me to come with you?'

Suzy snaps round to face her. Sudden, violent hurt on her face, as if Wren has punched her, and Wren sees right away that she shouldn't have asked: that the asking has made everything a lot worse.

'Yes, right, of course,' Wren says quickly.

But the damage is done. 'No, you know what?' Suzy says, her voice peaking as she fumbles with the door handle. 'Forget it. I'll call when I'm finished. If it's not too much fucking bother to pick me up.'

Wren watches her go. She crosses the road, every movement of every limb dragged with exhaustion as she steps onto the pavement.

Wren is supposed to be thrilled about this child. If not thrilled, at least nervously excited. Dread is a very poor substitute for any of those things. And that is exactly what it is, coiling knowingly inside her whenever she sees the bump, whenever she takes delivery of another consignment of muslins or sippy cups or nipple cream. Dread that she can't do it. That she isn't competent, isn't reliable – is just simply not *good* enough. Because where is her template for doing this? She has no example to follow – she's only ever seen how not to do it. Where Suzy is excited, settling into a new nurturing groove of her life, ready for the shift, all Wren can feel is terror. It's made her almost – she can hardly bear admitting it – it's made her wish it wasn't happening at all.

There is still time to go after her. But Wren stays where she is, watching as Suzy is absorbed by the automatic doors. And she drives away.

The city farm has been an institution for years. Tucked up an unlikely side street between the brothels and discount shops of Bedminster and the railway sidings just south-west of Temple Meads, it serves two distinct sectors of the community. On the surface it is a place for middle-class lefty parents to kill a few hours with their Boden-encased toddlers, but its real mission is something nobler. Every year, dozens of desperate Bristolians find within its greenhouses and outbuildings an escape from addiction, depression, crime and desperation. Rehab units across the area send their struggling clients to the farm's projects to learn skills and break the cycles of self-destruction.

Which is why, when her search for information on Jake Slater came up with a mention of a nearby drugs project, the farm was her first guess. A combination of this intuition, a phone call and an alarming lack of front-of-house confidentiality had given her a positive match. All she has to do now is hope he doesn't do a Leah and refuse to talk to her on the grounds of perceived allegiance with law enforcement.

In the cool of the reception, she gives her name and asks to speak to Jake about a family matter.

'He know you, does he?' the young man behind the desk asks.

'It's a family thing,' Wren says, dodging it. 'I'll be in the café. Only need ten minutes.'

She crosses the courtyard, passing a mother casually breastfeeding a baby in a patch of sunlight. This place, with the comic troupe of Indian Runner ducks streaking over to where a welly-wearing volunteer fills their pool with a hose, is exactly the kind of place Suzy will want to bring the baby. *And you,* she tells herself. She waits for the fizz of excitement to accompany that thought, the warm glow. But it doesn't come.

Wren takes a small table by the window in the café, and waits. After a few minutes a young man comes in. He is stringy, clean-shaven but slightly shaggy-haired, and his jeans are shiny with want of washing. He puts a well-used mug on the counter and the woman fills it for him, gratis. As he speaks to her she glances over and nods in Wren's direction.

He comes across, holding the mug with both hands. There is an uncomfortable energy about him, from his quick footsteps to the dart in his eyes as he scans the room. Though she doesn't doubt he is in recovery, recent addiction is betrayed by the grey of his skin.

'You asked for me?' he says, putting the mug on the table but staying standing. His fingertips play anxiously on the back of the spare chair.

'Thanks for coming over,' Wren says, rising. 'Do you fancy something to eat? Cake?'

But he is shaking his head before she's finished the sentence. 'Look, I don't know who you are,' he says, his voice thin, almost pleading, 'but I'm straight now. I've done everything I had to do, I really have, OK?'

'I only want to talk,' Wren says.

'They all say that!' He wraps his arms around himself, telling Wren the whole story of who he is in a single gesture. 'Who are you then? Social? Police?'

Behind his head there is a clock. If the trip back to the hospital is fifteen minutes, that leaves her with about the same again before she has to leave. So the choice is either tell him the truth and spend the next ten minutes unravelling his prejudices, however understandable they are, or bullshit him.

'I'm writing a book,' she says. 'It's about kids in care, how they get forgotten.'

His eyes narrow, but his fingers stop tapping. 'Right.'

'Your sister wasn't properly looked after. That's not OK. I want to do something about it.'

He turns that over, measuring it against the complex circuit board of suspicion that Wren can sense in his every movement.

'She's dead,' he says after a pause. But he doesn't move.

Wren inclines her head. 'And I'm so, so sorry about that, Jake.'

'She wanted kids.' His eyes are still on her but have

defocused, like she's turned to glass. Wren gestures again to the chair, but he makes a face, glances around. 'Can we do this outside? Just, you know. Small spaces. Being inside.' He shoots her a look of apology. 'Can't do it for long.'

She follows him through the door, past the busy courtyard and the pond, out to the perimeter. Once they are out of earshot, Wren starts with the easy stuff: asking how Makayla found herself in care in the first place, when things started to go wrong. Given his reticence of thirty seconds previously, Jake needs surprisingly little prompting once he gets going.

They'd ended up in care via the most common route. Although the ratios were variable, the ingredients were common in most cases Wren knew of: drugs and/or alcohol, poverty, abuse and/or neglect. The Slaters had been no different – mum in and out of rehab, dad in and out of prison until he overdid the sampling on a consignment he was running and ended up dead.

'We got split up,' Jake tells her. 'I was in another unit, ten other kids. Soon as I could I got out of there and just stayed on people's sofas for a bit until I got a place in a squat,' he says. This part of the story is his legend, something he's evidently recounted before, because it is interspersed with smiles and shrugs like, *that's how it is, what can you do?* Wren nods, makes a few notes.

She waits for a pause. Lets the pause expand until she can be sure he knows what's coming. Then says, 'Tell me about when she died.'

Jake Slater goes still. 'She didn't leave a note. Nothing.' His pockmarked, reddish forehead softens from a frown into something emptier, like the years between that day and this have contracted into seconds. 'I didn't – when they called me, I didn't believe them. It was like I skipped the bit where I thought, *oh shit, my sister's...*' he lifts a hand like it weighs ten stone, trying to wave the word into existence, then goes on without it. 'And I went straight to thinking, *we're going to laugh so much at this later, we're going to dine out on this mess-up.*'

But it hadn't been a mess-up.

He missed the funeral, he says. Didn't mean to get high, thought he could tough it out without pharmaceutical back-up but somehow—

'I can't remember it. One of her teachers took me outside, and by the time I came down the whole thing was over.' He shrugs, the pain of it tight and permanent on his young face. 'Told myself it was better that way, at the time. But I wish I'd been there, you know? Been there for her. Can't be helped though,' he concludes, looking up from the patch of gravel he's been kicking. 'That's drugs for you though, not much that's good about them.' He gives her the least convincing grin she's ever seen. 'Except making you skinny. I was pushing nineteen stone until I discovered amphetamines.'

She returns a small fraction of the smile, then says, 'I can't begin to imagine how that must have felt, Jake. To miss the funeral.'

'Long time ago,' he says, but his eyes and his words don't match.

He says he has a few errands, so they start walking, out on a pitted concrete path towards the livestock.

'Did you visit her much when she was in care?'

He shrugs. 'Not much. Too far. I was in Bristol, she was out in Burnham.'

'And your mum?'

A rapid shake of his head, and Wren takes the hint and lets it go.

They pass a pig shed, where he fills a bucket with feed and jumps the low wall. Half a dozen piglets swarm over, snorting with excitement, and he mutters to them like they're old friends. After depositing the food, he casts his eye over the brood then selects one, pins it under his arm. He takes hold of a hind trotter and inspects it, then, satisfied, lets it go.

'I did go there a few weeks later though,' he says, climbing back over. They carry on walking the loop. 'There was this inquest, but it was just a piss-take, took about two hours and then they were done. No answers, you know?'

'Answers to what?'

'How come she'd stopped going to school, or good as.'

'She'd been doing OK at school, right?'

The memory of it makes him smile, revealing for the first time his crazy-paving teeth that justify the tight-lipped way he speaks. 'Put us all to shame. Mum used to say maybe she wasn't my dad's after all because she sure as shit didn't get it from either of them.' He pauses to pull a bent roll-up from the top pocket of his shirt. 'She knew it too, mind. That she was bright, like. Probably didn't make her many friends.'

'Did she get on with the staff? At the home?'

He motions weighing scales. 'Some of them. One was really nice to her, she said. Oliver – whatever it was.'

'Polzeath?'

'Yeah. You know him? Same as the owner at Beech View.'

Wren stops. '*You* were at Beech View?'

He shrugs. 'For a bit. Got moved after that girl disappeared.'

'Paige Garrett? You knew her?'

His shoulders come up like a barricade. 'Yeah. Why?'

'Where do you think she went, Jake?'

He pulls a hand down his face, scratches at his stubble. 'I – I don't know.'

Wren waits.

'That fucking girl,' he says eventually. 'So fucking special, everyone thought she was this perfect—' he says, then cuts himself off and moves the hair away from his temple to reveal a faded pink scar. 'That's from where she smacked me round the head with a saucepan, this one time.'

'Blimey.' Wren gives that a moment. There's no easy way to ask what she needs to ask next, so she just makes her voice soft and says it. 'Jake, do you think there was any chance Makayla was being abused?'

He sighs. He's not shocked; it's clearly not the first time he's considered it. But it takes a while for him to answer. 'I don't think so. I think she would have said. But who knows. One minute we'd be talking every night, then it just…' He mimes a sad, slow explosion with his hands.

'What happened?'

He looks away. 'Went off the rails. Drugs, mostly.'

'Where'd she get the money?'

Jake takes a lungful of smoke and points at her with the cigarette between his fingers. 'That's the question, isn't it? Where'd the money come from? Or did someone give her drugs for free? None of them knew. I read the inquest report. It's only about this thick.' He indicates a millimetre between his index finger and thumb. 'Nothing about the money, nothing about school. They didn't even try to find out who knocked her up, before.'

Wren stops dead. 'What? When?'

'She had an abortion. Few months before she died.'

Wren runs the maths. If Makayla had been even three months pregnant, that would have made her fourteen at the time of conception.

Fourteen.

'Did you know who the father was?'

'No,' he says. Too fast.

'Did you, Jake?'

He looks at his feet, and Wren waits, trying to decipher it. This isn't shame, not family shame at least. There are families that would be sent into a tailspin by a teen pregnancy, but she'd stake money on the Slaters not being one of them. Wren is no newcomer to shame, though. She knows it well enough to understand it has more than one face.

After a heavy sigh he lets it out. 'She tried to tell me. I said I didn't want to know. I got wasted a lot, you know? I was – unpredictable. I didn't want to end up high and doing something I'd regret. That was the person I was back then, more interested in how it would play out for me than looking after someone who needed my help.'

There's a moment of still air. When he looks up at her, there are tears in his eyes. 'She wasn't a slag.'

'Oh, goodness.' Wren touches his shoulder. 'Of *course* she wasn't, Jake.'

'I didn't hear from her for months,' he says, his voice so small now that Wren has to bend towards him to hear over the sounds of animals and the shrieks of children. 'Kept trying, just nothing. And then eventually I get this call in the middle of the night. She'd wanted to keep it. Said they wouldn't let her.'

'Who's *they*? The father?'

'I don't know. She just kept saying they'd made her get rid of it, and what if she went to hell. Our mum was Catholic,' he adds, by way of explanation.

'Do you think she meant the staff pressured her?' Wren says. He shrugs, but in her head, the gears are engaging. Because it wouldn't have looked good for the Polzeaths, would it? Especially not if they knew who the father was and had done nothing to stop it.

Especially if it was Oliver Polzeath.

'Have you got any guesses, even, about who might have been responsible?' She speaks as softly, as gently as she can. 'She was very young, Jake. I mean, fourteen, that's—'

'I know what it is! All right?' His eyes connect with hers. 'I *know*. But I don't know anything else to tell you.' He breaks off, the tears streaming down his face now. 'I could have saved her. She wanted to tell me. She was asking me to save her and I didn't. I didn't.'

27

Before

As soon as Luke gets home from school, Geraint ushers him into the office. Luke hasn't spoken to the fucker since he dobbed him in to Mr P about being in Paige's room that time, but he knew he could only avoid him for so long. Geraint gets behind the desk and he puts on his get-ready-for-the-shit-news face.

'So we heard from your social worker today, Luke.'

'Right.' He makes his gut go hard, ready.

'Your brother had a hearing in the family court about an application for guardianship. I think you knew that was coming up?'

He shrugs. In the bottom drawer of his desk there's a piece of paper with a grid on it that he drew up twenty-two days ago, like a calendar, counting down the days with a felt-tip X every day until today.

Geraint says, 'I'm afraid things have changed slightly, Luke, since the incident at your old house. With the threat to the baby.'

Luke's eyes cram with tears. 'I didn't—' he starts to say, his voice cracking. 'I wasn't going to—'

'But, mate, it's what it looked like. No one called the police, you don't have it on your record, so it could be a lot, lot worse. You know that, right?'

The files on the shelves are mostly red, and some of them are blue. It would look better if all the red ones were on one shelf, and the blue ones underneath.

'I know this isn't really what you wanted to hear.'

Through the open window that looks out onto the side path there's the sound of a bird.

'Luke.'

'Yeah?' He looks him in the eye. Geraint's waiting for him to reply, but he doesn't know what the question is.

Geraint lets out this massive breath like Luke is literally the most disappointing thing in the universe. 'Did you hear what I said, Luke?'

'Yeah.' He bends, gets his bag. 'Can I go?'

He spends the afternoon in his room. He doesn't go down for dinner. He waits for Rob to ring, but Rob doesn't ring. In the end he has a shower, makes it last ages. He puts everything out of his head, and he starts thinking about Paige. He gets hard thinking about her.

Paige, kneeling in front of him and taking him in her mouth and the water raining down over her naked back and—

Standing. Kissing him on the mouth. And then he pictures turning her around and fucking her and holding her wet tits in his hands and

and then she turns around to kiss him but oh God—

It's not her

His eyes fly open and he slaps his hands high against the tiles and stands blinking against the water because the face—the face he saw wasn't Paige.

It was his mother.

And he drives his fist into the tiles, again and again until the water running down them is tinged red with blood, because everything's fucked now. Everything. He bends in half and whips the towel from the floor and stuffs it in his mouth.

And he bites down hard, his body rigid with horror and rage, each muscle in spasm and each bone crushing against the next like he's at the bottom of the sea. And with the water at his feet getting redder, getting darker, he clenches his eyes shut and he screams and screams.

Mel's on the eight-till-eight, and he hears her come in but he doesn't go down. One of the twins is kicking off about something, but once everything's gone quiet, there's a knock.

He lets her in and she goes straight over to sit on his bed. He shuts the door, stands there with his back to it.

'I'm really sorry about your guardianship thing,' she says, and she means it. She looks at his hand, goes out, comes back with a bandage and a pad and some antiseptic in a blue tube. She doesn't say anything, just gestures for it. But he doesn't move.

She puts the first aid stuff down on his table. He picks up the cream, smears a white glob of it on his knuckles.

'I know you're angry with me,' she says. She doesn't know the fucking half of it. She didn't have to tell the panel about the flowers, did she. Or the baby. It wasn't like he was going to hurt anyone.

The cream stings like fuck but he puts some more on. 'I read that booklet, the one they sent before the hearing. Says if they turn it down we can reapply in a month.'

She shuts her eyes and when she opens them again she sighs. 'Listen, Luke…'

'And then I'll be out of this shithole. And you'll never have to bother about me again.'

'Luke.'

'And I'll be fucking fine, thanks very much, I don't need any of you—'

'*Luke!*' He's never heard her shout before. 'Listen to me,' she says. She looks really, really tired. 'I know you were holding out hope for this. We *had* to disclose it, about the…' she pauses, fumbling for the word, 'the incident. At your old house. I didn't want to do it.'

The bed creaks and Mel's standing behind him. She puts her hand on his shoulder, and he shakes it off, but she puts it back and he just stands there.

'We all know you didn't mean anything, my love, but the fact of it is, there's some serious child protection issues around what happened. If your care gets transferred anywhere else, we have to be able to show that your new guardian is completely across all of that.'

He knows what she's saying now. She's saying he has to stay. And if he has to stay—

He spins round. 'What about Paige?'

Mel blows out her cheeks and looks at the ceiling. 'What about her?'

'The guardianship. Once Rob got me, I thought he could apply for her too. And she'd be out of here—'

'Fuck's sake,' she says, and turns her back to him, her hands in her hair.

'What?'

Mel drops onto his mattress again, plants her hands on her knees. 'Luke, Paige is not going to live with your brother. That's never going to happen.'

'But Rob said—'

'Well, he's full of bullshit, isn't he? He's not someone you can rely on! It should have been him telling you he'd withdrawn the application, you shouldn't be finding out from us.'

Luke gapes. 'Withdrew it? No. They turned it down.'

She's shaking her head. 'They didn't. The hearing was cancelled. The panel contacted Rob about the incident and he backed out.'

'What do you mean? He promised me—'

'Well, he talks out of his arse, doesn't he? And how the hell did you even think that was possible about Paige? What was even going through your—'

She cuts herself off, but her shoulders are right up and she's angry. Well, fuck her. She doesn't know what the fuck she's talking about.

After a silence she takes a deep breath and she says, 'OK, I'm sorry. That was unnecessary—'

'She's being abused right under your fucking noses.'

Mel pulls her hands down her face. 'What?'

'Paige. She's being sexually abused.'

She turns to him and he meets her eyes and although he knows he has to hide it, he almost wants to smile. He's done it. He's done it and Paige is going to be all right.

'Who by, Luke,' she says flatly, and the feeling disappears. Because he promised.

'I can't.'

Mel tips her head, eyebrows up. 'What?'

'I can't tell you.'

'Well, firstly, you *can*, and secondly, if you don't, I'll have to go straight downstairs and call my manager, and then you'll have to tell them. That's how this works, Luke.'

It's right then that he sees it. It's not a choice, even though it seemed like one. Because he doesn't get to make choices, does he. Things happen to him. He's not master of a single thing.

He says the name, quiet as dying.

'Mr Polzeath,' she says, repeating it as if it's in a foreign language. 'Oliver Polzeath.'

And then she laughs. 'Oh, Lukey, for fuck's sake.' But she doesn't laugh for long. 'You're going to tell me exactly what you think you saw.'

He opens his mouth, closes it. This is not going the way he expected it to go.

'Tell me what you saw.'

He folds his arms. 'Stuff.'

'Stuff?'

He says nothing.

'What *stuff*, Luke?'

'Just – he was – in the car—'

'And?'

He just wants her to stop looking at him like that. Like he's any of the others, giving her gyp.

'I'm sorry,' he says, sitting next to her. 'Sorry.' He doesn't understand. He doesn't know what else to say.

She shifts so she's facing him, making it so that he has no choice but to look at her. But not in a way like she's worried. In a way like she's so fucking furious with him that she might smack him.

'Listen to me, Luke. If you do this, if you let your little crush *do* this – no, let me finish – not only will it ruin that man's life, but it will be the end of anything you think you might have with her. Do you understand what I'm telling you?'

His mouth is clamped so tight shut that he can feel the roots of his teeth. Her fingers dig into the shallow flesh on his shoulders and he wants to cry out.

'Do you understand?'

'Yes,' he says, his voice breaking. He sounds about six.

'You start mucking around with that kind of shit, Luke, things get pretty fucking serious pretty fucking fast. I've seen it happen.'

'I don't care.'

'No? Well, I do.' She goes to the window. 'Let me explain how this goes. You make an accusation like that, the first thing that happens is we call the police. The police will interview you, and they'll interview Paige, right? They will go through every little detail of your statement, they will check where Paige has been, who she's seen, who she's spent any time with. What she was wearing and when. They will go through every inch of her background.' She pins him with her eyes, and he understands without a doubt that she knows he's read Paige's files. 'All of it,' she says.

She knew, and she never said a word.

Why?

28

Now

Callum Roche tucks the phone between his ear and his shoulder and waves Wren in. She closes the door behind her and takes the chair he gestures her into.

'I've already got half of them doing extra shifts,' he groans into the receiver, elbows on the desk and fingers splayed across his scalp, which is noticeably sparser than it was a month ago. 'Fine, fine. Yes, I'll find a way. Well, I'll have to, won't I?' He mutters a beleaguered formality to end the call and replaces the handset. Then, glancing up at Wren, he delicately removes two pencils from an overstuffed desk tidy, inserts one into each nostril, and mimes slamming his own face onto the table.

Wren laughs. 'That bad, huh?'

'You don't know how lucky you are to have such a caring and sharing boss, Reynolds.'

'Is that so.'

He casually removes the pencils and makes a big deal of looking at the clock behind him. 'Glad you could make it.'

Wren apologises. 'We had a scan, whole thing took twice as long as we thought.' He doesn't need to know that the scan itself had only overrun by ten minutes, and that the bulk of her tardiness was down to the argument they'd had afterwards.

The default irritation on his face gives way momentarily to a grudging concern. 'All well with the baby, though? And your…' he pauses, waving an awkward hand, 'your girlfriend… wife… she OK?'

'Partner,' Wren says, putting him out of his misery. 'Both fine.'

'Right then,' he says, clapping his hands together, pleased to have dispensed with the niceties.

The news he needs to share with her is that the deadlines are tightening.

'Whole team,' he says. 'You need to clear up on Ashworth by the end of the week. Think you can manage that?'

Wren lets her head drop back. 'Seriously? After I came here asking for more time, you're telling me I have to do it in *less*?'

'Or shall I find someone else who can?' Callum picks a piece of lint from the cotton stretched across his gut. 'Let me not have to remind you that you're on a three-month trial here.'

She gives him a look. 'You're not going to swap me out now, and we both know it.'

'Try me,' he says, but she's not convinced. 'I understand he still hasn't got work? That hospital job didn't work out?'

'They didn't want him. I am trying, Callum! But I can't possibly get all the visits done *and* set him up for work *and* write it all up in that time.' She's supposed to have another week. 'What happened?'

'Search me. Came straight from the Home Office. Twenty-five per cent funding drop as of next month, so Upstairs says we have to pre-empt it.'

'But the project was all costed out! The funding was rock-solid, that's what you said.'

Roche spreads his hands. 'Welcome to the era of McProbation. Same as the NHS. They make it impossible, set us up to fail, and when we do, they privatise the lot and pick over the carcass. So you're OK to start with… who is it again?'

'O'Shea. Wife-beater.'

'Right, right. Beginning of next week, then.'

'Come *on*, Callum.'

He holds up his hands. 'Not my call. That person I was just talking to? Two down from the bloody Justice Secretary. You want more time to cuddle your offender and tell him how much the world's missed him since he got locked up, you take it up with her.'

She mentally runs over what there is left to do. Maybe she can get the four remaining knocks done, and set up a job for him if she's extremely lucky. But there's more to it than that: the extracurriculars. What about finding Luke? What about Rob and that phone?

What about Paige?

'There isn't time.'

He gets up. 'You'll have to make time.'

On the way back to her desk, still fuming, she texts James. *I need that contact for Luke*, she tells him, *and we need to talk about the Polzeaths*. Not even bothering with the *hi* or *bye* this time. She drops the phone into her bag, and draws up a list.

If she can get hold of Makayla Slater's social worker, sweettalk them into sharing the notes, maybe there would be something in there, and then—

Then, what? She shoves the keyboard angrily away. If there was anything in Makayla's notes identifying Polzeath, or anyone else, as a potential sexual abuser, it would have been acted on. She has three days. If she can't get Rob to talk, and she can't get Melanie Pickford-Hayes or Leah to talk, she needs Luke. He's the only one who was there at Beech View with Paige who might volunteer something useful.

Five o'clock. She powers down the screen and heads

outside. Suzy needed the Kangoo so Wren's taking the opportunity to get a decent walk in, clear her head on the way to pick up her car, which she's hoping will be ready by now.

She waits until she's cleared the noisy motorway bridge, then gets her phone out to call the garage to check. But the thought leaves her head as soon as she sees James's text.

Still working on Luke, it says. *But got something else. Be at yours in twenty.*

She dials his number, heart hammering. Voicemail. *Shit.*

'James,' she tells the machine as she turns one-eighty towards the taxi rank and breaks into a run, 'please, *please* do not go to my house.'

By the time she gets home, James's car is parked outside, and James isn't in it. She pays her driver, sprints up the path, goes inside.

'Wren?' Suzy's voice, pitchy but polite, rings through the house as if it were empty, and tells Wren everything she needs to know.

The two of them, Suzy in the slackest of her maternity slacks and James in a crumpled linen jacket and jeans, are sitting at the kitchen table. Suzy beams at her as she comes in, her eyes unnaturally wide to match the big, plastered-on grin that confirms Wren's fear.

'Here you are!' James says warmly.

'James has just been telling me about that bar you went to,' Suzy tells her. 'And I feel *so* silly, because I'd got it totally mixed up. *I* thought you were working late.' She makes a *silly-me* face, rolling her eyes at her mistake, and the smile doesn't move, not even when she gets unsteadily to her feet. 'Anyway, I'll leave you to it. There's wine in the fridge, if you feel like another party.'

Wren waits until she hears the living-room door close, and the sudden burst of noise from the TV.

And then she rounds on James. 'What the *fuck* are you doing here?'

James recoils. 'What? I just – I thought you'd want to—'

'Well, I don't!' Wren hisses. 'How do you even know where I live?'

'I brought you home,' he says, visibly hurt at the insinuation. 'In the taxi?'

Wren sinks into a chair. 'Right,' she says, the fight going out of her with the scrap of a memory – her spilled bag, his kindness at her messy display of emotion. 'Look, I'm sorry,' she adds. 'I just – things are kind of tense.'

'Sure, sure. I get it.' He reaches for the leather satchel slung on the back of the chair. 'Shall we do this another time?'

'You're here now,' Wren says. 'Just – I need a minute.' She makes her way to the living room like a woman headed for the gallows.

Suzy doesn't even turn her head when Wren sits down beside her.

'I should have told you—'

'Yeah,' Suzy says dully, cutting her off.

'But I knew you'd—'

'I'd what? Prefer you didn't lie to me?' Suzy sighs heavily and turns off the TV. 'Did you engineer this, Wren? Did you make it so that you got the case about a girl in a children's home?'

Wren opens her mouth to reply, but Suzy holds up her hand. 'I googled it, just now. Paige Garrett, right? And then I realised I remembered it from before. Because you got so upset about it, when she disappeared.'

Wren looks at her feet. She doesn't know what to say to make this better.

'We hadn't been together that long, had we?' Suzy says. Her voice softens slightly, but Wren's heart just accelerates because if she knows one thing about how Suzy works, it's that a gentle voice doesn't mean she's off the hook. 'I begged you to explain it to me, why it got to you so much.'

'And I told you,' Wren says weakly. 'It's because of… when I was a kid.'

'But what does that mean, Wren? Look at us, we're about to start a family, and stuff like this happens and all I can see is this vast history to you that you won't even share with me. It's like…' she pauses, and looks away. 'It makes me feel like I don't even know you.'

Wren winces. 'I'm sorry.'

Suzy glares back at her. It was the wrong thing to say. 'Sorry's not enough. You lied to me. You could have talked to me about it, Wren. Back then, or last night. Any fucking time would have been fine. I would have understood.'

Wren can't even meet her eye. At first, Wren hadn't even wanted Suzy to know where she'd grown up. She'd been evasive, careful even to never mention schools or anything about families. But Suzy had been through her flippant fob-offs and vague half-truths until one day, she'd broken down in tears and told her that she couldn't be with someone who completely refused to share her history. And so eventually and under duress, Wren had given her the bare bones. That she'd been in the care system, that she didn't have any contact with her family. It wasn't much, it certainly wasn't complete, but it was enough to stop her from leaving.

Wren sees now that it was a window. She could have opened up. Not just that she'd been in care herself, not just that *she* could have been Paige: but all of it. The whole story.

But not now. It's way too late.

Levelly, Suzy says her piece, addressing it to the space just above Wren's heart. 'Listen, my love. I want this to work. I want our child to have a better childhood than you had. Even all the stuff that you've never told me and—' she raises up a hand to silence her, 'I *know* there's a *lot* of stuff you haven't told me. And that's your choice. But a family needs stability and honesty and—'

She is interrupted by a soft knock at the door.

'I can come back another time,' James says through the door.

'No, no,' Wren calls through, 'I'll be there in a sec.'

Suzy holds her gaze. She shakes her head, slowly, as if against the drag of all that disappointment.

'No,' Wren says quickly, recognising her error, watching it gather speed and career away, 'James, I mean, let's do this another time.'

But it's too late. Suzy looks around the room, nods to herself, and leaves Wren there alone with the realisation that this is worse than a mistake. It's more like the back end of her last chance.

James is waiting in the kitchen, chin propped on his hands, eyes closed. He straightens as soon as she enters the room.

'Micro-meditation. Keeps the focus,' he says by way of explanation, clearing his throat.

'Right,' Wren says, not giving one ounce of a fuck.

'Everything OK?'

Wren nods. It isn't. Upstairs, Suzy is storming around, and even though Wren knows she should go up there, she just can't. The only thing that could make a difference would be telling her she'll drop the case.

'What was in the box, then, that Leah was holding for him?' he asks.

She doesn't answer. Because actually, there is *something* else she could do, to limit the damage.

'I think we're going to have to part ways, James.'

James laughs, then realises she means it. A weary, reluctant frown descends. Then he pulls his satchel over and brings out a battered manila file. It is maybe three inches thick, and looks as if it contains mostly loose leaves of paper.

'This,' James says, pushing the file towards her, 'is everything I could find—'

He pauses, his eyes moving to a space behind her head. Wren turns, following his gaze. There at the door, tears on her face and a suitcase in her hand, is Suzy.

'—on Luke Ashworth,' James finishes. Then, 'You OK?' as if he's known Suzy for years.

Suzy doesn't even look at him. She lets her eyes linger on Wren's face, as if committing her to memory. And then she turns, and she walks out of the door.

'Suze, please,' Wren says, getting up.

'Fuck you, Wren,' comes the reply. And then the door slams, and the only thing holding back the silence is Radclyffe, whining plaintively in the hall.

Wren sits back down at the table, slumping onto it with her forehead into her hands. 'Shit.'

James clears his throat. 'Do you think you better…?'

'No,' Wren says. Because there is nothing she can say to Suzy, nothing she can promise that wouldn't be a lie. She sighs hard, then turns her focus to the file. But she finds James's hand is still on it.

There is a condition.

'We're still doing this together, all right?'

She feels her sails sag. 'I'm in probation, James. I'm not running a vigilante gang.'

'I know that. But we both want to find out what happened, and we both know that doing it by the book doesn't get results.'

A timer sounds, and she goes to the oven. There is a lasagne in there. She opens the door to a blast of heat, turns it off, and turns to face him.

'I've already broken the law,' she says.

'Yeah. You have,' he says flatly, making no attempt to assuage her feelings. Not that she can blame him. He is a victim of crime – a victim who has been as positive as he could possibly be about rehabilitation, about forgiving his attacker. He'd gone out of his way, a *long* way out, and Ashworth had thrown it back in his face. And now she is doing the same.

'I'm sorry,' she says. 'I need to just do the rest of this above board.'

He stands up, riffling in his pockets for cigarettes.

'It's your call,' he says. 'I'm not making any demands of you. I just – I don't know. When I met you, I could see straight away you were in it for the right reasons. I thought maybe there was a chance we could actually do something here. But anyway. Have a look in there,' he says, indicating the file with an unlit Marlboro, 'and we'll talk.'

He goes into the back garden to smoke, and Wren begins to read.

It is a complete history. Everything from Luke's school reports to his referral forms to social services, pupil premium applications from the school, social work assessments, contact agreements with his mother. She turns the pages gingerly. Where has all of this come from? There has to be, what, ten, a dozen sources – and she knows from personal experience the hoops a person needs to jump through to get access to it.

The door cracks back open and James returns. He sits at the table, trailing a rich smell of tobacco behind him.

'Helpful?'

'I don't know. I mean, yes, probably. Where did you get all this?'

He raises his eyebrows. 'Do you want to know?'

She flaps the folder shut. 'No. I'm not taking this.'

James laughs. 'You're actually serious?' A flicker of indignation on his forehead, gone before it takes anchor.

'Not if it's not legit.'

He gives her an indulgent smile, as if they both know this is just lip service.

'I'm not joking. This is… seriously confidential stuff.'

'Yeah. And there might be something in there that'll lead you to him. Or have you changed your mind now? Decided Paige is just, what,' he says, turning the corners of his mouth down, 'just one more kid in care, and who gives a toss?'

'It's not like that.'

'No?' He sits back, the file like an unexploded bomb between them. 'Do you know what she said to me once, Paige? That she never used the word *care*. Didn't know what it meant, couldn't make it work. Because all her life, people had used it to refer to what she got in the homes. Everywhere else, it was supposed to mean love. And the two things weren't the same.'

'Look, I'm sorry.'

'Yeah,' he says, the muscles in his jaw tight. He draws the file back towards himself. 'I get it. You don't want to get your hands dirty. You've got a job to do, family to support, all that.'

'It's not that. I appreciate what you've done. You're a good guy—'

'For all the good it does me.'

She ignores that. 'But I can't share this. I need to do this on my own.'

'I can help you, Wren. We can work this out together. For Paige.'

She glances at the folder. Stuffed with things she can use, material she can't get anywhere else. But it is criminal, accessing this information without proper consent. It isn't a grey area: it's straight up against the law.

She slides it back.

But he doesn't pick it up. He opens it, starts flipping slowly through the pages.

'No one knows what it's like, being in care. Living with

however many other unwanted kids they can fit in a building. No one giving a toss about you, except that you stay out of prison and off drugs until you're not their problem any more.' He rubs his hands over his face, shakes himself. 'I'm sorry, this isn't—'

A thought comes to her, something that, until now, she would never have even considered as a possibility. It wouldn't make sense, not with his money and obvious breeding and connections. But she has to ask. 'James, were you were in care, too?'

He won't meet her eye.

'Oh my God. You were. I'm – I'm so sorry.'

Eventually he relents. 'Worst year of my life. Worse than anything Robert bloody Ashworth could throw at me.'

She would never have guessed. There are markers, tics that veterans of the system collect, buzzing like little psychological tattoos under the skin that only others who've been through it can recognise. He has none of the markers. A nasty little thought surfaces unbidden – *Well, it was only a year. Lucky him!* – but she is instantly ashamed of herself. Because a year is a year, and no child's tragedy starts and ends with their time in care. It is the final act, the nadir of a childhood that they will likely spend decades, if not their whole lives recovering from.

'How did it happen?'

He shakes his head. 'My parents died and I…' he trails off, and she thinks she sees it. Something left of a little kid in his face.

'I'm sorry,' she says. She waits, giving him space to tell her more of it, but he clears his throat and she knows he's shared enough.

He stands up, tucking the folder under his arm with some finality. 'Just do me a favour and don't tell anyone I had this, OK? I had to pull a lot of strings.'

She follows him to the hall and opens the door, grabbing Radclyffe by the collar as he bumps past, trying to chase after his favoured mum. 'I'll keep you updated,' she says. 'I just, I have to be professional, you know?'

He dismisses it with a wave of his hand. 'Sure. That's fine.' He takes a few steps, then pauses and turns, pulling his satchel round to the front of his body. 'I almost forgot,' he says, lifting the flap. He holds out an orange supermarket bag.

'Found it when I got out of the cab the other night.' He shakes it, impatient. 'Take it, it's yours. Must have fallen out of your bag.'

He meets her eye, transmitting something that she doesn't quite want to receive. Something she will have to store and process later on.

'We did have a bit of a skinful, didn't we?' he says.

She goes to take it but he holds the package for half a second, just long enough to mismatch the release and the resistance so that Wren finds herself pulling too hard.

'You're not the only one with an agenda, Wren. That man ruined my life. He ruined Lucilla's life. I don't even know who she is any more. So if you think he killed Paige, I want to be the one to prove it. I want my face to be the one he sees in the witness box before he's sent down for life. *That's* justice. *That's* what I'm after: for me and for Paige and for all the people your project is really supposed to be about. We're close – you know we are. I can't just walk away from that. Not again.'

Wren opens her mouth, closes it, and nods. James stares at her for a moment longer, his eyes dark and simmering. And then he turns and walks up the path, leaving Wren holding a bundle of letters that she took – stole – from Paige Garrett's room.

She says it so quietly the first time that it takes him a

moment to register it. He turns. 'What was that?' His hand is on the gate.

She clears her throat. 'It was a phone,' she says. 'The reason Ashworth was so anxious to get those boxes from Leah. He was after a phone.'

He nods, slowly, not taking his eyes from hers. 'Then I guess that's what we need to get hold of, isn't it?'

29

Before

Oliver fucking Polzeath has come to the house and there's no reason for it. Mrs P is there too, staff meeting, and yeah, that's OK, there's a reason for *that*, it's fine. But him? No. He isn't a carer, he isn't a member of staff, he's not having a meeting, he's got nothing to do with any of the kids. Nothing he'll admit to anyway. And Luke was supposed to be going round Rob's to play on his new Xbox but he's texted him to say he's staying in. Because he's not letting that wanker out of his sight.

Luke sits on the sofa, phone in his hand. Polzeath's doing the same, keeps glancing over. No one's saying anything. After about ten minutes Polzeath gets up.

'You off?' Luke says.

Polzeath's mouth flaps a few times. 'No, I'm just, uh,' he says, gesturing at the door. He leaves the room and Luke gets up when he hears his footsteps on the stairs. Paige is on the first floor. Surely he wouldn't just go up there and… when the house is full of people?

But he's a paedo. You can't know.

Luke follows him. Polzeath gets to the top step before he looks down and sees him. And Luke just stays where he is, halfway up. *I know what you are, you fucker.* Polzeath turns left like he was going to the gents all along.

As Polzeath disappears into the toilet, Paige's door opens.

'Luke,' she says. She's bare-faced, pale as a block of chalk. 'Come in here.'

He does what he's told. Inside, the room is stuffy and disordered. Her clothes are piled up, and at first it looks like it's just a mess but then he sees that's not it: she's sorting them. She's got a big rucksack bulging with stuff and her schoolbag's full but it doesn't look like books in there.

'Sit down.'

He finds a space on the bed. She moves some scraps of lace from the stool of her desk onto the floor, then he sees that they're not scraps, they're underwear. He looks away.

'Luke, I need to talk to you.'

He squares up. Whatever she needs from him, he's ready to give it.

She lowers her eyes, looks at her hands. 'I know you've talked to Mel. But you've got to keep away from me for a bit, all right?'

White heat rushes to his eyes. He gets up, sits down again. He doesn't know what to do.

'I don't need your help. You'll understand why,' she says, her voice barely there. 'I really care about you Lukey but you have to back off.'

'Why?' he says, and the force of it surprises them both. She looks at him properly for the first time and it's not just her skin that's grey. There's no life around her eyes at all, her cheeks are sunken. She sees his shock and covers her face with her hands. 'What's going on?'

'Jesus Christ, I feel awful,' she says. He can see the nausea in the hunch of her shoulders, can almost smell it.

'You need a doctor,' he says. 'I can take you.'

But she glares at him. 'That's exactly what I mean. It's not – you just need to leave me alone. All right?'

He realises, horrified, that the heat in his eyes is tears.

'Come on, Luke,' she says. Everything about her is exhausted.

He brings his knees up, stops a pile of her sweaters from tumbling to the floor. 'What is all this?'

She glances at the piles. 'Sorting out.'

'Why?'

'Because I'm selling some stuff.'

'But it's your best stuff.'

Then they both think the same thing at the same time. She gets to her feet, scanning the floor with her eyes wide, but he sees it first.

The hem of a dress, hanging out the edge of a binbag. Silver and weightless. The one he bought.

He pulls it free. There's a crashing inside him that he can't hear through, can't think through, because it's too many things at once. He brings it up in his fist like he's going to throw it but then he sees her shrink back.

Scared of him. Terrified.

He goes to take her hands but she flattens herself against the wardrobe. Hands across her belly.

And when he looks back up at her, and she won't meet his eye, he knows.

'Fucking hell, Paige.'

All this stuff on the floor. How she's given up smoking, just like that. How ill she looks. She's selling her stuff because she needs money because she's pregnant. She's leaving, because she's pregnant.

'Where are you going to go?'

She leans her head back against the wardrobe door and then slips down into a squat. Closes her eyes.

'I don't know.'

'But like, another place like this? Or a mother and baby unit, or something?'

She laughs, like it's the most ridiculous thing in the world.

'What?'

'You think they'd let me keep it? Social would have it out of my hands in ten seconds flat.'

It takes him a minute to work out what she's saying. She's not just leaving. She's running away.

'Do they know?' he says. She won't meet his eye. 'Tell me you've told them.'

She hasn't told them. Which means she's going to be on her own. Unless—

'Whose is it?' She won't look at him. 'Is it – is it him?' he says, spitting it, jerking his head towards where Oliver Polzeath is supposedly taking a piss.

'Oh, for Christ's sake – whatever Rob's told you...'

'Rob? What the fuck's it got to do with Rob?'

From the hall there's the sound of the flush, then footsteps. Luke knows the bastard has dragged it out in the hope that he's gone back downstairs. There's a knock at the door.

'Paige?' A hushed voice.

It's Mr Polzeath. A ball of rage starts spinning in Luke's throat.

Paige casts a panicked look around the room, the stuff everywhere, bags half packed, then she glares at Luke and puts a finger to her lips.

Moments pass. He doesn't knock again. The creak of the top step, then a soft padding as he goes back down. And it's like the air in the room goes slack again.

'Does he know?'

Paige sighs like she's just too tired of him to even answer.

'Do *you* know?'

'Luke, *please*—'

'*Whose* is it, Paige?'

'Keep your fucking voice down, all right? I'm asking you to help me by staying out of it. I've got enough to worry about without you messing it all up.'

'Messing what up?' He laughs, and it comes out angry and cruel and he does not give a toss. 'How can this be any more messed up?!'

But she looks away, like he doesn't know the half of it.

And he makes up his mind right then that this is one of those times you've got to do the right thing. He doesn't care what Mel says, or Rob, or Leah, or anyone else. Even if Paige says she's going through with whatever it is she's got planned, if it's just him who can see that it's not right, he's got to do something about it.

He drops the dress, the one he bought her, and it drifts back to earth, half on the binbag and half on her floor, forgotten and discarded whatever way you look at it.

She'll thank him. Might not be right away, but she will.

30

Now

Wren pays the taxi driver and heads down the cobbles beneath the approach to Temple Meads station to the garage under the arches. Of Suzy's multitudinous cousins, Paul is the one you go to when you have car trouble. When he called her a few hours ago to come and collect it, he was friendly but to the point. Either he doesn't know about the recent developments between her and Suzy, or he doesn't want to get involved.

She dodges the perennial oily puddles and goes inside. As bad luck would have it, there is Marty, Paul's brother, the one with the point to prove on the news desk.

He smiles broadly when he sees her. 'I was talking to Paul, he told me your ride was fixed. I was passing, thought I'd drop it home for you.'

'You didn't need to come,' she tells him. They haven't spoken since he'd mentioned the article he was doing on Ibrahim. 'I'm not going to change my mind, if that's what you're thinking.'

He pulls in his chin, feigning offence. 'I just thought as I was here, I'd do you a favour.'

'I don't need favours,' she says.

Paul appears and ushers her through to the workshop. The tinny sound of something by Phil Collins emanates from a radio balanced on the bonnet of a BMW.

'Good news?' she asks, ignoring Marty hovering behind her.

'Well, kind of.' Paul wipes a sheen of moisture from his forehead with the back of his hand, leaving a swathe of dark grease.

He clicks the radio off. 'I mean, I've diagnosed your problem, it's not a complicated fix.'

'But?'

'I found something kind of strange,' he says. 'You got many enemies, Wren?' He's joking, but there's a ghost of concern behind the smile.

'I annoy ex-convicts for a living, mate.'

He laughs, but the frown stays put. 'Come and have a look.' She follows him through to where her car is. 'So it wasn't your battery.' He opens the driver's door, pops the bonnet, and comes round the front to prop it open with the rod. 'The first thing I thought was that it was the alternator.'

'Feel free to simplify this for me,' she says, peering at the mysterious entrails of the engine.

He takes a step back. 'Your fuel line's been severed.'

'What?'

He twists his face into an awkward apology. 'Yeah.'

'You can't be sure, though? I mean, presumably it could have just… I don't know, broken?'

He wrinkles his nose. 'No. Look.' He directs her attention to the section in question with a torch. There are two pieces of a tarnished metal tube, one about six inches long, the other half that. 'It should be one piece. But it's been cut in half. I mean, deliberately *cut*, Wren, not just disconnected, even. See where it's compressed next to the break. Someone's used pliers of some sort,' he says, peering at the severed ends. Then, decisively, 'No, not pliers: diagonal cutters. You don't get that shape with the flat-blade kind. See how the cut is pinched at the top?'

Wren does. Alarm bites in her stomach. 'When – I mean—'

Marty is behind her, leaning in for a better look. 'Who would have done that?' he says.

Wren straightens up. To Paul she says, 'How long until you can fix it?'

Paul regards her. 'I can do it in an hour,' he says, 'but that's not the point. Do you want to, I don't know, take pictures?'

'What for?'

'Insurance,' Marty puts in. 'And, you know, the police? Just tell Suzy. She'll know who you need to talk to.'

She doesn't deem it necessary to tell her partner's favourite cousin that they are not currently under the same roof. 'Yeah, maybe,' she says, poking at the break.

'No, not *maybe*. Someone's sabotaged your bloody car.' Marty slaps her hand away. 'Fingerprints,' he says. And he is serious.

'Marty, can you back off, mate?' she says, snapping.

'Jesus,' he says, and slinks back inside.

Paul says, 'You got any idea who it could have been?'

She forces a smile. 'I did break Cathy Bennett's ruler on purpose when I was eight,' she muses. 'Do you think it could have been her?'

Paul folds his arms. 'It's not funny, Wren. You work with some pretty dodgy characters, don't you? People with grudges?'

She rolls her eyes. 'Come on. This isn't downtown Chicago. Can you just fix it?'

He makes no secret of his reluctance, but relents in the end. Wren goes to the hipster bakery a few doors up for a coffee, then sits turning the thing over in her head as she sits on the bench outside. Who would even think of sabotaging her car? Who could benefit from that? It wasn't like she'd parked anywhere she couldn't get a bus from, wasn't as if it was going to cause her to lose her job or miss a court appearance. So what, someone wanted to scare her, then? Who?

Ashworth?

After a few minutes, Marty comes over. Wren immediately gets up to go.

'Wait, Wren.'

She huffs. 'What?'

'Look, I just want you to know. They're not letting it go, in the office. They've really got it in for the CAP, they're trying to discredit it any way they can. If you would just talk to me—'

'No,' she says.

He sighs. 'Someone else is writing something up. They're saying the team – your team – are underqualified—'

'I don't care.'

There is a pause. 'I shouldn't be telling you this but… they've got someone in your office. Apparently you don't have any GCSEs; they're saying there's no proper background checks.'

Wren's heart does a bellyflop. Gary fucking Kitchener.

'And they're trying to make out that's why Ibrahim got out. Because you're…' he says, but he can't finish it.

'Incompetent?'

Marty scratches his neck, looking mortified.

'But is it true, Wren, about you not finishing school? Because I can put it right, if you can just give me something else…'

'Like what? What could I possibly tell you that's going to be of any fucking interest to a newspaper that just wants to make it look like we're choosing to let violent criminals out willy-fucking-nilly? The prisons are bursting at the seams, Marty! Something had to happen!'

He looks at her for a moment. Then, quiet as anything, he says, 'Suzy told me about Paige Garrett. How you got obsessed when she disappeared.'

Wren stares him out for a moment.

'OK, you know what?' she says eventually. 'Print whatever the hell you like. But you and me are done.'

And then she walks past him, back to the garage.

Paul's apprentice comes over wiping his hands on his overalls and tells her the job is finished, and within a few minutes, Paul brings the car round to the front.

He gets out and hands her the keys, telling her about another few tune-up jobs he did while he was there. He won't accept payment for any of it. 'But if it happens again,' he says as she gets in and starts the engine, 'I'm going straight to the police.'

She thanks him and goes to close the door, but he stops her and holds out the two sections of metal that he's replaced.

'Look. I know Suzy doesn't want looking after. But, please, look after her, won't you?'

Wren takes the pieces. 'Of course,' she says. Because what else can she say?

The whole way to Ashworth's, Wren thinks about that fuel line. He worked in a garage before he went inside, was on a post-sixteen scheme as an apprentice mechanic. But can it really have been him? What possible gain could he have made from stranding her at work?

She parks in a quiet side street round the back of his block. She drops open the glovebox and tucks the two pieces of metal inside.

Diagonal cutters. Can't be everyone who has a pair of those.

Does Ashworth? Right at the back of the glovebox is the envelope with his spare key in it. She brings it out, turns it over a few times. Then she gets out. She starts walking, and pulls her phone from her pocket.

He answers on the second ring.

'What do you want?' Ashworth says, annoyed. The sound

of traffic and wind in the receiver tells her everything she wants to know: he's out. 'I thought I was free until two.'

'You are,' she says. She passes the corner shop and his block comes into view, its mirrored windows blazing back the sun. 'I'm just checking in. Staying out of trouble?'

He sighs. 'Goodbye,' he says, and hangs up.

The lift is out of order so she takes the stairs. An elderly woman nods at her solemnly as she passes, and Wren has to resist the urge to turn, check she isn't being watched or followed. And if she is? If someone comes to the door while Wren is inside, what then? Fact is, it was Wren who'd found him the flat, negotiated the rent with the housing association the NPS dealt with. Wren who'd picked up the keys, stocked the fridge and bought the toilet paper the morning before he got out.

It isn't like he doesn't know she has a key. It isn't like she's *breaking in.*

Forcing confidence into her stride, she makes her way to his front door, and lets herself in.

The flat is musty inside. Gloomy, blinds drawn. She turns her attention to the search. Two things she's after. That phone, which she *knows* he's got, and the cutters, which she suspects.

The kitchen, barely three units wide along one wall with a sink under the window, yields nothing more than an insight into the culinary life of a man accustomed to prison food. The basic provisions the state provided – cans of chopped tomatoes, pasta, rice – are still exactly where she left them the day before she brought him here from HMP Bristol, and have been joined on their shelf only by a packet of Jaffa Cakes. She rummages under the sink, looks behind the pipework, but there is only a tacky layer of something spilled, plus a dusty half-bottle of drain cleaner.

If I were you, Rob, where would I put them?

Further into the flat, she feels around the threadbare,

sagging cushions of the sofa, then gets onto her knees to peer underneath it. Junk mail, a discarded battery, wrappers. Dust. She gets back up, eyeing the room. The boxes she brought from Leah are side by side next to the TV, their contents jumbled. With less care than the day before, she sifts through their contents again, but doesn't find the phone.

She stands in the centre of the room and turns a slow circle. There is a slim bookshelf in the corner but it's empty except for a small, battered toolbox that looks promising until she opens it. Nothing but a hammer and some broken Rawlplugs. A chest of drawers, incongruously solid, stands beside the door that leads to the tiny bedroom. She searches it methodically. Although they're at least clean and odour-free, his meagre selection of clothes have been thrown into the drawers at random. Wren sighs through her nose, gets to her feet, takes a step towards the bedroom door. But then she has another thought.

She bends and carefully slides the bottom drawer open again, all the way this time, and then out entirely.

Time slows. Face down, on the carpet beneath, is the phone. Without making a sound, without breathing, she reaches in. It is matte black, an old-model Samsung. She briefly presses one of the buttons to see if it'll wake, but it is switched off. With infinite care, she turns it over, runs her thumb over the peeling scrap of a sticker on the back. A unicorn.

She hardly breathes again until she is back in the car. As soon as she sits down, her own phone buzzes with a text from James.

Did you find it?

And Wren understands the mechanics of this now. He knows she took the letters. It doesn't even matter if he knows why. What does matter is that she keeps him at bay.

So she sends back a single word. *Yes.*

Seconds later: *Bring it here. Don't do ANYTHING with*

it. I'll be outside the donut drive-through at St Philips in five minutes, OK?

Wren replies with a cursory *OK*, puts both phones, hers and Ashworth's, beside her, and starts the engine. She moves off, making her way to the retail park James is referring to. But as she gets close, she flips on the indicator, turns into a sideroad, and stops.

She stares out of the windscreen. She stares for a long time, and after a while, she gets out. She walks round the block. When she goes back to the car, there are three texts from James, asking where she is with increasing urgency.

She doesn't answer. She just sits for a while longer.

Thinking, *what happened?*

What am I doing here?

She's there for five minutes, ten. She ignores a call and more texts from James. And then she makes up her mind.

Her message to Suzy is simple.

Please let's try again. I have one thing I have to sort out, and then I'm coming home. I love you so much.

Then she drives back to Ashworth's. She gets out of the car with the stolen phone in her hand, and she goes back to the flat. Because this is madness. She's going to return it. Putting the key in the lock, she opens the front door. On entering, she nearly trips over a wet carrier bag that she didn't notice before, the handles tied together. She nudges it against the wall with her toe, grimaces as it leaves a streak of diluted mud on the lino.

It is at this moment that the door to the bedroom opens. Ashworth, bollock naked apart from a towel slung around his waist, freezes where he is.

'What – what were you doing in there?' Wren says, stupidly, every shred of her attention on the phone she is holding in her left hand behind her back. In one deft movement she slips it into her trouser pocket, thanking her lucky stars that she hadn't gone for a skirt that morning. 'I mean, I didn't know you were in.'

'You broke in,' he says matter-of-factly.

She lets out a stammer of a laugh, makes an incredulous face. *Think, woman.* 'I just had to do an inventory check,' she says, amazing herself with the speed of the lie. 'For the landlord.'

'Bullshit.'

And even though she's desperate not to do it, her eyes travel to the chest of drawers, just beside him.

The bottom drawer is slightly ajar.

He follows her gaze. He crosses the room in half a second and drops to his knees, wrenching the drawer out.

'Fuck!' he screams.

She turns to run, but he's fast and the room is small. His hands are on her shoulders before she can dodge him, and he's forcing her back. The towel has fallen but he doesn't care.

'Where is it?' he spits.

'I don't – I don't—'

'*Where's the fucking phone?*'

Pain explodes in her collarbone as she hits the wall. She ducks low and twists hard to get away from him. *Just get out,* she tells herself. *Deal with the fallout later.*

'Give it to me, you bitch.' He lunges at her but somehow, this time, she is faster, propelled by what he's giving in his desperation to get it back. This is it. This is the key. She bolts away from him, crashes hard into the front door, shoves the handle, pulls it open.

And stops dead.

On the other side, his hand up as if to knock, stands a uniformed police officer.

'Robert Ashworth?' he says, peering in behind Wren.

Wren stands aside, panting. 'Here.'

Ashworth, scrabbling for the towel, recedes into the

bedroom. 'Let me just get some—' he says, but the uniform barges past.

'Police. Stay where you are,' he bellows, charging in and swinging the bedroom door back open.

'Do what he says, Rob,' Wren calls, but the damage has been done. She follows the policeman into the bedroom. There is barely room for three adults to stand in there alongside the unmade bed but there they stand, the cop holding Ashworth against the wall, pressing him in by the back of the neck. He reaches for his radio and gives his number.

Shit, Wren thinks. This is bad. If he gets arrested, he'll be recalled, and if he is recalled, her access to him disappears.

'Suspect resisting arrest,' the cop says into his radio, and Ashworth groans.

'He's not,' Wren shouts. Then calmly, palms up, says, 'I'm his PO. He's not resisting, are you, Rob? You're not.'

'I just need some bloody boxers,' Ashworth says through a squashed cheek.

The cop looks her up and down, and releases Ashworth with a shove. 'Get them on then, now.'

Wren retrieves underwear, jeans and a T-shirt from the drawers and hands them to the cop, then leaves the room.

Moments later, both men emerge, the cop holding Ashworth by the elbow and issuing a calmer edit into his radio. He pushes Ashworth into the sofa.

'You want to tell me where you've been today, sir?'

It is easy to read malice into Ashworth's every expression – he is a man with a face made for it – but right now, there is nothing but utter confusion.

'Today?' he says, as if he doesn't understand the question. 'Here, mostly. Went out for some food just now. Had a walk a bit earlier, about six.'

'Six in the morning, was it? And where was that you went?'

'The river. Same as every day.'

‘Whereabouts? Crew’s Hole, by any chance?’

Ashworth’s forehead rucks with bewilderment. ‘What? No, other way, out towards—’

‘Prove that, can you?’

Ashworth shakes his head. ‘No, I went on my own, but—’

The cop gets closer, gets right up in his face. ‘What were you doing there?’

‘Can I ask what this is about?’ Wren says.

He asks for ID, which Wren gives him.

‘We had a call about suspicious behaviour from a gentleman walking his dog this morning. Recognised Mr Ashworth from the coverage of his release in the *Post*. Apparently Mr Ashworth was seen digging in a clearing near Crew’s Hole—’

‘I never went *near* Crew’s Hole!’

‘—and removing something from the ground.’

Wren goes cold.

‘Removing what?’ she asks quietly.

‘Well that’s what we came here to ask. Because we had a look at that hole, and recovered some very alarming evidence.’

Right in the bottom of her heart, a door creaks open, just a crack at first. ‘What kind of evidence?’

The cop gives her a look, then squats in front of Ashworth, who is refusing to meet his eye. ‘You got anything you’d like to tell me at this stage, Mr Ashworth?’

Slowly, Wren turns. Goes to the door.

From the sofa, Ashworth says, ‘Please. I don’t know what you’re talking about.’

With shaking fingertips, she loosens the knotted handles of the carrier bag she stumbled over on her way in. She inhales, deep, deep as she can go.

‘Don’t you?’ says the officer behind her.

And he is only just there, a few feet away, but somehow his voice is stretched and distant, as if she’s hearing him from the other side of the universe.

'No? I'm sure you'll be quite happy for me to have a bit of a look around then?'

Wren swallows, and pulls it open. Then she lets her eyes close, because maybe if she looks again she'll be given another chance. She forces herself to look properly.

'What have you got there?' the cop is asking her. He peers into the bag, then turns to Ashworth, his eyes wide. And once Ashworth sees what she is holding, he takes matters into his own hands.

He gets himself free and onto his feet, and then he is coming towards her. But Wren doesn't even flinch. Not even when he shoves her aside, crashing through the front door, followed by the police officer. She hears but hardly registers the cop screaming at Ashworth to stop, then shouting the address into his radio as he charges after him, out of the flat and along the walkway.

It is as if all the hope in her body, everything that has held her together, is suddenly just blood and bone again, and it turns out to be not enough. And then she is on the floor, her heart clenching and her mouth open. A long, high, empty sound coming from right down inside her.

Because inside the bag is a checked shirt, red and black. Tangled into that, some denim. The glint of silver: a clasp at the end of a fine silver chain. A tiny pendant shaped like a star, covered in little gemstones.

With the grief gathering fast and heavy in her chest like beads of mercury, she sees there is something else too. Not much of it, but enough to be sure.

Long strands of blonde hair.

31

Before

Luke gets to the Kingswood garage where his brother works at twenty to six. He's early on purpose so he can get him on the way out. As he comes to the turning into the dead end, he finds a low wall and sits down.

He gets out his phone. Two more missed calls from his mum. He'd spoken to her this morning, and she'd gone on and on about how they'd all be together again soon, that Rob had sorted everything out. And he'd pretended to lose reception because he didn't know what to say.

There's the slam of a metal door opening hard against brick, and he sees Rob. Coming out of the side door, swinging his bag onto his back. Luke runs over, but the first thing his brother does when he sees him is roll his eyes. He doesn't break his pace.

'Fuck are you doing here?'

'You're not answering my texts.' Luke tries to fall into step with him but he has to jog to keep up.

Rob groans. 'All this crap about Paige. You need to leave her alone.' He pulls earbuds from his coat and starts to stick them in his ears.

But Luke shoves him, hard. 'Why didn't you tell me the guardianship went tits up? They said you withdrew it. *You* did it.'

'That's what I went to Leah's to tell you the other day,' Rob says, angry. But he won't meet Luke's eyes, because what he's saying is not true. He didn't even know Luke was going to be there. 'It's your own fucking fault for going to the old house.'

Luke grits his teeth, but he says nothing because he needs him on side.

Neither of them speak until they arrive at the flat. Rob puts the key in the lock and shoves the door open. 'Why are you here, Luke?' he says, dumping his coat on the floor and turning to face him. He's furious with him, and Luke doesn't understand why. 'What do you want?'

He's never asked him that before. He's always pleased to see him. Luke pushes it away. 'I need a car.'

'Oh, for fuck's sake. Why?'

'I want to follow Oliver Polzeath.'

Darkness rises on Rob's face and Luke takes a step back.

'She's pregnant, Rob. That fucker's got her *pregnant*, and she's running away. And we've got to prove it, that he's a nonce. So I need a car.'

Rob's nodding really slowly. He's breathing hard through his nose, and his eyes are white all around. Luke doesn't like it.

'Rob,' Luke says quietly. 'Please.' He wants him to stop.

Without taking his eyes off him, out of nowhere Rob grips hold of Luke's arms, hard.

'Keep. Your fucking. Mouth. Shut,' he says, shaking him.

'Rob,' Luke says, pleading, 'you're hurting me. *Rob.*'

'Do you know how fucking long I spent trying to sort shit out for you to come and live here? How hard I've worked to sort things out for Mum, pay for her to be somewhere else, somewhere they're going to actually make her better?'

'But that's – we're never going to afford that!' Luke cries

out. They'd looked on the internet about private care for her, this psychiatric unit up in Redland, just to see. But it was stupid money. Thousands a week.

'And all I'm asking is for you to keep your fucking mouth shut, so I can make something work, just one thing, without you ballsing it up!' Rob shouts at him, not letting go, rage in his face.

It comes to Luke, then. The call with his mum. It's not just her being nuts. Rob's been telling her this stuff. Making promises that he can't keep.

Rob releases him, slamming him hard against the wall, and he walks away. 'Get the fuck out of my flat, little man,' he says. He goes into the bathroom and swings the door shut with a bang.

Luke stands there, his arms burning where Rob had gripped them, just staring ahead.

Rob's not his brother any more. And if he doesn't have a brother, he doesn't have anyone.

The boiler on the wall whooshes into life as the shower goes on. Luke makes his feet move towards the door.

Then something stops him. It's a croaking sound, three regular blasts of it, then a pause, then another three. It's coming from Rob's bag, by the door.

Luke crouches down and undoes the zip. It's not a croak. It's the sound of a duck. Like Paige's message tone. And either that's a coincidence, or—

He flips it over. There's a unicorn sticker on the back. Rob has Paige's phone.

The questions crash into each other in Luke's head like a motorway pile-up as he turns it over. Luke doesn't waste a second. He gets up, clutching the phone in his fist, and goes to the front door. He pulls it shut behind him, and runs. All the way out of the estate, along past the shops, the other direction from the garage. There's a playing field just down there, and he finds the break in the fence where it's been trampled down and he goes in, drops down onto the bench.

Breathing hard, his chest burning with the run, he touches the screen.

There's a code. But he saw her enter the code, two days ago, under the stairs. And he might not have much but, like Mrs Shah told him, he's got a head for numbers.

He types in 7031. The phone lights up. There's no picture on the homescreen, no selfie or photo of her mates or anything, just a factory-settings picture of a beach that no way Paige has ever been to.

He's in.

Everything swirls tight and dense inside. She would go absolutely mental if she knew he'd even touched it.

But all he needs is one text message from Polzeath to her, one thing proving that he's the filthy nonce Luke knows he is, and everything changes. Paige will get the help she needs, Polzeath will go to prison, and Luke will have made that happen. It'll end up OK. They'll make the social see sense about the baby too, because she's a good person and she's kind. She can be a mum.

He's going to do what he has to do, and take it back to her. Prove that whatever else goes wrong, she can rely on him.

He goes straight to the texts. The one that's just come in is part of a long thread between her and a number that's not saved with a name. The message just says: *I can't wait, you filthy bitch.*

Luke feels his face harden. He scrolls down, spinning past message after message, frames of unloaded pictures. He stops at random, and starts reading.

And then what are you going to do?

I'm going to let you do it like you did last night

You liked it hard didn't you?

Yes

Tell me how much you liked it

I can still feel it

Show me how much you liked it, dirty girl

There is an empty frame with a green circle chasing its tail, telling him a picture is loading. He waits.

And once he realises what he is looking at, he holds it away from him, free hand over his mouth.

32

Now

'For fuck's sake,' Callum Roche says, his voice creaking with frustration down the line. 'It's fucking Younnis Ibrahim all over again.'

'I just – I didn't expect him to ever do that,' Wren tells him, eyes closed, rubbing her forehead. Ashworth has officially absconded. She is still shaking. 'He wasn't a flight risk. He just – he just *wasn't*.'

'Well, let's fucking hope whoever's running the manhunt hasn't got any mates at the *Post*, Wren, that's all I can say. Fuck's sake,' he repeats, shouting it. 'How, *how* did you not see this coming?'

'How could I?' She waves her hand pointlessly, swaps the phone to the other ear. On legs that feel as if they can hardly hold her, she starts walking back to the car. 'The police want me at the station now, the Bridewell. They're preparing a spit kit for me.'

'For what?'

'Because of the… the bag,' she says, hardly able to say the word without the conjuring of what was inside. Involuntarily she clenches the hand that touched what was inside that bag. 'Said I might have contaminated it.'

'Oh, for – *seriously*?' She can practically see him screwing his face up and jamming the heels of his hands against his temples the way he always does when he is stressed. But he lets out a breath and asks, a little softer, 'You're sure the clothes were hers? The victim's?'

Wren shuts her eyes.

'Wren?'

'They – they're testing it. I don't know.' But it's a lie. The shirt, the necklace, the scrap of denim she saw before she dropped the bag and threw her hands back, away from the horror of what it meant: well, either it was a hell of a coincidence or… no. They were Paige's. That was the evidence: that the clothes of a girl who had been missing for years had turned up, all in the same place, in the flat of the man who had been the prime suspect in a case that had never quite shifted over into a murder inquiry.

All that's going to change now, of course.

'Why were you even there?' Roche is saying. 'I thought you were prepping for O'Shea this afternoon.'

'I was tying up some loose ends.'

He growls in frustration. 'Great. Just great, Wren, this is exactly what we needed. First tranche of fucking offenders, two weeks in and we've already got the police applying for immediate recall. They're coming out here for your notes in about ten minutes. Anything you want me to say in your defence, or shall I throw you to the fucking wolves like I was planning to?'

Wren sighs heavily. 'Do what you want, Callum. I've said I'm sorry.'

'Fine. Just – fine then. You've already given your statement?'

'Not fully.' She'd waited in the flat until the backup arrived, sitting on Ashworth's sofa, rubbing at the muddy water mark on her trousers like Lady Macbeth. A uniformed officer, a woman whose name and face she can't remember, had made her a cup of sweet black tea and sat her on the sofa until she'd been able to form sentences again. *Just shock,* the woman had said. *They'll find him though, don't worry.* Wren had nodded, letting her believe that her tears were for her oversight, for the loss of her offender. 'I told them what happened but I didn't have much for them. They said I can do the formal statement when I go to the station.'

'You've got no idea where he's gone?'

She opens her mouth to reply when her phone buzzes against her ear. It's James, for the hundredth time. 'I'll call you back,' she tells Roche.

Wren hangs up, relieved, and answers James.

'Why are you ignoring my calls?'

Walking fast, Wren comes out of the estate and onto the main road. 'Something's happened,' she says.

'Are you there? At Ashworth's?'

She stops at her car, gets inside. 'He's run off. Absconded.' She lets her eyes close, hardly able to make herself breathe.

'Right.' She hears him take a long breath. 'Why didn't you meet me like we arranged? Where's the phone? Have you still got it?'

'Yes, but—'

'You need to bring it here, OK? Right now.'

'I – I can't, James. Everything's changed now, I've got to—'

'Yes you *can*,' he tells her, gently. 'You can. We can look at what's on it, and then you can take it wherever you need to.'

She puts him onto hands-free, then moves the stolen phone from her pocket to the passenger seat, along with her jacket, neatly folded, and her bag. She sits in the driver's seat and rests her hands on the wheel.

'I found something. In his flat. It's… it's bad.' Her voice cracks. *Do not cry. Do not fucking cry.*

'Shit, Wren, what?'

He waits, patiently, and when she can breathe, she tells him falteringly about the bag. The fabric, the mud, the few threads of hair.

'Is there a chance it was something else?'

'No! It was hers! The shirt was the exact one she was last seen in. Skinny jeans. There was a necklace even—' She breaks off. *Breathe, Wren.* Then she tells him in choked fragments how the whole thing had been taken off in a sealed bag, how the forensics crew are all over his flat now, looking for anything else.

'Look, are you still there? At his flat? I'm two minutes away,' he says. She hears the rumble of his engine as he starts it up. 'Stay where you are.'

'Yes, but I have to go and give samples,' she tells him. 'Because I touched it.'

'We can meet before you have to—'

'And a statement!' she adds, her pitch rising again. 'I don't know what I'm going to say. I let myself in, James. He found me with the phone in my hand. Why didn't I just tell them? What was I *thinking*?'

There's silence for a moment. Then with a calm in his voice that strikes the crest off her panic, he says, 'All right. Nothing has changed. We still get one step ahead of him with whatever he's hiding on that phone—'

'No *way*. I'm handing it in.'

'You're not. Wren, look. I've worked with the police dozens of times, child protection stuff. And we've got two very big problems here. The first is that you have taken that phone out of his possession. Whatever they find on it is going to be inadmissible.'

'But I haven't even turned it on!'

'They don't know that. When he gets prosecuted, and you get put up in front of the jury as a witness – which is what is going to happen by the way, if you do this – they are going to tear you apart.' He lowers his voice. 'We both know there's things you've done in the last few weeks that aren't… strictly professional.'

She shuts her eyes, saying nothing.

'And me, I'm on your side. I'm happy to let that stuff slide. I won't pry. But a defence lawyer, trying to save their client from a murder charge? That's going to be a different deal altogether.

'The second thing,' he goes on, 'is that anything might happen to that phone when we turn it on. It might somehow have the GPS data from her last movements, which could get wiped if it updates.'

This isn't something she's heard before. 'Look, I don't know how all of this stuff works—'

'But I do. If Ashworth is half as slippery as he was when he went to prison, he's going to have protected it.'

Wren rubs at her wet eyes. 'No,' she says, finding the level in her voice again. 'He doesn't know stuff like that. Honestly, he's not like that.'

'You don't know that for sure,' James says, raising his voice over hers. This could be crucial. Whatever it is that he so badly wanted to get hold of could be destroyed, if you don't do what I'm telling you.'

'But the police… their forensics people…'

'They have no idea what they're doing half the time! Where do you think the best and brightest minds in IT work? Because I can tell you for a fact it's not the public sector. I would put money on them wiping or losing or corrupting that data before they've even got it out of the fucking bag. Do you want to lose your career for that? And not just *your* career, either,' he adds.

He doesn't have to say the next part.

Suzy, her partner, the mother of the child they are going to raise together, is a police officer. And despite being pushed away, held at arm's length because that's what Wren has always chosen over risking judgement and rejection, Suzy has persevered and shared her life, and loved her.

Right now, they are on a knife edge. Will she really stand with her through this?

Would Wren, if it was the other way around?

This, everything she's done in the last few weeks, culminating in these last few hours: *this* is a fuck-up of monumental proportions. All she'd wanted was to know for sure what had happened to Paige.

All she can do now is own it. She isn't going to let it get any worse. As if by divine intervention her phone buzzes. It is a message from Suzy.

I love you too. Do what you've got to do, then come back. I'll see you at home.

It is all she needs.

'Sorry, James,' she says. 'But I'm doing this my way.'

'What the hell does that mean? Stay where you are, I'm right around the corner—'

'I'm going home,' she says. 'I'm going to go home, take a shower, sort things out. And then I'm going to take the phone to the police station, and it'll be out of my hands.'

Then, with James bawling at her down the line, she cuts the call. And it is easy. It is the only option she has left.

33

Before

The pictures from that screen burn through his dreams, but it's her face that propels him awake. Rocketing closer and closer until he felt that her darkness would just swallow him whole.

He wakes ten, twenty times in the night, until he gives up at half-five. He sits on the edge of his bed, staring at the wall but not seeing it. Not seeing anything but her.

His own phone is on the desk. He goes over and turns it on. The calls from Rob had started last night maybe half an hour after he'd left the flat, and after that they'd come every ten minutes until he turned the phone off. Luke hadn't even gone to the window when he heard the stones hitting the glass. He'd known it was Rob without even looking. So he'd just put his pillow over his head and waited for him to go away.

His own brother. Knowing she was being treated like that, taking pictures of herself for someone like that, and doing nothing about it.

Why? And why did *he* have her phone?

Luke's got fifteen voicemails, but he doesn't listen to them. As he deletes the notifications, it dawns on him that he didn't hear her come back last night.

On his way to the bathroom he pauses by her door, but

he can't tell if she's in. Luke showers and dresses, and by the time he's ready, the night shift is swapping with the day and there's movement in the kitchen. Just before he goes downstairs, he thinks of something. He tears off a scrap of paper from a piece in his bin, and places it between the door and the frame when he closes and locks his door.

He goes down. Paige's shoes are in her box.

Fat Jake's in the kitchen, spooning sugar onto his sugar-free cereal. He jumps when he sees Luke, and looks away. The bandage across the side of his head is gone now and the black eye is fading into a bluey green, but that's just what's on the outside. Jake's sort of disappeared, since the thing with the saucepan. He stays in his room, doesn't even talk to Cameron. Luke had heard him complaining to Geraint a few days back about how Paige wasn't bollocked, and it wasn't exactly true but Luke gets his point. She basically got away with attempted murder.

Funny that, Luke thinks bitterly. Because from where he's standing, it's almost like someone's pulling strings for her.

He microwaves a mug of milk and adds chocolate. He takes it into the dining room, trailing circles in the mug with a spoon, watching the granules melt. Upstairs, one of the day staff is banging on doors to get everyone up. He doesn't recognise the voice; it's someone new. He's given up keeping up with who's actually working at Beech View, they change so often.

He plays a game on his phone but half-arsed, his mind drifting up to the first floor, into Paige's room. Listening and waiting for her, until eventually, at half-seven, down she comes.

Out of the corner of his eye he watches her put the usual three spoons of muesli into her bowl – a small bowl so it looks like more, she reckons – and cover it with about a thimbleful of red-top milk. She's humming as she brings it to the table, sits down.

Luke keeps his eyes on his game, scraping away in his head for the explanation, any explanation for what the fuck is going on. The first thing she does in the morning is check her phone. He's seen her coming out of her room scrolling through her feeds before her eyelids are even really open. But he stole her phone back from Rob, and it's been down the back of his desk since midnight. She hasn't had it since at least five o'clock yesterday, and she's not even bothered.

There's only one explanation. She knows Rob's got it. He was supposed to have it.

'All right, Luke,' Geraint says with a laugh, coming in. 'Tough level?'

'What?' Luke says, emerging from his churning thoughts, and Geraint gestures to the game he's pretending to play. 'Oh, yeah. Yeah.'

Paige glances over, gives him a smile. There's a beep and she puts the spoon down and digs in the pocket of her blazer. And as if nothing's wrong, as if it's completely normal, she brings out a phone. A different one, recognisably expensive.

'That new?' Luke says.

She shrugs. 'Yeah.'

'Been saving up?' He bores into her with his eyes and she meets them. She knows what he's saying, what he really means, and without saying it she's begging him to leave it.

But he's not going to leave it.

'What's that worth then. Five hundred quid?'

Fat Jake looks up, his stupid forehead rising. Paige gives him a look like *yes?* and he makes a face like someone's shat in his mouth. He gets up with his bowl, slamming his chair into the wall as he goes.

'Bitch,' he says.

Paige doesn't even flinch. She keeps looking at Luke.

'What happened to the old one?' She doesn't know it's hidden in his room. 'Just, what? Threw it away?'

The one she's holding beeps again with a message. She reads it and slowly, slowly, her face falls. 'Shit,' she says, almost to herself.

Then she gets up, does it so fast she knocks the table and hot chocolate sloshes out of Luke's mug. The phone's against her ear as she leaves the room, ignoring Geraint telling her to clear her breakfast.

Luke goes out too, but her door closes before he's halfway up the stairs. He hovers on the landing, leans against the wall. Through her door he can hear her hissing half a conversation.

'What the fuck do you mean, Rob? You *had* it! It was in your bag!

'Where is it? Well, who?'

Then, muffled, her hand over her mouth maybe, 'You are fucking kidding me.'

Clearer, smaller: 'Oh, no. No. You promised me this wouldn't happen.'

There's movement then – she's coming out. Luke slips down the stairs, gets to the front door as her bedroom door opens.

She calls his name but he doesn't stop. He pulls on his trainers, puts his bag on his back. He goes to open the front door but then she's there, her hand on his shoulder.

'Luke,' she whispers, panic on her face.

'What.' He knows he shouldn't be angry but it's all so messed up now.

Because what he's got in his room is *her* phone. *She* took those pictures. And yeah, she was asked to do it, told to do it, and the messages sent to her were fucking disgusting, but she'd replied, hadn't she? So did she want it?

'Come on,' she says, her eyes watery. 'I need it back.'

He straightens up. It's cruel, but he makes himself smile at her. 'Need what back, Paige?'

She wraps her arms around herself. 'Stop it, Luke. Just give it back. Please.'

'I don't know what you're talking about,' he says. And he opens the front door and leaves.

He's never been much of a runner but he walks fast the whole way, and by the time he gets to school his lungs are burning and the sweat is trickling down his spine. He's the first one there for Tutorial, but he stares out the window the whole time.

And then he goes to English, and that's when it all goes tits up.

Cameron's in his class, always chucking stuff at him and giving him gyp. It's been way worse since Fat Jake got smacked because Cameron's lost his only mate, and so all that anger, all that *stupid*, has got to go somewhere else. And today, that somewhere happens to be Luke.

Cameron comes in just before the bell, and he slings his bag down hard next to Luke, deliberately catching him on the side of the head with it. He gets a chair and turns it round the wrong way and sits down, legs wide open like his balls are as big as his brain is small.

'You missed all the fun this morning,' Cameron says, all singsong.

Luke ignores him.

'Must have done something *preeetty* bad to your batshit little girlfriend.'

Luke unpacks, placing his pencil case on the table with his forefingers and thumbs, lining it up.

'Don't know what it is you've got of hers in your room but she is not fucking happy. Took two of them to stop her trying to smash your door in, mate.'

Exercise book next to the pencil case. Straight and neat.

Cameron leans in. 'What is it you've got up there that she wants back so bad, Lukey-loo? You sneak a pair of panties out of her dirty washing?'

Textbook. Highlighters.

'Or did you forget to give her dildo back? Yeah,' he says, face brightening, leaning back with his hands behind his head. 'That'd be it. Bitch like that's gonna have a great big one too! Oh! Oh!' he goes on, high-pitched, miming it with his empty fist at his crotch.

And then it happens. It's not like Luke makes a decision. It just happens.

Luke's on his feet. He kicks out the back legs of Cameron's chair and he does it so hard and fast that the whole thing pitches forward with Cameron in it. His face hits the edge of the desk and he screams as he smacks into the floor. But he gets straight up, and there's a scraping of chairs behind Luke and all around, everyone standing up, getting out of the way, and someone shouts, 'Fight!' and then it's a chant, all around him. *Fight! Fight! Fight!*

But it isn't a fight. It's Cameron, twice Luke's size and with his eyes on fire and hate snarling up in his face, launching a fist into Luke's head, just once.

And then it goes black.

34

Now

Wren is nearly home when she pulls over to take an incoming call. It's from the uniform who'd made her the tea in Ashworth's flat, asking her to come to the station later than planned.

'We're on skeleton staff as it is because of the Rovers game,' she explains, sounding exhausted. 'And we've got to prioritise tracking Ashworth down.'

'OK,' Wren says, relieved. She's on the edge of the dual carriageway heading towards St Philips, and the little Corsa rocks from side to side as an artic passes. 'Guess this means you haven't found him.'

'Nope. I've got someone here going through your notes – but you said there's nowhere you can think of that he might have gone? No family?'

'Have a look at his visitor records. There's no one.'

A heavy sigh comes down the line. 'Fine.' She signs off, telling her she'll be in touch about the formal statement within a few hours. 'But if you think of anything, or anyone who he might have gone to…'

'Sure, yeah, I'll call,' Wren finishes. But as she hangs up, she realises two things. Firstly, that the phone she had been planning to hand in on her visit to the Bridewell is still in her glovebox.

And secondly, that maybe there *is* someone, after all.

Carefully, the thought still taking shape in her head, she flicks the indicator and moves into the traffic. Then she circles the first roundabout she comes to, and turns back the way she came. Heading west, towards where Leah Amberley works.

For just a moment she considers calling back, letting the police deal with it. But she's seen how these things work. It'll be out of her hands and there'll be nothing she can do to soften the blow, the ramifications.

On the way she tunes in to the local radio, waiting to hear if Ashworth's made the news, but it's all nineties hits and traffic updates so after a while she turns it off.

She pulls up outside the nursery and checks her face before she gets out. Everyone keeps telling her she should sleep as much as she can before the baby arrives, like sleep is something you can stockpile. But when she thinks about it now, pulling the puffy skin around her eyes taut and then releasing it, she's been averaging about five hours a night, and it shows. Wren sighs, flaps the visor closed, and gets out.

A tiny woman with a brisk manner buzzes her in and when Wren asks for Leah, she rolls her eyes and instructs her to wait in the corridor. From there, Wren can see into the main room through the strip of glass in the internal door. Two dozen toddlers are sitting in a haphazard circle, raptly watching an expressive, chubby twenty-something read from an oversized board book. Leah is at the back of the room, washing paint from little white dishes. The tiny woman who answered the door goes over to her, looking annoyed and gesturing back towards Wren, who steps away from the window.

Leah comes out wiping her hands on her apron. 'What now?' she asks when the door closes behind her. 'Because I've already told him I'm done with it.'

'Listen, I—' Wren starts, but then she catches up. 'Told who?'

'Rob, obviously. Couldn't get rid of him, was only about half an hour ago. I'm going to get docked if I miss any more of the shift.'

'Rob came *here*?'

'He was in a right state. Wanted somewhere to stay. He had to leave his flat or something, right?' Leah tips her head. 'Didn't you know?'

She resists laughing at this. 'No, I knew. So what, he wanted to crash at yours?'

'Yeah.'

'And you said…?'

Leah gives her a hard stare, but after a few seconds the wind goes out of her sails and she looks away. 'I just want to get on with my life, all right? I don't want any more drama.'

There's a vulnerability to her that she hasn't seen before, and Wren knows her instinct to come alone, giving Leah a chance before it defaults to the hard option, was right.

'He's absconded,' Wren says gently.

'What?' Leah says, eyes going wide. 'Why?'

It takes about a second to weigh up telling her about the clothes. 'We're not sure,' she lies, 'but I need to find him. The longer he's gone, the worse it gets for him.'

'Yeah, well, we'd already kind of parted ways, to be honest.'

'How do you mean?'

A rap on the glass makes them both turn. The small woman is scowling at Leah, tapping her watch. Leah makes a pleading gesture and holds up a finger. She turns to Wren, but Wren speaks first.

'Please, this is the last time you'll see me, Leah, then I'm out of your hair. Tell me what happened.' Then, sincerely: 'I don't want to cause you any trouble, and I know you don't trust me. But Rob's disappeared, and that means sooner or later the police are going to be here asking you questions. And they're going to be a lot less understanding about you holding back.'

The younger woman wraps her arms around herself. 'Fine. He came round, wanted me to help him with something. Few days ago. I said no, I didn't want to. I thought I could trust him, you know? But then he was so wound up about this thing and I was… I started being scared of him. I asked him to leave and he wouldn't. He kept saying how I must know where Luke is but I *don't*.' Tears in her eyes. 'I'd do anything to know what happened to Paige, or to see Luke again. He was my mate too, you know? But Rob kept hassling me, and then he wanted me to do this – thing – for him.'

They're running out of time. 'What kind of thing?' Wren braces herself, knowing what's coming, almost deciding then and there to tell her she already knows about the clothes so it's easier for her to come out with it.

'He wanted me to make a phone call.'

This isn't what Wren was expecting. 'What?'

She speaks urgently now. 'He'd tracked his mum down; there was this mental hospital she was in. He'd gone there but they wouldn't let him see her, said it was against patient confidentiality. So he wanted me to call and pretend to be a doctor or something, to find out how she is.'

'And you said no.'

She pauses, looks away. 'It took a long time to get away from trouble. I'm just putting myself first.'

Wren wants to hug her. 'I think that's a very admirable thing to do.'

Leah just shrugs. 'Yeah, well. Tell him that. We fell out big time, him saying I never cared about him or his family and what a selfish fucking… Anyway. I thought that would be the end of it, right? But then today, he turns up at work and he's saying how sorry he is, how I'm the only one he's got, and can he come and stay with me.' She shakes her head and laughs bitterly. 'Didn't think to mention he was on the run, mind.'

'You did the right thing,' Wren says, no doubt in her mind that she's being told the truth.

Straightening up, Leah says, 'You said this would be the last time, right? Then I've got nothing more to do with it.' It's more of a demand than a question.

Wren nods. 'None of this is on you. You deserve your fresh start.'

Leah gives a nod, and her decision is made. 'It's called Meadowside. The hospital he wanted me to call. Up towards Yate.' The betrayal flushes red across her face. 'If he's got nothing to lose, that's where he'll have gone.'

35

Before

He comes round in the school nurse's office. The striplight's burning into his eyes so bright he almost shouts out in pain.

He says about a hundred times that he's fine, but Mr Yardley, who heard about what happened, isn't having it. They go to Southmead A&E, driving in silence, Luke with his eyes shut the whole way. It takes ages to get seen, and then the doctor pokes him about for what seems like forever, uses some long word for what's happened in his neck and jaw but says he got off lightly. She gives him painkillers, and a note for Yardley to give to Beech View saying Luke has to go for a check-up in two days.

They emerge into bright sunshine blazing white on rain-wet tarmac. Yardley's ride, an Audi A6, is parked right over the other side. Every step jars, twisting the ache in Luke's head until he feels like it's going to snap.

Yardley spots him wincing. 'Take it slowly,' he says.

'I'm all right.'

Yardley rolls his eyes at him, kindly though. When they get to the car, he starts to help him into the passenger side. But before Luke's strapped in, there's the sound of brakes slamming on, another car right behind them, and Yardley looks up. The look on his face goes from surprise to confusion before it settles into just pure pissed off. Luke shifts round, the movement discharging a vicious bolt of pain in his skull. As his vision clears, he sees Yardley marching over to the other car, and leaning in through the window.

'He's fine,' Yardley's saying. Shouting it, good as.

It hurts to even put his feet down but Luke makes himself get out again. He goes down the space between the Audi and the next car, trying to work out what's going on. Yardley's got his hands on the driver's side window frame, holding it so whoever's inside can't get out.

'No,' Yardley's saying. 'I'll take him. He's seen the doctor, she says he's all right, you don't need to be here.'

'*I* don't? You shouldn't even have *brought* him here,' comes the voice from the car. Fury cracking at the edge of it. 'We're the ones *in loco parentis.* I don't care what... what you think you've got over us. You can't just do whatever you like.'

'Can't I?'

There's a pause. Luke stays still. Yardley takes his hands off the door and straightens up. It's Oliver Polzeath he's talking to. Red in the face, staring at Yardley with murder in his eyes.

Yardley folds his arms. 'I think I can, Oliver. I think I can take care of the kids. Better than you, when everything's considered.' He turns his head, and Luke knows he's seen him. Polzeath sees him too, and his shoulders give.

'Luke, buddy, are you OK?' Polzeath says, and Luke knows that he's never, ever going to hate anyone as much as he hates this man.

'Buddy?' Yardley mimics. He slaps the top of Polzeath's car and turns away. 'You head off now, Oliver. I'll drop him home.' Then to Luke, he says, 'In you go, then. *Buddy.*'

They get back in the car. When Yardley closes the driver's door, the engine behind them revs hard and Polzeath screeches off. Yardley watches in his rear-view.

'*Not* my favourite guy,' he says simply, putting the car into reverse.

Luke stares ahead. The same sentence running on a loop. *I don't care what you think you've got over us.*

They drive back towards the school. They hit some traffic and Yardley takes a hand off the wheel to flip open the glovebox. He gets out another one of the instant icepacks the school nurse gave Luke, wraps it in a soft leather cloth, and hands it to him.

'So,' Yardley says, eyes front, and Luke sighs, thinking he knows what's coming. *Want to tell me what all that was about, Lukey.* But Yardley says, 'There's a boxing club I know of.'

Luke glances at him.

'Just seems to me that a little shit like Cameron shouldn't really be able to land a punch like that on you without you getting something in first,' Yardley says.

Luke laughs painfully. 'Yeah, all right.'

They drive in silence for a while, until Yardley gestures to the radio. 'Find us some tunes.'

So Luke does. One of the stations is playing some old Kano, radio edit but it'll do. Yardley turns it up and lowers the windows. The wind blows through Luke's hair.

And even with the pain in his face that's radiating right back to his spine and all down his shoulder, even knowing he looks a proper fucking mess, he lets his arm drop out the window, and he feels *cool.*

His head is throbbing angrily and he realises he hasn't had anything to drink, so he leans forward to get the water bottle out of the schoolbag that Yardley had brought along to the hospital. When he puts the bottle back, he clips the catch on the glovebox, which drops open and releases a phone onto the floor. 'Oops, that's my spare,' Yardley says, lunging over and making a grab for it before it slides under Luke's seat. 'Need to get it fixed. Battery's been playing up.' He tosses it back into the glovebox and snaps it shut.

But Luke's plunged back into thinking about Paige's one.

What the hell he's supposed to do with it. Who he should tell.

They're taking a route he doesn't know. Luke can't piece it together until suddenly they emerge next to a big park he used to go to with his mum. Yardley pulls up outside a café hut and gets out.

He comes back with a couple of paper cups and a Kit Kat each. 'Not every day you get a free pass out of school,' he says, handing a cup and one of the bars to Luke. 'Might as well make the most of it.' He puts his own in a cup holder and Luke opens his lid. Coffee, black. Not hot chocolate like you'd get for a kid. It's bitter, he wants sugar and milk in it, but he doesn't ask. He just drinks it.

Yardley turns the radio right down. But he doesn't say anything.

Luke finishes the chocolate. 'He started it,' he says.

'OK.' Yardley dips a Kit Kat finger into his coffee and bites it. 'Like I said. Boy's a little shit.'

Something in Luke flexes. 'Probably does his best.'

'You're sticking up for him? After he knocked you out?'

Luke shrugs, winces again. 'It's not easy, being…'

'Being what? In care?'

'Yeah.'

'It's brutal. I remember. You end up feeling like the people looking after you are just there because they're paid. And some of them are. But it doesn't mean it's always going to be—'

'If I tell you something,' Luke says, interrupting, 'will you have to dob me in?' He sniffs hard.

'You can tell me whatever you want.'

'But will you tell anyone? I need to know.'

Yardley looks him right in the eyes. 'No,' he says. 'I know how hard it can be to trust people, Luke, but you can trust me.'

Luke lets his shoulders drop. He believes him. He takes a deep breath, and he tells him everything. All of it. Polzeath;

the bite mark; the late nights out unchecked, unmonitored; the money she's obviously got. And the pregnancy, and the pregnancy before. And then the photos, pictures that are just – they're just not her, and that wanker Polzeath is getting her to take them and send them. And how does she know what he's doing with them? Is he sharing them with his filthy fucking mates? Is he selling them? Is he selling *her*?

Yardley doesn't rush him or interrupt. He just listens and nods, and as Luke's speaking, the thing happens that he had hoped would happen when he told Mel. The load gets lighter, even when he gets to part that's almost worse than any of it: Rob knowing. Rob knowing about all of it, but doing nothing. Telling *him* to do nothing.

'Rob, your brother?'

'Yeah. And what I want to know is—'

'Where's this phone now, Luke? Have you got it?'

'No. It's at home.'

'And your brother had it.'

'Yeah.'

'And Paige was OK that he had it.' Yardley's eyes are shut. He's piecing it together, or trying to. Luke knows exactly how it feels.

'How do you know it wasn't him, then?'

'What?'

'How do you know it wasn't your brother sending those texts?'

Luke shakes his head. 'Wasn't his number.'

'He could have used a different one.'

'I don't think so.' Not because Rob wouldn't – he doesn't even know what Rob would and wouldn't do any more – but because Leah would have known, and he can trust Leah.

Can he trust Leah?

Yardley is nodding slowly, staring straight out of the window, fingers lightly on the wheel.

Abruptly, Yardley reaches for his seatbelt and tells Luke to do the same. And then they drive.

'Where are we going?' Luke asks, holding on to the handle above the window. He glances at the speedo. Residential streets, but they're doing forty-five.

'We're going to sort this shit out.'

'No, look, I just wanted to talk about it…' Luke's flung against the window as Yardley corners hard.

'Sorry, Luke. I can't stand by and let this happen.'

'But you *said*.'

'Things change.'

Luke works out where they're going pretty quickly. Out to Muller Road and over. They're going to Beech View.

'Please,' Luke says. 'Please, Mr Yardley.'

But he's not listening.

Minutes later they arrive. Yardley doesn't park outside. He slows, goes past the house, then pulls into the next side street.

The engine goes silent. He turns to Luke. 'Listen. Here's what we're going to do. You go and get that phone. Don't do anything to it, don't tell anyone, don't show anyone you've got it. Just come straight out again. And then we're going to work out what's going on. You and me. All right?'

Luke stares at his knees. 'I want that fucker in prison,' he says.

Yardley nods. 'I'm not surprised.' He puts his hand on Luke's shoulder. 'You did the right thing, telling me. All right? We're going to fix this. For Paige.'

Luke nods. He's not sure. Then he takes his chance, because something tells him it's now or never. 'Mr Yardley, what did Polzeath mean, about you having something over him?'

Yardley meets his eye. For a moment, Luke thinks he's going to tell him. But then Yardley leans across him, opens the door. 'I'll explain, all right? But later. Come on, Luke. Go and get it.'

As quietly as he can, he goes in the house and creeps up the stairs. The piece of paper's still balanced on his door and the phone is where he left it. He wakes the screen – there's a single bar of battery left.

He takes it back downstairs and out to the car. Carefully, because there's no protective case or anything on it, Luke takes the phone with the unicorn sticker out of his pocket, and passes it to Yardley through the window. Then he goes to open the door, to get back in.

But it's locked.

'I'll take it from here,' Yardley says, and before Luke can argue, the window is rolling back up. And Luke, gaping in confusion, has to jump backwards to get his feet out of the way of the wheels.

The car streaks up to the crossroads, pauses, turns. Its fancy indicator ticking on and off, a line of yellow lights made to look like a moving line.

Luke tilts his head. He's seen that before. And then—

Then he remembers. That time, weeks ago, when he watched Paige leave.

He's got this all wrong.

The world dips. He's thinking about the conversation he had with Paige about Polzeath. Except he never said his name.

She never said his name.

She could have been talking about anybody.

Luke goes back inside, up to his room, and closes the door. And he recalls each of the eleven digits of the phone number of the person who had been texting Paige.

He writes them down. And then he calls it.

He puts his phone next to his ear as it connects, thinking about that car with its sweeping indicator, his heart finding its pace now, thumping low and slow.

It goes straight to answerphone, and Luke knows why. *Battery's been playing up*, wasn't that what he said?

It's Yardley. It was Yardley all along.

36

Now

Suzy Wood pulls up outside the house and turns off the music. She undoes her seatbelt and presses the palm of her hand to the side of her belly, where a hard limb has been jabbing her from the inside for the last ten minutes.

'Would you mind just, down a bit… Thank you,' she whispers, manipulating the foot or elbow back into its rightful place. The miracles of conception and gestation she can rationalise, but sharing her body with another person is still incomprehensibly freaky.

Several minutes of hauling and groaning later, Suzy is at the front door, her hastily repacked suitcase at her feet. A surge of hope as she steps inside. Her mum, who she stayed with last night, had been right, as always. *This isn't the hill to die on*, she'd said.

Suzy puts the case down, lets her shoulder bag drop to the floor, and closes the door. And she just stands there for a moment, feeling their home greet her. She breathes deep through her nose, filling up with the familiar alchemy of dog and residual baking and just… them.

Her and Wren.

The thing people say more than anything else is how tough the two of them are. It has become a bit of a joke between them. People can't see past their jobs, the stereotypes, whatever, but the truth is, what they have is strong and warm and loving. Maybe they *are* tough, but they are tough like a tree, or a bridge. She'd just needed a day outside it, on her own, to see that. But a day was long enough.

They are going to be great mothers. It is going to be worth the work.

Radclyffe comes trotting up, claws clacking on the hardwood. Although she wants to just drop to her knees and hug him, she heads out to the conservatory at the back. She sits down on the cushioned wicker sofa and pats her legs.

'Come on then, sweetheart.' He jumps up and licks her face, and she jerks her head back, loving his simple affection. Then the baby shifts and kicks out suddenly, and Radclyffe jumps back, surprised, and barks at it.

Suzy laughs aloud. She rests her head on the back of the sofa, and closes her eyes, rubbing the dog on the bumpy crown of his skull.

A noise in the kitchen. Breaking glass.

Radclyffe instantly gets up and starts barking.

In one movement she stands, faster than she's got to her feet in months. The training kicks in instantly; it doesn't give a fuck that she's spent the last twelve weeks on desk duty. Assess exit, assess weapons. On the coffee table there's a fat remote, an empty pint glass, and a foot-long, boat-shaped clay dish full of batteries and pens and change. She grabs the dish, jettisons the crap, goes to the door. Radclyffe runs out ahead of her.

'Police officer!' she shouts, holding the dish in front of her with one hand, using the other to swing the door open. There's a squeak, a series of light thuds. She knows without any doubt it's footwear, it's trainers on her kitchen floor.

Someone is in her house.

Her phone is in her bag, all the way through the house at the front.

Two options: try to get to the door before he sees her, or stay and defend. Can she get to the landline? Bottom of the stairs?

Not without passing the kitchen door. But she glances over at it, thinking does she have time to—

No. She doesn't. Because emerging from the kitchen into the hall is a man, his nose and mouth obscured by a bandana. The dog runs at him, then bottles it and runs back to her, barking all the time, his eyes wide with terror.

Her two options reduce to one.

'Police!' she shouts again.

He freezes. 'I'm sorry,' he says. In his hand, he's got a crowbar. In her house, with her and her unborn baby, there is a fucking stranger carrying a weapon.

'I'm sorry – I thought—' he says, then, 'I didn't think—'

But Sergeant Suzy Jean Wood doesn't hear any of it. She sees red. She wraps her free hand around her belly and lifts the dish, ready to swing.

And before she runs at him, she looks him in the eyes, and she roars.

37

Now

The Meadowside psychiatric inpatient unit is a nondescript two-storey affair sitting in an appropriately depressed-looking border of garden and hedges, and Wren can see something is wrong before she's even parked. Several members of uniformed staff – too many – are standing outside the main entrance, facing the short driveway as if expecting someone. As Wren pulls her jacket closed against the cold and heads over, a black-clad female security guard, vaguely familiar, breaks away from the group and approaches her.

'No visitors I'm afraid,' the woman says, before frowning slightly. 'Do I know you?'

Wren stops halfway up the steps. She struggles for a few moments to place her, then a lightbulb goes on. 'You go out with Cara, right? She's my partner's ex. Suzy Wood, you know her? The cop?'

'Shit, right,' she says, satisfied. 'Small world. But Cara's my ex now too, *Jesus*.' She rolls her eyes, grinning lopsidedly. 'Your girl made a lucky escape. But look,' she says, squinting back towards the building, 'your visit's going to have to wait I'm afraid. We're in lockdown.'

'*Lockdown?* Why?'

The woman pauses to regard her. 'You police too?'

'Probation. I've come to check on a… someone I'm working with.'

The guard nods, then drops her voice to a conspiratorial low whisper. 'Guy came in demanding to see a patient, no ID or appointment. Staff tried to deal with him but he just lost it. Went round opening doors, trying to find this person – I was on my break, never run so fast in my life.'

'Where is he now?' Wren asks, her heart galloping. What she doesn't ask is, *who is he*.

'Waiting inside.'

'For what?'

'The police. Should be here any minute. We put him in one of the secure rooms. Not locked or anything,' she adds quickly. 'In all honesty he's not a threat, we could probably just sit him in reception. Feel a bit sorry for him really – he said he really wanted a cigarette, so I snuck him one of mine. After all that, turns out the patient's not even here. Hasn't been for a couple of years. Fight totally went out of him when he found out. It was him who asked us to call the police – though we had already, obviously. He wanted us to tell them he was co-operating.' She checks her watch, then puts her hands on her hips. 'Who was it you wanted to see?'

'Actually, I think it's him. Robert Ashworth, right? He's my offender.'

The guard's eyes go wide, and she leans back on her heels. '*Oh*.'

It takes Wren a lot of charm and a bit of wheedling, but it isn't long before she's convinced her to take her to him. She knows she's got minutes, if that, before the cavalry arrive.

When the guard pushes the door to the secure room open, Wren's first thought is that he's done another runner. But then she sees him. He's crouched in the corner, almost behind the door. His head turned away from her, face in his hands.

'I'll leave it open,' the guard says softly as she leaves.

The room is thick with the smell of the illicit cigarette. 'Rob,' Wren says, then again, more firmly, '*Rob*.'

He looks up at her. His eyelashes are peaked into wet clumps, and as he meets her eye, he lets out a sob.

'Fuck,' he says.

'What are you doing here, Rob?'

This is a man brought as low as he's going to get, but even though she's itching to dig out a tissue for him, show him that there's still compassion in the world, she's not going to. Front and centre in her head is that wretched, sodden bag. Those clothes.

'I wanted to find my mum. I told you that's what I wanted to do, and you wouldn't *help* me, you wouldn't…' he breaks off, screwing his face up like he's got to shut himself up tight. 'All of this, all this stupid shit I've had to do, it – well it doesn't matter now, does it?'

Right on cue, there's a siren. Rob jumps to his feet. He takes a step towards her and for a second she thinks he's going to hit her.

But he doesn't. He says, 'I'm going to do whatever they say, all right? But you've got to tell them. I don't know why you did it, and I know you think I'm this fucking monster, but you've got to change your mind, all right?'

She glares at him. 'About what? What is it *I've* done?'

'I was doing everything you said. Wasn't I? I was doing all the visits, I was doing the interviews, keeping my head down. I've done my time, right?' The siren gets louder. 'Why are you setting me up?'

'Setting you up?' She laughs bitterly. 'No, Rob. That bag, those clothes, were in *your* flat.'

'You're the only person who knows where I live!' he shouts.

From just beyond the door the guard says, 'You need help in there?'

'We're fine,' Wren says, feeling anything but. She turns back to Ashworth, incredulous. 'Someone *saw you digging.*'

'No, Wren, look—' His eyes are filling with tears again.

'No, *you* look. Did you think you'd get away with it? Just because she was in care? You deserve everything you're about to get. And I hope you fucking rot.'

'*Listen to me.*' The meniscus breaks and Ashworth is crying. 'I made some mistakes, OK? I really did. I let my brother get into some serious trouble, and I let my mum down, and I got Paige wrapped up in something fucking lethal when I should have just walked away. I know that. I'm a bad person, all right, I get it. But I'm not—' He stops, his breath ragged. 'I'm not a fucking *killer*.'

'Who did it then? Huh?' Half of Wren is still furious with him. The other half is weighing this up. Because this doesn't sound like the Rob Ashworth she knows.

'I don't know. I thought… I thought if I could find Luke, and find my mum, I could find Paige too and it would all – it would all be OK.' He glances towards the window and a flash of blue light hits his face. They're here. 'You've got to believe me.'

She doesn't know what to say. There's a commotion outside and then male voices, heavy footfalls.

Robert Ashworth lets his eyes close for just a moment and then he releases a long breath, stands tall, and faces the door. Hands empty and by his sides, ready. This is his last moment of liberty, certainly for some time, possibly for decades.

But just before it happens, he turns to her. This time, when he speaks, it's in a voice belonging to someone much younger, and so quiet that she can hardly hear him.

'Is Paige dead, then?' he says. 'Is that what this means?'

38

Before

Luke sits motionless on his bed, a blackness sweeping up inside him. The phone is gone.

So what now? Without it, he's got nothing at all. No one's going to believe him, not if it's his word against Yardley's, not without proof. And the proof just sped off on five-hundred-quid tyres. If Yardley's got half as much sense as Luke thinks he has, that phone's going to be corroding on the bottom of the Avon by teatime.

He gets up, and aims a kick as hard as he can at the wall. Then he gets his coat and goes back outside.

He doesn't know where he's going, or what he's going to do. It's four o'clock in the afternoon. School's over. Paige will be on her way back now. Just as he's wondering which way she'll come from, whether he should try to intercept her, a car passes him, then screeches to a stop, reverses until it's level with him.

It's Rob.

And in the passenger seat, her face blotched white and red and her eyes so swollen with tears she looks like she's been punched, is Paige.

The door behind Paige clunks open. Rob doesn't even look at him. 'Where's the phone?'

'I haven't got it.'

Paige turns to Rob; she lets out this sob and says, 'He has! He did, this morning, I know he did.' Then she turns back to him. 'Please, Luke. Just give it back.'

Luke can't even look at her. 'I told you I haven't got it.'

'Then who has?' Rob barks.

Luke says the name so quietly he can hardly hear it. His brother turns his eyes on him and Luke manages about half a second before he has to look away. He tries Paige, but the horror on her face is even worse.

'Oh, Lukey,' she says, crumpling. 'Oh, no.'

'Right. Get in the fucking car,' Rob says, hardly moving his lips, his knuckles tight on the wheel. 'Now.'

They drive, lefting and righting until Luke's pretty sure that Rob doesn't know where he's going, hasn't got a plan. The car – one he's either stolen or borrowed from the garage, Luke guesses, because he sure as hell wouldn't have *bought* a Volvo estate – has that sickening smell of plain-can air-freshener over cigarettes.

No one says anything. When they stop, it's in the car park of the Maccy D's they went to just a few weeks ago, before any of this happened. Back when Luke was a little kid, and his brother was someone good that he could rely on.

Now the engine's off, all he can hear is Paige crying, softly, like she doesn't know how to stop. He reaches forward and touches her shoulder but she shrugs him off.

Rob undoes his seatbelt and he turns all the way around. 'You want to tell me what the fuck you think you're doing?'

There isn't an answer to that, so he continues.

'Because I had a plan, little brother. And we need to get that phone back, right fucking now. All right?'

'Just leave it!' Paige says, covering her face with her hands. 'It's over, all right?'

Rob turns to her, fury igniting. 'It's not over! That money, Paige, is going to change everything.'

Luke looks up. 'What money?'

Paige lets out a little moan.

'What money, Rob?' he asks again, louder.

And then Luke gets it. He lets his head sink back against the rest. 'You were going to blackmail him.'

There's a jolt, and the engine roars into life.

'What are you doing?' Luke asks, but he needn't have bothered. Rob stands on the revs, pushes down the handbrake, and Luke's forced back again.

'Stop! Stop it!' Luke screams. Then the squeal of brakes, and he's flying forward, smashing his nose on the back of Paige's seat. The car stops, but Rob's pumping his foot and making the engine pulse.

'I did all of this for you. You understand that?'

'How is *that* for *me*? Getting yourself fucking locked up? Huh?'

Rob slams his palms against the wheel. 'I had a *way out.* For you, and for Mum.'

Paige turns to him. 'And me,' she says quietly.

'Fuck's sake, for all of us!'

Luke says nothing. He tastes blood, and his nose gives when he touches it. His whole face shrieks with fresh pain.

'We're going to get it back,' Rob tells him. A thick vein is snaking in his forehead, and Luke doesn't see his brother now. He sees their dad, the face on him the day he left, pissed out of his head, terrifying everyone around him. Take away the drinking, and it's basically Rob now.

And that's what makes up Luke's mind. He leans forward again towards Paige, doesn't care if she rejects him, because this is the end of the road. He's got fuck all to lose.

'I'm not having anything to do with this. You don't have to either, Paige,' he says, putting his hand on her shoulder. 'It's not too late. You can walk away.'

In the mirror ahead of her, Luke meets her eye. She blinks

once, presses her lips into the weakest of smiles. Then she twists and reaches her arm behind her seat, and for a minute he thinks she's going to touch him, hold his hand, squeeze his leg, something.

But she doesn't.

She opens his door. 'You should go.'

39

Now

Suzy's car is already there when Wren arrives, her parking immaculate, wheels a perfect three inches from the kerb. Wren checks her face in the mirror, flips open the glovebox for powder, and sorts the shine on her nose and cheeks. She smooths her hair, knowing how silly it is. Four years in, definitely too late for first impressions. But still.

She pauses in the front garden before she goes in, noticing the space, the variety of colour there, even at this time of the year. There is a corner where they can make a mud kitchen when the baby is a toddler; Marty's girls spent hours in theirs when they were small, making potions and dinners. She'd like that for their child.

Smiling as she digs in her bag for her key, she goes to the door. But as she lifts her head, key in hand, her mood drops.

The front door is open.

The door drags on something as she pushes it wide. Suzy's handbag is next to her suitcase on the wooden floor, caught under the door, its contents scattered. Radclyffe, obscuring something larger behind him at the foot of the stairs, lifts his big head and whines, but he doesn't come to her. And then, behind him, she sees the leg.

Suzy's leg.

Something brittle cracks underfoot as she runs to her. She

pushes Radclyffe out of the way and drops to her knees. Suzy is lying on her side, one arm caught underneath her, the other thrown out sideways. Her eyes are shut, but only just.

'Suzy. *Suzy*, can you hear me?'

Nothing. Wren leans across her, over the powerful bare arm that is now pallid. Careful not to move her she hovers a hand in front of her mouth, praying.

Breathe.

Please, Suzy. Please breathe.

She gets up, races to her bag, then she's back beside Suzy with her phone wedged between her ear and her shoulder, each pulse of the ring in her ear taking a lifetime.

'Ambulance,' she says when it is answered. She gives her address, Suzy's name. 'I think she's fallen down the stairs. She's pregnant, thirty-eight weeks. Our baby—'

'All right, we're already on our way, someone else has called this in as well. You just stay there with her. Is she breathing?'

'I don't – I don't know.' She puts her hand up to Suzy's mouth again. She waits. 'Oh God, oh God,' she whispers. 'I don't think she's breathing.'

'OK, you're doing fine,' the call handler tells her. 'If you've got something there like a glass or just the screen of your phone, pop that in front of her mouth and nose for me, can you do that?'

Wren does as she is told. She puts the phone right up to Suzy's mouth.

She waits. The call timer on the display ticks up the seconds. They are the longest, darkest, emptiest seconds of her life.

'Anything?' the tinny voice says from the speaker.

She tries to speak. All that comes out is a high, wavering note. A keening, the exact frequency of grief.

Please let her live.

Please let our baby live.

Please.

And then, faintly, the slightest bloom of condensation, there and then gone. Wren crumples back onto her heels, tears blistering in her eyes.

She's alive.

The crew arrive, two guys, and suddenly her house is full of noise and movement. And in the pause, where Wren can do nothing but watch, she replays in her mind what the call handler said.

Someone else has called this in.

The impossibility of that clatters over itself in her head. How? Who?

Then are more instructions, and Wren does as she is told, stepping back and giving them room to check Suzy. The older one applies an oxygen mask while the other jogs back to the van for a stretcher. They want to know if Suzy has any blood pressure problems, or pregnancy complications. Who is providing her care, the due date. And Wren finds that she knows all the answers.

She stands with her hands cupped around her mouth as they manoeuvre Suzy onto the stretcher, a wide one so they can lie her on her side to avoid compressing her spine. And as these strangers take control, she replays the thing that she compartmentalised for later – whatever it is that is broken on the floor. She glances around. It is the clay dish they bought in Peru. The largest piece, the size of a jagged palm, had been right next to Suzy's hand – she notices it just as its corner is caught by the heel of one of the ambulance crew's boots. It pings off towards the wall and spins to a stop. Careful not to get in their way, Wren goes over to it. She bends to touch it, but withdraws her hand.

Across one ragged edge, blood. And as she peers closer, something else, too: threads of hair. Not Suzy's.

She'd used it as a weapon.

In her mind, the teeth of it suddenly engage. Suzy's handbag, emptied on the floor.

She hadn't fallen down the stairs. This is a crime scene.

40

Before

It takes Luke an hour to find his way back to Beech View, and once he's there, he's a ghost. He sits at his window from dinnertime to nine, waiting, but she doesn't come back. There are no calls from Rob or from Paige.

When the house falls silent and the other kids are finally harassed into their beds, he sneaks down and sits in the dining room. Midnight comes. Geraint is on the waking night shift but Luke can hear him in the office watching American soaps. So he gets his coat, goes into the kitchen, turns the key in the rusty lock and shoves the back door open. He closes it behind him and crouches there in the blackness, listening to the not quite silence of the city at night, studded with shouts and sirens and the rise and fall of engines. Through the open window back into the kitchen he can hear the rhythmic beeping of the faulty freezer that's been trying to get someone's attention for weeks.

She should be back by now. Something's gone wrong.

There's a sweep of headlights up the narrow path beside the house, and a car pulls up, followed seconds later by another. Luke stands. If he goes back in he'll be seen and sent to his room. He stays where he is.

Car doors are opened and closed. Two low voices speak as the people approach the house. The front door opens, closes softly.

Even from where he is he can hear the stairs creak. He treads soundlessly round the front.

An Audi A6 and a Discovery. Yardley and Polzeath.

When he returns to the kitchen door, the light behind it is on. He slips past the door and crouches right under the kitchen window.

There's nothing for a minute. Then, through the open window, he hears a kettle click off, a cupboard door opening, closing. Then a voice.

'She's not here, James.'

It's a woman's voice. It's Alice Polzeath.

Yardley makes a low growl of frustration. 'Shit.'

'Where else can she be?' Mrs P says, sounding close to tears. 'We've got to find her before she talks to anyone else.'

'I know.'

'For Christ's sake! You promised me you'd stopped all this. You swore to me that this would *not* happen.' She sounds close to tears.

'We all make mistakes.' There's the rattle of a teaspoon, a long pause.

'This is more than a mistake,' Mrs P whispers at last. 'I should have reported you the moment I suspected you were behind those bitemarks Melanie saw.'

'Yeah, well. You got someone else on that committee, have you? Someone else blowing little clouds of money your way?'

Luke breathes out. She knew. She knew, and she did absolutely nothing.

'Here,' Yardley says. 'Take this.'

'What is it? A bracelet? Oh good God, James, the size of it, I can't take this!'

'It's a smokescreen. Police think that's what they broke in for. Too suspicious if we say they left without taking anything.'

'But I don't want it!'

'I'm not giving it to you, for fuck's sake, it's only for a few weeks. I can't have it on me right now.'

It sounds like Mrs P is crying. 'You ought to go.'

'Go where?' Yardley hisses. 'Hmm? The police already told Lucilla they're going to be all over Ashworth's place. We've got nowhere else to try.'

'I'll wait here for Paige. She'll have to come back for her things, even if she is planning to abscond. Oh, bloody hell,' she says then, muffled like she's hiding her face. 'I'm going to have to report her missing within an hour or so. What a mess. What a bloody awful mess.'

The kitchen light goes off. A few moments later he thinks he hears the front door open again. There's a hushed exchange Luke can't make out, and one of the cars starts up again and leaves. A few minutes later he hears Geraint and Mrs P talking inside, and more lights go on downstairs. They're up, waiting for Paige.

Luke gets his phone out to ring her, to warn her not to come back, but then he thinks about it.

He can't ring her, doesn't even know what number she's on, and Yardley said the police were at Rob's place, waiting for him, so he can't ring Rob either. What would he even say to him, if he could?

The cold is making his skin and the muscles beneath hard like he's growing a shell. He has to go inside. But just as he starts to stand, he hears a crunch of gravel. Someone's coming up the side path, very slowly, like they're sneaking up.

He darts left, ducking round the edge of the house, and peers around. The sound has stopped – did they hear him? He stays where he is.

Another footstep. And then out of the darkness, a small figure, eyes flashing like a fox.

It's Paige.

He steps out from behind the wall and she gasps, hand on

her chest, then softens. She opens her mouth to speak but he puts his finger to his lips, motions to her to move back. Then, keeping low, he creeps over.

'Go,' he says. He turns her back along the path, and she doesn't resist.

Just before he follows her out, he has a thought. If he's going out past curfew, he can't just walk back in through the front door. Staff think he's in bed, so he might get away with it, but he's going to need the key. So he eases the back door open just enough and reaches round for it, working it until it comes free. Then he follows Paige out into the night.

'They're waiting for you,' he hisses, catching her up at the front of the path where it meets the pavement. She quickens her pace. End of the road, cross, keep going. 'Said they were going to call the police when you got in.'

She bites her lip.

Luke says, 'What happened?'

She shakes her head, but he catches her sleeve. 'Tell me.'

'What do you think? We had to get it back,' she says. 'So we got it back.'

'Did they see you?'

She laughs like she can't help it, but her face isn't laughing. 'Yeah, you could say that.'

'Where's the phone now?'

'Rob's got it.'

'Right, but where's Rob?'

'I don't know. We got the phone and got outside but the police were coming and we split up. Yardley's wife called them, they had this panic thing on their CCTV—'

'They have CCTV?'

She presses her hands around her face. 'Yeah.' She's been talking mechanically, but now she blinks and looks away, like it's just sunk in. 'His wife was… she was really upset… I think – I think I might have hurt her.'

'What did you *do*, Paige?' he says, slowing. But she won't answer.

After a while they pass the garage where the guy sits behind the glass for night orders, and then there's a bus stop. They sit down. Luke checks his phone: if anyone notices him gone, he knows the first thing they'll do is ring him. But there's nothing, no missed calls, so he's safe for the time being.

'What now then?' Luke asks her.

She shrugs. The narrow bench is too high for her, and her feet dangle. She looks about eight years old. 'He said I should go back, pretend nothing's happened.'

Luke laughs out loud because he wants to cry.

'Don't,' she says. Then, quietly, 'He wants to go ahead with it. Use the photos, I mean. Make Yardley pay us.'

Luke turns to her. 'Listen.' He takes her hands, and she doesn't pull away. 'If you're telling me what I think you're telling me, Rob is going to go to prison.'

'What do you mean?'

'Rob's eighteen. Think about it. When it comes down to it, who's got possession of naked pictures of a kid?'

She looks incredulous. 'He has, but—'

'But what? It was only so he could use them to blackmail Yardley? I don't think that's going to sound great in court.'

She slumps like someone's just let the air out of her.

'Did you steal anything else?'

'No!'

'Did he?'

'No,' she says again, fast enough for him to be sure it's the truth.

'Good. But if you hurt someone, and they've got CCTV—'

'I know! All right? I fucking *know*.'

A bus rumbles past and whips up the wind and Luke shivers. Paige has only got that thin black jacket, her red-and-black shirt and jeans. The tiny silver star with the gemstones on it hangs on a chain round her neck, catching the light from the streetlamp and glowing like a tiny sun.

He looks away. 'You didn't need to lie to me, Paige. What you said, before.'

She doesn't even ask what he means. 'You want to know the truth? I've never had any sex that I've really wanted. Every single time, it's been because someone's talked me into it, or because I thought they'd – I don't know. Care about me. I told you I was a virgin still because I wanted it to be true.'

They just sit there for a moment. Then almost to herself, she says, 'Pathetic, really. I just wanted someone to love me.'

And Luke leans over and bumps the side of his head gently against hers. He looks her in the eyes, and smiles. He doesn't need to say it.

'Yeah, OK,' she says. 'But you know what I mean.'

He nods. 'It wasn't love though, with him. No one who loves you is going to want that from you.'

'But that's the thing. He didn't, to start with.' And she tells him how Yardley was good to her, never touched her, not for ages. And then slowly, he got affectionate, and she never told him not to. She never told Leah, or anyone, because he made her promise. Said all the gifts, all the good stuff, would have to stop if she did.

And then Rob saw them together in Yardley's car. Saw her kissing him. To start with, Rob said he was going to the police. But then he had a different idea.

'I should never have gone along with it. It was stupid.'

'He can sweep you up into things. That's what he's like.' Luke tips his head right back and looks at the stars. 'I thought it was Polzeath.'

'Yeah,' she says. 'I realised that, later.'

'I just wanted to stop it happening to you, Paige,' he says, his teeth chattering and his voice as brittle as ice.

'It's not like I was—' she says, stopping before she can say the word. 'No one forced me.'

'OK,' he says. But even he can see there are different kinds of forcing. 'Maybe no one pointed a gun at you. But why do you think he chose *you*?'

She shrugs, miserably. She wants him to say because she's beautiful, or because she's perfect. And she is. But it's not about that.

'Because you needed a way out. It comes off you like a stink, and don't—' he says, holding up a hand, 'don't take that personally. It comes off all of us. Because if you've got nothing, and someone says do this and I'll turn that nothing into something, that's pretty much the same thing as forcing you.'

She sniffs. 'That's quite a speech. For you.'

He shrugs.

And then, suddenly she sits up straight, turns to him, slowly. Her eyes have come alive, properly alive.

'Luke.' She puts both hands up to her mouth, but it's not horror in her eyes. It's something else. Something better.

'What?'

'I think I've got a way out.'

41

Now

Time stretches out like a universe expanding, and still no news comes. Reluctant to leave her spot beside the closed door, behind which Suzy and the baby are being measured and probed and monitored, Wren waits in the hospital corridor. She is unbearably redundant. A phone rings almost continuously, and men and women in colour-coded uniforms move around ceaselessly, not seeing her.

She buys chocolate from a machine a few paces away, but she can't eat it. She sits motionless for a time, elbows on her knees, staring at a spot between her feet on the tiled floor for so long that it starts to warp. Catastrophic worst-case scenarios advance in ranks through her mind.

They had lived, she and Suzy, before the prospect of a child. They had thrived and grown and loved and been happy as a complete unit of two. But there is no going back to that. If the baby doesn't make it, they will be minus one, defined by the absence of something that never even arrived, an impossible loss to overcome.

A pair of shoes stops in her field of vision and she looks up. A doctor, green-rimmed glasses jammed up high on her head atop an inch of afro. A sincere but practised smile.

'You're Suzy's partner?'

Wren makes to stand, but the doctor gestures her to stay where she is, and takes the seat next to her.

'She's stable, she's awake and lucid. We're going to move her shortly. And the baby, as far as we can tell, is doing OK.'

Wren presses a hand over her mouth. The doctor gives her shoulder a squeeze.

'Thank you,' Wren breathes.

'You are very welcome. There's some swelling though, which is impacting on the cervix. So we're going to recommend a C-section.'

'Yes. OK.'

'We're not in panic mode or anything, but I'm going to speak to the surgeon in a minute. It's looking like a few hours' time, assuming baby stays happy for now. It might not be what you both really planned for, but—'

Wren waves it away. 'Whatever we need to do, it doesn't matter.' She gets up. 'Can I see her?'

'Of course. Just don't tire her out, all right? She's got a long night ahead.'

The lights are low in the side room but Suzy is wide awake. She struggles against the pillows to sit up as soon as Wren steps inside.

'Did they get him yet?' she asks.

Wren kisses her forehead, then pulls up a chair and sits close, reaching for her hand. She looks oddly flushed, her neck and cheeks flaring patchily against a pallid background, as if her body can't decide what temperature it should be. Her knees are up, making a tent under the latticed hospital blanket, and her feet are already tapping alternately as if planning their escape.

'I haven't heard,' Wren says, placing what is meant to be a calming hand on a foot.

'He was local, from his voice, they know that, right?' Suzy

says. 'So weird though – he kept apologising…' She drifts off, frowning out of the window.

'He'll do more than apologise when I get hold of him,' Wren says, getting up to let in some air. At home, Suzy always insists on open windows at night, whatever the weather. But as the window reluctantly gives a few inches and the room freshens, Wren turns to see Suzy gathering the blanket higher, her forehead puckered with something that doesn't suit it, something new.

She is afraid.

Wren slides an arm behind her shoulders in an uncalibrated hug, but Suzy pulls back, meets her eyes.

'Did you sort it out? Whatever it was you were supposed to be sorting?'

Wren nods. Now isn't the time.

'Good,' Suzy says. She reaches for Wren's hand and squeezes. 'Because I need you here, properly here. Everything else we can just – just *forget*, for now. OK?'

Wren returns the pressure on her hand. 'OK.'

She thinks about the phone in her car, how she is going to go about getting it back to the station. Then there is a cursory knock, and the door opens.

The doctor strides over to collect the clipboard at the end of Suzy's bed. 'You girls ready to be mums?' she asks, making a note, replacing it. 'You're booked in for 7 a.m. We'll keep an eye on you and baby in the meantime, but I'd get some rest.' She gives them a thumbs-up, and then she is gone.

Suzy watches her leave, her face slack. 'Holy fuck,' she says at last. 'It's happening, then.'

Wren grins. 'You'll do brilliantly.'

Suzy tries to return the enthusiasm but there is an obvious effort to it. Her fingers move, seemingly unconsciously, to play at the butterfly stitches on her head.

Wren cranes to see the wound, and is instantly gripped

with fury. Suzy's injury is swollen but clean, the broken edges of skin already knitting together.

'What kind of arsehole hits a pregnant woman, though? In her own house?'

'He didn't hit me. I mean, he's still an arsehole, but I slipped. I ran at him, and he backed off, and then I hit the floor. Blacked out. But – I don't know. He didn't seem right, Wren. It all seemed so… off.'

'Like what?'

Suzy frowns. 'I've done hundreds of burglaries, you know? So many interviews and arrests. But this one, it was like he didn't want to be there.'

'Bit early for Stockholm syndrome, isn't it?' Wren says, which wins her a smile. Then Suzy sniffs the air and looks suddenly shocked. 'Wren! Tell me you haven't been smoking again!'

'No. It was Ashworth. He was desperate so I just let him get on with it.'

'Desperate how?'

Wren doesn't want to lie about it. 'He absconded. It's fine now,' she adds hurriedly, 'but he was missing for a good while and when I found him he was, well, not in a good way.'

But from the expression on Suzy's face, she's not thinking about Wren's offender's state of mind.

'What is it?'

'When did he go missing, Wren?' she asks gently.

'Few hours ago? Three?'

Suzy nods. 'And how does he… feel about you?'

'I imagine he thinks I'm a tosser, they tend to,' Wren says, trying to deflect it. But Suzy's not smiling.

The implication of Suzy's question suddenly breaks. Ashworth. Could it have been him? She does the sums: had there been time for him to get to her house before he went to Meadowside? Maybe. Wren glances at the clip on Suzy's finger, and the monitor attached to straps circumnavigating her belly.

The machines monitoring every peak and trough of her vital signs. And she forces a smile, wrinkles her nose, and lies.

'Nah,' she says. 'It couldn't have been him. Timing doesn't work.' Because putting it down to a random break-in is surely less terrifying than the alternative: that Wren's work brought this to their door.

Suzy shrugs. Then from under heavy lids, she gestures with her eyes to the door. 'You want to pick us up some snacks and stuff? I'm going to get some sleep. CID should be here soon. And my mum, actually.'

Wren kisses her hair and gathers her bag, dimming the light as far as it will go as she leaves.

She walks down the corridor towards the lifts, hardly looking where she is going.

Someone else has called this in, she thinks again.

The metal doors slide open and she goes in, hitting the button for the ground floor. She stands aside to allow a porter to back in with a sleeping teenager in a wheelchair.

Forcing herself to concentrate, she goes into the little shop in the main hospital concourse, but thirty seconds' browsing tells her she isn't going to get anything Suzy wants from there. But there is a decent supermarket maybe five minutes' drive away.

Outside, the usual wall of cigarette smoke hits her and she slows her pace, her cravings instantly igniting. She is just starting to consider whether the events of the day warrant a cigarette, just one to take the edge off, when her phone rings.

'Wren Reynolds.'

'Hi, Wren. This is Sergeant Mahmood from the Bridewell? I've just booked Robert Ashworth in. He wanted to use his phone call to speak to you.'

'Right.'

'You know the drill?' the sergeant asks. 'You've just got a few minutes, all right?'

'OK. Put him on.'

There is a pause. 'Wren.' Ashworth's voice is tight. He draws a breath but Wren cuts him off before he can start.

'Were you at my house, Rob?'

There's a pause. 'I don't know what you're talking about.'

'Were you *at my house*?'

'No. I wasn't. I don't even know where you live, how could I have been—'

'Fuck you, Robert.'

'Please, Wren, listen to me.'

Face knotted in a furious grimace, she passes the phone to the other ear. 'What.'

'Can you do something for me?'

'Ha! Are you serious?'

He ignores that. 'If you find them, my mum and Luke, can you tell them something for me?' He drops his voice low, as if they're some kind of friends. 'I didn't have that bracelet. I never had it, never even saw it. I want them to know because if they think I kept it for myself—'

She can't believe that this is what he's wasting his phone call on. 'You do realise what's going to happen to you, right? *You had her clothes in your flat.* You're going to prison for murder. Your mother isn't going to give a flying fuck about any jewellery.' She doesn't need to do it but the rage has taken hold of her and all she can see is hatred. So she twists the knife. 'If they didn't want anything to do with you when you were in for aggravated burglary, Rob, I don't think you're going to get a whole lot of visits when you're doing life for killing a young girl. Do you?'

Ashworth makes a choked sound. 'Please,' is all he says in reply.

And then Mahmood is on the line telling her that the time is up, and the line goes dead, but then instantly buzzes again in her hand. It's a message from Roche.

Forgot to tell you, he says. *Spoke with colleague who worked care placements. Got a lead on Leanne Garrett, the mum. Strange you missed it. Can we talk.*

Wren breathes out a long, slow breath. Before she's even had a chance to put the phone away, she hears a shout.

'Hey! Wren!'

She turns to see a suited man, youngish, jogging across the road. As he gets closer she recognises him: Andy, who got his sergeant stripes with Suzy last year but has moved to CID.

'How's she doing?' he asks as they shake hands.

'Shaken, but OK, we think. Got anywhere yet?'

'Not yet. But don't worry, we'll get him.'

'I know you will. Look, can I ask – are you across what's happening with Robert Ashworth?'

Andy regards her uncertainly.

'I can keep a secret,' she adds.

'You're his PO, right?'

She nods and makes a pleading face. 'I just really want to know what the deal is for him. Off the record. The bag of clothes, all of that.'

Andy nods slowly. 'Far as I've heard, they've got a team down at Crew's Hole looking for remains, but nothing yet. Your boy says he knows nothing about the bag, but,' he makes a dismissive face, 'obviously he's going to say that. Said something about a catflap, reckons someone must have planted the bag in his flat. My guess is they'll put a rush on the lab work, get the DNA done in forty-eight hours.' He pauses, then says, 'There was this one thing – they can't get hold of the bloke who called it in. Dog walker, saw him digging the hole.'

'What, he called anonymously?'

'Apparently. Ashworth's shouting the odds about it, saying someone's setting him up. Reckons it must be us because no one else knows where he lives.' The expression on his face invites her to laugh.

But she doesn't laugh. She thinks, *maybe it's true.*

Maybe he hasn't told anyone where he lives. But there is someone else who knows, other than the NPS and the police. There is one person who's been guided there in the back of a taxi, who's had the flat pointed out to him.

James Yardley.

'Wren?'

She blinks, looks up. Andy has asked her a question.

'I'm sorry, what?'

'I said, do you know if Suzy's got her phone?'

'No, why?'

'Just, we think the intruder emptied out her handbag, like he was looking for something. And he didn't take the purse, even though there was over a hundred quid in cash and all her cards. Pretty unusual, but I don't know. Maybe they took her phone. We couldn't find it.'

'She always keeps it in her bag,' Wren says, bringing out her own phone to call Suzy's number. But Andy puts his hand out to stop her.

'Tried that, goes to voicemail. Got someone tracking it now.' He flips out his notebook. 'What model was it?'

Wren grimaces, trying to remember, and reels off a couple of makes it might have been. 'Old and crap, honestly. I've been trying to get her to upgrade for years. But she doesn't use it much, she's pretty strict on having it out at home. Leaves it at the door – if anyone needs to call her in they use the landline.'

As she's saying that, thinking about Suzy's phone, something else occurs to her.

They didn't take the money, but they took the phone? A crappy old thing she'd had for five years? It's probably even older than Paige's—

That's what the masked burglar was after. That's the reason Suzy could have died, the reason her unborn child might have never drawn breath. The phone.

'You OK?' Andy's asking.

Wren cracks a smile. 'Fine!' She mumbles something about supplies, the birth, and says goodbye.

She resists the urge to shoot a glance over her shoulder until she is well out of sight, around a corner and shielded by a thick hedge. She keeps walking, beyond the entrance to the hospital complex, keeping its low perimeter wall beside her. She finds her car, gets in. She brings up Facebook and finds Cara, the ex-girlfriend that Suzy and the security guard had in common. Skimming that feed, she finds the guard's name. She drops her a friend request, adds her own number into a message to go with it, asking her to get in touch. There's a green dot next to the woman's icon, meaning she's online right now.

Seconds later, Wren gets a text. *Hi, what's up?*

Hey, Wren texts back. She doesn't waste time with small talk. *Just crossing some ts here re my offender this afternoon. What time did he turn up?*

The three dots jump in their wave pattern, telling her a reply is coming.

I'm just writing it up, the text bubble says, and it's followed by a photograph of a paper form. Wren zooms in, scans down. It says the police were on site seventeen minutes after the call. Wren squints at the sky, working it out. She knows Ashworth went to the nursery in Westbury after he fled his flat. There's no way he could have got to Meadowside in that time if he'd gone to hers for a spot of housebreaking in between.

But it was never just Ashworth who was interested in that phone, was it?

From the glovebox she retrieves it. She holds it in the palm of her hand, replaying James's warnings.

And then she turns it on.

42

Before

Luke's breath clouds in front of his mouth and his face is freezing already. Frost sparkles on the roofs of the parked cars all along the street. He's out of breath keeping up with her. Treading softly is hard to do in Caterpillar boots but he's keeping his distance, and anyway, she hasn't looked behind her once. She takes a left onto Feeder Road and it's wider, more open. She reaches the end of the road where it meets the river, turns right over the bridge, then along the overgrown alley. A hundred years ago when he came here with Leah, there were flowers. But they're gone now.

His lungs are burning by the time they reach the old warehouse.

From where he's standing, tucked around a hedge fifty metres back, he follows Paige's gaze to the roof, but there's nothing there. She darts off around the building. He loses her for a moment, until a scrape of metal screams in the silence and there she is, crouching, teeth bared as she yanks the wire mesh of the fence, a weak spot.

He gives it to a count of ten and then he goes after her. A spike of exposed wire scrapes hard against his hand and he almost cries out, and when he brings it close to his face he sees black spheres of blood springing out against the white of his skin. He wipes it on his thigh and keeps going. Into the building, silently through a wooden side door almost off its hinges. The dark in there almost complete.

As his eyes adjust he finds a slip of light, maybe three metres up, the other side of the floor. There is a moment when she is suspended impossibly on the wall, halfway up, and then he sees the metal staircase she's standing on, and that massive steel frame bolted to the wall beneath it. She goes higher, careful to navigate the missing steps, moving out to the edge and climbing along the safety railing until she's past the big hole. Her hair is loose, lifting in the draught.

She takes his breath away.

Suddenly she stops, as if startled.

'Luke?' she whispers into the gloom, stock still now, hands on the rail.

Luke says nothing. There will be time to talk later, when it's all over. She can thank him then.

She carries on, and when a moment has passed he goes up after her, taking the steps, sticking to the shadowiest part against the wall. He hauls himself past the missing section with his hand on the scaffolding pole.

Up higher it's easier to see, empty windows all around. Right across the other side of the wide-open building is another flight that's so steep it's nearly a ladder, ending in a narrow door.

The exit to the roof.

From his side, he waits. Paige makes it to the top and pushes open the door. It cries out as it swings wide, open to the night, and she disappears from his view.

With numbing hands, Luke grips a rung and starts the final climb, placing each foot as softly as he can manage.

When he's up, he pauses, tucking himself behind the door. He makes himself open his eyes, and forces himself to look at the sweep of the roof, at the lights of the city beyond. But he can't quite look at the building's edge. That drop to the concrete below is beyond terrifying, but he can't trust himself to resist it.

Paige is standing in the middle of the vast flat space. And there's someone else there.

It's Yardley, sitting right on the edge.

Luke's guts turn to oil, and he puts out a hand on the doorframe and it's like his body wants to lurch forward.

'You came, then.' Yardley says it without looking around. 'Thought maybe you just asked me here to stand me up, humiliate me a bit more.'

There's a click, and a soft flare of brightness as he lights a cigarette. He pulls his legs back around and stands, facing Paige.

'I'm… I'm sorry,' she says.

He cocks his head. Then wheezes out a laugh, looks away like he can't believe what he's hearing. 'You're *sorry*? Paige, your little plan is going to ruin. My. Life.' He jabs the cigarette in her direction with every word. His face twists, tight and furious. 'I had to spend the last hour with the police, do you realise that? Lying. Telling them you're just a student, that I have no idea why you broke into my fucking home. I thought I could trust you. I loved you, Paige.'

'I'm sorry,' she says. 'I didn't mean for this to happen. It wasn't my idea.'

'No? But you went along with it, right? You and your *boyfriend*,' he says, venom in the word. He means Rob, Luke thinks. And he's wrong. But none of that matters now.

'James, please.' Paige walks towards him, her hands outstretched. 'I need your help. Please. I never meant for any of this to happen. They're going to—' she says, and her voice catches. 'I think they're going to take the baby away.'

The wind picks up and Yardley staggers, his jacket flattening against his stomach. 'Yeah, well,' he says. 'You're on your own now, you little bitch.'

Luke takes a step forward. His hands go loose by his sides. He stands full height.

And he says, clear and strong, 'She's not on her own.'

Yardley whirls round. Looks from Luke to Paige, then back. 'What the fuck are you doing here?'

Paige wraps her arms around herself. 'You followed me? All the way here? What the hell, Luke?'

He doesn't look at her. Everything he needs to say, he's going to say to Yardley. 'You've got to help her.'

'Have I? I don't think I have, Luke. I don't think I'm going to do anything for her, after what she's done to me.'

'I've seen the pictures. The messages you sent her.'

'Oh yeah?' Yardley sucks hard on the cigarette, and his face glows orange for a moment, and Luke sees him clearly, the way he really is. In that moment, he's not a human being at all. He's a wolf. 'And?'

'And I can get the phone back. He's my brother. He'll listen to me. But you've got to help her,' Luke says evenly. 'You're the only person we know who's got money. She needs to get away, start again.'

'Ha!' There's brutality in his eyes. 'Only because she just committed aggravated fucking burglary!'

Luke doesn't blink. 'Do you know what they call it when a man like you fucks a fifteen-year-old?'

Yardley's lip curls.

'I thought so,' Luke says.

'You know what?' he hisses, turning to Paige again. 'I don't give a toss about your brat. They can drown it for all I care. My life is over now, because of you.'

Luke takes another step. 'But it's *your* child!'

There's an awful noise from Yardley. It starts like a wheeze, but then it's not. He's laughing.

'*My* child?' he says, catching his breath. 'You think I'm

that fucking careless, mate? Take a risk like that, with a slag like this one? Christ, no!'

'James, please. *Don't,*' Paige says.

'Oh, this is priceless!' He throws his head back. 'Did you tell him it was mine?'

'*Just stop it!*' Tears on Paige's cheeks, bright in the moonlight.

Luke swallows. 'So… so whose is it?'

Yardley's still grinning hatefully. 'Go on, Paige! You tell him. *Go on.*'

She puts her hands to her face. 'Don't. Please.'

'She's been fucking your brother,' Yardley says, and he's not laughing any more. 'The baby's his.'

Luke turns slowly to Paige. It's not true. He can't bear it to be true. But she won't look at him, and so he knows.

But also – deep down, he already did. He's known for ages.

Before he gets to say it, Paige runs. Barrels past him, head down, back into the building, feet clanging on the ladder. It takes him a few seconds to process it. But then, all the doubt is gone. There is a moment of perfect, unshakeable clarity, and he finds he understands exactly what has to happen next.

He goes after her.

'Paige!' he shouts. At the bottom he turns, follows the black shape of her running to the staircase. He sprints, catches up with her, and grabs her arm.

'Luke, please!'

He grips her hard. He can hardly see it through the dark but just behind her is the hole where the steps are missing. The drop, if you fell, would be about ten metres.

'Luke, *please,*' she shouts, 'I'm sorry!' But she's not looking at him. She's searching behind him, for Yardley. Luke turns, sees him coming down from the roof.

When he looks back to Paige, her eyes are already on him.

And there is a connection, like a clear pathway of electricity, and everything, every screaming, twisting thread of it in his mind goes quiet.

He sees her. Really *sees* her. And he knows that she sees him, too.

He smiles, and she stops struggling. She's right on the edge of the step, so close, like the last few inches at the limit of the earth.

'*Luke*.'

Out loud, all he says is, 'I loved you, Paige. I always did.'

She's leaning back, pulling away from him. She opens her mouth to say something else.

And then he lets her go. She cries out, and then there's nothing.

Luke closes his eyes.

Then Yardley's down the ladder, and pounding across the floor to the top of the broken steps.

'Shit,' he says. 'What happened? Where is she?'

Luke is frozen to the spot. Seconds pass. He can't speak.

Yardley's hands go to his head. 'No. Oh shit, no.' He grabs the rails to go down, but Luke is in his way and he can't get past. 'Move, Luke!' he shouts.

Luke uproots himself and slowly, carefully passes the gap on shaking legs, keeping Yardley behind him. The knackered stair hangs down like a broken arm.

He finds her directly underneath, on the floor. On her side, one arm splayed behind her, the other flung right up above her head. Legs bent. Her head twisted into her armpit. Luke kneels, puts his hand to her throat, and then Yardley's there next to him. He reaches out to touch her, and Luke elbows him hard.

'Get back. Don't touch her.'

The older man rocks back on his heels. 'What have you done, Luke? Is she alive?'

Luke takes his hand from her neck. Slowly, he bends lower, putting his head, his ear, against her ribs.

He stays like that for a long time.

Then he looks up at Yardley. Makes the slowest, smallest shake of his head.

Yardley walks away, his hands in his hair, just saying, 'Shit.' Over and over again.

Luke moves Paige so her neck is straighter, and her arms are comfortable. He doesn't look at her face.

Yardley crouches several metres away. He looks up at Luke.

'Well, you're in the shit now, aren't you, Lukey?'

Luke's eyes go wide. 'She fell.' His voice trembles.

'Did she?' Yardley shakes his head. 'I don't know. We all know how you feel about her, don't we? Then all I heard was you shouting. And now she's…' he gestures towards her. 'It's not looking good for you, my man.'

'It was an accident. Please, Mr Yardley. James. Please.' He lets his voice break. 'My mum. Rob's going to prison already. If you say it was me, if I go away for this, she'll—' he breaks off.

'She'll what?' Yardley waits, arms folded, his mouth working like there's something disgusting on his tongue.

'She'll have nothing left.' He drops his gaze. 'It wasn't my fault. She *fell*. Please.'

Yardley stands then. He jerks his chin at Paige. 'You want me to help you, Luke, you're going to have to do something for me, too.'

'Yeah, OK. Anything you say.'

Yardley gives him a long look. Eventually he says, 'I'll keep your secret for you. But I'm going to need you to get me that phone.'

Luke draws in a breath, all the way to the bottom of his lungs.

And he nods, just once.

43

Now

Wren stands glaring at the camera on James Yardley's inter-com box.

'Let me in, you perverted fuck.'

There is a long pause. She hits the button again. 'I said—'

'Please,' comes a woman's voice, a harsh whisper, almost inaudible. 'I – I can't.'

Who is it – the wife or the housekeeper?

Wren leans closer. 'You can let me in now or I can go straight to the police.'

Another pause. Then, through the crackle, 'I think that's exactly what you should do.'

Not the housekeeper. Too old. Too… bitter.

'Lucilla.'

'Yes.'

Eyes closed, Wren rests her forehead against the wrought-iron bars of the gate. 'Why should I go to the police, Lucilla?'

'Because,' she starts, still whispering, 'because of that poor girl.'

'You need to let me in.'

'I can't. They're *here*.'

'Who's *they*?'

But Lucilla doesn't answer the question. 'I tried to put it right, as soon as I found out what he'd done. But there's no proof – there's never been any proof. He tells everyone I'm insane, traumatised,' she says, her voice sharpening, 'so no one will believe me. He's *evil.* You need to get that phone to the police, right now—'

Wren's eyes fly open. 'How do you know I've got it?'

'Because they're *right here* arguing about it!'

The last scrap of doubt Wren had about the source of those messages to Paige dissolves.

'Please,' Lucilla is saying. 'Just go and—'

Through the little box, the sound of a voice approaching in the background, male, saying her name—

But Lucilla raises her voice '—they'll take it! They'll get it from you—'

'*Who is that?*' comes James's voice, roaring.

There is the indistinct sound of a scuffle. And then silence.

'*Lucilla?*' Wren presses the button again. But the connection is gone.

Then there is a whirring and a clunk as the gates open, and Wren strides in. On the drive, two cars. James's and one other, which gives her pause for half a second because she's seen it before. She knows that ostentatious white 4x4.

The front door flies open. James stands there, arms folded, a loose smile on his lips. Wren speeds up. By the time she is on his steps, she is running, and he is stepping backwards.

No sign of Lucilla. But she hasn't come for Lucilla.

Wren slams into him, drives him back into his hallway. She pins him against the wall, hands on his shoulders, sending a low table crashing sideways.

'What did you do to her?' she spits.

'Wait – wait—'

'*You* put those clothes there. *You* sent the police around once you knew I'd got the phone out for you. You're setting him up and it wasn't him. So I'll ask you again. What did you do to Paige, you filthy bastard? Where is she?'

He gapes, eyes wide, saying nothing.

Wren transfers a hand to his throat. 'Where. Is. She?'

His eyes start to bulge and she doesn't care. After what she's seen on that phone, the things he'd got Paige to do, the pictures he'd told her to send to him: he can fucking choke, for all she cares.

'Wren.' A woman's voice. Coming towards her with a gentle expression: not James's wife, but Alice Polzeath.

'Wren,' she says again, and touches her fingertips lightly to the hand across James's neck. 'I don't think we quite need this, do we?'

Wren shoves him hard against the wall and lets go, then stands back as he coughs, rubbing his neck.

'Jesus Christ,' he splutters. 'Just give me the damned phone and get the hell out of my house.' He puts out a hand to take it from her. He actually puts out his hand.

'You think I came here to give it to you?' Wren laughs. 'I don't fucking think so. You came to my house to steal it from me. My partner's in hospital right now because of you.'

He frowns, affronted by the idea. 'I was nowhere near your house. I've been with a patient.'

'Didn't want to get your hands dirty? So you sent someone else to do it.'

'Let's just be grown-ups here, shall we?' Alice says.

'The hell have you got to do with it?' Wren hisses, wheeling around to face her. 'Why are you even here?' She is trying to fit the pieces together but nothing will stick, it all keeps slipping, the questions clambering on top of each other.

But the answer, when it comes, nearly takes her breath away. Because if Alice Polzeath is here in James Yardley's house, and if she knows about the phone, then that means she knows what he's done. And that means there has to be a reason she kept it quiet.

Wren sees the beautiful carpets, the carved wood of the

staircase. She sees the whole house, the drive, the electric gates. The immaculate cars, not just his but *hers*, too.

The answer is money. The answer is always money.

'You needed him. You let him do whatever he wanted, so he'd scratch your back in return.'

'It's funny,' Alice tells her, righting the overturned table, 'because when you came to see me, I suspected something was a little bit… off, shall we say. And then a couple of days later, it all started to make sense. Didn't it, James?'

Wren folds her arms. 'What are you talking about?'

'I got a call from Melanie Pickford-Hayes. Used to work for me. Liked Paige, I thought at the time. Anyway, you went to see her, didn't you?' She cocks her head, the picture of innocence.

'It's my *job*.'

Alice glances at James. 'Is it? You didn't take Robert though, so it can't have been *approved*, could it?'

'Get to the point.' A knot of dread forms, but Wren doesn't let it show.

'Melanie called me after you paid her a visit. She wanted to see Paige's letters. The ones she'd got from her mother. I asked why,' Alice says, feigning confusion, 'but she wouldn't say. We're not exactly close. All she said was that she wanted to compare something.'

'Right. And?' Wren says, as dismissively as she can. The knot hardens and metastasises as Melanie flashes into her mind. The way she'd looked at the note Wren had written.

'I said no, obviously, but I remembered how Paige and Mel would sit and read those letters together. I went to look for them, and I found that they weren't there. Which was funny, because only that morning, I'd shown them to someone for the first time in goodness knows how long,' Alice says, letting her eyes linger on Wren's. 'Robert Ashworth. And you.'

Wren puts a hand to the doorframe.

'You didn't have to say much, Wren,' James says. He goes to a mahogany coat stand, retrieves his jacket, and from the inside pocket pulls a thick, loose fold of A4 sheets and leafs through them. There are printouts, records, but also photocopies. The handwritten letters to Paige, in familiar handwriting.

Familiar, because it is her own.

'I started with the letters,' James says, 'and worked back from there. You really went to town, didn't you? Starting again, making a nice little life for yourself after Paige was taken into care.' He flicks through the sheets as if examining a shopping list. 'If I didn't know better, I'd say you wanted shot of Paige. Maybe she was holding you back.' He shrugs. 'No wonder you're feeling ambivalent about the new baby.'

Wren stands against the doorframe, stock still.

'Weston-super-Mare, you lived before. In a particularly nice neighbourhood. Couldn't exactly go *down* in the world after starting there.' He glances up, poison in his eyes. 'But you left, changed things up a bit. Got yourself a different name, wormed your way into a respectable profession.'

'This isn't about me.' It comes out as a whisper.

'Oh, I think it is. You want to tell me why you did all of that? So you could go and stalk her? Find ways to get close to her even after everything you did, see if you couldn't damage her a little bit more?' He is hitting his stride now. 'I wouldn't be too hard on yourself. Classic psychological paradox. You didn't get enough love in your own childhood, so you sought it from your daughter who was ill-equipped to give it.' He waves a hand dismissively. 'And so the child suffers the same fate. Explains how Paige was always so keen to please.'

She doesn't move. She can't.

'And you *did* hurt her, didn't you, Wren? I mean, neglect, abuse,' he weighs them both in his hands, 'same thing, really. Says here that she was on her own three days straight at one point, aged three, when you were out on a drugs binge?' He looks up, his confidence returning, the swagger coming back. He tuts. 'Don't think we're in much of a position to point fingers, are we?'

The blood is hammering in her ears, and she tries to speak.

'What was that?'

Wren fumbles again, trying to articulate any one of the excuses that she draws around herself every night like so many threadbare blankets. *I was young. I was a drug addict. I needed help, and no one helped me.* But the words tangle themselves in her throat because they are, have always been, so utterly inadequate. Because nothing excused it, what she'd done to Paige. How she'd let her down. How she'd been led by her weakness, allowing her addiction to pull her around like a chained animal while her daughter, her precious child born into need and addiction herself, followed her, believing with the single-mindedness of extreme youth that Mummy loved her, would put her first, and would protect her. That if Mummy said she would change, then she would change.

But she hadn't changed.

Not in time to save her. And now Paige is dead. Stripped of everything, right down to her innocence, right down to the clothes on her back.

'She had nothing,' Wren manages to say past the choke in her throat. 'She was vulnerable. You knew that. You knew what it was like, being in care.'

James gives a slight shake of his head, incredulity giving way to sneering amusement.

'I wasn't in *care*, for goodness' sake! People like me don't end up in *care*, Wren! Surely you didn't believe that.'

He comes over, places a hand on her shoulder. She can't even move away.

'Not nice when people start digging things up, is it? But it's all over now. You can go and have your baby, and no one needs to know about who you really are. How you shouldn't really be allowed to be near children at all.' He leans in close, so his face is almost touching hers. Close enough to smell the nicotine, to see the flecks of yellow in his drinker's eyes.

'And we certainly don't need Suzy knowing about this, do we? Not with all she's got to lose.'

Maybe it is Suzy's name in his mouth that breaks the spell. Whatever it is, it's powerful enough to shake her out of it, to make her meet his gaze. She blinks, and finds her voice.

'You know what they say, though,' she says softly.

He frowns, confused. 'What?'

'You can take the girl out of Weston.'

And then, after a pull-back as short and swift as a pinball spring, she drives her forehead into the bridge of his nose. He screams as he goes down, holding his face, instantly bloodied, in both hands. As he drops, Wren grabs the bundle of papers in his hand, and she spits in his eyes.

The gate is still wide open when she strides straight across James's tree-lined driveway, big enough for a coach to turn. But as she approaches the yawning gates, she is stopped by the buzz of her phone.

'Where the hell are you?' comes Suzy's mother's urgent voice. 'They've brought it forward. The baby's heart rate is slowing.'

'Shit,' Wren says, running now, her car in view. She can hear James's indignant howl, Alice Polzeath fussing angrily. 'Is Suzy all right?'

'She'd be a hell of a lot better with you here. They're going to be prepping her in a few minutes, Wren. She needs you.'

'I'm coming.'

Wren runs.

But just before she gets to her car, she pauses. Feeling eyes on her, she spins around to the house and locates Lucilla at an upstairs window, one hand on the glass, raised in farewell.

A look of determination on her face. And something else, which could be hope.

Wren raises her own empty hand.

Then, she looks at the papers in the other. Her past, an endless humiliation, used only as a threat, or a ransom.

There will be more where this came from. There already is: that text from Roche, sitting unanswered on her phone, demanding a new layer of lies, more sleight of hand, another misdirection. She can bury it this time, she can pack it all away again and hope it never resurfaces, but she'll never outrun it. Not for good, and not forever.

So she brings her arm up, and she opens her hand, and she lets the papers fly.

She isn't going to hide any more.

44

Now

There is solid traffic on Brislington Hill, as far as she can see. So she veers right, off the main drag of the A4, narrowly avoiding a L-plated moped that has been too close almost the whole way since James's. She takes the back way through St Anne's. The satnav tells her she doesn't have a hope of making it to the hospital before they slice Suzy open, but she'll be damned if she's going to give up. Her twenty minutes dwindles into eighteen as she hurtles through the thirty limit, the sky draining from orange to pink. Past the defunct police station, riding the speed bumps, hyper-alert but smooth, somehow.

Calm.

He thought he could use her. The more she thinks about it, the straighter the line between all the points appears. How he'd practically petitioned her for an audience with Ashworth; how he'd plied her with booze, finding her weaknesses, using them against her, all to get hold of the evidence of what he'd done to Paige. Well, fuck him. So maybe she does have weaknesses. But if he thought he was going to lay her low by exposing that, he'd read her all wrong. It isn't going to be something she'll ever tell him, but he's done her a favour.

There is a smooth run of clear junctions and green lights

all the way down to Arnos Court, and she'd be forgiven for thinking someone is smiling on her. But all of that is about to change.

She'd wanted to drop the phone at the station before heading back to the hospital, but there is no time now. To make matters worse, as she pauses at a crossing, the engine coughs and complains. The fuel light glares – how long has it been on? The learner on the moped comes up right alongside her and scowls in through the window as she tots it up: she's probably covered twenty miles since it appeared, meaning she's running on fumes. She adjusts her route, heading to a garage with the pay-at-pump machines; a stop will cost her sixty seconds, if she just takes enough to get her to the hospital.

She pulls up on the forecourt, gets out and sinks the nozzle into the tank before she notices the sign: *All Transactions To Be Completed In Shop*. Bollocks – but she doesn't have a choice. She takes the minimum five litres, simultaneously scrabbling in her bag for her card, then darts inside to pay and is back out in less than a minute.

Mirror, signal, out of there, past the moped at the pump right ahead—

Movement in her wing mirror, drawing her eye towards it. Someone running. Right towards her.

The rear passenger door opens, then slams.

'Eyes front. Fucking drive.' A muffled voice, close against her headrest. And more than that.

A fine finger of cold against her neck. Metal. A knife?

'Turn left.'

She risks a moment's glance in the rear-view, and a moment is all it takes. The rider of the moped is in the back of her car, black helmet obscuring his face, visor up only a fraction. And his hands are white, unnaturally so. He is wearing gloves.

Latex gloves.

'Go left,' he growls, and she jolts into action. Her knuckles bone-white on the wheel. Angry tears blistering in her eyes.

Her phone, even Paige's phone – both are in her bag, on the back seat. Shit. Can she just open the door, slow down, roll out? No. Grab his arm? No. Just speed up, hit a wall, hope he's knocked out? He isn't wearing a seatbelt, sitting that far forward – that could work…

No.

She has to do what he says. There is no choice. But she will not cry. She will stay alive.

'What do you want,' she asks, flat and clear.

'I want you to drive.'

Time, impossibly, compresses and stretches simultaneously. The minutes pass so quickly that, before she knows it, she is in a completely different neighbourhood, and yet somehow everything is heightened, playing in HD and super slo-mo. There is time to analyse every peak and trench of his voice, running it against some subconscious database of every voice she has ever heard, in the hope that she can identify him.

'Please,' she says, her voice brittle. 'I need to get to the hospital. Just take the car, OK?'

In the rear-view mirror, there is a fraction of a second where he dips his head, and she lets herself believe that he will change his mind.

'We can't. Just *drive*.'

He pushes the metal harder against her skin and she rises from the seat with the pressure. But she is no longer thinking of what he is going to do, but why. *We can't?*

This is no opportunist car-jacking. He's been sent. There is only one person she knows of who'd send someone.

'You can just take the phone, OK? Just take it and let me go.'

But he doesn't respond. She presses her lips between her

teeth and she instructs herself to stay calm, keep it together. Because she is 3.2, 3.3, 3.4 miles from the hospital, from putting things straight with Suzy. In a matter of minutes, she's going to be a parent. And he is going to kill her, because James Yardley has told him to.

He continues to direct her, monosyllabically. First up to the St Philips Causeway and then off, north and then east and then she is lost. She keeps her hands on the wheel. An invisible fist at her windpipe tightens with each breath and her body, her skin, is alive with the sheer injustice of it. She wants to put this right. That is all she has wanted to do.

Does that filthy, privileged prick really get to win?

They come to a road that will take them under the M32. No houses, just a long high wall one side and a fence on the other, holding back a tangled mass of bramble and nettle.

A flood of darkness, a change in volume, as they pass under the thundering bridge, and then they emerge.

'Pull in here.'

She turns, slowly. A gap in the green behind the fence, a flash of what it conceals.

The river.

The window is open, and she inhales deeply. Beneath the car fumes there is a rainy freshness there. Something sweet.

'Stop the car.'

Honeysuckle? Yes. Growing wild somewhere. And conifers.

'Get out.'

She doesn't falter. The metal leaves her neck and she moves her legs, noticing for the first time the catch of the fabric seat against her clothes, the almost inaudible creak of skin loosening against plastic as she unpeels her hands from the wheel. She is almost weightless as they walk through scrubland, no discernible path underfoot.

'Down on the ground,' he says, after a minute.

'Will you leave them alone?'

'Down on the *ground*.'

The sound of footsteps going back towards the car.

'It's in my bag. In the zipped bit,' she calls to him.

The song of a single blackbird pierces through the rumble of the traffic above them. His footsteps sound on the rough, stony earth as he returns. On her knees now, the dampness seeps through her tights in a second and she thinks of the same thing from only a few days before. Melanie Pickford-Hayes, who gave her blue roll and was kind to her.

And then Wren opens her eyes.

Some people, they'll manipulate literally anyone, Melanie said. *Even the best-hearted children you'll ever meet.*

She knows who he is.

'Luke.'

He is right behind her. She tries to get to her feet.

'Stop,' he says. 'Stay where you are.'

But she can hear it now. His age, and his fear, his reluctance.

'Whatever you've done, Luke, you do not have to do this.'

Something slack hits the floor just behind her. Her bag, she thinks. But she doesn't turn.

'Did you find what you wanted?' she asks. She has to speak up to be heard over the boom of the motorway, but he says nothing.

'You don't have to help him. I know you were involved in whatever happened to her,' she says, even though she hasn't ever been sure, not until now. 'But whatever you did, giving him that phone is not going to make it better.'

Still nothing. But he is still there.

'He's not on your side, Luke. He's evil. Even his wife says so.'

She can hear him pacing. She is too terrified to turn.

'Do you know what's on it? The phone?'

'Yes,' he spits. 'Yes, I fucking do.'

And because Wren has nothing to lose, she asks, 'Why do you want to destroy it for him, then, if you loved her? Why are you helping him?'

Then he is right next to her ear, so close she can feel the spit against her skin and the smell of him. Sweat and petrol and youth.

'Because there is only one way to put this behind me. You think I want any of this?' Venom in every word. 'This is because of *you*.'

So *he* knows who she really is, too.

'All Paige wanted was to know someone was there for her. That was *your* job. That's what mothers are supposed to do.'

'Please, just let me—'

'No. You want to know why I'm here? You can fucking listen. Everything she did was because of that – that *hole* you left in her. You think anyone's ever going to be all right after being dumped by her own mum like that?'

She takes her time. She will answer the question.

'I was an *addict*, Luke.' It is the first time in her life that she has ever used that word aloud to describe herself. 'I made some really bad mistakes. Paige was the one who suffered. And I've been trying all this time to put that right. I just wanted to hand the phone in. If you loved Paige, you'd want to do that, too.'

'Why did you steal it from Rob, then? Huh? Why did you make me go to your fucking house with that poor fucking woman there and, and—' he breaks off, and there is a sound like a gasp. A sob, even. 'Why didn't you just give it to the police? I had a plan, all right? Get the phone, put everything right. But you had to go and steal it. Paying you, was he? James? Or did you have the same plan as my brother?'

'No! That's not—'

'I'm not fucking stupid. You're just like everyone else.'

Wren tries to force it all together. He is working for James, but he loved Paige. And: he hates James, yet he'd come for the phone, he'd even broken into her *house* for the phone.

'I can't trust you with it any more than I can trust Rob,' Luke is saying. 'I thought he cared about us. And *Paige* did. But all he wanted was his stupid plan. Even when it went wrong the first time, he just took the prison time so he could try again, blackmail him when he got out. No,' he says, breathing hard. 'I'm the only one that really cares about her. I'm the *only* one who wants to make Yardley pay for what he did.'

'And so you set your own brother up? You put those clothes in his flat?'

A pause. 'What clothes?' Genuine confusion.

'Paige's clothes!' Grief surges again.

'I've got nothing to do with any clothes,' he says. Something in his tone makes her sure it is the truth.

'Let me help you,' Wren begs. 'I loved her, Luke. You can't imagine how much.'

There is no answer.

'Luke. Please,' she says, her voice rising. 'Luke!' Where is he? She gets up and rounds on him, ready to take whatever she has to take—

She gasps, claps both hands to her mouth, unable to speak or scream or breathe.

He's gone.

She stands there shuddering, forcing down each breath. After a few moments she takes her hands from her face.

Her bag is on the ground. She knows without checking that her keys will be gone. But next to it, there is something silvery.

She picks it up, understanding as she turns it over that this is what he'd been holding against her neck, in the car. But it isn't a knife at all.

It is a pair of what look like pliers, but which she knows, upon expert inspection, will turn out to be diagonal cutters.

45

Before

Luke's never seen anyone drive as carefully as Yardley is driving right now. It makes no difference that his knuckles are pressed white on the wheel: the needle might as well be glued to 29 mph. Not that Luke's complaining. Considering the cargo they've got in the boot, he's not exactly desperate to get pulled over either.

It's close to one in the morning by the time they get into the car park near Crew's Hole. Luke knows it like the back of his hand; he's been here dozens of times since he was little. The car park is edged with trees, the tall narrow kind. They sway and twist, looking down on the single car, slowing to a halt.

'You sure there are no cameras?' Yardley asks.

Luke isn't, because he's never thought of checking before, but he gets out and peers into the gloom. Standing outside the car, he realises he's never seen real night before. And instead of his eyes getting used to it, the blackness is crowding in on him, and he takes a step backwards without even meaning to, feeling for the door handle again.

Take it easy, he tells himself. *It'll all be over soon.*

He tells Yardley he doesn't see any cameras, although he doesn't really know what he's looking for. There's nothing man-made there except a dog-shit bin.

Yardley shakes himself and gets out, then both of them are by the boot. Luke goes to open it, but he pauses, says again the thing that matters most.

'I'm carrying her.'

'Fine.'

'I'm doing all of it. I don't even want you looking at her.'

Yardley glares at him, his lips tight. 'This is me helping you out here, Lukey. Don't forget that.'

'Is it?' Luke plants his feet. 'You can get the phone yourself then, can you?' They both know Rob is already in custody, and that means there is no way Yardley has a chance of getting it. Only Luke. 'If you want me to get it back, we're doing this my way.'

And even though his heart is thundering, he keeps his eyes on him and he doesn't look away until Yardley sighs, furious, and moves off around the front again.

The boot clicks open. Things have shifted around back there on the journey but the tarp he used to cover her with is still roughly in place. Her face is covered, which is the main thing. He lifts the canvas, and Paige is a little doll, eyes closed, her hands in loose fists. Luke's never noticed how tiny her hands are before.

He leans in close, his lips right next to her ear. 'We're here,' he tells her.

He takes a deep breath, steeling himself, and then he leans in again. Gets his arms round her, careful to keep her mostly covered. He gets low, bracing his knees, and does it in stages, but eventually she's up on his shoulder.

'Get the spade,' he says to Yardley. 'And don't use the torch unless you have to.'

He makes Yardley walk ahead of him. They start on the path, then they come off it and snake through. Yardley's got his arms up over his head, batting away branches. Luke's struggling with the effort but he keeps going. He's holding her in place with one arm, and the other is up in front of him, shielding her from the brambles and the twigs.

'That way,' he says. 'Between those trees there.' Yardley heads where Luke points, the spade over his shoulder glinting for a second as he turns. They come to the clearing just past where his mum was found that time, right up next to the river.

Luke finds a place. He kneels and sets her down, lying on her side. Yardley comes over, holding out the spade. Luke jumps up. 'Don't. Fucking. Look at her.'

The spade thuds to the ground. 'Dig the hole then,' Yardley says. He goes to the edge of the clearing, sits on a fallen log.

Luke turns back to her. He pushes the hair from her lips, pulls the tarp back around so it covers her from Yardley's view but so that if he gets down really low, he can still see her face. Her mouth.

'All over in a minute,' he whispers.

And then he starts to dig.

46

Now

Wren sits motionless in the maternity ward's waiting area. The concerned-looking receptionist had ushered her into a chair before somehow finding the time to get her a mug of sweet tea. Wren is to wait there while the midwife makes her way down from theatre.

Because she's missed the birth, of course.

Once she'd found her way back onto a main road and located a cab office, and sat, shaking and catatonic, until someone arrived to take her to the hospital, by then Leo Wood-Reynolds was already being placed on his mother's chest, cautiously opening half-blind eyes for the first time.

With the moment gone, the adrenaline of the journey has given way to a cold shroud of shock. The only evidence that might have helped to plot Paige's last moments, that could have brought her some justice, has been lost.

She sips her tea, not tasting it. Tells herself again – *I missed the birth of our child.* But it still sounds like a punchline in a half-joke about a shit husband. Ex-husband. It won't sink in.

The midwife appears through the double doors. She exchanges a few muted words with her colleague at the desk before coming to sit beside Wren.

'You'd be surprised how often this happens,' she says.

Wren attempts a smile, and is rewarded with a sympathetic

pat on the back. 'Well, the main thing is she's fine,' the midwife tells her. 'Mum's fine, baby's fine. Lovely little chap, eight pounds exactly.'

Wren turns to ask if she can go up but the midwife, reading her mind, wrinkles her nose kindly and touches her shoulder.

'Let's give her a little while. She'll be out of recovery within an hour. I can let you know when she's settled?'

Wren nods. 'Maybe I should go out, get some flowers and things,' she says, half to herself.

'I really think it's probably best you stay in the building, don't you?'

The hour passes torturously slowly. When at last the receptionist beckons her over and tells her she can go up, her legs are blocks of stone, entirely numb. She climbs the three flights to the floor where she will meet her son, and the only thought that she can keep in her head for more than a couple of seconds is that this could be it. This could be the end of them.

Suzy's mother Shirley is on her phone in the corridor, but hangs up as soon as she sees Wren. She opens her arms and strides over. 'Come here.'

Wren allows herself to be enveloped. Years have passed since Wren's own mother died, and Shirley will always be the person she thinks of whenever she hears the word *mum*.

With her arms around Wren, Shirley sighs, squeezes hard, then holds her out by the shoulders. 'You got a good excuse ready?'

Wren wants to laugh, but the breath comes out rather more like a sob. 'No,' she says simply. 'Not really.'

Shirley kisses her cheek and wishes her luck. 'And congratulations,' she says, mischievously. 'He looks just like you.'

Wren can't help but laugh.

As she enters the room, Wren is met with the soft sound of Suzy singing. In Suzy's arms, his mouth against her breast and his eyes closed, is a black-haired boy, beatific peace on his snub-nosed, furry-cheeked face. Without looking up, Suzy reaches for her. Wren sits beside her and lifts a fingertip to her son's face. He is a living, breathing thing. He is real, and he is theirs, and the miracle of it is more than she can comprehend.

Suzy turns her head. She acknowledges the thing with a single nod. 'You're here now,' she says.

The apology evaporates unspoken on Wren's lips.

And what comes out instead, as the first blue light of the rising moon casts their single, amalgamated shadow on the wall, is something else entirely.

Paige Garrett was three months old when the fabric of her family life first started to fray. Her mother, Leanne Garrett, had been known to social services since she was a toddler, and once she hit double figures she had spent most of her life in care. At fifteen, she'd been referred by the local NHS to a clean-needle programme. But when sixteen-year-old Leanne had become pregnant, she'd initially straightened out. Something had clicked in her, she told her social worker: she knew she could be a good mother. She'd get clean, find a job, enrol in all the mother-and-baby support programmes that she was offered. And at first, it had gone well. She managed the rehab with determination, she learnt how to cook, she read books on parenthood, sleep, childhood illnesses. Despite a complete lack of family of her own, with no contact with the father of the child since the night of conception, Leanne bonded with the baby better than anyone had expected. She attended all the appointments, said all the right things. But after a few months the grinding reality of single, unsupported motherhood set in.

At times of crisis, when the membranes between intention and reality are at their thinnest, all it takes is a little tear.

For Leanne, that tear came shortly after a move to one

particular flat, when a well-meaning neighbour took a shine to Paige. She offered to babysit while Leanne went out. *Have some fun,* she told her, *see your friends.* The neighbour would never know that Leanne, a newcomer to the town, didn't have friends. She used the time instead to find drugs, the way a recovering addict always can, as sure as water will find a way to sink lower.

Waking up after the first relapse, Leanne panicked. She returned to her flat hours late, and the neighbour was furious. But the baby was clean and fed and *content.* Her nails were clipped, the sheets of her cot were fresh and dry, and she was fast asleep. Oblivious.

And the seed was planted.

In Leanne's absence, Paige had been better cared for. She was happier, and she was safer.

Leanne could have admitted defeat then, and given her daughter up for adoption while she was still an infant – and a white, pretty, healthy infant at that, the kind in highest demand. But what Leanne did was persevere.

It was the fork in the road that would haunt her for the rest of her days.

That night, Leanne borrowed money from her new dealer, the only person she could ask, and bought flowers for the neighbour as an apology. The neighbour forgave her, believed her promise that it would never happen again.

But even as she reached the end of her teens, Leanne was still a kid. She didn't know how to meet her own needs, and how to keep herself safe, and the deck was stacked against her. With help only available to those who admitted their struggles, and the near certainty of Paige being removed if she asked for help, Leanne entered a slow, spiralling slump of drugs and prostitution, until one day, after years of concern, the neighbour reported her.

The process of removal was swift. Within a few weeks it

became apparent that Leanne would be lucky to avoid prosecution. She was told that although Paige was five and a half, there was still a really good chance she could be adopted. A child psychologist claimed that the damage from a lifetime of exposure to drug addiction, dangerous men, neglect: all of that might be remedied, if her daughter got a clean break. And although Leanne realised by now that Paige was the only thing preventing her from sinking all the way down, she relented. She sent a frenzied series of letters, explaining herself, desperate that her child should know how dearly, how desperately she had been loved.

Three weeks later, a stranger found Leanne on the Easton bridge of the M32, incoherent and disorientated. When she was released from hospital a week later, Leanne cleared her flat, sold everything she owned. She bought a 25cl bottle of fizzy white wine from a corner shop, and made a vow to herself that if she wasn't clean in a year, she would return to that bridge, and she would do the job properly.

And twelve months and one day later, she took that bottle onto the bridge. She smoked a single cigarette, and drank the wine, and watched the sun go down as the cars full of lucky people with jobs and families and futures shot by underneath her. A year of constant, aching graft and perseverance had convinced her that she deserved another chance. So she left Leanne Garrett behind and she chose another name, and another path.

She stopped writing the letters, in case they became a trail of crumbs that Paige could follow, leading not to the safety of home but to the witch herself.

But even though she knew she could never have her back, she hadn't quite been able to say goodbye to Paige. So she followed her doggedly whenever she could scavenge information about her, from foster home to foster home, stealing glimpses of her through windows and on her way to school.

Getting close enough to hear her voice, watch her grow and change, but always maintaining a safe perimeter. Because no matter what she called herself, or how she changed inward or out, Leanne would always be toxic.

As the years passed, the woman who had become Wren Reynolds realised that she had, after all, left it too late. Every time her daughter was moved on and Wren lost sight of her for a while, she believed that maybe this time it was for good, that a permanent family had been found for her precious child. But it never was. Paige never did get adopted, never put down roots. Was never loved, not properly.

Or at least, that was how it would have seemed to her.

Leo is asleep by the time Wren finishes the story. For a moment, Wren thinks that Suzy is sleeping too, her breathing steady and slow with her head resting on Wren's chest. But then she clears her throat.

'You know the first thing they teach you in forensics?'

Wren frowns. 'No.'

'They say, "Every contact leaves a trace."' She shifts and turns, looking up at Wren. The air pulls tight around them, like they are the only three people in the world.

Suzy finds Wren's hand with her own and guides it over to Leo's inert fist, the size of a small plum. Wren holds it in her palm, stroking the plump dents of his knuckles.

'I know this is literally the worst time to burden you with this,' she says quietly. 'I'm sorry.'

Suzy weighs that up, a small smile on her mouth. 'Well, there is that, yeah. As timing goes, it's – I mean, it's—'

'Horrendous.'

'Couldn't be more inappropriate.'

They laugh. Suzy rubs her thumb gently over Wren's hand.

'But look. This is us now,' she says. 'I love you, Wren. I wouldn't have gone this far with you if I didn't love you. And that doesn't just mean loving the things about you that you show. It's all of it. You think anyone has the humanity you've got without shit happening to them? You think I believed you were perfect?' She turns down the corners of her mouth, as if the very thought of it is something incomprehensible. 'I didn't once think you were perfect. That you had somehow just materialised, without a past, without family, the way you wanted people to believe. It was always obvious you had a past. And when Paige went missing – I mean, I found the pictures of her, Wren. And I've seen photos of you at that age. You may look different now but, back then, you could have been twins.'

'So why didn't you say anything?'

The baby sighs, and Suzy shuffles back, sitting up straighter. She goes to lift him, but grimaces. 'Ow. Hurts, when they slice your guts open.'

Wren smiles. 'Let me.'

She moves round and lifts him into the clear plastic cot beside the bed. When she comes back, Suzy takes her hands.

'I asked. I asked you so many times what it was about that case. You chose not to tell me. And if you remember, we nearly split up over it. Actually I left, at one point – I never told you that. Packed up in the middle of the night and left. I sat in a Lidl car park for two hours and cried.'

Wren hangs her head. Suzy touches her chin, lifts it. 'And then I came back. Because you're mine. Whatever you are. We've got a lifetime to pick it over. Right now, you need to tell me what you know about Robert Ashworth and that bag of clothes.'

For the next twenty minutes, Wren tells her everything. She holds nothing back, not the complicity with James Yardley, not the theft of the phone. She tells her about how it must have been Luke who sabotaged her car, and as she says it, she realises why.

'So I'd need a lift back,' Wren says, wincing at how stupid, how utterly reckless she'd been. 'So bloody Yardley could come and save me and ply me with booze.' She pauses again. 'And find out where I lived.'

Suzy looks almost impressed, then she pauses, struck by a thought. 'Not just where we lived, though.'

'No.' She'd led him right to Ashworth's door.

Suzy closes her eyes, nodding, and neither of them speak for a while.

Wren sighs. 'He killed her, then. Yardley did. He spent all this time talking out of his arse about forgiveness and redemption, when he just wanted to use me to get close to Ashworth, and get rid of those pictures of Paige.'

'I suppose so.'

'And once Yardley was sure you were out of the flat with the phone, he dropped the clothes at Ashworth's, and set him up. *He's* the dog-walker.'

'Yeah.'

'And then Luke tries to steal the phone back, so – so what?'

Wren stands up, starts to pace. The thing is still just beyond her grasp. 'Luke was furious with Yardley. He didn't believe that I was going to hand the phone in, and he clearly hadn't wanted to break in to the house. He mentioned you. *That poor fucking woman*, he called you.'

Suzy concedes it with a nod. 'Makes sense. He kept saying sorry. I kind of – I almost feel sorry for him, now.' Then, darkly, deadpan: 'Tell anyone on the force I said that and, so help me God, I'll break your legs.'

Wren smiles. 'But that's it – he didn't want to be doing it, there was no bravado or anything. He just said how much he cared about her.'

She runs it back, then frowns. How had he put it? *I'm the only one that really cares about her.*

Cares, though, not *cared*?

Suzy studies her. 'What is it?'

They lock eyes for a single moment, and then there is a knock on the door, and a nurse puts his head into the room. 'Call for you,' he says. 'For Wren?'

She goes out and is handed the receiver at the desk.

She clears her throat. 'Wren Reynolds.'

There is a moment's hesitation, but then a voice.

'Wren. It's – ah, it's Oliver Polzeath. I think we've got a few things to talk about.'

47

Before

Luke finishes digging. Any deeper and it's just going to be water, this close to the river.

He turns on the torch and looks around for Yardley, finds him crouching the other side of the clearing, his head in his hands.

'Ready,' Luke tells him.

Yardley comes over. It's so dark Luke can hardly see his face, even standing a metre away.

'Anyone finds it, it's on you.'

'I know,' Luke says.

'I still think we should burn it.'

Luke doesn't. He gives him the reasons he's already given: the rain, the smoke.

Relenting, Yardley says, 'Let's get it done then.' He touches the tarp with his toe, just where Paige's elbow is.

'No!' Luke shouts. There's the commotion overhead of several birds taking flight, disturbed from their roost.

'Jesus. What?' He puts his hands up, sneering at him like he thinks this is funny.

'Don't even fucking *touch* her.' Fury boils up in his throat.

Yardley turns away. 'Do it then. Go on.'

Luke gets down into the pit again, and he lowers her in. He moves her so she's lying on her side, her back to the man, and lays the tarp out again, taking care to keep it a little way from her face.

'What are you doing? It's not like she's going to suffocate.'

There's nothing he can say to that. Luke takes a last look at her, and starts to climb out.

But then the terrible thing happens. 'Hold on,' Yardley says. And he throws down a knife. Tells Luke to cut her clothes off. Because of fibres, evidence. 'We're going to burn them,' he says. 'And ours, to make sure.'

And Luke knows this could go two ways. He could do it, or Yardley could come down and do it. And he can't have that. So, as carefully as he can, he peels off her jacket, and her shirt, and everything else. Yardley makes him take her necklace, everything.

He folds it all up, and Yardley takes it from him, tucks it inside his coat.

And then an idea slips into Luke's mind.

'What about her hair? Fibres. There'll be my hair in hers, probably. And yours.'

Yardley folds his arms. Agrees, tells him to cut it close.

The whole thing takes a few minutes. He twists the hair into a loop and zips it into his jacket pocket, then climbs out, teeth chattering, and faces Yardley.

'We should split up,' Luke says. 'You go back. I'll walk home after. Don't want to be seen together, do we?'

'You're sure they don't know you're out? And you can get back inside without being seen?'

Luke gets his phone out, checks the screen. 'No calls. They think I'm still in bed. I'll go in through the back door.'

Yardley looks at the hole, then back to Luke. 'You're going to fill it in?'

'Of course I'm going to fucking fill it in.'

'And cover it over. Leaves,' he says, gesturing to the ground. 'Make sure it's hidden.'

'I know.'

'I'll throw the spade in the water. Burn these later on,' he says, gesturing to the clothes. 'Give me the hair.' He puts a hand out.

Luke shakes his head.

'Give it to me.'

Luke sighs, knowing he can't win. He unzips the pocket and reaches in. But – without knowing why he's doing it, without even thinking – before he pulls his hand back to pass it over, he parts the hair with his fingers, saving just a finger-thickness of it for himself.

Yardley takes it and looks at him hard. 'How do I know you'll do your side of it properly? Given how badly you've fucked everything else up?'

'Because it's me going to prison if I don't, isn't it?'

'And your mum left with no kids.' Yardley keeps his eyes on him. 'No one taking care of her.'

Luke doesn't look away. 'Yeah.'

Eventually Yardley looks up at the sky, sniffs in a long breath.

'Right then, Luke. But I promise you this.' He points at Luke's chest, his face an animal snarl. 'What you're doing here is making a deal, like a man. I have helped you. I will keep my word. And if you go soft about this, mate, if you decide you're turning yourself in, or if you don't complete your side of the bargain and you don't get that phone back for me: you'll wish you'd never been born.'

And then he leaves.

Luke watches him duck through the low branches, back towards the path. He listens to his footsteps cracking the twigs, getting softer and softer. He closes his eyes and strains his ears, stands there for five minutes, longer, until he hears the faint boom of the Audi starting up.

He waits even longer than that.

And then he goes over to the pit, and he gets back in. He shrugs off his coat, and crouching, he lifts the tarp.

'He's gone.'

And Paige opens her eyes. The last severed strands of her beautiful hair fall away and she smiles, taking the coat and pulling it tight around her perfect, living body.

'Thank you,' she says. 'Thank you.'

48

Now

Wren waits outside the hospital, right next to the main entrance. It is dark now, into the evening, and most of the traffic is leaving the complex. She hopes this will make it easier to spot him on his way in.

But when he arrives, Oliver Polzeath is an entirely different person to the man she'd met at Beech View the previous week. So much so that when the battered twenty-year-old campervan pulls up, initially she looks straight through it.

He winds the window down. 'There's a bay just over there, to the left and back a bit. Nice and private, OK?'

She nods and follows him. Pulling the van into a layby there, he silences the engine, and hops down.

Since she saw him at Beech View, he's had what is left of his hair cropped tight against his skull. He is wearing clothes that suit the person she'd met there better: a faded khaki coat over a grey-brown jumper, possibly hand-knitted; well-loved corduroy trousers. There is nothing of the businessman about him now: she can't see anything in this man that would make sense alongside a woman like Alice Polzeath.

Which, she supposes, is probably what divorces are for.

'I'd invite you in for a chat, stay out of the cold, but I imagine you're not too trusting of people at the moment,' he says grimly.

Wren eyes him. 'How did you guess that?'

He gives her a serious smile and glances behind him. Following, Wren peers more closely at the van. On one of the back seats, his face obscured by his hand, is a young man.

Luke Ashworth, complete with an angry crescent-shaped gash on his head where Suzy had given him a run for his money.

Wren draws back. 'What the hell is *he* doing here?'

'Wait,' Polzeath says, putting his arm out, 'please. Just give me a moment.'

'No. *No*.' The undiluted terror of her abduction hits her at full force. 'I thought he was going to kill me. I thought I was going to *die*!'

'*Wren*,' Oliver says, hands up. 'You said you wanted to help. You said that to Luke. I came here because there's something you can do.'

She rounds on him. 'Have you still got the phone?'

'Yes, but—'

'Why?' She shoves him hard, both hands into his chest. 'Why is it not with the police?'

'Because – stop, stop! Listen to me! Luke wanted that phone to be found by the police, OK? That's what he's been here trying to do. He's been stringing Yardley along for years, making him believe he's on his side; he's put himself on the line, many times. When you told Yardley it was at Leah Amberley's grandfather's, Luke tried to get hold of it before you did, but it got moved.'

'*He* broke into that garage?'

'All he wanted was to bring Yardley to justice.' He speaks in a calm, measured voice. 'But when those clothes were planted, everything changed. Luke called me in a massive panic. It got – out of control.'

Wren stares at him. 'So you knew, all along?'

'I helped him before, when he needed it most. And we can do it again, Wren, we can still put this right.'

'You've got the phone, though, you've got the evidence! Why not use it?'

'Because unless the police find it in his possession, it's useless.'

'What? Why?'

'Because of lawyers! This is years-old evidence. And Yardley's not stupid – he may not even have registered the SIM he used to exchange those messages with her. He definitely wasn't using his usual number. It might have no link to him.'

'Bullshit. Why did he want it so badly then?'

'Because he knows what Rob was planning before, and doesn't want to take the risk that he'd do it again. Rob wasn't exactly desperate to get that phone to the police, was he? Wren, listen. Calm down. I need to ask you something.'

'*You* need to ask *me*?' She laughs bitterly. 'My baby son nearly died because of him. *Fuck* you.'

'It's not for me,' he says, dropping his voice to an urgent whisper.

'Then who? Huh? *Him?*' she says, waving a wild arm at Luke.

'No. For Paige.'

'*What?* How—'

'She's alive, Wren.'

There were a few minutes after that which, when she tried to recall them later, took on the sense of being underwater. Everything around her slowed, went loose somehow. He helped her to a bench, where she sat for a few minutes while he got a bottle of water from his van. He offered her a cigarette, which she took and lit and smoked halfway down before she remembered that no, she didn't smoke, she hadn't smoked for years.

He was saying that Paige was alive.

Her daughter, Paige.

She finds herself sitting beside him in the back of his van now, listening to what he has to say. And slowly, her sense of who she is returns.

'Are you all right?' he is asking. 'Can I get you anything?'

She casts around for words. 'Is she – is she all right?'

He nods at his shoes, then looks up, giving her a smile. 'She is.'

'Where is she?'

He doesn't answer immediately. 'I can't tell you that just yet,' he says. 'She's got a lot to lose, Wren. It's why we had to keep it so secret. I had to get rid of Mel to try and limit what she could find out. Paige never even told her best friend about it. If she comes back, if anyone finds her, she could still find herself prosecuted for what happened.'

'But she was a kid. She'd been groomed. She'd been – it was statutory rape.'

'I know. And she understands that, too. But she would have had a custodial sentence for what she'd done. Young offenders unit, sure, but it would have meant being locked up. She couldn't do it. And what she has now, she can't risk losing. Even if it means letting James Yardley get away with what he did.'

Saying the name sends a bite of tension across him. He loathes James, she can feel it like an aura. Maybe she can trust this man, Wren thinks.

'But letting him just carry on like nothing happened, letting it go – that's not enough for me. And it's not enough for Luke.'

Wren sits with her hands in her lap, running over it. 'What happened to Makayla Slater?'

He lets out a long breath. 'She'd been pregnant. We covered it up because it made us look bad.'

'Because it was James?'

He looks her in the eye. 'Honestly, I don't know. He spent

a lot of time with her. She refused to name anyone, but I had my suspicions. I begged Alice to cut ties with him.'

'So what happened?'

'My wife decided that the best course was to bully her into a termination.'

'But you were supposed to be her carer, weren't you? You could have done something.'

'Yes.'

'But you didn't.'

'No. The abortion, it sent her…' he casts around for the words, the shame and sadness of it written on his face. 'I didn't realise until after the event that Makayla was so desperate. Alice told me she was dealing with it, but actually she'd just put all her efforts into covering it all up, as usual.'

'How do you mean, as usual?'

'She did it all the time. Kids ran away, drugs were found, sex, booze – Alice was constantly redacting our records or making sure things weren't recorded in the first place, for the sake of our reputation.'

'So what happened then?'

'Makayla kind of receded. I liked her. She was so, I don't know, *sparky*. But it just ruined her, and then… well. You know what happened. And when I discovered what she'd done, I removed myself from the business – resigned as a director, stopped work altogether for a while.'

'And Yardley?'

He shrugs. 'He got more involved in Beech View and the whole thing started up again. I tried to catch him in the act but,' he shrugs, 'he was careful, I suppose. Paige refused to admit what was happening, however carefully I approached it with her.'

Wren thinks about that. 'You suspected what was happening. You saw how it had ended before. But you just let it go.'

He uncaps a bottle of water. 'We have a son,' he says after a moment. 'I wanted custody. Her lawyers were going to make the argument that I was reckless and insolvent.' He shrugs resignedly. 'Alice took it all over on paper and I did another year, helped her get the contract so she'd be kinder when it came to the custody arrangements.'

Wren listens. 'So you were a pussy,' she says.

He sniffs out a single syllable of a laugh, takes a mouthful of water, nods sadly. 'I hope that what I have done since then goes some way to redeeming who I was before. But yes: in short, I was indeed a pussy.' He nods. 'And after all of that, after James fucking Yardley worked his magic and Acumen ended up with God knows how much money to open new homes, she took my boy anyway. I get every other weekend.'

'So everyone turned a blind eye to him grooming my daughter,' Wren says quietly, 'because your wife needed him to swing the contracts her way?'

'That's exactly what happened.'

They sit there for a moment, acknowledging it.

He takes a deep breath. 'You said to Luke earlier that Yardley's wife hates him.'

'That's what she said.' Then she thinks about it again. 'Not a huge fan of yours, mind.'

'I remember. And so we get to why I'm here.'

From the inside pocket of his coat, he produces a bag. Holding it cautiously, he opens it up. Inside is the phone. But as Wren peers in, she sees that it isn't just the phone. There is something else in there, as well.

'I wondered if you might want to go and ask a little favour from her.'

49

Now

Saturday morning. The house is full of flowers, so many that they've had to use pint glasses and measuring jugs and everything else they can lay their hands on. It is cold but glorious, the spring sky an unbroken expanse of vivid cobalt blue. Leo, a week old, is asleep in his Moses basket; Suzy has gone out for croissants and the paper, and Wren is writing a stack of thank-yous to Suzy's army of aunts and uncles and cousins and family friends. The card to Callum Roche has been started many times, but it turns out that there's no standard wording for a note that simultaneously thanks someone for both a delightful Scandi-chic baby-gro *and* fighting tooth and nail for you to keep your job despite demonstrable gross misconduct. He says she's in with a good chance, but time will tell. For the moment, Wren's little family will manage. And if they have to adapt, that's exactly what they'll do.

In the back garden, Marty is planting willow saplings in a circle. When they grow, he's going to show Wren how to weave them into a living bower, a den for Leo and the friends he'll make. His editor was furious when he left, Marty said, but he'll get over it. Wren's discovered a newfound respect for the man: once Leo was born, he'd decided that no number of promised bylines could justify the kind of betrayal the publication wanted from him. He'd explained this to his editor, and had been escorted from the newsroom for his trouble, but that was fine with him. He was talking now about maybe combining his skills, writing freelance pieces for gardening magazines. He's not sure yet but Wren, watching him entirely absorbed by his task outside, suspects he'll make a go of it, whatever *it* ends up being.

After she refills Radclyffe's bowl and takes it back through to his spot under the stairs, through the open front windows Wren can hear Suzy coming down the street, laughing with someone. She goes to the door.

'Look who I found,' Suzy says as it opens, handing Wren a carrier bag. Andy, her friend from CID, steps inside, a paper under his arm. 'I made him come for coffee. He has an interesting story to tell us,' she adds, the tiniest sparkle of mischief in her glance.

Wren makes the coffee, and they go outside into the bright morning. While Andy vapes, Suzy treats him to what is fast becoming her set piece about Wren missing the birth, minus a few details.

'And I'm like, "Fucking *petrol*? They're slicing me in half in five minutes' time and you're getting *petrol*?" And then – you tell him, Wren.'

'They'd run out of petrol at the petrol station,' she says simply. 'I had to get a taxi.'

'Oh, for – *really*?'

Suzy takes Wren's arm and squeezes it. 'Really. Took twenty minutes to arrive, by which time she's frantic, trying to flag people down—'

'And no one at the garage would give you a lift?' Andy says, aghast.

Wren shrugs, grimaces. 'People, eh?'

Suzy hands Andy a mug of coffee, then sits back and folds her arms. 'Go on then, tell her what you just told me.' She probably thinks she is disguising her glee, but Wren can read her like a book.

'We had a bit of a development with your Robert Ashworth,' he starts.

And he tells the story of how, two days previously, they'd got a call from a lady by the name of Lucilla Yardley. She'd been doing a spot of gardening, weeding out a section beside the vegetable patch that she had been asked by her husband not to touch – there was a lot of broken glass there, the husband had said. But she hadn't found any broken glass. What she'd found, when she dug a little deeper, was a watertight box.

'And inside the box there was a mobile phone.'

Wren keeps her expression absolutely neutral. 'Right.'

Andy leans forward. 'And on that mobile phone, there was a string of text messages, of very explicit content, and hundreds of pornographic images, sent between James Yardley and,' he pauses for effect, 'Paige Garrett.'

Suzy looks over at her. And Wren tries to say something, to express some kind of surprise, but the words just burst and go to nothing in her throat.

So Suzy speaks for her. 'The bastard,' she says.

'Exactly what I said,' Andy agrees. 'But that's not all. Under the phone, in another bag, was hair. Human hair. We tested it against what we got from her hairbrush when Paige disappeared, and from the bundle recovered from Ashworth's flat. It's hers.'

With a discreet toe, Suzy nudges her foot under the table. *Listen to this*, her eyes say. Wren turns back to Andy.

'And then, right at the bottom of the box, there's a zip-lock bag. And in that bag there's a twenty-grand bracelet. Solid platinum, diamonds, emerald the size of a Creme Egg.' He leans back, folds his arms. 'Working theory is that the phone is what Paige and Ashworth went to find in the first place.

They never did steal anything – Yardley just hid it to put us off the scent. So then we fingerprint it – no sign of Ashworth's on it anywhere, but what we do get is some prints we took for elimination when Paige went missing.' He pauses for effect, really hitting his stride. 'Alice Polzeath, the woman who owned the children's home. And your boy Ashworth took the rap for the bracelet even though he'd never even seen the bloody thing, because Paige Garrett didn't want it coming out about the phone.'

Wren opens her mouth, closes it again.

'Something like that, anyway,' Suzy says.

With coffee finished and the catching up done, Andy gets up and stretches his back out. He puts his head in on Leo, who is just beginning to stir, and then says goodbye in the hall.

As he steps outside, though, he turns back, suddenly grinning.

'I know what!' he says. 'I'll get hold of the CCTV of the petrol station for you. Birthday present for Leo, seeing what his other mum was doing while he was being born. Something to show the grandkids, eh?'

Suzy and Wren smile, and exchange the briefest of glances. Then Suzy wrinkles her nose. 'Nah,' she says. 'I think she's suffered enough.'

Epilogue

The flight is only an hour and a quarter from Bristol, but to Wren it feels like days. She gets her phone out again, looks at the picture she took of Leo and Suzy, waving her off. He's grown so much in just a couple of months, with creases of fat round his wrists and ankles that she can't wait to tease him about when he's bigger.

When he's bigger. When he's a man. She can let herself say things like that now, because whatever happens next, she knows she's going to be in his life. She's his mother, and she's not perfect, and both of those things are all right. God knows she doesn't have to be perfect to do it better than last time.

The steward comes around and she sits up straighter, gets a lemonade. Ireland from 25,000 feet is a thing of unparalleled beauty, she thinks. And she leans her head back against the seat.

After a while the announcement comes on. They're descending into Knock airport.

It's nearly time.

Wren's the last one off the plane. She gathers her things, and she takes her time.

Luke is there in the airport, waiting for her. He doesn't wave – he's not a waver – but he lifts his chin in recognition and when she goes over, he smiles.

'Good,' he says. 'Here we go, then.'

The drive to the house is directly south, and longer than she thought. While they travel, they talk about everything it took to get them out here in the first place. Oliver had needed to pull a lot of strings for Paige.

'She knew it was the only way,' Luke says, 'but Jesus, it was hard to start with.'

Between them, Oliver had told her, they'd made the decision that Luke would stay behind for a while to avoid suspicion. His mum was released from hospital a month after it all happened, and they'd gone up to Yorkshire for a while before making the move out to Ireland to be with Paige.

'She missed Leah more than anything,' Luke says. 'It was – well. It was bad, especially before we managed to get over.'

But now, with everything that's happened, things have changed. Leah's going to come over in a few weeks' time, he tells her. Leah was pretty angry when he first got back in touch, but she's coming round. Especially after Luke explained exactly how Paige had executed that fall in the warehouse: how without that day when she and Leah practised it to wind Luke up, it might never have worked.

And Rob – well, everyone's going to need a bit longer with Rob. But they'll give it a try.

'Takes time though, doesn't it?' he says. 'Trusting people.'

Wren smiles. 'It does. Yeah.'

They talk about how the investigation into the housebreaking has trailed off, how Suzy's description of the young man who entered their home turned out to not be all that clear.

'I know I've said sorry before,' Luke says, 'but—'

Wren holds up a hand. 'We're past it, Luke. It's finished.'

Their place is out on its own, he tells her, but not too far from Ennis. They've lived there since they left the UK, bought it with some money his mum was left by her uncle, straight after she came out of hospital.

'It wasn't loads, mind,' he says, bracing himself against the wheel because the road has become a track, and it's bumpy. 'We had to find somewhere that was going for pretty much nothing. But it's OK. We're all right. We've made some friends.' Then, shyly, he adds, 'I've kind of got a girlfriend, too. Maybe you'll meet her.'

'I'd like that,' Wren says.

Maybe it's something to do with the time of day, the quality of the light, but it's like the saturation of colours has gone wild. Everything is so green, vivid against the thick slate-grey sky. A house comes into view, just over a low wide hill, bright walls under a long, black roof. As they get closer, she can see the house is a single level, with an outhouse off to one side.

'Where my mum paints, when she's got time,' Luke says, pointing. 'She's at work now though. Cooks lunches at the school up in the town.'

There are a few cars outside, neatly parked. 'You fixing those?'

He nods, a flash of pride. 'Bit of a mechanic,' he tells her, pulling up the handbrake. His voice is different here. He's not angry any more.

They get out of the car and walk up to the house. Everywhere is dewy and green and there's a smell of moss, something earthy that she could just stand and breathe in all day long. The house is really old, foot-thick whitewashed walls and the paint peeling from the single-glazed windows. But it's perfect too, the kind of house a child would draw.

The kind of house her child drew, once upon a time.

Wren hangs back. She tries to find a place for her hands but everything feels wrong, and all of a sudden she loses her nerve. Luke says they've had a lot of long conversations since what happened a few months back. That things are different now. That everyone's ready.

But what if they're not? What if this just makes everything worse? She shouldn't have come. What if it's a mistake?

'It's all right,' Luke says gently, and he loops a long arm across her shoulders. 'Deep breath.'

She takes a breath, and meets his eye.

'OK.'

And she lets him take her to the door. The moment they're on the doorstep, a little girl with paint on her face bowls out. Head down, running comically, straight-legged because she's not even three years old. Wren laughs, watching her waving her paintbrush, curls of spun gold bouncing round her head.

Then, from inside the house there is a sound, a mother's call.

'Leah, wait!'

And for a moment, Wren forgets to breathe. Because the warmth of that voice, the love it holds, winds its way inside her, and pulls her fractured heart whole again.

And then, standing in the door, is Paige.

'Hello, Mum,' she says. And she opens her arms.

Acknowledgements

This book has been rattling around in my head for a lot longer than it took to write it. During my former career in TV production, I was tasked with working undercover in children's homes, investigating bad practice and profiteering at the expense of some of the UK's most vulnerable children. Although there are still huge problems with social care in this country, the tireless dedication from the huge majority of the foot soldiers in this industry is enough to break your heart. So my first thank-yous are to the real-life Melanies out there, and to the world's greatest TV producer, Andrew Smith, who gave me the opportunity to meet them.

Nina Whittaker and Noelle Holten deserve a special mention for their help with my research and insight into probation: Wren doesn't exactly play by the rules here but your help in explaining them was greatly appreciated!

The first draft of this book was written under the unparalleled tutelage of Laura Ellen Joyce and Henry Sutton during my time at UEA, for which I am forever grateful. Heartfelt thanks also to my friends and classmates Merle Nygate, Marie Ogée, Jenny Stone, Suzanne Mustacich, Geoff Smith, Shane Horsell, Stephen Collier and Caroline Jennett, and especially to Harriet Tyce and Trevor Wood, who continued to read draft after draft until the book was finished.

I have found a huge amount of camaraderie and support in the crime fiction community in the last couple of years, without which this would be a lonely profession indeed. Special thanks for laughs, feedback and motivational speaking go to Susie (S.E.) Lynes, Garry (G.D.) Abson, Niki Mackay, and the hilarious and brilliant members of the Criminal Minds alliance.

I was lucky enough to get a giant leg-up by winning the 2019 Bath Novel Award for this book, so a special mention goes to Caroline Ambrose, Hellie Ogden, and everyone involved in the judging – it was such a blast.

Oodles of gratitude go to my ludicrously brilliant agent Veronique Baxter. Your insight, enthusiasm and candour have smoothed the otherwise arduous process of getting this book into print, and I can't thank you enough. Likewise my editor, the stellar Miranda Jewess, without whom this book would be 300,000 words long, and a lot less coherent. It has been an absolute pleasure and an education working with you. Let's hope the reading of this book doesn't cause any further retinal trauma. Thanks also to the rest of the team at Profile, especially Graeme Hall, Hayley Shepherd and Rebecca Gray.

Finally, a word of appreciation to my stupendous family, the greatest cheerleaders a person could have. Thank you, Mum, Faye and Dad for everything. Tom, thank you for your unending patience, your insistence that I tough it out, and for taking up the slack so that I could get this done. Mo and Sid, you pair of plonkers: your pride and enthusiasm about what I do with my time makes it all worthwhile. I love the lot of you very, very much.